THE PLEASURES OF A ROGUE

David stroked her cheek, down her throat, and all the way to her belly. He did it again, just one lone fingertip trailing over her skin, and her nipples hardened as if in longing for the touch of that finger. "Tell me what you like," he said.

"I don't know . . ." She gasped as his fingertip retraced its path, but this time taking a slow circle around the very edge of her breast.

"Say yes if you like it." David moved, sliding down her body. "No, if you don't."

"Yes," Vivian whispered as his finger continued to blaze a path of sensation across her skin. It dipped into the hollow of her navel, and then climbed her ribs to skate along her collarbone. "Yes."

He traced the line of her breastbone, then slowed as he crossed her belly. He drew lazy circles there that made her hips rise of their own volition. "Do you like this?" he whispered.

"Yes," she said. "Yes!" She wanted him to move lower, to the place between her legs that she knew was his ultimate destination . . .

Books by Caroline Linden

WHAT A WOMAN NEEDS

WHAT A GENTLEMAN WANTS

WHAT A ROGUE DESIRES

Published by Kensington Publishing Corporation

WHAT A ROGUE DESIRES

CAROLINE LINDEN

ZEBRA BOOKS
Kensington Publishing Corp.
www.kensingtonbooks.com

Chapter One

There comes a reckoning in every rogue's life when he will be called upon to give up his vices, repent of his wild ways, and become a respectable man. It is a known truth that scoundrels do not long survive the passing of their youthful looks and charms, to say nothing of their fortunes. David Reece knew this, had accepted it, and even told himself he was prepared to embrace it. He was lucky enough to have survived this long, and had decided it was best to stop thumbing his nose at Dame Fortune.

He just hadn't realized her vengeance would be quite so harsh.

"I've made all the arrangements with Adams," Marcus said. "He'll be ready to assist you in every matter, as will Mr. Crabbet, my banker, and Mr. Rathbone, my solicitor."

"Excellent," David said, adding under his breath, "thank heaven." For the last hour he'd been listening to all he must attend to while his brother was abroad, and this was the first mention of any help. Surely Marcus knew he wasn't ready to handle everything on his own. Surely Marcus wasn't ready to *allow* him to handle everything on his own. David had been counting on that fact when he had agreed to see to Exeter business.

Marcus shot him a glance. "Yes, excellent. However . . ." He paused, straightening the many documents on his desk. "Adams is a fair secretary," he said in a dry voice, which David immediately interpreted to mean Adams was a borderline fool. "He is young and inexperienced." Another pause. "You mustn't rely on him too much, as he is capable of following directions, but not giving them."

Just bloody brilliant. David had been hoping Marcus's secretary would know how everything ran, and do most of the running. "What about Father's man?" he asked, remembering the highly efficient man who had worked for their father. "What was his name? Er . . . Holt?"

Marcus sighed. "Mr. Cole has been forced by his health to retire. If you can restore him and get him back to work, you would have my undying gratitude."

David slumped a little. Blast. Just his luck, that the capable man who knew Exeter business up, down, and sideways would have recently retired. "But he's passed on his, er, knowledge, to this Adams fellow, hasn't he?"

Marcus's dour look quashed that hope. "One would hope, but sadly, it seems not." He got to his feet. "That is why I need you, David. There is no one else I trust." David nodded, partly in acknowledgment, partly to conceal his continuing surprise that it did seem to be true. Not since they were young boys could he remember his brother expressing trust in him, and even then not on such an important matter. And after the events of the past spring, it was a bloody miracle his brother still spoke to him, let alone asked David to look after all his business affairs for three months. Yet more pressure that he must not make a mess of things now.

Resolutely he got to his own feet, watching his brother pack an alarming number of documents and books into a large leather case, which he then strapped closed and set upright on the edge of the desk nearest David. "These are the most current," he said, deepening David's gloom. "The rest will be in London, in my study. I suggest you work there, for convenience's sake."

David mustered a smile. There were more? How many more? "Right. I do like convenience."

Marcus smiled back briefly, then came around the desk. "It is a great relief that you're to manage for me," he said, clapping David's shoulder. "Otherwise I doubt I could be away for so long." Barely a month ago, Marcus had married, and was now taking his bride on an extended wedding trip. For three months they would be traveling the continent, enjoying the finest entertainments money could buy, wallowing in love and happiness, while David would be, apparently, buried beneath a mountain of ledgers with only an incompetent secretary to advise him.

But that was fair. David pushed aside the urge to recant his offer of help and nodded, laying one hand on the leather case. He owed this to Marcus, this and much, much more. Sitting at a desk and reading papers was far better than what he deserved, so he would do his best. Nearly getting someone killed was a large debt to repay.

There was a soft noise at the door, just before it slowly creaked open. "Look," said the little girl who entered. She was lugging a large basket that appeared far too heavy for her. "Look at my kitties!" She waddled across the room and set her basket down at Marcus's feet, then pulled off the cover to reveal three small kittens of decidedly mongrel heritage.

David watched as his brother smiled and placed one

hand gently on the little girl's curly blond head. "How charming. Where is their mama, Molly?"

"In the stable," said his stepdaughter blithely, scooping up one tiny kitten. "This one is my favorite. I named her Moon. She likes to ride in my basket." The kitten was squirming against Molly's hold as she spoke. "Stop it, Moon!" Molly ordered, pressing the wriggling animal to her chest. "Stop!"

David couldn't hold back a chuckle as the two other kittens took advantage of her distraction to leap from the basket and scamper across the floor, one to play with the fringe on the rug and another to chase dust motes in the sunlight streaming through the windows. "They're getting away," he remarked.

Molly swung around to glare at him with suspicious brown eyes. David cocked his head and grinned at her. "Shall we collect the kittens?"

Molly turned, caught sight of her kittens scampering away, and squealed, "No, no, come back!" She ran after them, catching the gray kitten who was too busy playing with the fringe to run. "You come back here, Butter!" Butter, a yellowish kitten, had left the dust motes and was climbing the drapes. "Butter!" Her arms full of wiggling, meowing kittens, Molly turned to Marcus in appeal. "Catch them for me, Papa, please?"

David's eyebrow quirked upward as he watched his somber, serious brother retrieve the kitten from his fine velvet draperies, unsnagging its tiny claws with great patience, then replace all the kittens in the basket and securely tie the cover down, all under the approving gaze of his stepdaughter. Molly clapped her hands. "Good, now they can go for a ride again!"

The door opened again. "Is Molly—oh, Molly." There were equal parts laughter and fatigue in the woman's voice. "We agreed the kittens would stay in the stable with their mama cat, Molly," she said. "Why are they in here?"

The little girl's chin sank. "I wanted to show my new papa," she said, beginning to pout. Her mother's lips parted in surprise, and she looked at Marcus. He merely shrugged, but the set of his mouth made David think he was enjoying being called Papa.

"You must still mind Betty," said her mother in a softer tone. "Now take the kittens back to the stable, please."

"Yes, Mama." Dragging the basket after her, Molly trudged toward the door, head down. Her mother caught her up in a hug until the little girl shrieked with glee. "Put me down, Mama," she cried, still giggling. "My kitties!"

Laughing, her mother put her down. "Go, then." Molly toddled out the door, her high sweet voice rising as she was intercepted by her nursemaid, and then the door latched behind her.

David looked at his brother. "Papa?"

Marcus gazed back. "She asked if she might call me that," he said. "I had no objection." Then he ruined his appearance of calm by darting a questioning glance at his wife. They exchanged a look, and apparently an entire conversation passed between them as well. Marcus's face relaxed again, and he gave a small smile. That look gave David an odd feeling. Marcus had never been one to care what others thought. And David couldn't recall the last time he'd seen Marcus smile so often.

"I suppose next she'll come up with a name to call you, David," said Hannah with a laugh as she came across the room to join them.

He groaned. "She already has. Liar, liar, she called me a month ago, and barely anything since."

Again his brother and sister-in-law shared a glance. David wished they would stop that. It felt as though they were talking about him without his having any idea what was said.

"She's a child," said Hannah at the same moment Marcus murmured, "Observant child." Hannah shot her husband a warning look. "She'll forget," she said kindly. "Would you care for tea, David? You've been locked in here an age."

Tea was too weak. In fact, whiskey sounded too weak. David was tempted to drive straight to the nearest pub and stay there for a month. "Thank you, no," he said, patting the leather case on the desk and trying to hide his rising apprehension behind a front of confidence and cheer. "I've quite a bit of studying to do, so I shall make for London."

"Before luncheon?" she exclaimed. David paused, thinking of the excellent chef at Ainsley Park, but shook his head. The longer he stayed, the greater the odds that he would lose his nerve and back out. He would not back out. He would do this.

"I should make an early start, I think," he said. "I don't wish to make a fool of myself."

"Of course you shan't," said Hannah staunchly. "Mr. Adams will be there to assist you."

"Before I forget," Marcus said, going back around his desk and opening a drawer. "I've had something made for you, David. It will make things easier." He handed David a small jeweler's box, which turned out to contain a copy of the signet ring Marcus wore on his own hand.

David slid it on his finger, flexing his hand and taken aback by the weight of it. With this ring, he might as

well *be* the duke of Exeter, he thought, vaguely alarmed
at the thought. David had never envied his brother the
title. It had suited him much better to be the younger
son, never expected to do much beyond cut a dashing
figure. He was a rogue by nature, he always told himself, and while it was very convenient to have Marcus
step in and right his ship from time to time, David was
quite content to sail where the wind took him.

But now he wore a copy of the Exeter signet on his
hand, and the responsibility for the Exeter affairs rested
heavily on his shoulders. He summoned another careless smile, saying a quick prayer that his sister-in-law
would return from her wedding trip expecting the first
of three or four sons, to obliterate any possibility of in-
heriting the title himself.

"I'll be on my way, then," he said with a hearty—and
completely false—grin. "A very safe and happy trip to
you, Marcus, Hannah."

Marcus shook his hand, and Hannah kissed his
cheek. Still grinning determinedly, David lifted the
leather case, and made his escape before anyone noticed
he was sweating, and before he opened his mouth and
wormed his way out of this. Responsible, sober, and de-
pendable, he repeated to himself.

Hannah watched her tall brother-in-law stride from
the room, his shoulders back, his spine ramrod-straight.
He looked like a man marching to his doom. "He'll be
all right," she said.

Her husband sighed. "No doubt. The question is, will
my affairs?"

She turned and gave him a reproachful look. "Now,
you promised . . ."

He smiled, his expression softening dramatically.
"Yes, yes. I will have made him a useless man if I do not

trust him and give him a chance to redeem himself. He will never become competent if I do everything for him. I was quite awake during that lecture, I assure you."

She quirked her brow. "I never said you must put him in charge of everything. A single estate, perhaps."

Now there was a positively roguish twinkle in his eye. He glanced at the door, securely closed behind his brother, then pulled her into his arms. "Sadly . . ." He kissed her nose. "Events have conspired against me." He kissed her right eyelid, as Hannah let her head fall back and slid her hands up his arms and around his neck. "I cannot leave Adams in charge for so long. He would bankrupt me within a fortnight." He kissed her left eyelid as she laughed. "Someone must watch him, and someone must watch David, so I give them each other." He kissed her forehead. "Perhaps between the two of them, there will be enough of Exeter for us to return home to. Because I intend to see that you enjoy every moment of your wedding trip." He kissed her mouth, long and deep.

Hannah smiled mistily. "Mmm, do you?"

His lips brushed her temple, stopping to nip her earlobe. "It is my mission in life."

"David will do well," she said again, as he came to that sensitive spot behind her ear.

"Well enough, I hope," Marcus muttered.

"And you—oh!" She shivered as his lips continued their assault. "You're already doing well."

"And we've not even left the house yet," he replied.

And that was the end of the conversation.

Chapter Two

David was halfway to London when he knew something was wrong. One of his fine new chestnut horses had developed an odd lilt to her stride and, despite slowing to a more cautious pace, David realized she needed attention. He turned into the next carriage yard before a bustling inn and pulled his team to a halt.

"Need help, sir?" called a young stable hand as David jumped down.

"My mare. She may have gone lame." The boy trotted over and checked the mare, running his hands gently down the horse's legs and murmuring to her as he did. After a moment he glanced up.

"Not lame, sir, not quite. She's got a stone in her hoof here. With a bit of rest and care, she'll be fine."

David frowned. "Can she make it to London with the stone removed?" But he knew the answer, confirmed with a shake of the boy's head.

"Ought not to, sir. That might make her lame, it might. But a night in the stable, we'll soak her hoof, and she'll be right as rain in the morning."

Even if he left early, he wouldn't make it to town

before dinner, especially not with a horse with a tender hoof. This pair had cost him a pretty penny, and it would serve nothing to abuse them. Resigned, he handed over the reins and told the boy to take the team to the stable and see to the mare's foot. Perhaps he could hire another team and be only an hour behind.

That idea died as well, with a firm shake of the stable master's head. "No, sir, I've not got a one, not even a pair of mules." David slapped his gloves into his palm, eying the stalls of horses behind him. Not nearly in the class as his chestnuts, but there were a few sturdy-looking beasts all the same. And he only needed one for a single day's journey.

"Surely you've got something; a single horse. I cannot afford a delay. I'll pay well for your trouble." The stable master cast him an assessing glance. David cocked his head and lowered his voice a tone. "Very well, indeed."

The man hesitated, then shook his head again, reluctantly. "Your pardon, m'lord, but I can't oblige. I haven't got the horses to hire. These are spoken for, and I cannot let them go." This time David did swear. It was utterly unacceptable that his good intentions be upset so easily and so soon. But what could he do, if the man wouldn't listen to money?

"Then I shall have to take my custom elsewhere, I see. Where might I hire a carriage?" He had to raise his voice to be heard over a burst of shouts and a rumble of wheels.

A stagecoach was just turning in, and with a flurry of activity the stable boys rushed to stand ready. The stable master turned from David, saying quickly over his shoulder, "The Golden Bear, two miles distant, might be able to assist you, sir."

David watched him go, simmering in silence. He was quite sure the man wouldn't have turned Marcus away like that. But then, Marcus would have left early, and most likely his horse wouldn't have picked up a stone in the first place. Between the two of them, David was quite sure his brother had gotten more than his fair share of luck. And then, of course, made the most of it with his methodical, calculating nature.

Swearing again under his breath, he turned on his heel and strode into the inn, just barely avoiding running down a stable boy behind him. The passengers from the coach were climbing down, and David had no desire to wait and watch them all be served ahead of him. He flung open the door, a little too roughly, and hailed the innkeeper.

"Yes, sir? Will you be wanting a room for the night?" The man's eyes ran over him in a split second, and he bowed, wiping his hands on his apron. "I've got my best room still."

No doubt all his rooms were his best, if they were unoccupied. "I suppose, since it appears your stable master is unable to oblige me," David said coolly. "I must say, I've found this establishment rather lacking thus far, so perhaps I should examine the room before I take it."

The man puffed up obsequiously. "My stable master? Why, if he didn't oblige you, sir, he must not be able to. If he simply hasn't got the horses, he hasn't got them. But my rooms are fine, and I vow, if you're—"

"No doubt." David glanced around the room as if he found the entire inn rather lacking, although to tell the truth, it looked like many a tavern David had spent time in. He simply didn't want to spend time in this one. "But I don't require a room. I require a horse, for I must return to London this day, and now, due to your stable master, I shan't be able to."

The innkeeper abandoned his defense of the stable master. "And I'll speak to him about it, depend upon it, sir. He'll have a horse for you by first light, if I have anything to say about it. But in the meantime—"

"I don't want another answer, in the meantime," said David testily. The man's mouth, still open in mid-sentence, snapped closed.

"The only other thing I can suggest, sir, is the stage to London, just arrived and soon to depart again. Will you take a place?"

David almost said no; he almost snapped back at the man that he would not ride the public stage like a common farmer. But he caught himself in time, realizing the innkeeper was no longer looking at him with respect and deference, but with weary impatience and even veiled contempt. Because he was behaving like a spoiled child.

There were two choices open to him: ride the stage and reach London today, or stay the night and reach it tomorrow. If he left tomorrow, he would either be driving a strange team or a team with a tender-footed mare who couldn't travel at any decent speed. The second choice admitted little to no chance of making his appointments. The first choice, however unpleasant at the moment, would reap benefits tomorrow.

David sighed. "A place on the stage, then."

The innkeeper bowed his head. "I'll see to it at once, sir."

He reached for his purse. "See that my baggage is transferred as well, if you would. I'll send a man for the horses in a day or two. See they are well tended." The man took the generous sum David counted out, bowed a trifle more respectfully, and hurried off. David took a deep breath, relaxing his shoulders and trying to let go of his irritation. Normally he wouldn't have minded the delay so much; the taproom, and perhaps a barmaid or two, would have consoled him for his inconvenience. David was well used to consoling himself in pubs and taverns, and it was extremely tempting to do so again.

But he had made a promise. It would be appalling if he broke it not even six hours after making it.

Straightening his shoulders, he turned away from the taproom, ducking through the low doorway into the afternoon sunshine. The ostlers were changing the horses while men tossed trunks and bags off the top of the coach and secured others thrown up. Passengers, hot and dusty, brushed past David in search of a drink in the taproom or a bit of exercise in the shade. David eyed the coach with resignation. Instead of bowling along in his comfortable, well-sprung phaeton, he'd be packed in with half a dozen other souls, covered in dust kicked up by the team of six, bounced this way and that by every lurch of the heavy coach. He calculated the time until they would reach London and sighed. Being responsible was proving to be extremely burdensome.

He caught a passing boy and gave him a coin to fetch a mug of ale. He would stand out here and drink it, to avoid temptation as much as to stretch his legs in anticipation of being jammed inside the coach for the next few hours. The boy returned with the mug, and David retreated into the shade of a tree to nurse his pint and study his soon-to-be fellow passengers.

A widow in unrelieved black sat on a small trunk, her bonnet concealing her face. A tall man who was taking care to flash his shiny pocket watch was ordering the post-boys about, or trying to. A middle-aged couple in sturdy clothing was sharing a basket of food on a patch of grass. A portly man lounged on a bench near the inn, yawning and scratching himself. David tipped his mug to his mouth. Lord, there was always one. He made a mental note to avoid sitting by that man, who would no doubt smell of onions and pass gas the entire trip.

When the call went up that the coach was departing, David went, still not at all happy. The inside of the coach looked stuffy and dusty and just as cramped as he had expected, and his mood did not improve when the middle-aged couple took their seats first and beckoned to the widow to join them. Clutching a small reticule, she came forward slowly, hesitantly. The stable boys were tossing her trunk to the top of the stage, and she seemed worried about it, stopping twice to peer up at it. At the step of the stage, she paused again, gathering her black skirts in her hands. She was a small woman, and the high step appeared difficult for her. David stepped forward and offered his hand, anxious to get this trip begun as soon as possible, all the quicker to end it. "Allow me."

She turned her face to him, beaming as she thanked him, although he didn't hear a word she said. David had never seen such a face in his life. It was the face of an angel, a perfect heart shape with skin like fine china. Her eyes were a soft clear blue, her lips full and pink, and even her nose was simply perfect. Thoughts both reverent and wicked blossomed in his mind. Struck dumb, it was all David could do to nod and hand her into the coach. He climbed in after her and took a seat opposite her, all but staring.

"Right on time, right on time!" The portly man plumped himself next to David, taking up half the seat. Distastefully David moved over as far as he could, but when the last passenger climbed aboard, he was promptly squashed again.

The coach was off with a lurch a moment later, and David leaned his face nearer the window, only to recoil in disgust as a cloud of dust blew at him. "Best close the window, sir," said the older lady. "Mr. Fletcher and I have been on the coach since Coombe Underwood, and the roads are very dusty, sir, very dusty. We'll all be dust-covered."

And now we'll all be suffocated, he thought grimly, tying the shade down. The man beside him moved, squishing from side to side, and David caught a whiff of, indeed, onions. He angled himself a little more in the corner, trying to find a more comfortable position, and winced as the coach hit a rut and bounced him backward. The seat was too narrow; he felt perched on the edge. But his legs were too long, and he couldn't stretch them out to brace himself. He had to draw up his knees to avoid kicking the woman opposite him.

Now there was the only attractive thing about this ride. Wedged between the window and the fat man, dust drifting between the window frame and the curtain to cover his coat, unable to move or sleep, David took full advantage of the opportunity to admire the young widow. He had seen pretty girls before, and more than a few beautiful women. Women in artfully designed gowns that showed off their figures, women with cosmetics that emphasized their good features and covered their flaws, women who used flowers and jewels and perfume to enhance their appearance. He couldn't recall seeing someone dressed so shabbily and primly who looked so breathtaking.

It might be her eyes. As blue as the summer sky, he thought, amused at his own poetical turn. It might be the soft pink color that bloomed in her cheeks as she talked

with the older woman beside her. The shy smile that followed showed a trace of dimple in her cheek, and lifted
her mouth into a perfect curve. A hideous bonnet covered most of her hair, but the bit that peeped out around
her temples was a light brown. If she wore perfume he
couldn't smell it, although she might have bathed in it
and he wouldn't know, thanks to his neighbor. Every
other inch of the woman was covered in black, from the
scuffed toes of her boots peeping out from under her
skirts to the black lace mitts on her hands.

He slouched lower in his seat, his eyes sliding over. Her
traveling cloak had fallen open, and he was quite sure she
had a nice figure. Her bosom was nicely rounded, under
the high-necked dress, and his imagination filled in other
nice curves: the gentle flare of a waist, the rounding of a
hip, the slim line of a leg. And that exquisite mouth. He
could imagine quite a bit about that mouth, and what he
might teach her to do with it that could make this trip pass
much, much more enjoyably.

She caught him looking at her then, her eyes meeting
his for a moment before she looked away. She wasn't
afraid, he thought, but on guard. So she'd be a challenge
to seduce; David rather liked the prospect. He felt the
beginnings of a lazy smile on his face before he remembered himself.

Good God, he was nothing more than a tomcat if he
could sit here and imagine seducing a woman he didn't
know anything about, had never seen before, and probably would never see again. They were strangers on a
stagecoach, crammed in with four other people, and he
was thinking of having her naked.

What kind of man was he, precisely? Whatever was
left of his smile vanished at the question. Had he
learned nothing in the last few months? This was not

responsible, respectable behavior; this was not part of his vow to reform himself. Was he to be the sort of man who grew old alone, reduced to ogling women's ankles with his quizzing glass as they laughed behind their fans at him? The lecherous old man, they'd whisper. It was bad enough what they whispered about him now.

He pushed back further into his corner, turning his gaze away from her. She was safe from him. No matter which sensual direction his imagination ran, he would not act on it.

They rattled onward for some time. David made good on his vow not to stare at the pretty widow, but only by closing his eyes and pretending to rest. From time to time he would take a quick look out the window, and usually also stole a quick glance at her, catching the smooth pale curve of her cheek as she chatted with the other woman, the flash of her smile. That much he was helpless to resist. He told himself he could just as easily be stealing glances at the other woman, although why anyone would do that, he couldn't imagine.

He heard bits of their conversation, too, over the rumbling of the wheels. The older woman introduced herself as Mrs. Fletcher, and seemed to take great delight in drawing out the quiet young widow. Her voice was often too low to hear, but what David heard was soft and gentle. She had the accent of gentry, and he pieced together a tale of genteel near-poverty, then her husband's death. She must be on her way to relatives, he thought, wishing he had anything else to do but think about her. He was behaving himself, but it would be easier if the other men were of a sporting inclination. Or if he hadn't so recently vowed to become an upright model of respectability; he and his friend Percy had once taken the reins of a coach and driven it on a mad race for a smashing good run. There was no time to think about women while careening along atop a coach. Percy and the other rogues David kept company with would roar with laughter to see him wedged respectably, boringly, inside the coach, opposite a luscious young widow and not doing a blessed thing to seduce or even flirt with her. Even though he had imposed it on himself, David was beginning to think his penance was extraordinarily harsh.

The noise and the shaking were mind-numbing. Incredibly enough, the man beside him had gone to sleep, his head lolling on his broad chest, his mouth agape. David leaned further away in disdain. He finally closed his eyes, determined to try to sleep as well, when he heard a distant crack. A sharp, ringing report almost like a gunshot. In fact, *very* like a gunshot. He opened his eyes.

"What, what?" The man next to him jerked up abruptly. "We're stopping!" he said indignantly.

"Indeed," said David dryly, pushing up the shade and putting his head out the window as the coach shuddered from side to side, swaying like a sapling in high wind but most definitely slowing down. He could see nothing on his side of the vehicle, but heard shouts, and then another shot, much closer and this time unmistakable.

"We're being robbed!" cried the older woman opposite. "God have mercy on us!"

How utterly splendid: highway robbery. The only thing lacking in his day so far.

As Mrs. Fletcher continued calling out to God, David mentally said a few choice words to that deity himself. The two men beside him began arguing over the best way to proceed, and Mr. Fletcher had his head out the window, spurring his wife to latch onto his back and plead with him to be cautious and not get himself shot.

The young widow sat motionless, her eyes wide, and her reticule clutched in her hands. She looked petrified.

David leaned forward. "Are you going to be ill?" he asked. His boots were directly in front of her, and he could ill afford to replace yet another pair.

Cornflower blue eyes turned in his direction, but she made no sign she understood him. She was completely terrified.

The coach door flew open barely a moment after the coach jerked to a halt. "Out," grunted a mountain of a man. He wore a long black coat, a dark hat pulled low on his head, and even his face was dark. Blackened with soot or dirt, David decided as the man raised a pistol in threat. It was difficult to make out his features in the encroaching dusk, as shadows slanted across the road. Silently the passengers climbed from the coach. Mrs. Fletcher clung to her husband's arm, her face twisted with fear. The tall gentleman stood aloof, frowning furiously, and the portly fellow looked as though he would wet himself with terror. The young widow stood mute and pale, her huge eyes fixed on the highwayman. David remained at the back of the group, wary but resigned.

"The baggage," called a voice. There were three robbers, it turned out: the large man who stepped into the coach's doorway and sliced through the baggage traps with a wicked-looking knife; another man, seated on his horse several yards away who appeared to be the leader and who kept his own pair of pistols trained on the driver and outriders; and a tall, thin man who moved toward them as the first man began kicking open trunks and rifling the contents. All wore dark clothing and had their faces blackened.

"Your valuables, if you please," said the thin one, holding out a sack. "Jewels and money."

"This is intolerable," burst out Mrs. Fletcher with a sob. "You brigand! You thief!" Her husband quickly put his arm around her and turned her into his side, silencing her. Without a word he fished a pocket watch from his waistcoat and dropped it into the bag.

"Any jewelry?" asked the thief. His voice was very young, David thought, and perhaps Irish, from the faint lilt to his words. He raised a pistol at Mrs. Fletcher. "Any rings, mum?"

She clutched her hands together, and sobbed louder, but her husband spoke into her ear, and she wrenched off a glove and added a thin gold band to the bag. The portly man tossed in a silver snuffbox and his purse, and the tall man handed over a purse, thin-lipped with anger.

"You, mum? Give it over," said the thief to the widow. For a moment, she hesitated, her eyes flitting around the group. Slowly she opened her reticule and dug out a single shilling. She dropped it into his sack with trembling hands, and David felt an unexpected burst of outrage that she'd been robbed of her last coin. The highwayman turned glittering eyes on him.

"Hand it over, guv," he said with quiet menace. Silently David took out his pocket watch and purse. He pulled the pearl stickpin from his cravat and dropped it in the sack, too. He never took his eyes from the young thief's face. The highwayman's eyes scanned up and down. "And the ring," he ordered.

David glanced down involuntarily. He'd forgotten about the signet ring on his hand.

"Oh, no! Not such a ring!" the young widow whispered then, sounding horrified. David looked at her in surprise. Color had returned to her cheeks in two bright pink spots. Why she was protesting the loss of his ring after the thief had relieved her of her last shilling, David couldn't guess, but he wished she hadn't. He wasn't about to lose this ring, but he didn't want to see her get hurt over it.

"Hand it over," repeated the highwayman. The pistol wavered in his grip, and sweat beaded his upper lip. "All valuables."

David curled his hand into a fist, never taking his eyes off the man. "No."

The thief's eyes widened; he hadn't expected to be denied. "Do you want me to shoot you?" he exclaimed.

The widow gasped. "No! Oh, please don't shoot him! Over a ring? Have some compassion!" She put out her hand beseechingly. The robber started as she touched his arm, whirling about and bringing his arm up, catching her across the body and knocking her backward into the dirt. She hit the ground with a soft thud and didn't move. Instinctively, David stepped toward her.

"Hie!" shouted the man on the horse. "Hie, there!" The highwayman spun around again, his throat working. The other bandits were retreating, pistols still trained on them. The rifled baggage lay strewn about the ground, and the driver and his men still had their hands on top of their heads. The widow lay in a huddled heap on the ground, and David glanced at her again. The lady had stood up for him, defended him to an armed bandit, and now she lay senseless at his feet.

There was another shout. The thief near David turned again. "You bloody bugger," he said furiously, raising his gun. David ducked, but too late, and the last thing he saw was the ground rushing up to meet him.

He came around with a splash of water on his face. With great effort, David pried open his eyes and squinted up at the darkening sky. "Are you awake, sir?" asked a female voice.

He pushed himself upright, squeezing his eyes closed against the violent clanging inside his skull. "Yes."

"Do be easy. That outlaw gave you quite a blow." It was Mrs. Fletcher dabbing at his face with a damp handkerchief. David took a deep breath, and gave his head a tiny shake to clear it. "Unfortunately they got away," she went on. "If only the constables had been a few moments sooner. I vow, they should be shot! Striking a lady and leaving you for dead!"

"Not to mention stealing," he mumbled.

"The outrage of it! Why, I told Mr. Fletcher we ought not to take anything valuable with us on our travels, and wasn't I right? Now he's gone and lost his pocket watch, and you, sir! Wasn't I right, I asked Mr. Fletcher, just wasn't I right, these roads are still dangerous. I never thought I'd see the like, a thief ripping the ring right off a man's hand!"

David thought to himself she'd see a lot worse in certain parts of London, but he was just then realizing that his whole hand felt as though it had been stepped on. He turned it over, holding it up to his face in the weak light. It was swollen, with a scrape along the side of his palm, but when he flexed his fingers everything still seemed to work. The signet ring, though, was gone.

He swallowed a curse as Mrs. Fletcher continued to fuss over him. It was just a ring, he told himself, and another one could be made just as easily as Marcus had had that one made. It wasn't really his fault it was gone, either. But David felt the loss like a hot coal in his gut, a searing taunt that he wasn't up to his task. That Marcus has been right to keep tabs on him all these years, that he would never be more than a hapless scoundrel who got by on his family name and his brother's money. He couldn't even make it to London without mishap.

Ignoring Mrs. Fletcher's protests and the ache in his head, he staggered to his feet. Somehow, he would get back that ring, he vowed to himself. And he would make that highwayman regret ever picking up a pistol. "The lady," he asked, as something else occurred to him. "The widow."

"Oh, she was so upset! When she came to and saw you lying on the ground like the dead, with blood all over your face, she set to weeping and carrying on like I'd never heard before. Not until Mr. Fletcher assured her you weren't actually dead did she calm herself a bit, but when the constable came, she went all to pieces again. He had a man escort her to the next town to rest. But it's very good of you to ask, sir. Are you acquainted with her?"

David shook his head, very carefully. "No. I wanted to be certain she wasn't hurt. That highwayman struck her."

Mrs. Fletcher nodded vigorously. "He did. Another reason for her to go on to the next town and rest."

"Yes. Thank you, madam." David began walking toward the cluster of men who appeared to be in charge. "Who is the constable here?" he asked.

A tall man with iron gray hair spoke. "I am. And you are, sir?"

David introduced himself. "Have you any hope of apprehending the thieves?" he asked, cutting to the heart of the matter.

The constable swelled with offended pride. "Of course we have, of course," he huffed. "Not the first time those brigands have struck hereabouts. We'll have them soon enough, sir, depend upon it."

"Not soon enough, clearly," said David. The constable flushed. "What are you doing to find them?"

The constable and his men began talking at once, gesturing in every direction while making no effort to move in those directions. They hadn't a prayer, he realized, as the pounding in his head worsened. "And are we to stand here in the middle of the road while you argue over it?" he interrupted to ask.

The constable closed his mouth. "What was your name again, sir?"

"Lord David Reece. I'm expected in London tomorrow on business for my brother, the duke of Exeter, and have little patience to wait here in this thief-infested county until you reach a decision."

As usual, Marcus's name worked wonders on the man's attitude. "Yes, sir," he said with a bow. "No, sir. Thomas!" He waved one of his men forward. "See that the passengers are carried on to the next town at once. We'll conduct our investigation from there." With a flurry of activity, everyone was returned to the coach, the constable and his men rode on, and at last they were off. The other passengers gave him a little more space than before, and David leaned his aching head into the thinly padded corner of the coach, his eyes falling on the empty spot opposite him.

"What was her name?" he asked.

"Who? Oh, you'll mean young Mrs. Gray," said Mrs. Fletcher, who seemed intent on mothering him. "Such a poor girl, widowed and left alone so young! She's on her way back to her family, although I don't think she's happy about it—we had a nice long chat at the Three Roosters, you know—and now this! I vow, the poor dear has suffered enough . . ."

David quit listening. Mrs. Gray. He wondered what her first name was. A poor relation, it seemed, unhappily sent back to her family. He half-smiled to himself; he seemed to have a partiality for poor young widows—especially attractive ones—although of course he couldn't pawn this one off on his brother. Not that he particularly wanted to do that.

His head felt like it would split open. Mrs. Fletcher talked on and on, as if the trauma of being robbed had relieved her need to breathe, and each word was like a pebble striking him in the temple. He opened his eyes a slit, hoping to look so invalid she would take the hint and be silent, but she wasn't even looking at him as she recounted every moment of the robbery and her own outrage. David let his eyes fall closed in defeat, and tried to refocus his thoughts on something more pleasant. Like the pretty widow, and where she might be now.

After what seemed an endless journey over a thousand ruts and bumps, they reached the next little village along the road, barely more than a coaching inn, as far as he could see. The coach lurched to a stop, and David gingerly climbed down, wincing at the loud bustle of the yard. The constable and his men had already arrived, and were issuing meaningless announcements in a booming tone that made David consider murder. He ignored them and went straight into the inn, catching the innkeeper by his sleeve.

"A private parlor," he said. "At once."

"Ah, yes, sir, yes, sir, right this way." David followed him to a small parlor that thankfully didn't face the road. He dropped onto the tiny sofa with a groan, resting his head with a great deal of relief.

"Will you be wanting anything, sir?" asked the innkeeper.

"Privacy. Quiet."

"Yes, sir." The man bowed, rubbing his hands on his apron, but didn't leave.

"I was robbed, my good man," said David wearily. "Put it on account."

There was a pause. "Shall I add it to the rest, then, sir?"

Again David pried open his eyes. "The rest of what?"

"The rest of your account, sir," said the innkeeper, deferential but firm. "From your last visit?"

David just blinked at him. Had he ever been to this place before? He certainly couldn't recall it, at any rate.

"Two broken pitchers, several pieces of smashed crockery, a chair leg broken off, and one mattress fair ruined with water, sir," the innkeeper added. "Eighteen quid, two shillings, and nine pence, sir."

Mention of the chair leg stirred a vague memory. His friend Percy, several bottles of wine, and two barmaids figured prominently, at least in as much as he could remember. When had that been? Last year? No, this spring, perhaps. "Oh, yes," he murmured. "Yes, add the room to . . . that."

The man sighed. "Yes, sir." The door closed behind him, filling the room with heavenly silence. David made a mental note to send payment as soon as he returned to London, and to ask Percy what was what with the chair leg, then let his head fall back.

All too soon the constable himself knocked at the door, and David dutifully related his tale. The constable asked several questions about the thieves, but David had little to say. He hadn't seen where they'd gone, or where they'd come from. He couldn't describe them, because they'd struck at the perfect time, when the onset of dusk would obscure their darkened features while still leaving enough light for them to see. He described what he had been robbed of and what he recalled of the robbery. All his questions about the chances of recovery and the highwaymen's capture were vaguely brushed aside.

"The widow," he said as the constable was preparing to leave. "The highwayman struck her when she said a word in my defense. Is she recovered?"

"Don't rightly know, m'lord," said the man. "We're looking for her, to take her statement, see, but she's been hard to track down."

"I'd like to make her a small reward for her effort on my behalf," David said, thinking of the lone shilling in her outstretched palm, winking sadly against the worn and darned lace of her glove. He told himself it was pity, and chivalry, and honor that prompted him, but he also knew the mention of money would make the constable not only look for her, but report back to David where she was, particularly if a coin or two were in it for himself. And in spite of his vow, David was still curious about her. When he had fulfilled his duty to Marcus, he wouldn't mind seeing if she were still available. A lovely little thing like her ought not be dependent on inhospitable relations.

"When I find her, sir, I shall inform her, depend on it," said the constable, ducking his head.

After the man had left, David leaned back again. His head felt a little better. He didn't relish the idea of staying the night in this inn. The whole reason he had taken a place on the coach was to reach London today, and thus far it had not been worth the trouble. He got up to ring for the innkeeper, trying to decide if he could sit a horse, but had to abandon the idea when he nearly fainted crossing the room. Perhaps his head wasn't so much improved after all.

The innkeeper came eventually, bringing a tray with food and a bottle of surprisingly good wine. "I remember you favored this wine," said the innkeeper, setting out the plates. David eyed him askance, wondering how much of his own life he had been too drunk to remember. He had only the barest memory of this inn, but he'd obviously been here a while. The girl who had come to assist in serving the meal kept winking at him behind her employer's back, wiggling her eyebrows in a suggestive way. David tried to ignore her, not having the slightest memory of ever seeing her face before, but she contrived to linger after the innkeeper bowed his way out of the room.

"Delighted to see you again, m'lord," she said coyly, bracing her arms on the table and leaning forward, displaying her breasts in front of his face. "What's your adventure this time? Highway robbery?"

"Er, yes." He took a long sip of wine, avoiding looking at her. "I was robbed and assaulted."

"That's so cruel." She drew nearer and slid her fingers into the hair at his temple. "Shall I make it all better, like last time?"

He finally looked up into her smiling face. She was fair, a little on the plump side, and rather plain. She was an ordinary country maid who'd obviously fallen into his bed before, and he hadn't the faintest memory of it—or her.

"I'm sorry," he said regretfully. "I took a dreadful knock on the head. I can barely stand on my own two feet."

She giggled. "I can help you stand," she said. "Not on your feet, but tall and straight enough for a bit of fun. Shall I—?"

"Not tonight," he said, catching her hand as it dipped toward his lap. He brushed a gentlemanly kiss on the back of her knuckles before tucking her hand into her apron pocket. "To my everlasting sorrow."

Her face creased with sympathy. "You poor, dear

man! Too knackered even for a tumble. Here! Let me tend you." And she busied herself pouring more wine into his glass, stirring up the fire, and plumping a cushion behind his back. David forced a smile for her as she finally left with another giggling smile, and the room was finally quiet again.

He finished his glass of wine and stared into the now-roaring fire. Good God. No matter how hard he probed his memory, this rustic inn and the plump little serving girl remained stubbornly vague. He must have been here only two or three months past, while he and Percy were jaunting about the countryside avoiding London, Marcus, counterfeiters, and Percy's overbearing father. They'd meant to go to Italy, but Percy had lost half of his funds on a cockfight and David, of course, had had none. A series of inns and taverns blurred together in his mind, soaked with wine and populated with women like the maid who'd just left. Only . . . he couldn't remember most of it. His memories only became clear at the point when he'd returned to London and gotten soundly beaten. That, he remembered with painful clarity; his broken rib was still tender.

But that was in the past. He was determined to do better in the future. Beginning tomorrow, when he would rise at first light and hire a horse for the remaining bit of his journey, no matter how much his body and head might ache. He would devote himself to Marcus's business, tidy up his own affairs as well, and survive this episode a changed man, reformed and respectable.

And the first order of business was retrieving his ring.

Chapter Three

"You bloody idiot!" Vivian Beecham was so furious with her brother she could have hit him. "What the devil were you thinking? Or were you even thinking at all? Sure, and it didn't look like it to me!"

Simon scowled and hunched further into the corner where he sat. "It wasn't so bad, Viv. If that bugger of a mark hadn't been so bull-headed—"

"Then what, you'd have slipped a knife into him and got us all hanged for murder?" She paced back and forth in front of him, her black skirts swinging. "It was a ruddy stupid thing to do and you know it," she said in fury. "Are you trying to get us hanged?"

"No," he muttered. His lower lip trembled, and he scuffed at his eyes with the back of his hand. "I thought the extra blunt would come in handy. I was only trying to help, Viv."

She sighed and ran her hands over her head, trying to rein in her temper. The sad thing was, Simon was telling the truth. He *was* only trying to help. He didn't mean to do everything wrong, he just couldn't help it. There was no question that her brother was simply not cut out to be a highwayman. "I know, Si," she said more kindly. "But you're not to think—you're just to do what we planned. What good can that ring do us? Chances are, we'll have to get it melted down to be able to sell it, and we'll have to find someone who won't ask questions to melt it for us. It gains us nothing, does it? The watches, the smaller jewels, and especially the money—that's all we want. Things that can be sold in a hurry, and that won't be easily traced to us. Because I'd rather not dance at the end of a rope, thank you very kindly."

"I'm sorry," her brother whispered, now thoroughly cowed. "I'm just dense, is all."

"You're not that dense," she said with another sigh. "But when I remind you what to do, in the midst of a job, and you shove me to the ground, I'd like to drop a brick on your head."

He shifted uncomfortably. "I ought not to have done that."

"At least you realize it now." Vivian closed her eyes, counting as high as she could. She crouched down so her eyes were level with Simon's. "Look at me," she commanded. Simon did so, warily. "I'm trying, Si, I truly am," she whispered. "But you've got to follow my lead in this until we come up with something better—"

"I ought to slit your throat, you ruddy fool," boomed an irate voice above them. Vivian shot to her feet.

"I've already scolded him, Flynn," she said.

The big man glared at her. "For all the good it does. He's trouble, he is, and I don't fancy waiting for him to get us all killed. You know they hang people for stealing, don't you?" he demanded of Simon, as indignantly as a parson might. Flynn's indignation, though, was for the fact that thieves like him were hanged, and not for the fact that they stole.

"He knows," said Vivian sharply. She might privately agree with every word he said, and not hesitate to give Simon a brutal dressing down herself, but she would defend her brother to the death before Flynn. Simon would have done the same for her, had the places been reversed, and besides, it was Vivian's fault Simon had been pressed into stealing anyway.

Flynn's jaw worked for a moment. "You're a right lucky bloke," he said to Simon. "If not for your sister, you'd have already been found belly-up in the river."

Simon flushed dull red with anger. He wasn't a child to be cowed by Flynn's threats anymore, Vivian realized. Her brother would soon be seventeen, a man old enough to give in to his temper and a man big enough to think he could take on Flynn.

"What's done is done," she said, trying to end the argument. "You'll not cut his throat and he'll not make such a mistake again." *I hope*, she added silently. Flynn still glared at Simon.

"What about his take?"

Vivian raised her eyebrows. She was not going to let Flynn cheat her out of Simon's share of the profits. "What of it? He was there, he gets a share."

"It might have been a larger take if he'd done what he's told and not gone after that bloke," said Flynn. Vivian saw he was holding the ring that had caused all the trouble, and was rolling it around in his hand.

"I'll get rid of the ring," she said, putting out her hand. "Give it to me. We're near enough to London, there are a hundred places to sell it unnoticed. I'll give the usual tale and we'll have an extra profit. It's worth a mint."

Flynn kept the ring. "I don't know."

She withdrew her hand. "Then you sell it. Take care

to have an answer ready for why a man such as you would have such a thing."

Flynn scowled. "All right, then. But you take care to get a good price." He shot another deadly look at Simon. "Or I'll take it out of his skin."

Vivian waited until he had stomped out of the room before hitching up her skirts and sitting on the floor beside Simon. The old miller's cottage was damp and falling down, but no one bothered them when they were here. She heard the squeak of a mouse as she settled herself, and moved aside with a grimace. She hated mice. Someday, when she had her own little cottage, she would have a big fat cat to keep them away from her.

"We've got to get out of this," said Simon, in a low voice so as not to be heard by Flynn and the others in the next room.

Vivian sighed. "I know. Especially you."

"It's bad for you, too, Viv," her brother returned. "You're the safest of us lot during the job, but then you're on your own. How many times can you throw a fainting fit and not have to answer any questions? What if some constable puts together how you're on every stage that gets stopped?"

"That's why I'm acting a widow," she said. "No one wants to ask a poor, grieving, young widow any harsh questions."

"And what happens in a few years?" he pressed. "You won't be young forever. And Flynn is waiting for you to be less important so he can toss your skirts, whether you say nay or yea."

"I'll kill him if he tries it," said Vivian.

Simon shook his head. "Flynn's a bad sort. I don't like him."

She shifted. Flynn wasn't her ideal, either, but he kept

them fed. And she didn't know how they would accomplish that if they left the protection of his little band. "It's so difficult to find honorable highwaymen these days," she said, hoping to make Simon laugh. Instead he just put his head back against the wall and let out his breath.

"I hate this," he said softly. "Not the stealing—don't mind that at all, since there's no choice except to starve, and any nob what wears a ring like that can afford a donation to the poor. But I hate feeling like we'll get caught any day, and it'll likely be my fault. Everything I do is wrong, Viv. I'm going to get us all in prison, or worse."

That was probably true. Simon had no sense for thieving. Unlike her, he was not a good liar or a good actor. He got nervous. He overreacted. He made mistakes. Today his persistence in taking that bloody signet ring had held up the job, and put them all in danger. They could be sitting in a jail cell tonight instead of in an abandoned miller's cottage, damp and cold but fed and free.

Wordlessly she took his hand. If only she had a little bit more money saved. She had always hoped to start Simon in a safer occupation, and now it seemed imperative. Their mother wouldn't be proud of Vivian for leading her younger brother into a ring of thieves and scoundrels. "I'll take care of everything," she said. "You keep your mouth shut around Flynn. He's a blooming idiot for sure, but he's an idiot with a sharp knife. No one but me would care if he cut your throat, but if he killed you, I'd have to kill him, and then we'd all be dead."

He was silent for a long time. Vivian heard the skittering of tiny feet and tried not to shudder. "I don't want to hide behind my sister all my life," came Simon's voice at last, thin and plaintive. "I'm a man now, Viv."

"A young man," she corrected firmly. "If Mum hadn't died, you'd still be under her hand, so mind you don't make me smack you for her."

He huffed with a reluctant laugh. "Aye, you would. But I should be able to stand on my own two feet."

"Someday you will," she promised, hoping it was true. "But first we need to eat, so you don't take faint and end up lying on your own backside."

Simon shrugged and got to his feet, then helped her up. Vivian swatted at the black fabric of her dress, hoping no mice had gotten to it. "You go on," she said. "I've got to put away this rag." Her brother gave her a half-hearted grin and left, pulling the warped door closed behind him. Vivian retrieved the old valise that held her things and set about changing out of the shabby, secondhand widow's weeds that had been her costume for the day. The widow's pose usually worked very well for her. Today had been no different. That older woman had all but held her hand on the trip, so concerned for her tender feelings that Vivian had wanted to snort with laughter. Anyone in her supposed penniless state had better not have such tender feelings, not if they wanted to survive. The gentlemen on the coach had alternated between sneaking looks at her bosom and trying to look righteous whenever she glanced their way.

Well, not quite. The rich one hadn't hidden behind any such look. He didn't keep the interest off his face. He was a right handsome one, she thought, although not too bright. A clever chap would have handed over the ruddy ring without complaint when Simon pointed a pistol at him. Thanks to him, she'd been forced to abandon her faint-with-fear pose and actually speak up for him in a vain attempt to warn Simon off. And all she got for it was a shove to the ground.

It was doubly galling that he'd only had a pair of guineas in his purse. From the moment he'd driven his flashy carriage into the coaching yard, Vivian had been certain he would be worth their while, a spoiled dandy ripe for the plucking. She saw the way he demanded a horse as if the world should bow to his wishes, and then how he handed over a handful of money for the care of his very fine horses. The bloke was rich, she knew it, and so she'd made her move, dropping her handkerchief in signal to Simon. He'd gone off to alert the rest of the gang, and she'd gotten on the coach. And then the bloody cull only had a few guineas. It wasn't even repayment for all the time he'd spent staring at her bosom.

She inspected a rip in the elbow of one sleeve of the black dress, and cursed. Now she'd have to stitch the bloody thing. That was not the dandy's fault, she conceded, pulling on the loose trousers and sturdy shirt she usually wore at nights. Simon should have known better. She didn't know what had gotten into her brother lately.

Ah, well. What was done was done. She ran a thin cord around the waist of her trousers and knotted it tightly. At least if Flynn tried to grab her bottom she'd have warning and a chance to get her knife before he could get the trousers off. Vivian's mouth twisted as she folded her widow's dress and put it away. Simon was right; Flynn was just waiting before he tried anything on her. Now he wouldn't dare touch her, because she'd leave the band, if she didn't fight him to the death for it. Vivian was well aware of the importance of her role to them all. It was she who chose their targets, she who rode the coaches as the decoy, and she who provided diversions by fainting or having a fit of hysterics that allowed the rest to get away. Flynn would be reduced to random robberies without her, and everyone knew he wasn't clever enough to get away with it for long.

But they had worked this stretch of road for too long, and Vivian couldn't shake the sense that they ought to move on. Simon's mistake today only made the feeling stronger. Perhaps they should lie even lower than usual for a few days, letting any fuss over the botched job die down, and then pick a better spot. Two jobs in any neighborhood was enough for Vivian, and already Flynn had put them to four in this corner of Kent. If someone recognized her, the game would be up before they knew it.

She packed away the rest of her costume and followed Simon into the other room, where everyone else was already eating. She stowed her valise in the corner and took the bowl of stew Alice handed her. Simon scooted sideways, making space for her by the fire, and Vivian sat. No one said a word for a while; it was the first they'd eaten all day, except for a bit of oatcake in the morning. Vivian ate ravenously, even though the stew was redolent of onions, bringing back memories of the horrid man on the stage who had breathed on her with that wretched leer. It was rabbit again, just as it had been for the last three days. She knew it should be enough that they had meat at all, but one of these days she would shake some coin out of Flynn and buy a chicken for the pot.

Across the circle from her, Flynn shoved aside his empty dish and produced a leather bag from his jacket pocket. Simon and Crum, Alice's man, also put aside their bowls and sat up straighter, intent on what Flynn poured on the ground in front of him. With the keen eye of a moneylender, Flynn divided the money into five equal piles. Then he plucked a few coins from four stacks and added it to the fifth. That was his, as the leader, he claimed. Vivian gritted her teeth, saying nothing as Flynn shot her a glittering glance. He knew she thought it was unfair that he took more than the rest, but he also knew she had only Simon on her side. Crum was pacified by Alice getting a share, even though poor Alice never participated in their jobs. So Vivian kept her silence, and skimmed a little off the proceeds of the items she sold. If Flynn deserved a little extra for being the brawn of the group, she deserved a little extra for being the brains.

The take was only modest. "Barely four quid," said Flynn grimly. Again he flashed her a look, as if it were her fault the dandy had only carried a pair of guineas. She'd been sure he would have a nice fat purse, and never would have decided to rob him if she'd known otherwise.

"What else?" Vivian prodded him. He grunted.

"One plain ring of gold, a snuffbox, two pocket watches, one jeweled, and one cravat pin with pearl." He lined them up.

"And?"

He glared at her, but pulled the wretched signet ring from his pocket. "One signet ring."

"Of good gold, and thick and heavy," she pointed out. "That'll bring a guinea at least." Beside her, Crum perked up. He had been watching with his customary glumness. Crum never said much, good or bad. He was a big thick fellow, and only in defense of Alice did he show any animation.

"That's not so bad, then," he said.

"It's passing fair," she said before Flynn could speak. "It's our best take in a month."

His mouth twisted. He didn't want to admit that, after

the way Simon had blundered. Vivian put up her chin and met his glare head-on.

"We ain't sold it yet," he growled. "It might be trouble to sell." He was rolling the ring in his palm again. She could see he had taken a fancy to it, for all his complaints about the way Simon had gotten it. She felt a whisper of dread. One never knew what Flynn would take into his head, and he was as obstinate as a mule once he set his mind on something.

"I'll take it tomorrow," she said. Best to get rid of the blasted thing as soon as possible. "I'll take the stage from Wallingford and find a pawn shop. It'll be just another bit of gold." She put out her hand for all the jewels. Still glowering, Flynn scooped them up and handed over everything but the ring. She kept her hand out, waiting. For a moment they stared at each other, neither willing to give. Vivian hid her clenched free hand in the folds of her shirt; if Flynn didn't give over the ring, came the sudden thought, she could take it as a sign that it was time for her to go. She could sell the little things, hand over Flynn's and Crum's and Alice's shares, and then go away with Simon. For the space of a second, she almost hoped he would refuse to hand it over, effectively announcing his lack of trust in her.

Flynn tossed the ring at her. With a flick of her wrist she caught it, dropping everything else in the process. Flynn barked with laughter as she collected it again, her lips pressed tight together. It was time to go, all right; she hated Flynn worse than ever then, for his mocking laugh and leering looks.

"We need to move on," she said abruptly. "This bit of road is too dangerous now."

Flynn quit laughing and frowned. "We move on when

I say," he snapped, "not until. You mind your role, girl, I'll mind mine."

She swallowed the protest that leaped to her lips. She forced herself to nod, and hide her thoughts. That was her sign, she thought furiously. They nearly got nabbed by the constables, and Flynn would ignore it out of bullish pride. Because he hadn't said it first, he would refuse to do what any sensible person would do.

She put the valuables with her widow's dress and got her blanket. There was a general shuffling as everyone shook out their blankets and Alice banked the fire for the night. Vivian rolled up in her blanket and lay down next to Simon. Her brother's frame loomed larger than ever over her, and she felt another pang of worry for him. He would soon be too old to become anything but a hardened thief. In the faint firelight, she saw his crooked grin.

"Cheer up, Viv," he whispered. "All will be well."

She mustered a smile. "I know." Somehow, someday, she supposed, it would. She would do her damnedest to make it so—beginning tomorrow, when she headed into London to sell those stolen pieces. Simon knew she was angry at him, and he knew she'd stuck up for him tonight. She couldn't do it forever, though. Sooner or later she or Flynn would run the other through in a fury, if Flynn's stupidity didn't get them killed first. Long after the snores around her indicated everyone else had gone to sleep, Vivian stared at the ceiling.

She thought about Alice, asleep beside her, lying flat on her back with her mouth open a little. Alice had an unfocused, vague look in her eyes, and Vivian dimly remembered hearing something about her being kicked in the head by a horse. Alice never complained, never protested, never said much of anything. She went about her business with plodding determination, cooking for all of them and darning Crum's old coats and socks. Vivian supposed Alice was sweet enough, but the sad truth was that Alice was simple, and would be lost without Crum.

Crum would be no help to her, either. He was Flynn's man, through and through. He was kind and patient with Alice, but that was it. Flynn must have decided tolerating Alice was a fair price to pay for Crum's unwavering loyalty, because Flynn never said a word against Alice, even when he didn't mind tearing into Simon or Vivian for the smallest thing. It was as if Crum and Flynn had made a pact that they would leave each other alone and blame any misfortune on the two Beecham brats. As everyone knew, the Beecham brats had no one else to turn to, and nowhere else to go.

So it was only she and Simon, and her brother was more hindrance than help at times.

She sighed, stuffing an extra fold of the thin blanket under her head. She hated sleeping on the floor. When she had reason to take a room at an inn, Vivian went to bed early and stayed in it as long as she could. Linens, even coarse, not-entirely-clean ones, on top of a mattress, even a scratchy, lumpy, straw-filled one, made for much better sleeping than a threadbare blanket and a hard floor. In her cottage, some day, Vivian would have a nice soft bed to sleep in, even if she had to eat nothing but oatcakes for a year to buy it.

Across the room, Flynn grunted in his sleep, and Crum snored a little louder. Alice's still face looked corpse-like in the wan moonlight. Vivian closed her eyes, hating it all. But how was she to get away from it? She'd been a thief for most of her life, and Simon had never known anything else. What could two thieves do besides steal?

She set off early the next morning in her worn gray dress, with some of the valuables in her reticule. Flynn and Crum still snored away, although she knew they'd be at the local pub by noon, drinking away their shares. Alice handed her a cold oatcake with a shy smile before dragging the bucket out to the brook for water. Simon alone got up and walked her partway to the nearest coaching inn.

"Be careful, Viv," he said as they drew near the parting point. "That cove might put out a reward."

She smiled. "That's why we sell it today, see? No pawnbroker in town will know today about anything stolen yesterday."

He frowned uncertainly. "I know. You're quicker at this than me, for certain. Still . . ." His voice trailed off as he squinted into the rising sun, breaking over the trees. "I ought to start taking care of you now, not the other way around."

Vivian almost rolled her eyes with impatience. "We take care of each other, and ourselves," she said firmly. "Now get on back and tend to your chores." Simon had the care of the horses when they weren't working. Vivian would take the dusty stage into town and back. Alice would cook. Flynn and Crum would sit on their fat arses all day and do nothing, or even worse, walk into town to drink away money that should last them a month or longer. Bloody fools.

She squeezed her brother's hand in farewell and continued into town. She counted out the coins for outside passage to London, readily telling her simple story to anyone who asked: she was a poor governess on holiday, going to visit her mother who was ill with consumption. By keeping her eyes downcast and her mouth shut, she wasn't interesting enough to draw any notice, and arrived in London just after noon.

She disembarked at the Elephant and Castle and made her way into London. Being back in the city always made her a bit edgy. She didn't like it here, with a thousand people pressed close around her. It was loud and dirty in the city, at least the parts Vivian knew. She'd grown up here, but never missed it. She walked quickly with her head down, clutching her reticule tightly, until she reached the edge of St. Giles. Here the houses were more crowded and dingy, the streets filled with ragged, dirty children. Vivian especially didn't like it *here*, but here were the pawnshops.

She never visited the same one twice. She always had a different story. People in St. Giles didn't ask many questions, but Vivian wanted to be certain no one could connect her visits. She knew she was exposed again, and she knew what would happen to her if she were caught with stolen property. So she walked and walked until her feet felt blistered, and finally found just the sort of shop she was looking for.

Vivian pushed open the door, making her eyes wide and nervous. The shop was small and plain, but fairly clean. It looked like a place a naïve young widow would think reputable. Clutching her reticule in front of her, she took tiny, hesitant steps to the counter where a rotund, balding man of indeterminate age watched her without a trace of expression, his chin propped on one hand.

It took only a glance to size him up. Expecting something dodgy. The sort who had seen everything and then some. She decided to try being pitiful and stupid. "Your pardon, sir," she said in her youngest voice. "Might you be Mr. Burddock?"

"Aye." Only his lower lip moved with the word. She swallowed and edged closer.

"Please, sir, I—I have some things to sell. They tell me you give fair prices."

Still his face didn't change. "Aye. A fair price for fair goods."

"I have that," she hurried to assure him. "My husband—that is, my late husband . . ." She shook her head and went to work on the reticule strings, bending her head as if in shame or sorrow. "I have some things of his," she whispered. "Very fine."

"Let's have a look, then." He spread his hands on the counter and cocked his head, waiting. Slowly Vivian brought out the pocket watch from the onion man yesterday. Mr. Burddock took it and examined it coolly. "Passable workmanship," he said, sounding bored.

Vivian's blush was real, although not from shame but anger. It was a fine watch, and he knew it. Just let him try to cheat her. "And this." She drew out the pearl pin.

Burddock held it up to the light and yawned. "Is the pearl genuine?"

"Of course!"

He twisted his lips and put it down on the counter, but didn't argue with her. Vivian was quite sure it was a fairly valuable piece. "That all?"

She bit her lip as if in indecision. "Yes. No. I—I don't know." Taking care that her fingers trembled, she reached into the reticule again and took out the signet ring. Just its weight guaranteed a good price. It gleamed of riches even in the dusty light of the little shop. "His ring," she said softly, keeping it in her hand instead of adding to the other items on the counter.

The man looked at it for a moment, and then finally a flicker of interest showed on his face. He reached for the ring and she let him take it, blinking rapidly. Mr. Burddock turned the ring from side to side, studying it, weighing it in his palm. "Family crest?" he asked with a keen glance.

"Yes," she said. "He was the last of his family. And now—not even a son to follow him—" She broke off and bit her lip, looking down.

Burddock continued to roll the ring between his fingers. "Well, it seems a well-made piece." He put it down. "A fine piece, in fact. I'd say it's worth a fair sum." His attitude had thawed considerably in a matter of seconds. Vivian gave him a cautious smile.

"Is it? Oh, I cannot tell you how that comforts me, that dear Charles may yet provide for me."

"Left you badly off, did he?" Burddock nodded, peering at her face.

"It is a familiar tale to you, I'm certain," she said with a sigh. "This is all I have left of him. Oh, sir, you wouldn't cheat a poor widow, would you?" She assumed an expression she knew made her face look young and hopeful. "You have raised my hopes tremendously."

Something like a smile flitted across his face. "Never say Thaddeus Burddock is a cheat, madam. Fair prices for fair pieces, is my creed." And he named a sum that made Vivian almost gasp aloud, act or no act. It was even more than she'd hoped for. Flynn would have to shut his mouth about Simon's rashness in taking the ring. With her share of that, plus the funds she'd already saved, she could apprentice Simon to a decent businessman. And with Simon safely settled, she could even think about extricating herself from thieving. An image sprang into her mind, of a small quiet cottage, with flowers and honeysuckle growing wild about it, and a fat cat sunning in the window.

She forced her imagination into submission and concentrated on the matter at hand. She mustn't get ahead of herself. "Sir, that would be most acceptable," she said breathlessly.

"I thought so." He put the ring down. "It's such a sum, though, I haven't the funds on hand to pay you today. If you come again tomorrow morning, I shall have it."

Vivian's disappointment was tempered by anticipation of the lovely, high price he would pay. "I believe I can manage it," she said. "And the other two pieces?"

With newly attentive eyes, he examined the pin and the watch again. "Perhaps these are a bit finer than I first thought," he said. "Shall we make a deal for all three pieces? To be purchased tomorrow?"

Vivian agreed, especially when he named a sum within reason for the other two pieces. She slipped all three items into her reticule. "Until the morrow, then, Mr. Burddock."

"The morrow," he said. "I shall expect you."

She ducked her head. "I will. Early tomorrow. Thank you, Mr. Burddock."

"Thank you, madam." He nodded, and Vivian left. She walked along as sedately as she could, clasping her shaking hands together in relief. She'd feared it would be a terrible task, selling that ring. Of course it was valuable, and a shop on the edge of St. Giles likely took in items of that kind every day, with no questions asked. Still, after she'd feared having to find someone to melt it and sell it as just a lump of gold . . . Even though it would mean another early morning trip into the city, she hurried through the streets all but wiggling with excitement.

The note arrived just before dinner. After a long and torturous day, David had finally succumbed to the headache that had never completely faded after his encounter with the highwaymen the previous day. He had accomplished his goals for the day, and felt rather proud of himself for doing so, but now his skull seemed to be squeezing his brain to the point of strangulation. He was lying on the sofa in his small drawing room, with a cushion over his face, when the bell rang. After a few moments it rang again, and then once more. David uncovered his face. "Bannet!"

At last shuffling footsteps sounded in the hall. The door opened, then closed. The servant tapped at the drawing room door. "A message for you, sir."

David grunted, but the bell had disturbed his rest already. He levered himself into a sitting position, closing his eyes against the renewed dizziness the action caused, and tore open the note Bannet held out to him. David gazed blearily at it for a moment before realizing what it was. The message inside lifted his spirits greatly. *Come early tomorrow to meet your thief. –Burddock*

"Excellent," he breathed to himself. At last, his shady past had come in handy. Immediately upon his return to London in a hired carriage, David had taken the time to personally visit each and every fence and pawnbroker he knew in London. Thanks to his highly varied gambling history, David knew quite a few fences and pawnbrokers, and all of them had been delighted to do business with him again. But instead of his silver or his pocket watch, this time he had offered them a reward: twenty pounds to anyone who recovered his signet ring, and double if they helped him capture the thief. Thaddeus Burddock, who had once extended David a loan against his best hunter, had had a visit from the highwayman, it seemed.

"Bless you, Burddock," he muttered. He lay back on the sofa and frowned in thought. It was best, perhaps, not to summon the Runners at once. Not because David feared they would object to his plan, but because they would be noticeable to a practiced thief. David didn't want to risk giving himself away and letting the thief escape; oh, no. David did not take kindly to being knocked senseless. Without thinking, he flexed the fingers of his sore hand, imagining the pleasure of driving his fist into the cowardly criminal's gut.

These thieves weren't entirely stupid, given their efforts to unload their stolen booty as soon as possible. Within a day reward notices could be posted, and robbery victims could hire thief-takers to track down their property. David doubted any had done so yet, for the simple reason that they could only have arrived in London today. Had the thieves' plan gone off successfully, the stolen goods would have already been sold, and any chance of capturing the thieves would be greatly reduced. David knew it had been a good idea to see to the pawnbrokers first, even though he'd had to postpone a meeting with Marcus's banker to do it. The banker could wait. David meant to catch those thieves, and smile at the shock on their faces when he did it. And then he would hand them over to Bow Street and applaud at their hanging.

Smiling with grim anticipation, he rang for dinner, his headache miraculously improved.

Chapter Four

The next morning David was at the pawnbroker's shop before it opened. Burddock, still in his nightcap, let him in and showed him into a small office at the rear of the shop. He offered tea, which David refused, and then went back upstairs to his lodgings. By the time he waddled back down the stairs and unlocked the front door, David had already explored every inch of the cluttered shop. Now there was nothing to do but wait.

He settled himself in the back room, but found it difficult to be patient. David shifted his weight and sighed. He'd been here an hour already, but it felt like an eternity. Burddock had assured him the thief would be returning early, but that was all. David was quite tired of waiting in the cramped, dingy back room of Burddock's shop, which smelled faintly of meat pies and sour ale. He peered through the threadbare curtain again, observed Burddock's wide backside reposing as indolently as ever on his stool, and cleared his throat.

"Patience," said Burddock without turning around.

"I've had patience," said David with an edge. "Have you anything else to suggest?"

Burddock glanced over his shoulder. "Have a seat, m'lord. Thieves ain't the most punctual sort."

Fair enough. David dusted off the end of the dingy bench and gingerly sat. He resisted the urge to drum his fingers. He couldn't afford to give in to his urge to go pace the streets until he found the thief and thrashed him. Tracking a criminal into the rookeries was madness, and David knew it; odds were, *his* throat would be in more jeopardy than the thief's. He had to wait, at least for a while, and see if this plan worked.

But sitting and waiting were almost impossible. The walls of the tiny room seemed to close in on him. The smells seemed to grow stronger and stronger until the air was too thick to breathe. He jumped up and peeked through the curtain again. The shop was still empty. "I'll wait outside," he said. "When he comes in, make certain you get the ring, then show him out. I'll watch for it."

"As you wish, sir," said Burddock, who seemed unconcerned about anything but keeping his ample body stationary. David set his mouth impatiently, then let himself out the back door into an alley. He strolled around to the front of the shop and across the street to where his carriage waited. His eyes swept the crowded street, but saw nothing exceptional. He spoke to his driver, who gave a discreet nod and sat back to wait, subtly shifting his position. Still unhurried, David bought a hot bun from a street vendor and leaned against a lamppost to eat it, keeping Burddock's shop in sight.

He waited a while. Several people entered, and all left alone. He finished his bun and took his time wiping his fingers on his handkerchief. Where the devil was that thief, he thought in aggravation. If Burddock had told him a tale, he would . . .

David left that thought unfinished. The door of the

shop had opened again, and Thaddeus Burddock himself was holding it open for the thief who had just sold him David's signet ring.

It was a woman. Not just any woman, he realized, his mouth dropping open in shock, but the pretty little widow from the stagecoach. Mrs. Gray, he remembered, the one with the face of an angel.

David snapped his sagging jaw shut. Not an innocent victim after all. He'd stood up for her and gotten knocked unconscious for it, never dreaming she would turn out to be in league with the thief who hit him. She'd played him for a fool—but would not do so again.

He raised his hand and adjusted his hat, the signal to his driver, who nodded once in response. Taking his time, but never letting her out of his sight, David drifted into the stream of passersby. It wasn't hard to overtake her; his stride must be half as long again as hers. Hard to believe such a dainty little woman was a hardened criminal, but David knew looks never did tell true. She paused at the corner, waiting for a produce cart to rumble past, and he made his move.

"There you are," he said, sweeping her into the curve of his arm and taking a tight grip on her elbow. "I thought I'd never find you."

Shocked blue eyes flew to his. "S-sir," she stuttered, then gasped as she looked at him. "Release me, please," she continued, masking her recognition well, but not well enough. "You've mistaken me for someone else, I fear."

"I fear much the same thing, but let's sort it out properly, shall we?" His carriage drew up, and David pulled open the door with one hand and shoved her inside with the other. She braced her arms against the doorframe, trying to resist, but David made short work of that by stepping onto the step, wrapping one arm around her, and bodily boosting her into the carriage as if she were a large sack of wheat. The carriage was off even before he pulled the door shut behind him.

His quarry had tumbled to the floor in a heap of shabby gray skirts, and was struggling to right herself. David watched in dark amusement as she scrambled to her feet, crouching a little in the carriage. She was breathing hard, and her eyes were like saucers. She stared at him for a moment, then lunged for the door. He put his boot on the opposite seat, extending his leg across the door. She drew back as if singed, huddling in the corner farthest from him.

"Mrs. Gray, I believe," he said easily. She was rattled, and he wanted to rattle her more. "My memory's not terribly good for names, but being robbed and beaten about the head does tend to impress things even on my mind."

"Oh," she said in an odd, choking voice. "Oh, yes— now I remember you. From the Bromley stage."

He tilted his head. "Only now? I would swear you remembered a few moments ago."

She licked her lips. She had such a perfect mouth, he thought. What lies would come out of it next? "I—I wasn't certain. You took me very much by surprise, sir. I certainly never expected to be accosted on the street by someone with whom I'm hardly acquainted." There was just a trace of stinging censure in her words, which David found highly entertaining. She was a very good liar, it seemed.

But unfortunately for her, so was he, and one liar could always sniff out another liar. He leaned forward, watching her draw back and widen her eyes in alarm. "Ah, but we've a much closer bond than that, haven't we?" She blinked, an uncomprehending angel. "Since it *was* my ring you were trying to sell Burddock," he clarified.

If possible, her eyes got even bigger. "Oh, no!" she gasped. "No! Your ring? Why, I've no idea what you're talking of! I'm just a poor widow, sir—I have no other means of support than to sell some of my late husband's things—"

"A tragic tale," he agreed. "If only it were true. Stealing is a crime. Did you know they hang thieves?" She didn't move a muscle, her eyes fixed on him. The carriage jerked to a halt. "Ah, excellent. We've arrived. Care to tell me the truth? Last chance," he added with a dangerous smile.

"The truth? But I've told you . . ." Her voice trailed off, her eyes darting to the window. As directed, the driver had gone around to the alley behind Burddock's shop. The shopkeeper was waiting for them.

Without comment, David pushed open the door, keeping his leg across the opening. Burddock waddled closer, peered into the carriage, and said, "Aye, that's the one. Sold me this." He produced a pearl stickpin and a watch ornamented with tiny rubies. David frowned.

"Where's the ring?"

Burddock lifted one shoulder. "She didn't bring it today."

"Oh, sir!" cried the widow pleadingly. "Say you aren't in league with him! This villain snatched me off the streets and won't let me go! Please help me!"

Burddock gazed at her with his opaque black eyes, then turned back to David. "I bought 'em both, as you asked," he said.

David took them, holding his pin up to the light. "Good work. Your compensation will be sent over directly."

Burddock smirked. "Very good. A pleasure serving you, sir."

"But the ring?" David prompted. Burddock hesitated. "She didn't have it. At least she said she didn't." David shot him a dark glance, and Burddock backed up a step, spreading his hands as if to plead helplessness. "What was I to do? I expect you can handle it from here better than I could."

David turned back to his thief, the lovely, white-faced widow opposite him. "Yes, I believe I can," he said grimly. He thumped a fist on the roof. "Drive on."

Her gaze veered from the jewels in his hand to his face. "Release me," she said, her voice a thin thread of sound. "Please, sir, I beg you . . ."

"Yes, I expect you do." He held the watch up to the light. "This was from the Bromley stage robbery, isn't it? The fat man who smelled of onions, I believe. What was his name?" David turned the watch from side to side, pretending to study it but watching her from the corner of his eye. She was tensed like a cat waiting to spring, her hands curled into the cushions. "No matter," he said, putting it in his pocket. "I can send word to the constable. He'll have the man's direction."

His companion said nothing, her unblinking gaze fixed on him.

"I expect you're in it with them," he went on, as casually as one might discuss the weather. "There's really no other explanation for how you came into possession of items stolen from passengers on the coach. Fortunately for you, I don't particularly care. All I want is my ring. And you might as well give back my pocket watch, since I've gone to a lot of trouble to track you down. But once you return those things, you'll be free."

"I don't have them," she protested.

He smiled gently. "You'll have to get them. Send word to your associates."

"But I can't!"

David sighed, still smiling. This was really quite entertaining. "Then you'll just be my guest until you can."

She jerked, yet more color fading from her face. "What?"

He leaned forward. "My guest," he repeated. "I don't appreciate being robbed, my dear, let alone coshed on the head and left for dead. It was quite a fit of nerves, was it, that you had after that. I heard all about it."

"I—I was so sorry to see you hurt," she cried.

"No doubt. And yet, when I acted on my gentlemanly instincts and tried to make certain you were recovered, no one seemed to know precisely where you had gone." He put his head to one side, smiling a smile that made Vivian's blood run absolutely hot with fury. He was toying with her. She wanted to claw his eyes out for it.

"That was very kind of you, but—"

"But completely pointless," he finished for her. "Did it take long to rejoin your accomplices?"

"I—but—no—" She covered her face with both hands, trying to gather her panicked thoughts. How had he sussed out most of their operation, just from looking at her? She had to get away, had to warn the others that someone was on to them and would be setting the constables on them. It was definitely time to move on, all the way to Scotland perhaps. "I don't understand what you're saying," she bleated piteously.

"There, dear," he said. "Don't worry your pretty head about it. Rest your nerves. The answer will come to you soon enough, I expect."

Vivian finally decided to resort to weeping, something she only employed in desperate circumstances. It was always useful to keep one weapon in her arsenal in reserve. But these circumstances were desperate, like no others she could remember, and so she scrunched up her face and set to crying in the most pathetic manner she possibly could.

"A magnificent performance," he commented after a few moments. Vivian swiped at her eyes, trying not to glare at him.

"What else can I do? You won't believe a word I say."

"True," he agreed. "I won't." But the carriage was coming to a stop. She risked a glance out the window. If he would get out, or better yet, let her out, she would be gone in a flash.

Her captor pushed open the door himself and jumped down. His figure filled the doorway. "Come along now," he said.

She clutched her reticule in front of her chest. "No."

The wretched man's face didn't change. Vivian swallowed hard, battling back fear and fury. "I said, come along," he repeated. "Or I shall make you."

What the ruddy hell did he plan to do? Terrible images whirled through her mind. She dug the worn toes of her boots into the carriage floor, bracing herself. "No."

He leaned toward her, his hands on either side of the doorway. "Come," he said in a silky voice that almost sounded seductive. Vivian balled her left hand into a fist. She had to time this just right. . . .

"If you insist." Faster than expected, he lunged forward and seized her wrist, dragging her half out of the carriage. Vivian gave a startled little shriek, swinging wildly as he pulled her off balance and sideways. Her fist connected, pretty well to judge by the pain that shot up her arm, but he just gave a tiny grunt and then laughed. The blackguard *laughed*.

Now fighting in earnest, Vivian still found herself hauled out of the carriage and held upright against him, his one arm around her waist and his other around her shoulders. He adjusted his hold, and she found herself on her tiptoes. She clawed at his hand, scrabbling with her toes for balance, and his hand came to rest at her throat. He had a big hand. She could feel his fingers sweep lightly across the base of her neck, and she went still, her heart about to burst from beating so hard.

"You've lost the fight," he whispered in her ear. "I don't intend to hurt you, so cease trying to hurt me."

She swung her feet a little, desperately trying to get some leverage. Her worn half boots wouldn't do any serious damage, even if she could kick him. "Let me go," she said between her teeth. "I'll cry murder!"

He sighed. "The neighbors won't pay it any mind, my dear." With a squeeze around her waist, he lifted her a little higher and proceeded to walk up the steps into a house that looked immensely forbidding to Vivian. In fact, now that she looked around, she realized how deep in trouble she was. This was a fancy neighborhood, with clean-swept walks and wide streets and houses that gleamed in the morning light. As he mounted the steps, seemingly untroubled by her writhing, a man opened the door, his expression completely neutral.

"Help!" she cried, not having to feign her fear. "He's hurting me!"

The man didn't even look at her. "Welcome home, my lord," he said, stooping to pick up the hat her struggles had knocked from his master's head.

"Ah, Bannet," said Vivian's captor, setting her on her feet but keeping a tight hold on her. He sounded a trifle out of breath, nothing more. "Have a guest room prepared at once for . . ." He hesitated a moment. "My guest."

"I won't stay here," she shrieked, more, even more terrible, images filling her mind. Good Lord, this must be his home, and he could lock her up and do whatever he wished to do to her. Vivian had heard more than enough about the depraved behavior of upper-class gentlemen. At the realization that he meant to keep her a prisoner, subject to anything he wanted to do to her, she clasped her hands and jabbed her elbow back, right into his side. He gave a sharp hiss of pain, flinching away from her. Vivian lunged for the door, but his grip, though loosened, was still tight enough to keep her.

"Never mind, Bannet," he said grimly, dragging her toward the stairs. "She can sit in the dust."

"Very good, sir," said the servant. He hadn't moved a muscle since picking up the hat, which he still held. He wouldn't help her, Vivian realized. She would have to save herself. Each step up the stairs seemed another step closer to whatever horror awaited her, and she screamed until her throat burned.

At the top of the stairs he turned left, jerking her back to her feet when she tried to pretend a faint. "It's no use," he said, as he opened a door. "I'm not in the mood to be fooled any longer." And he gave her a little push, into a large, dusty room.

Then he stepped inside and closed the door behind him, turning the key in the lock.

Eyeing him warily, her chest heaving, Vivian took a step backward, and then another. He looked rather dangerous, to tell the truth. His black hair must have been tied back, for now it was falling loose about his face, much longer than most gentlemen wore their hair. His face was pale, but his dark eyes seemed lit by an unearthly light that was much more frightening even than his stance, arms folded across his chest and booted feet apart, like a sentinel at the door. He looked huge and dark and very threatening, and Vivian felt dizzy with fear as she caught sight of a bed, not four feet away from her.

"That was my broken rib, bloodthirsty wench," he said. "I promise not to hurt you, but only if you don't try to hurt me."

Vivian licked her lips, inching backward and thinking frantically. "I didn't know it was broken."

"Somehow I think it wouldn't have mattered."

Vivian kept her mouth shut. Of course it would have, she thought; if I'd known, I'd have hit it harder, and sooner.

"Nevertheless," he went on, "I shall overlook it. All I want are my belongings. Return them, and you'll be free to rob and assault any other chap you choose. Do we have a bargain?"

"I don't have them," she said again. "Truly I don't."

He started toward her, his boot heels thudding loudly and ominously. "You'll just have to get them."

She swallowed and backed away. "How could I do that, locked in here?"

His mouth curled in a frightening hint of smile. "That's for you to solve, isn't it?"

In spite of herself, her temper was getting away from her. "You liar," she cried. "How dare you say you want me to get you something I don't have, then lock me up so I couldn't get it even if I did! I'll fight you, I will, you won't have an easy time of it with me— "

"I've managed so far," he cut her off. Vivian didn't move, holding her ground but tensed for any action that might be necessary. His eyes were as black as night, and incredulously, she thought they were amused. Her stomach turned; this was all a sick joke to him. "Should you wish to tell me who has my possessions, and where that person is, I'd be delighted to have someone else do the fetching. And then you'll be free." He smiled charmingly. "It sounds so easy, doesn't it?"

"You can't keep me here!" she screeched. "This is kidnapping!"

He tilted his head, that infernal smile still on his face. How she longed to slap it away. "Shall I summon the authorities?" he asked conversationally. "You can tell them your story. No doubt they'll be very sympathetic, particularly when you explain how you came to be selling stolen goods to Burddock. And, of course, you can mention the kidnapping."

Vivian's heart thumped and her chest heaved with breathing. She thought furiously, but couldn't think of a single thing to say. She didn't have an excuse for having his belongings, let alone trying to sell them. She caught her breath and held it, then let it go in a little sob. "But I don't know anything," she said, screwing up her eyes and trying to conjure up some more piteous tears. "All right—the truth is, someone gave me those things to sell and said he would share the profits with me if I did. Please, sir, please let me go, I don't know anything about your ring—"

"You're very good," he said admiringly. "I'd wager a guinea you'd shoot me through the heart if you had a pistol. How much did he promise you?"

"Wha—? Why—" Vivian swiped at her eyes with her fingertips, trying to think. "Five shillings, sir."

"Five shillings is small gratitude for selling stolen goods," he commented. "You really ought to have asked for a percentage of the price, particularly on fine pieces. Why didn't you bargain with him after you spoke to Burd-dock yesterday?" Suddenly he leaned forward, and Vivian couldn't repress a small squeak. "Where is it?"

he asked softly. His dark hair fell forward around his face, which combined with his lethally quiet question to give him a deadly air. For the first time Vivian felt a shiver of fear, not just for her virtue but for her life. She was alone here, and no one she knew would ever find her if he made good on his threats to lock her up. "Where is it?" he demanded again when she said nothing. She jumped as he slammed his hand against the wall behind her—she hadn't even realized she had her back literally to the wall—and shrank back as he crowded even closer, towering over her. "Let me be clear," he said in the same terrifying tone. "I want that ring back, and I shall have it. Whether you cooperate or not."

"You'll never get it back if you don't let me go." The words flew out of her mouth before she could stop them.

He placed his other hand against the wall, trapping her in place. "Then you'll be my guest here, until you decide to be more cooperative."

At that, her temper abruptly overtook her fear, and she pushed at his chest. He didn't move. "Let me by," she said through her teeth, "or you'll sore regret it."

His only answer was a slow grin that seemed to dare her to prove her words. She ground her teeth and slipped her hands behind her back. "You've made a mistake, mate," she tried one last time. "I don't have your ring, and I can't get it, not stuck here blathering with you. You want it back? You let me go, then you pay another visit to your favorite fence in a day or two. He'll have the goods, I swear to that. We'll all be happy then, aye?" And she pressed her little blade against his side.

He looked down. "In your sleeve, I suppose," he said. "Damned careless of me."

"Aye, damned careless," she agreed. "Let me pass."

He tilted his head from side to side, studying the

blade. "Right." He leaned back, and Vivian stepped sideways out from between him and the wall, keeping the blade pointed at him. "I would, except," he went on, pausing significantly. Vivian scurried backwards toward the door, stumbling a little on the edge of the carpet. He followed at arm's length, moving slowly but with his attention fastened on her intently. Too intently. She reached the door and rattled the knob, remembering too late he had locked it.

"Give me the key," she said. He rocked back on his heels, and drew the key from his pocket.

"This key?" Now it was his turn to mock her. "Come get it." He tossed it in the air and caught it with his other hand, dangling the key from his fingertips.

Vivian swallowed. Damn him. Damn her for forgetting about the bloody key. She ought to have stuck him at the start and been done with it, even though it was highly unlikely her little blade would incapacitate him. His smile grew wicked. "We seem to have reached an impasse," he said, examining the key before stowing it back in his pocket. She eyed the pocket, and gripped her knife. If she threw it and hit him, she might be able to get the key and escape. Then again . . . They'd string her up for attempted murder if she so much as pricked a cove like him. She lowered the knife, glowering.

"As I was saying," he said. "I would let you go, but I've lost something important to me, something I want back. And like you, my dear, I'm hard-headed enough to stick to my course even in defiance of reason and logic." He smiled. "Unlike you, though, I shall get what I want."

Vivian threw the knife. To her shock he caught it, just *caught* it, straight out of the air as he ducked aside. Cursing, she scrambled for the window, preferring to be spattered on the ground than at his mercy, only to be caught by the arm and swung around until he had her around the waist again, her back tight against him. She kicked and swore some more as he thoroughly and roughly ran his hand over her, finding the second little knife she had in her stocking. He pulled that one out and held it before her eyes. "Mustn't be careless again," he murmured. "Is that all?"

She snarled at him. He laughed, and turned her loose. Vivian backed away, hating him for blocking her in, like a mongrel dog about to be put down. He picked up her reticule from the floor, took a quick look inside, and dropped it on the bed.

"Don't take on so," he said. "I've given my word I shan't hurt you, although only if you refrain from trying to kill me." He pointed the knife he'd just removed from her stocking at her in admonishment. "Not very well done." He paused. "What's your name, Mrs. Gray?" She glared at him. "Hmm. No matter. You know my terms. When you're disposed to talk, I'll be disposed to listen. In the meantime . . ." He gave a small bow. "Welcome to my home." And he left, taking both knives—and the key—with him.

David examined the wicked little blades in the hallway. Cheap, thin metal, barely a handle to speak of, but effective nonetheless. He took out his handkerchief and squeezed it around the cut her first knife had left on his fingers. He could hardly blame her for that, since she couldn't have expected him to grab it in his fist like a circus performer. That had startled her, he knew, and he grinned again at the memory of her expression. Oh, yes, he liked the mysterious Mrs. Gray. Which was surely proof beyond proof that he was a fool.

Because . . . what was he to do with her now? He had
expected the young highwayman, or even the older one;
he had expected the thief to crumble under threats of
being turned over to the Runners. David didn't especially want to involve the Runners, although he never
would have admitted it to his captive. He was quite
aware that some of his own activities in the recent past
would not reflect well on his credibility, and he preferred to keep a law-abiding distance from anyone with
the power to arrest him for misdeeds past, present, or
future. It had been a different matter when he'd expected
to have his belongings returned and could simply turn
the thief over to Bow Street. He wasn't at all certain
they would approve of his methods now, though. The
prickly Mrs. Gray had inadvertently called his bluff, and
now he had gone and locked her in his own house.

Well. In for a penny, in for a pound, he told himself.
He might as well follow through on his words and keep
her a while, to see if he could wear her down and get the
ring back after all. David knew he was quite good at
talking people into things, particularly when those
people were female. And if the opportunity arose to talk
her *out* of her drab old sack of a dress, he would probably sacrifice himself to that task, too. But only as a last
resort, he reminded himself virtuously.

He glanced back at the door, thinking. Was there anything in there she might use as a weapon or a means of
escape? He didn't think so, just because there was very
little in the room at all. His stepmother had made some
effort to furnish the house when he first bought it, but
that was years ago and no one had bothered to keep it
up since. He never had guests, after all. But now he did,
and no doubt he'd have to post someone outside the

door to make certain she didn't escape or burn down his house in his absence.

Punctuating that thought, his footman, or butler, shuffled up the stairs. Bannet was a rather dodgy fellow. He was one of the few servants who hadn't cut line and left during David's latest difficulties. That would all change, though, thanks to David's vow of responsibility and honesty, not to mention prompt payment of wages. He'd already found entries in Marcus's ledgers indicating his brother had paid his servants twice this year alone—not that it seemed to keep them from leaving without notice at inconvenient moments.

"Bannet, see to it Mrs. Gray has meals brought to her room, without knives, and take care of her other needs. She's not to go out, though." He handed over the key.

Bannet took the key without the slightest sign of surprise or alarm that his master intended to keep a woman locked up. David gave him a measured look; was that normal? Where had Bannet been previously employed, he wondered.

But the servant just gazed placidly back at him. "Yes, sir. What shall I serve her, sir?"

As tempted as he was to say 'bread and water,' David restrained himself. That was exactly what she would expect, no doubt. "She's my guest, Bannet," he said. "Serve her as you would a guest."

"Yes, sir," said Bannet, unfazed. "But what shall that be? Cook gave notice and left this morning."

David only just managed not to curse out loud. Why would Cook quit now, when he was back in town and feeling responsible? "Why?" he snapped. "Why did no one tell me?"

Bannet blinked. "She gave notice after you left, sir,"

he explained. "To me. And I told you, just now, as soon as you arrived home."

David closed his eyes. Brilliant, just bloody brilliant. "All right, I'll hire another cook. In fact, I'm going to re-staff the house, immediately." Bannet bobbed his head in acknowledgment. David turned to go, then thought of something and turned back. "But in the meantime, go around to Exeter House and have Cook there pack up a hamper for a day. And see if she has any talented helpers who might like to take the post of cook here."

"Yes, sir," Bannet said.

Feeling rather proud of himself, David took himself off to attend to his other business. By this evening, surely, Mrs. Gray would see that he meant what he said, and she'd tell him where the ring was. Then he would let her go back to thieving and throwing knives, and he could go back to being responsible and respectable.

Chapter Five

The door closed behind him, and then, ominously, she heard the sound of a key turning in the lock.

Vivian snatched up a candlestick with both hands and drew back, ready to hurl it at the door in a fury. Then she paused. The candlestick was heavy, but not massive enough to break down the door. And even if it took a chunk out of the door, it wouldn't free her, and most likely would just bring *him* back. Vivian didn't want to see *him* again.

She put the candlestick down and prowled around the room. It was a good size and, although dusty, still a very fine room. There was a rug on the floor, without a single worn spot that she could see. There were two windows, although they looked out on a neglected little garden, at least twenty feet below, without a single foothold she could use to climb down. She tapped her fingertips against the glass in ire. Perhaps she could use the bed linens? She crossed the room and yanked back the coverlet on the bed. A cloud of dust flew up, leaving her choking and even more frustrated. There were no linens on the bed.

But it was a fine deep mattress, and once she'd waved

aside the dust and sat on it, she decided it was very comfortable, too. Rich bloody sod, she thought furiously. She examined the coverlet for any chance of ripping it up and turning it into a rope, but it was thick and heavy. With her blades she could slice it to make a rope, but without them she had no hope. Everything in here was too well-made to help her escape.

She must think. Crossing her arms across her chest, Vivian rolled her lower lip between her teeth and tried to see the path out. He said he wouldn't let her go until he had the ring; she didn't have the ring. She couldn't even tell him where to go find the ring, for Flynn would move on once she didn't return or send word. And she didn't doubt that her captor would go to retrieve it with a brigade of constables at his side, ready to arrest Simon and the rest. Perhaps if she persuaded him to let her send a message to Flynn? But Flynn, shifty old bugger that he was, wouldn't set foot in London himself, and he certainly wouldn't hand over any valuables just to save *her* neck.

Not that she actually wanted to hand over the ring now. When the bloke had first snatched her off the street, she would have; if it had been in her reticule, she would have flung it at him and scampered into the safety of the rookery shadows. By making her his prisoner, though, he had worn out her goodwill, and now she was determined to escape without giving him the satisfaction of getting what he wanted. It would make things harder, but there was really no way she could get the ring unless she was free anyway.

So, she had to figure out a way around him. Why on earth did he want that ruddy ring so much, she fumed. Surely a nob like him could afford to get another, and another, and another. One for each finger on his hands, and probably enough for his toes, too, if he felt so inclined. And that Burddock! She'd spread the word on him, she would. He'd never see fresh goods again, if she had anything to say about it.

Of course, she couldn't do anything before she made it out of here. She went back to the window and examined it. It was well-fitted, and all the glazing was intact. It probably kept the wind out in winter, just as surely as it was making it warm in the room now. When she tried it, the sash went up easily enough, but then wedged fast after only a few inches. She pulled and strained, but it refused to budge. She got down on her knees and squinted at the underside, to no avail. Even his window wished to thwart her, it seemed. She cursed at the glass, circling the room in search of anything she could use to pry the window open.

Simon would be wild with worry for her. Flynn probably wouldn't care, beyond the lost money from her sale. She realized then that her wretched captor hadn't taken her reticule, and she dumped the contents out on the bed.

The coins from Burddock jingled out. She scooped them up with an apprehensive glance at the door; she didn't want *him* to come back and take them. She held them in her fist, trying to figure out where to hide them. Nowhere on her person seemed safe, after the way he'd run his hands over her. She could still feel his fingers slipping beneath the garter of her stocking to extract her little knife, and she shuddered. Thank God she hadn't put the knife in her corset. For that reason, she discarded the idea of putting the money down her bodice. On no account did she want to tempt him to stick his fingers *there*.

Finally she decided on the hem of her dress. With her

teeth she worked a hole in the stitching just large enough to force the coins through, and then painstakingly fed each one through it. There. She stood up and turned, watching her skirts swirl. They felt heavier, and fell straighter, but she didn't think it was obvious where the money was. Satisfied with that one small victory, she put her hands on her hips and looked around. What the bloody hell was she supposed to do now?

There wasn't anything useful in the room that she could see. The grate in the fireplace was cold and musty, as if it hadn't been used in a long time. She opened the wardrobe in the corner and found nothing except a huge amount of dust. She ran her fingers along the walls, trying to see if any of the moldings would come off and give her a weapon. Finally, in a huff of exasperation, she sat on the room's only chair. She could heave the chair through the window, but that would be pointless if she didn't have a plan for getting safely down. Drumming her fingers against the windowsill, she thought.

He'd said he wouldn't hurt her; he fancied himself a gentleman. He obviously had money, which meant he could be somebody important. Something resurfaced in her memory. She'd said she would cry murder, and he hadn't been the least bit disturbed. No one would pay it any mind, he had said. Vivian swallowed nervously. Perhaps he did this all the time, and his neighbors were used to women being dragged in and out of the house, screaming at the top of their lungs. He was so much bigger and stronger than she was, Vivian knew she wouldn't be able to protect herself for long. Not that she wouldn't try, of course.

But . . . if he fancied himself such a gent, he'd have to feed her, which meant the door would open.

She jumped when the door finally did open, the

metallic scrape of the key in the lock startling her. She backed up, bracing herself, but it was the servant who shuffled into the room. He carried a covered tray.

"Some luncheon, madam," he mumbled, setting the tray on the small table.

Vivian bolted. He was between her and the door, but she squeezed around him and out the door. In a flurry she ran through the hall, aware that the servant was calling out behind her. The stairs appeared around the corner, and she grabbed at her skirt, practically falling down the steps. Then she almost fell on her face as a tall, dark, dreadfully familiar figure appeared out of thin air in front of her.

Vivian shrieked, scrambling madly out of his reach. "Going out?" he asked, stalking after her, his eyes aglow with that unholy light. "I wasn't quite ready to say good-bye."

"Bugger yourself," she snarled.

He smiled, a devilish smile. A pirate's smile, she thought. "You didn't hurt Bannet, did you? He's my only servant at the moment, and I shan't look kindly on him being indisposed."

"I got no quarrel with him." She eyed the door, visible through the crook of his elbow. She stared at it long and hard, until he was most definitely aware of her interest, then feinted to his left. He lunged, and she sprang in the other direction. He cursed, but had overbalanced; he fell, landing on his knee, and the curse that came from his lips that time shocked even Vivian. He snagged a handful of her dress, stopping her in her tracks. Desperately, Vivian kicked, thinking of his broken rib, but he dodged her foot, grabbing her ankle instead and pulling her onto the floor as well. She felt him trying to rein in her flailing limbs, and then he fell on top of her with a thump that almost knocked her unconscious.

"You're downright vicious," he said in disbelief. "I see harsher measures are called for." He took advantage of her rather stunned state to scoop her into his arms, and then carted her up the stairs again. He dropped her none-too-gently on the bed, and Vivian flopped onto her back, still gasping for air.

"That will do, Bannet," said the black-hearted fiend to the servant, who was still standing by the door holding the tray cover. "I'll see to Mrs. Gray from now on."

The man bowed, mumbled something, and left.

"Bloody hell," she wheezed, trying to scoot out of his reach. "You're the devil, you are."

"Perhaps." He closed the door after his servant and propped one shoulder against it as he studied her. Vivian managed to sit up on the edge of the bed, bracing herself on both arms. Her chest ached with every breath. "But now you're completely at my mercy." She shot him a hateful look, but said nothing.

He picked up the chair and carried it across the room, setting it down right in front of her and then sitting on it. For a moment he just looked at her, as he might contemplate a puzzle. "You're a clever girl," he said at last. "Surely you see that I'm going to win. I'm being rather reasonable," he added when she only sneered at him. "If I turned you over to Bow Street, they'd send you straight to Newgate." Vivian seethed in silent fury.

"All you're accomplishing is subjecting yourself to further torment," he said in the same sympathetic tone. "Until you tell me where my ring is, I shall have no choice but to subject you to my charming presence. From this moment, you shall see no one but me, speak to no one but me, and hear from no one but me. Now,

I've already made clear my wishes. Speak now, and spare us both." He waited, watching her closely, but Vivian simply glared at him.

"Right." He got to his feet. "Bannet has already brought your luncheon, so you might as well eat." He stopped by the small table and inspected the dishes. "Don't worry that it's poisoned." He flashed her a faintly amused look. "Can't have you turn up your toes before you return my property, can I?"

Now that he mentioned food, Vivian realized how hungry she was. And how mouth-watering that tray of luncheon smelled.

"I'll be back shortly to take the tray. I suggest you reflect on the consequences of continued refusal," he said, his voice growing stern. She made a rude gesture with one hand, and he let himself out the door, laughing heartily. She could hear him still chuckling for several seconds after the key turned in the lock again.

Hateful wretch. Holding her side, Vivian gingerly slid off the bed and crept over to the table. Luncheon was a bowl of soup, some rolls, and a small glass of wine. Her stomach growled and her mouth watered. She was so hungry, she'd have eaten it even if she did suspect poison. Without hesitation she grabbed up the spoon and ate every last crumb on the tray.

When it was gone, she sat back with a sigh of pure pleasure. Food, glorious hot food, and not a bite of it rabbit. She ran her finger around the inside of the bowl and put it in her mouth, sucking off the traces of soup. That certainly made being a prisoner more enjoyable, to tell the truth; she hadn't had a meal like that in her entire life. She still wanted to escape, of course, but the food mitigated her suffering somewhat.

Her eyes fell on the empty plate that had held the

bread. It was china. And there was the wine glass. She could carefully break either of them and give herself a sharp little weapon . . . which her captor would probably use against her.

This was a quandary. It seemed she was stuck. There was no way she could send a message out to Simon and the others, not from this rich neighborhood, and she didn't dare let her jailer know where she would send word. For all she knew, he would see every last one of them hanged by the neck until dead. No, she didn't trust him. He'd caught her, which was bad enough, but she wouldn't help him to her brother, too.

At least he wasn't starving her to death. She licked the spoon once more and set it back on the tray. She would just bide her time, then. Until a reasonable avenue of escape appeared, it seemed best to outwait him.

He returned some time later and collected the tray. Vivian could feel his eyes on her the whole time, although she resolutely kept her back to him, staring at the wall.

David wanted to laugh at the sight of her, pert little nose in the air, arms folded, spine perfectly straight. She was the image of outraged dignity—she, who had thrown a dagger at him, punched him in the ribs, and called him any number of vulgar names. "The cut direct," he said. "I admire your spirit, madam. It won't do you any good, of course, but it's noble and heroic all the same.

"I have consulted Bow Street," he went on, watching carefully and noting her small start with satisfaction. Of course he'd done no such thing, but she wouldn't know. "The man I spoke to offered to come extract a confession from you himself, but he was a big brute. It seemed cruel to allow such a person to . . . persuade you. Surely

I can do so myself." She darted a scorching glance over her shoulder, and David smiled innocently. "I've always been rather persuasive with ladies."

That made her nervous. He could see the flicker of her eyelashes as she blinked several times, and the tiny twitch in her cheek. Good; let her worry. "How best to persuade you," he said thoughtfully, drawing his finger along his jaw. "I can see you're determined to be difficult. This may require . . . extreme measures."

Now she was completely motionless, except for the rise and fall of her chest. David was certain he would see smoke coming out of her nostrils if she were to turn around. Mrs. Gray, he thought, was furious. For some reason this delighted him.

"I shall have to think on it," he said, dropping his voice. Let her think about it for a while. "Until tonight, my dear."

He picked up the tray and left.

Chapter Six

After two days spent trying to find a way to escape, Vivian gave up. The servant seemed incorruptible, for he never came to open her door. She thought up an elaborate story sure to make him feel very, very sorry for her, to no purpose. The man brought clean linens for the bed, and then never came again. She never had the chance to use her tale of woe. No possible escape route presented itself, as the room proved as ordinary, and as secure, as she had thought at first. The only person she saw was *him*, that hateful man who'd locked her in here, and he only brought her dinner and breakfast. Even though she didn't want to talk to him, particularly not about his bloody ring, Vivian was growing a little edgy from having nothing to do and no one to talk to.

Frustrated and bored, Vivian took to pacing the room. What was she to do all day? Did he mean for her to fall into a stupor from sitting here staring at the walls? She dragged the chair over to the window and plopped into it, gazing out the window with longing. It was a lovely day. How she longed to be outside, to be free. . . .

Then she could return to Simon. She missed her

brother; she worried about him. What if he and Flynn came to blows over her disappearance? Flynn would be furious, no doubt, for not only was she gone and unable to set up other jobs, but she still had some of the profits from the last job with her. No doubt he would demand Simon hand over his share, to make up for what Vivian had hidden in her skirt hem. And her poor brother wouldn't be able to stop Flynn from taking it.

Of course, if she returned to Simon, she'd also be returning to Flynn. Even furious as she was with the gent who'd kidnapped her, she had to admit he was more pleasant than Flynn. Unlike Flynn, he fed her good food, gave her a luxuriously soft bed, and hadn't once tried to feel her bottom. Things could be much worse, and Vivian acknowledged it. Once her initial outrage had dimmed a bit, she even began to appreciate the advantages of being locked up. True, she was no help to Simon, but she also had a respite from Flynn. She had time to consider her future, what she would do once she managed to slip out of this spot.

That was a thorny question. Especially now that she'd had a taste of real comfort, it seemed harder and harder to return to sleeping on the ground, eating oatcakes and watery stew, and constantly moving around to avoid arrest. It was quite nice not to have to worry about her brother making a mistake, or about Flynn bringing disaster down on them in a drunken fit. Only now that it was lifted, even for a short time, could Vivian appreciate how oppressive that worry and responsibility had become.

It had always been her hope to find an occupation that was, if not completely respectable, then at least settled. Vivian had lived in more places than she could count, and she didn't care to remember most of them, cramped, dirty places that didn't offer an iota of the comfort of this room she was in. She had learned to keep her few belongings in a handy bundle, ready to be snatched up at a moment's notice in case the charleys had gone through in search of thieves. She glanced at the heavy wardrobe in the corner again, that big, solid piece meant just to hold a body's belongings in one place. The man who lived here had never had to leave in the middle of the night for fear of being thrown in prison.

For that, she envied him. For as long as she could remember, Vivian had wanted that security, that knowledge that she had a safe, cozy place to return to every night. She wanted not to be cold at night, not to be hungry during the day, and more than anything she wanted to feel in control of her own life. Now, she knew that the few things in life she valued could vanish at a moment's notice.

For a moment she closed her eyes. In her mind she could see the house, a small stone cottage with roses rambling over it, a prosperous smoke puffing out the chimney. The windows were open, and a yellow cat lay curled on one sill, tail twitching lazily. Vivian could see that house as clearly as if it were before her, even though she'd only seen it once with her eyes. The house was in Essex. She had seen it as she and Simon walked along the road toward Colchester, damp from sleeping under a tree, cold from having no fire, and so terribly hungry Simon had woken up crying from the pain in his belly. At that moment, that little cottage had been everything Vivian ever wanted in life: four sturdy walls and a solid roof, and a fire with a pot of food over it. She had wanted it for Simon, who was her responsibility, but she had wanted it most of all for herself.

She sighed and rested her head against the window

frame. On the other side of the glass, far down below, a small bird was digging in the garden for worms. He moved around with sharp, jerky movements that managed to cover every square inch of the sad little garden down below. His feet scratched at the dirt, his little brown head bobbing hopefully as he inspected his progress every few scratches. But the garden seemed as barren of worms as it was of flowers. With a sudden flutter of wings the bird was gone, off to seek greener, worm-filled, pastures.

Vivian's mouth twisted. Would that she could fly away, too, to someplace far away where life would be easier. Unlike the little bird, she was stuck with her bare patch of earth, scratching away day after day in search of bounty that never appeared. She heaved another sigh. Now the bounty was served to her twice daily, which she couldn't complain about, but she hated being caged in. This was by far the longest Vivian had ever spent indoors in her life.

A soft tapping made her sit up, alert. Someone was knocking, very lightly, on the door. "Who's there?" she said, getting her to feet nervously.

"Bannet, ma'am," said the servant's muffled voice.

"Aye, what?" she asked suspiciously. Why would he come knock on her door now, after two days?

"I thought you might like something to read," he replied. "Seeing as the master says you're not going out."

That was an understatement. "Will you let me out?" she said, unable to keep the eagerness from her voice.

"No, ma'am, I cannot. The master says not."

"But he's locked me in here!" she cried. "I want to go out! It's imprisonment!"

"But he's not mistreated you, has he?" asked the servant with infuriating calm. "I'd not stand for that, but he's a gentleman, and you're his guest."

"I don't want to be," she muttered.

"But the master's too busy to stay around the house all day, so I took the liberty of choosing a book you might find diverting." A thin volume slid under the door with a slightly gritty sound. "It took me some time to find something appropriate," he added apologetically. "The master's library isn't well-used, nor well-kept. But I once saw this play put on by a traveling troupe of actors in Plymouth, and hope you might like it as well."

Vivian picked up the book and frowned at the title. *The School for Scandal.* She wasn't much interested in school, nor a book about one. Still, it was a nice gesture, and it had brought the servant to her door. Perhaps she could work on him after all. She moved closer to the door.

"Oh, thank you. It looks wonderful. But I must tell you, what I long for above all else is a breath of fresh air. The window won't open. Might I please take a turn in the garden?"

"Oh, no, ma'am."

"But it's such a beautiful day," she pleaded in her softest, sweetest tone. "Just a brief turn?"

"No, ma'am," he repeated. "The master said not even a turn in the garden, nor sitting in the drawing room, nor leaving that room at all."

"But . . ." Vivian placed her palms on the door, the book tucked under one arm. She spoke right into the seam where the door met the frame. "But if he ordered you to do something awful, you wouldn't obey, would you?"

"No, ma'am, but he's never asked me to do something awful."

"He's told you to keep me locked up like—like an animal." She choked and affected a small sob.

"Now, ma'am, the master has his reasons. And as I said before, he's not mistreated you."

"His reasons are to torment me! He knows he is keeping me here against my will!"

"Now, madam." He was beginning to sound aggrieved now. "I'd lose my place if I let you out."

"I'll help you find another," she promised at once.

"But this one suits me. Thank you kindly, ma'am. I hope you enjoy the book."

"Wait!" she cried. "Wait! Please, don't go!" She pressed her ear to the door and listened, but heard only a faint sound of slow, shuffling footsteps, slowly fading away. She slapped her hand against the door in irritation.

"Sure, and you're such a good man," she muttered. "Keeping a woman locked up! Bugger the both of you."

This was always the way of it in her life: someone else decided, and she had no choice but to live with that decision. Vivian cursed them all, from her father who went away to war and left her mother destitute, to her current captor who imprisoned her just because he felt like it. Vivian hated not being able to choose her own path, even if the choices she faced were not always pleasant.

Her eyes fell on the book where it had fallen on the floor. A book about a school. Vivian rolled her eyes, but picked it up. Her mother had taught her to read, years ago, but she had never had a book all her own to read. She flipped it open, more for lack of anything else to do than because she truly wanted to, and started to read.

Chapter Seven

David's intention to hire a complete new household staff soon hit a snag. He had instructed Adams to send round to the agency requesting a butler, a cook, two housemaids, and a pair of footmen. The reply was swift in coming.

"It is from the agency," said Adams, reading a letter. He was sorting the post just delivered to Exeter House, where David was struggling to get through Marcus's daily workload.

"Yes, yes," said David distractedly, thumbing through the Ainsley Park estate manager's latest report. There were some queries he must answer at once. "Tell them all to start at once."

Adams cleared his throat. "Ah. Sir, there seems to be a bit of a problem."

David looked up with an impatient frown. "What?"

Nervously, Adams held up the letter. "Mrs. White, sir. She says . . . But I shall send around to another agency today, one better able to . . ." He fell silent, fidgeting with the letter.

"What?" said David. "What did Mrs. White say?"

Wetting his lips, the secretary said, "She is unable to fill your positions, sir."

"Why?"

"Because—because her people have heard of your past difficulties, sir. In paying wages."

David's frown deepened. "Surely you jest."

Adams shook his head, looking miserable. "No, sir." He held out the letter. "Would you care—?"

He flipped one hand in disgust. "No, no. Send around to another agency then. Bannet cannot run my household on his own."

"No, sir. Yes, sir." Adams shuffled the letter to the bottom of his stack of papers. "I shall see to it at once, sir."

The replies to those inquiries were swift in coming as well, though, and they were alarmingly similar. No reputable agency in London, it seemed, was anxious to assist him. One even went so far as to say that David had employed nearly all of their people at one point, and not a one of them would agree to return. At first David laughed it off, then he cursed in irritation, and finally he sat in grim, humiliated silence as Adams handed over yet another letter with downcast eyes. Never in all his life had he felt so low—rejected by employment agencies as unworthy! A Reece!

He leaned forward, folding his hands carefully on the desk. "Mr. Adams. I require a staff. See to it at once." He ought to have done it this way from the beginning, he thought, and spared himself the galling experience of knowing he was considered unsuitable by every scullery maid in London.

Adams swallowed, bobbing his head. "Yes, sir. At once, sir."

David jerked his head once. "Very good. Now, yes, back to work." Adams nodded again, readying his pen, and they resumed the Sisyphean task of dealing with Marcus's correspondence.

David waited until Adams took himself off to work in the small office down the hall before he flung his empty coffee cup across the room. It smashed into the fireplace in a tinkle of fine china. David ignored it, seething. Of all the nerve—how dare they—it was insupportable—

He unfolded his clenched fingers and stood, crossing the room with controlled steps. He chose a glass from the sideboard with equally deliberate care, unstopped the decanter, and poured precisely two fingers of whiskey. Calmly he lifted the glass, and tossed back the whiskey with one flick of the wrist. David stared out the window. Mocked and spurned by a pack of footmen. He poured two more fingers of whiskey and drank it as quickly as he had the first. He wasn't good enough to pay their wages, was he? He poured more whiskey, less precisely this time, and gulped it down, wiping his mouth on the back of his hand. Still holding the decanter and glass, he turned and went back to his seat behind the desk. Thumping the glass down, he poured another drink and slouched in his chair.

This wouldn't happen to Marcus, he thought grimly, tipping the glass to his mouth. Not that Marcus would find himself ostracized by *anyone* who wanted money, but his brother, David was sure, would have known how to present his request in a way that admitted no possibility of refusal. No one refused Marcus anything.

His eyes fell on the desk in front of him. The decanter was sitting on top of the account ledger from Blessing Hill, the farm in Essex where Marcus raised thoroughbreds. David didn't have to open it to know it contained columns of numbers indicating to the pence how much and how often each employee of Blessing Hill was paid.

If he looked in the London ledger, he knew he would find the same notations for every servant in Exeter House, to say nothing of some entries paying David's own faithless servants.

He sighed. Things like this didn't happen to Marcus because Marcus didn't let things get out of hand to begin with. Marcus paid his servants generously and promptly. Marcus didn't gamble his housekeeping funds away on cockfights and horse races. Marcus didn't get entangled with married women and then have to leave town to avoid their raging husbands. Marcus simply didn't make a thorough mess of his life. David poured the glass full of whiskey almost to the rim, and drank it.

Some time later someone tapped at the door, then again after a long pause. "What?" growled David.

Harper, the Exeter butler, appeared in the doorway. "Some gentlemen to see you, my lord."

"Who?"

"Mr. Anthony Hamilton, Mr. Edward Percy, and Lord Robert Wallenham, sir."

David sank lower in his chair. "I'm not in."

"Ballocks," said a different voice. "The devil you say you're not in to us." His friends had not waited properly in the drawing room to be announced, but had followed the butler to the study. Now they pushed their way into the room, ignoring Harper's cool disapproval. The butler stood, waiting for David's instruction like a proper servant, and David reluctantly nodded in dismissal. Now that they were here, he could hardly tell Harper to throw them out.

"I say," said Percy, glancing around somewhat nervously as he took a seat. "Odd to find you here, Reece. Gives me the shivers just to be in this room."

David lifted one shoulder. "I'm looking after the estate while my brother's away."

A burst of general laughter greeted this. Hamilton grinned, lounging in his chair. "Doubly odd, then, if you ask me. How did that come about?"

"He asked me," muttered David. Hamilton cocked an eyebrow. Percy shuddered in horror. "Do you question my competence, or his?"

"Not your competence, your sanity," exclaimed Percy. "What did he threaten you with?"

"Nothing." David frowned a little, cradling his glass against his chest.

"Ah, a debt repayment plan," said Hamilton. "It happens to all of us who haven't inherited our fortunes yet, from time to time," he explained to Wallenham. "Relatives require the damnedest things in exchange for their money."

"Don't speak to me about debt, you young pup." Wallenham glared at Hamilton. "I know all about debt. Got plenty of it myself. I just haven't got a wealthy older brother to pay it off for me."

"The debt was *to* him," said David. "Not something he could repay for me, were I inclined to ask for that."

"Well, enough about debt," said Percy. "Nasty, unpleasant subject. We hadn't seen you in over a fortnight, Reece. Hamilton feared you were imprisoned in the country, so it's most excellent to see you back in town, even if we did have a devil of a time finding you. Dine with us at White's?"

"Capital idea." Wallenham lurched to his feet.

David opened his mouth to say yes. An evening out with his friends, carefree drinking, a little gambling, and possibly some women, would surely improve his mood. No one at Madame Louise's or a gaming hall would refuse his money. It was what he usually did in London, and Lord knew he could use the respite from account ledgers and crop reports.

But then he remembered Mrs. Gray, locked in his guest room. Bannet would no doubt dutifully leave her be, and if David didn't go home she would have no supper, and likely no breakfast, either. Evenings about town with his friends rarely ended before dawn, and always left him useless for anything. Not only did he have to see to her, he had to be back here, at this desk, tomorrow morning. With a sigh, he slumped back in the chair. "Not for me. Not tonight."

All three of his friends paused, looking at him in surprise. "Have you taken ill?" asked Percy with a quizzical tilt of his head. David shook his head.

"I have some things to attend to. Another night, perhaps."

His three visitors exchanged a glance. "All right, then," said Wallenham. "Er, another night."

David nodded as they took their leave. He hadn't even really wanted to go, he realized with some surprise. It was rather a relief when they had gone and closed the door behind them, and he was left in the quiet solitude of the study. He had only been inclined to go because it was what he usually did in town. Had he become such a jaded creature that revelry was dull now?

He looked at the desk, and put down his glass. He'd had enough whiskey. He'd had enough work. He just needed a good night's sleep, he told himself, and by tomorrow his staffing problem would be behind him, his head would be clear, and he could face whatever came his way.

David stood up, wincing as he put his weight on his leg. The damned thing seemed to get tender and weak just from sitting at a desk. He walked around the desk and left the room, forcing himself to walk normally. In the hallway, Harper materialized at his elbow.

"Tell Adams we'll continue in the morning," David said. The butler bowed his head in acknowledgment. "And see to it another hamper is sent around to my house tomorrow. For another week, in fact." If not for the question of Mrs. Gray, David would consider taking up residence in Exeter House, just for the sake of convenience.

"Yes, my lord." Harper cleared his throat delicately. "If I may be so bold, sir, I may be able to assist in your hiring."

Already turning away, David paused. "Oh?"

"Mr. Adams mentioned you would be hiring a complete staff, sir," Harper went on. "I am acquainted with a man who will soon be seeking a position."

"Oh? Yes, yes, certainly," David said in a rush. He wasn't in any position to be particular. "By all means, give his name to Adams. He'll be handling the matter."

Harper bowed. "Very good, sir. Shall I send for your horse?"

David pressed the knuckles of his fist into the tense muscles of his thigh. His lower leg was throbbing dully. "No, I shall walk." He mustered a carefree grin. "Fresh air, you know."

"Yes, sir." Harper glided ahead of him, handing over David's gloves and hat. "A good evening to you, sir."

David nodded. "Good night, Harper."

The cloudy day had become even darker. It felt like rain. David walked purposefully, pushing through his heel with every stride. It wasn't far to his town house, but by the time he arrived, his leg felt as if someone had beaten it with a club. He knew he was limping as he climbed the steps and let himself into the house.

Bannet appeared as David was taking off his hat and

gloves. "I prepared a tray for Mrs. Gray, sir, just as you asked." And just as David had instructed, the tray was sitting on the table in the hallway. David was torn between being pleased his servant had followed his orders exactly, and exasperated that the man hadn't just taken her the damn tray and spared him the trouble. He eyed the staircase with resignation. He didn't look forward to carrying a heavy tray up all those stairs on his bad leg.

"Good work, Bannet." He couldn't afford to run off his last remaining employee. He handed over his hat and shed his gloves. Bannet trundled off with them, leaving David alone in the hall. He sighed, hefting the tray on one arm, almost wishing he didn't have too much pride to tell Bannet to carry it up for him. Gritting his teeth, he climbed the stairs and made his way to his prisoner's room.

He took the key off the top of the doorframe and rapped twice with his knuckle on the door before unlocking it. He heard a muffled scuffle of sound from within, but by the time he had opened the door she was sitting in the chair, staring out the window. He closed the door, then with slow, deliberate steps, he crossed the room and set down the tray on the small table. "Your dinner, madam."

She didn't look at him. David's calf trembled; he clenched his teeth against the pain. He should have told Bannet to prepare a boiling hot bath, the only thing David had discovered that relieved the ache. But now— the muscle was shaking. He could feel it on the verge of giving out. Not wanting to collapse in front of a woman, David quickly hobbled to the bed and sank down, hoping she didn't notice the bare groan of relief that slipped through his teeth.

It was blissful, to be off that leg.

Mrs. Gray darted a nervous glance his way. David realized he had never stayed longer than a few moments in her room. Well, well. Pretending he had intended to do so all along, he leaned back against the pillows and swung both his legs onto the bed. Her eyes widened before she jerked her gaze back to the window.

His mood suddenly improved, and his leg all but melting in relief, David folded his arms over his chest and settled back, watching her. She'd been here for four days, and he hadn't heard a word out of her since the first. He was growing tired of this escapade, and decided it might be time to rattle her chains a bit. "I apologize if I've been neglecting you," he said. "Very poor manners for a host, I know." He gestured to the tray. "I trust the fare has been satisfactory?" She said nothing. "And the accommodation, I hope, has been comfortable?" The bed was damned comfortable. David wasn't sure he would ever be able to get up and put weight on his leg again. Of course, he could have been lying on a stone slab and been reluctant to stand up again.

"We've had so little time to become acquainted," he went on, as if they were having a normal conversation. "Forgive me. I've had rather a lot to do of late, but in no way did I intend to slight you." She stole a hungry glance at the tray of food, and David hid his satisfaction. "I shall be a better host from now on, you have my word." He paused. "Have you anything to say?" All he got was an angry glare.

This time he didn't bother to smother his delight. She was a fiery thing, even if she had some control over her temper, and perhaps, if he applied just the right pressure, she would crack and tell him what he wanted to know. "Then I suppose it shall fall to me to carry the conversation." He stopped; what did one converse about with a woman? Any woman, let alone this particular woman. He hadn't the first idea.

But then again, what did it matter? Everything he said to her would be in strict confidence simply because there was no one she could tell. And he doubted he could shock her if he tried. He leaned back, made himself more comfortable, and, keeping a watchful eye on her at all times, began to talk.

Vivian was shaking with fury. How dare he sit there and talk and talk and talk, while the smell of meat filled the room? Wasn't it driving him out of his mind with hunger, as it was doing to her? Her mouth was watering at the thought of how tender and succulent it would be on her tongue, probably smeared with herbs and tangy with salt. Whoever cooked his food was simply an angel from heaven, to Vivian's hungry soul. Last night there had been ham and a treacle tart, and the night before some sweet custard. She had never had such delicious, sweet things before, just an occasional stick of hard candy. She couldn't imagine what would be on the tray tonight, and her hands were twitching from the effort of restraining herself from running across the room, tearing off the cover, and devouring every last crumb.

But instead he was sitting on the bed, his tongue running twelve score to the dozen about God only knew what. Even though he spoke in a light, conversational tone, she could feel his eyes on her, as if he were just waiting for her to lose her temper. She certainly was not so hen-hearted as that. She could sit here and ignore him for longer than he could sit there and talk, she was quite certain.

Or perhaps . . . not. The smell of the food was driving her wild. She pressed her lips together to keep from licking her lips in anticipation. She still hated him with all her heart, but she had to admit he had fed her well. Very well. And now if he would just leave, she would enjoy her dinner and only go back to hating him once it was gone.

But on and on he talked, about horses and gossip and other useless topics she barely listened to. Her dinner was getting cold, curse him! She tried turning her nose in the air and pretending to ignore him. It had no effect. She tried closing her eyes and feigning sleep. No effect. She tried shooting an angry look at him, but he just gave her such a sinfully wicked smile she had to look away.

"Do you know, I've never known a woman so resistant to polite conversation," he remarked at length. "It's quite lowering to a fellow's vanity."

Vivian scowled, but didn't say anything. Perhaps this meant his tongue was finally tiring. Lord above, he talked more than a fishwife. He sat up, swinging his feet to the floor, and her heart—and stomach—took a leap of excitement. "This dinner is going to waste," he said, looking at the still-covered tray. "Such a pity. My brother's cook is excellent. I confess, I'm quite peckish myself, and the smell is rather tempting." He lifted the cover and inspected the plate—oh Lord, it looked like beef!—and then, to Vivian's outrage, he picked up a roll and took a bite.

She sprang to her feet. "You've decided to starve me, then, have you? You wretched lying filth! First you lock me in here and refuse to listen to reason, now you eat my dinner?"

"So," he said, sounding pleased, "she can speak after all."

"Get out," snarled Vivian, "else I'll hurl myself out the window. Being smashed on the ground would be better than having to listen to your prattle!"

He laughed, and got to his feet, replacing the cover on the tray. "Never fear, my dear. I should hate to see such loveliness injured. I shall take my leave." He gave her a brief bow, his eyes still glittering with amusement. "My happiness is complete, now that I have heard your voice again. I bid you good evening." He strolled to the door and let himself out. She heard him whistling as the key turned in the lock.

Vivian didn't care, though. She dragged her chair across the room and leaned over the tray, inhaling deeply. It was a stew of some kind, beef with vegetables, and it smelled unutterably good. He had taken only one of the rolls, and she sank her teeth into the other. Even the bread here was lovely, as tender and soft as a cloud, nothing like the hard wheat bread she was accustomed to. She scooped up a bite of the stew, and moaned in delight. It was thick and juicy and so good. Colder than it should have been, no doubt, but now that she was eating, Vivian could overlook that.

As she spooned every last bite of the stew into her mouth, her thoughts turned back to *him*. He was trying to break her will, she decided. For the past few days he'd only asked a few questions when he brought her meals. It had been easy to ignore him. This new tack of his would be harder to ignore, especially if he meant to hold her dinner hostage every night.

She wished she knew something about him. My lord, the servant had called him, so he was nobility. He had a broken rib, and she wondered how he'd come by that. And tonight it had looked as though he had a bad leg, too. How she'd like to give him another broken bone, perhaps his head.

It was terribly unfair that such a nodcock was so handsome. That smile he'd given her . . . It brought back something he'd said before, that he was good at persuading ladies. Persuading them to lift their skirts, most likely, she thought with a sniff of contempt. He wouldn't persuade her to do so much as lift her finger. Vivian knew well enough what happened to girls who let gentlemen under their skirts for nothing more than a smile. More than one person had suggested Vivian could earn her fortune with her face—and on her back—but even a thief had to have standards. Vivian refused to do murder, and she refused to go whoring. This made her significantly more delicate in her sensibilities than most people in the rookeries, but she didn't care. It had served her well so far, and the day it didn't . . . well, she would reconsider the question then, but not until then.

And if this bloody rogue thought to change her mind about whoring, she'd just have to change her mind about murder, too. No one forced Vivian Beecham to do anything, and she'd die resisting any efforts to that end. For a moment she sat and reviewed her captor's known weaknesses: a bad leg, a broken rib, whatever sense of honor he thought he possessed. But then she was forced to review his strengths as well, notably brute strength, a marked size advantage, surprising reflexes and daring, and that smile. And that face. And the breadth of those shoulders—Vivian cursed at herself and jumped to her feet. She, of all people, knew not be swayed by a handsome face and a tempting smile. Not she, who used her face and form to her own advantages when she needed to; she would surely be able to recognize and ignore all his attempts to charm anything out of her.

All of them.

Chapter Eight

David's leg continued to ache through the night, even after he soaked in hot water for over half an hour. He lay awake until late at night, kept from sleep as much by the crashing thunderstorm outside as by the dull pain in his calf.

It was still sore in the morning. He felt like an old man, moving gingerly about the house. Dr. Craddock, the Reece family physician, was expected that morning, to examine David's broken rib and see if it had healed completely. David rather thought it had, no thanks to Mrs. Gray, but he was privately glad the doctor was already planning to call.

It bothered him that the leg injury still hurt. He had broken an arm twice, and both times it seemed but a few weeks before the arm was back to normal. He'd once won a hundred pounds from Percy for driving a demanding pair of bays with a broken arm. And he'd even broken his leg before, as a boy. He'd had to spend two weeks in bed, translating Latin passages as penance for trying to walk the roofline of the stable, but at the end of the month he was running and swimming and riding as if the bone had never broken. Yet now, here he was, still hobbling three long months after breaking his leg in a carriage accident. It was rather alarming to someone who had always taken his body, healthy and sound, for granted.

The doctor arrived soon after David finished breakfast. He examined David's ribs thoroughly, and pronounced them healed. "Although I do see a slight bruise here," he remarked, indicating the lower edge of David's ribcage. "Have you been taking proper care? It wouldn't do to re-injure yourself."

Mrs. Gray had left her mark on him. David pulled his shirt back over his head. "A slight collision. Nothing worth fretting over. It's hardly sore."

"Well, very good, then." He leaned back and gave David a smile. "You seem recovered from your injuries. I think my work here is done." David drew breath to speak, then stopped. The doctor's keen eye must have caught it, for he asked, "Is there anything else, my lord?"

David hesitated, then nodded. "My leg," he said. The doctor's brows arched.

"It has healed, I am quite certain. I examined it the last time I was here." He shook a finger good-naturedly. "You've been a terribly demanding patient of late, sir."

David grinned. "Always have been, as I recall. My father didn't retain you as his personal physician just for himself." Dr. Craddock might as well have lived at Ainsley Park when David was younger, so many times was he summoned to deal with injured limbs—from falling out of trees and off horses and once, out of a window—scrapes and bruises, including a magnificent black eye Marcus once gave him for cheating at cards, and the numerous fevers and chills a boy catches while swimming naked in the lake, hiding out in the rain to avoid his tutors, and one infamous stunt to hang his father's nightcap from the steeple of the local church at Christmastide.

The good doctor must have remembered it all as well. He just sighed and shook his head. "Boys. But your leg . . . ?"

His grin disappeared. "Yes. It still aches."

Dr. Craddock frowned. "Let's have a look, then." David sat down on the chaise, stretching out his leg for the doctor to examine and staring blindly at the ceiling as he tried to ignore the poking and prodding.

"Well, I can see no signs of infection or other weakness," said the doctor at last. "You are older, my lord, and your body will take longer to heal."

"But four months?"

Dr. Craddock pursed his lips. "Can you walk on it normally? I did not notice a limp when I arrived."

"Yes, I can walk on it," David said. "It doesn't always hurt."

"Late in the evening? When you are tired?" David nodded to the doctor's questions. "Then most likely it is still weak within the flesh, and needs more time to grow strong again. There is nothing I can do." Irritably David flipped the dressing gown back over his leg. "My lord, you had a very serious injury," the doctor went on in reproof. "There is nothing I can do to change that."

"Yes, yes, but ought it not be healed by now?"

The doctor finished packing his instruments in his bag before he replied to David's peevish question. "It has healed, sir. The bone is sound again. I know not what care you took whilst it was healing"—he shot a stern glare at David, as if he suspected some of the carrying on that had dulled David's memory of his convalescence—"but it is likely as healed as it ever will be. Some aches never go away."

"Never?" David exclaimed. Without thinking, he rubbed his palm down the outside of his calf, where the ache was most painful. "Are you certain?"

"No, not at all." The man put his head to one side and studied David's leg again. "It was well-set, and healed straight. You are fortunate in that, my lord. It may well fade in time. You are a strong, healthy man, and I give it an excellent chance of healing completely. You simply must give it time."

Time, time, time. Always more time. It seemed as though he could invent chaos and disaster in an instant, but everything he tried to do right took an eternity. David sighed.

"Perhaps a cane might help," Dr. Craddock added. "It might relieve the stress on the limb."

David closed his mouth into a firm line and shook his head. He would not walk around like an old man with a cane, not even if he walked in pain for a year. He thanked the doctor and the man took his leave.

His failings had never come home to David in such a physically painful way. He had always managed to escape his capers with mere flesh wounds, not lingering disabilities. And this ache in his leg was like a private punishment. He could walk normally; he wasn't obviously incapacitated. Only he knew when it felt like a barbed spur had been embedded in his calf, twisting and burning painfully with every step.

He got to his feet and began what had become his daily ritual lately, pacing the room with firm, measured steps. He flexed his foot each time it struck the floor, feeling the twinge deep within his lower leg and ruthlessly ignoring it. Surely if he worked the muscle enough, it would grow strong and steady again.

Five circuits of the room, ten, then twenty. Around he went, pushing his foot through a full range of motion even when it started to throb. When he was breathing heavily and his foot felt weighted with lead, David stopped, bracing one arm against the mantle. He hoped this was helping, but all he felt from the exercise was pain. Without thinking where he was going, he left the room and continued walking, only stopping when he came to Mrs. Gray's door.

David paused. For some reason he wanted to go in and talk to her again, not that he had much hope of her speaking to him. He didn't feel like browbeating her today. He just wanted to talk to someone, and she was the only person available. As he had told himself the previous day, it was rather safe to confide in her. She knew none of his acquaintances, and couldn't repeat any of his remarks to anyone.

He heard footsteps, and Bannet shuffled up, carrying a tray. "She's not had breakfast yet?" David asked, knowing as he asked that of course she hadn't. He hadn't brought it to her yet.

"No, sir," said Bannet. "You were occupied with the doctor."

David took the tray without another word, reaching for the key. He gave Bannet a curious glance, noticing the weight of his burden. "Quite a large meal for one small woman, don't you think?"

"She's a healthy appetite," replied Bannet. "The dishes are always near licked clean, no matter how large a meal it is." David's eyebrows went up. "I expect she's hungry, sir," Bannet added in his same bland tone. "A poor lass like her."

David had never thought of that. He glanced thoughtfully at the tray again, then opened the door and let himself in.

His captive scrambled out of bed in a flurry of bed linens and skirts. Her hair tumbled around her shoulders, and she held a corner of the blanket in front of her chest. She blinked at him in confusion for a moment, then her expression cleared, and she turned her back on him as usual.

David put down the tray. "Good morning." His leg still hurt a little, although just the dull ache. He was fairly accustomed to that now, but took a seat in the chair as a preventative measure anyway. "I apologize for being so late this morning."

She sniffed, her short, jerky motions indicating she was adjusting the front of her dress. After a moment she turned around, her mouth in a flat line. She glared at him a moment, then stalked across the room and inspected the tray. She grabbed a piece of toast and took a bite, then her eyes narrowed on David—no, he realized, on the chair. Her soft blue eyes shot daggers at him, then she turned her attention back to the food. He watched the way she attacked the meal, with a concentration he'd never seen a woman eat with before. As if it were her first meal in days, when he knew very well she'd had two large meals a day for nearly a week.

"I'm delighted to see breakfast meets with your approval," he remarked. She sniffed again, reaching for the plate of bacon. "I hope to hire a new cook soon," he went on. "It shall be so nice to have hot fresh meals again, instead of picnic fare sent over by my brother's cook."

Her eyes flashed his way again, bright with disbelief. She obviously found the food delicious, from the way she was systematically cleaning plate after plate. "I admire your forbearance," he went on, for some reason driven to poke at her until she said something, anything. It was beginning to annoy him that she was so stubbornly silent. "I find it virtually inedible." He shuddered as if in horror. In reality the food was perfectly fine. David wasn't such a gourmand that he discriminated much about food, so long as it was hot, decently prepared, and plentiful.

She looked at him in scornful disbelief. "Daft," she mumbled, applying the spoon to the bowl of porridge.

"It absolutely is, isn't it?" he agreed, purposely misunderstanding. "As soon as the new cook turns up, the food shall be much improved, I swear. No more of this . . ." He grimaced. "Porridge. Ugh. Ham steak, I should think, and perhaps some fresh kippers. Properly prepared eggs. Those tender little muffins ladies are so fond of, with sweet marmalade on them. My sister is particularly fond of those, although I have been given to understand they're not good for the figure. Far be it from me to worry about a lady's figure, but I confess, I'm quite happy to consume any of those little muffins as an assistance to any females at the table."

She had stopped chewing at the mention of the little muffins, her eyes perfectly round. She looked at him with rapt seriousness. David hid a grin, and leaned forward to inspect the tray. She liked sweets, it seemed. He pulled a frown, and exclaimed in disgust.

"Here, and no chocolate! My mother and sister swear by the little pots of chocolate they drink for breakfast. Too sweet for my taste, but woe betide the cook if the ladies have no chocolate. And now you have none." He looked up at her, his expression grave. "That shall be remedied as soon as possible. You are a rare woman to have endured the lack of chocolate so long without a word of complaint."

Vivian choked down the mouthful of porridge, her mind filled with images of delicacies she'd only ever seen in shop windows. Muffins. Pots of chocolate. He thought she was accustomed to such things, and promised to provide them in the near future. Just a bowl of hot porridge in the morning seemed a luxury to her. Chocolate! She had smelled it once, while shadowing a fancy gentleman through St. James's with an eye to lifting his purse. The smells from the coffeehouse he entered had stopped her cold, and she'd completely lost him as she just stood and inhaled the warm, rich aroma.

She shook her head. "Keep your chatter to yourself. Unless you've come to tell me I'm to be free, you might as well spare yourself the effort of speaking."

"It would be my pleasure to escort you out of my house forever," he said, his eyes lighting with that devilish light. "You have but to tell me what I need to know, and it shall be done."

She sniffed again. After all this time, quite likely she couldn't tell him anything useful even had she wanted to. Flynn, if he had any wits at all, would have moved on by now; it would take some doing for her to find the gang again. Even if she could say their whereabouts, so the rich cove could go looking for his bloody ring, she still had Simon to think of, and what might happen to him if this bloke fingered him as the one who'd rapped him on the head.

Besides, she wasn't really suffering here. She no longer lived in fear of imminent rape and murder. Sooner or later her chance to escape would come, but until then she saw nothing to gain by answering his questions.

David could tell by the change in her face that she

was done talking to him. He sat back with an inexplicable sense of disappointment. For no good reason, he liked this woman. She was nothing but trouble, and had done a masterful job of giving him a very cold shoulder, but David found her just as intriguing as he had that day on the stage coach. He was growing more and more determined to get her to talk to him—hopefully about where to find his ring, but any topic would do at this point.

He stretched out his bad leg and relaxed in the chair. "Oh, dear. You've gone silent again. I must have put my foot in it somehow. That always seems to be the reason ladies refuse to speak to me: I've said something wrong, or forgotten to say the right thing, or not said anything when I ought to have said something, even though I seldom know what I ought to have said, let alone that I ought to have said it." She made a funny little noise, and David heaved a sigh. "Yes, that must be it. I'm quite accustomed to the fact that these little misunderstandings are always my fault. I do wish someone would write a primer on the subject: *How to Handle a Lady*. Not that I'm the most studious chap, mind, but that manual I could most certainly read."

The food was gone. She was fussing with the spoon, scraping it along various plates and bowls, but he could tell she was listening to him.

"The trouble is," he went on, "you've become a challenge. I don't normally have trouble getting ladies to speak to me—at the beginning, that is. Yet you, my dear, are most hard-hearted. I cannot make you smile. I cannot make you laugh. I cannot tease one polite word from you."

"Bugger yourself," she muttered.

"There you go, two words, and neither of them polite.

What shall I do?" He put his head to one side, studying her. Her face was flushed, but she kept her gaze on the breakfast tray. "Perhaps if I put you on bread and water rations until you tell me your name?" he said thoughtfully. Then her eyes did turn his way, half alarmed, half contemptuous. It came to David instantly, that she'd lived on bread and water before. She wouldn't like it, but she wouldn't be broken by it. "No, that most certainly would not be the proper way to treat a lady," he said in the same tone. "Perhaps if I tempt you . . ." He smiled slowly. "Yes, that's it. I quite like tempting ladies. I shall have to think carefully about what will tempt you most."

He leaned forward, resting his elbows on the edge of the table and giving her a smile. "Talk to me, Mrs. Gray," he murmured. "I'll persuade you one way or another."

She stared back at him with narrowed eyes. There was defiance and scornful pride in her gaze. Just as she had become a challenge to him, resisting him had become the challenge to her. It was to be a battle of sorts between them, then. She didn't move except to follow him with those eyes as he got to his feet and crossed the room, then let himself out.

David locked the door without thinking about it, his mind flitting from one method of persuasion to another. Persuading ladies to his way of thinking was, perhaps, David's one true talent in life. If he couldn't loosen her lips—at the very least—by the end of the week, he'd give up drink for a week.

Vivian sat in the chair, her knees trembling. Oh, dear. This was taking a turn for the worse. She ought to have known he wouldn't simply feed her and wait patiently forever. That man burned with energy. It was likely a miracle he'd left her be for so long already.

Tempt her . . . What did he mean by that? She knew very well what he was thinking. She'd seen that look in a man's eye before. Not quite like that, though; she'd never seen anything quite like this man. She was afraid of what would happen if he did try to tempt her.

She rubbed her hands nervously up and down her arms, glancing around the room. But nothing about it had changed. She was still locked behind a stout wooden door in a room with a well-fitted window, some two floors up. She couldn't jump out the window any more than she could fight her way past her captor. But she saw now that she might not have been wise to delay her escape so long. A challenge, he had called her. Vivian snorted. This was all still a game to him, but to her it was life or death. He could hand her over to the Runners if she admitted to stealing his belongings, and then she'd hang for certain.

Of course, he could have handed her over to the Runners first thing, and they'd have hung her then. Vivian frowned a little as she thought. He said he would let her go once he had the bloody ring back. She still didn't see how she could accomplish that, but perhaps she should think about how to convince him instead of simply refusing to answer him.

She just didn't like that threat about "tempting."

Chapter Nine

David continued to be amazed at the breadth of his brother's concerns and interests. He had always known Marcus was the brighter of them—every tutor and professor had always said so, and of course their father had made it clear he was relieved it was Marcus who would inherit and not David. For the most part, David had simply accepted it. No one expected him to do anything else, until now. Now he was confronted daily with proof that he had not done very much with his life, while Marcus had become an authority on nearly everything. Every day something new and unexpected crossed the wide mahogany desk in Exeter House, and it seemed David hadn't the least idea how to deal with half of them.

"What the devil is this?" he asked, frowning at the densely-written document Adams handed across the desk late the next afternoon. They had already dispensed with most of the correspondence and necessary matters, and David was already thinking of dinner.

"It is a bill," said Mr. Adams. "Calling for the resumption of currency convertibility."

David dropped the bill almost reflexively. "Currency?"

"Yes, sir." Adams went on to explain. The sponsors wished to require banks to redeem all paper notes in gold bullion on request, a right which had been suspended due to the war against Napoleon.

"But I have no vote in Parliament," David said. "I've no say in the matter."

"His Grace gave his proxy to His Lordship the earl of Roxbury," replied Adams in reverent tones. "Lord Roxbury wishes to know how to cast His Grace's vote."

David's first instinct was to vote in favor of it, just to curb the use of bank notes. He had a hearty appreciation for the solid weight of coins in his purse now. But perhaps that was wrong; would people rush to exchange their notes for gold and bleed the banks dry? Marcus hadn't mentioned any thoughts on gold or currency; how was he to know how to proceed? Just tell Roxbury to vote as he saw fit? And if he decided wrongly, David thought morbidly, he could be the ruin of the entire English banking system.

He sighed. "Do you ever feel, Mr. Adams, as though you are utterly incapable of doing things correctly?"

"Indeed, sir, all the time," replied the man fervently. David glanced up with a rueful grin.

"Ah. Right. Working for my brother, no doubt you would have that feeling all the time."

Mr. Adams turned red, then white. "Oh no, sir. Not at all, my lord! I didn't mean to say—or imply—that His Grace is anything other than a model employer—"

"You're a dashed idiot if you think he's a model employer," said David. "He's demanding beyond all belief."

"Ah . . ." Mr. Adams looked as though he were being prodded along the length of a plank by pirates. "Yes, my lord," he said carefully. "But he is fair. I expect I shall learn a great deal from him before he sacks me."

"You expect it?" he exclaimed.

The secretary blushed. He looked very young when he did that. "Oh, yes, sir. Daily, in fact, sir. I can see that he hasn't much patience with my mistakes. He would never have given me the post if my uncle, Mr. Cole, hadn't written a letter. A letter full of lies, I have no doubt, as Uncle Cole must have known I would never be able to meet His Grace's requirements." His face fell.

David frowned. "Why couldn't you?"

Mr. Adams blushed again, but said nothing. David folded his arms on the desk and let his head hang forward, easing the tension in the back of his neck. "Well, thank God he hasn't given you the sack already. I'd have been hopelessly lost on my own, you know." He grinned humorlessly. "Perhaps we'll get the sack together."

"Oh, no, indeed, sir!" gasped the horrified secretary. "That is, *you*, sir, are doing splendidly. Surely His Grace will have no cause for complaint about your actions. I, though, have made one mistake after another. It's not difficult to see how impatient His Grace is with me."

David laughed. "Impatient with *you*? You've no idea what my brother's impatience looks like, Adams."

Adams opened his mouth to protest, then closed it, apparently realizing there was nothing he could say in reply. David sighed again, turning to the bill in front of him. "I've no idea what to tell Roxbury." He put it on the side of the desk. "I'll deal with that later." Adams bobbed his head, writing. Restlessly, David got to his feet. "I'll deal with all the rest later." Adams nodded again, still scribbling. "Until tomorrow, Adams."

"Yes, my lord." Adams jumped out of his chair, still clutching his pen and papers. He bowed as David strode around the desk. At the door, David glanced back.

"Go home, Mr. Adams," he said. "You have the evening free."

"Thank you, sir!" rang the secretary's surprised, but pleased, voice behind him. It brought a grin to David's face as he crossed into the hallway, where Harper was already waiting.

"Is the staff being given extra days out in the family's absence?" David asked, taking his things.

"Yes, sir," said Harper. "His Grace always orders it so, when he leaves town for any length of time."

"How often is that?" David donned his hat.

Harper hesitated. "Not often, sir."

"I thought not. He ought to go away more often, too. Good evening, Harper."

"Good evening, my lord." The Exeter butler bowed slightly as David walked out the door held open by a footman.

It was barely evening. David finished tugging on his gloves, breathing deeply of the warm air. Enough bother about Parliamentary bills and shipping contracts and drainage problems. He was free, for the night at least, and tonight he meant to make Mrs. Gray open her luscious lips and speak to him.

His leg felt better today. There was hardly a twinge as he covered the distance to his own house, and it gave David a thrill of hope. Perhaps the doctor was right, and the leg was just taking a bit longer than usual to heal. Lighthearted, he bounded up his front steps and let himself in.

"Bannet," he asked his servant when the man came into the hall, "have I any chocolate?"

"Chocolate?" Bannet blinked. "Perhaps, sir. Shall I see?"

"Yes. And if there's none in the house, go fetch some at once."

"Yes, sir." Bannet shuffled off, and David went up the stairs, smiling to himself in anticipation. This was going to be entertaining.

By the time Bannet had procured the necessary supplies, David had stripped off his jacket and put on his dressing gown. There were two trays waiting for him outside Mrs. Gray's door, the dutiful Bannet standing guard.

"I collected everything you might need, sir," said his man as David poked around the second tray. The first held her dinner, and it smelled distractingly good. David had not yet had his own dinner. The second tray held a silver chocolate pot, slightly tarnished, a kettle of hot water, two small cups, and the chocolate.

"Excellent work, Bannet." David nodded in approval, reaching for the key. He opened the door and beckoned Bannet to carry in the dinner tray, then once the servant had backed out of the room—he'd apparently accepted Mrs. Gray's presence, and the locked door, completely—David carried in the chocolate tray and set it on the mantle.

Mrs. Gray stood in the far corner of the room, as if to stay as far away from him as possible. Her eyes flickered from the dinner tray to David and the other tray. He couldn't guess what she was thinking. He gave her a smile. "Dinner, madam. And a little something else."

Vivian watched warily. What was he about now? He had another tray, with a kettle and a gleaming silver pot that would be worth a guinea in any pawnshop in London.

"Go on." He gestured toward the familiar tray. "I haven't come to disturb your dinner." He even turned his back on her as he poured water from the kettle into the silver pot, then took up a dark block and scraped it into the pot as well. She could see a pleased little smile on his face as he added more things to the pot, then closed the lid and began working a handle that fit in through the lid. An aroma, strange but wonderful, drifted from the pot. She licked her lips without thought as the answer came to her: he was making chocolate.

The dinner tray was forgotten. She craned her neck, wanting to see what he did without getting closer. He was perfectly at ease, spinning the handle between the edges of his palms. He set one little cup on the table, and poured the dark steaming liquid into it. Vivian couldn't stop a sigh at the scent.

"A peace offering," he said, curving his long fingers around the small cup. His dark eyes gleamed at her guilelessly. "Would you care for some chocolate?"

Was this what he had meant by "tempting" her? Vivian hesitated. As much as she longed to taste chocolate, she wasn't about to let him trick her into something she would regret.

"No?" he said with a raised eyebrow when she didn't respond. He sniffed the cup, then tipped it to his own lips. "Quite good, if I do say so myself," he said, sounding mildly surprised. He poured some more. "Are you certain you don't care for some?"

"What do I have to give for it?" she asked suspiciously. His smile was all charming innocence.

"Nothing more than your name. A cup of chocolate for your name."

If she had known what he was planning, she would have been able to resist. If he had asked for the ring again, she would have been able to resist. As it was, Vivian didn't see what he could do with just her name, and the smell from the cup was so enticing, so she told him. "Vivian."

His face registered a moment of surprise. "A lovely name," was all he said, extending the cup. Vivian took it warily, but aside from a slight brush of his thumb on her knuckles, he did nothing but hand her the cup. She put it to her lips and sipped.

Oh. Oh Lord in heaven. It was sweet and warm and rich, everything Vivian had never tasted in her life. She took another greedy sip, and another. All too soon the little cup was empty.

"Would you like some more?" asked her captor. He had pulled the chair up to the table as she drank, and now he looked up at her, his hair falling around his face, his chin propped on one hand. He looked harmless and beautiful and he had a whole pot of that lovely chocolate right by his elbow. Vivian nodded and handed back the cup.

"Where are you from, Miss Vivian?" He poured some more and held it out to her.

"Nowhere." Vivian reached for the cup but he drew it back.

"Nowhere?" He made a disappointed noise. "A little more specific, please." She hesitated, and he added, "Nowhere is so large a place."

"Here, there, everywhere, nowhere." She shrugged. "No place special."

"Ah." He looked at her a moment. "Have you been a thief all your life?"

Vivian straightened her back in affront. "Most. Beats starving to death." This time he didn't move as she reached for the cup again. Oh, joy, thought Vivian, unable to keep from drinking it straight off in one long sip.

"Did you ever starve?" he asked, and Vivian jumped. She had forgotten about him for a moment. She shrugged again, putting the little cup back on the table.

"A bit." She gave him a challenging glare. "Did *you*, your rich-and-mightiness?"

He started, then laughed. "Have I ever starved? More than once, love. But not always for food." His smile was wicked as he poured more chocolate. "Have you another name, Miss Vivian? Or is it Mrs.?"

She sniffed. "Aye, so you can hand me to the charleys?"

That sinful smile lingered on his lips. "Have I set the charleys on you yet?" She just glared at him. The little cup of chocolate sat at his elbow, wisps of steam curling from the rich brown froth. Her nose twitched involuntarily.

"Well, why haven't you?" she sneered, annoyed that he was just letting that cupful go to waste. "You said you would if I didn't hand over your bloody ring. I haven't got it, as you can see. Call the ruddy charleys, you lying bastard."

He leaned back in his chair. He seemed in a very good humor this evening, unruffled by anything she said. "But then they would take you away, my dear. We've hardly gotten to know each other at all."

Vivian snorted, retreating to the other side of the table and examining the dinner dishes. It would all smell much more enticing if not for the smell of that undrunk cup of chocolate. Any other night, the roasted chicken would have made her mouth water. Tonight she poked at it half-heartedly.

"For instance, I only just learned your true name," he went on. "All this time I could only think of you as Mrs. Gray. A bit formal, don't you think, given that you don't seem the least bit inclined to leave me and I cannot bear the thought of anyone taking you away?" Vivian snorted again, finally digging into the chicken. "And now I shall call you Vivian."

The way he said her name was wrong. He rolled the

first part around his tongue, as if tasting it, then said the second on a low murmur. No one said her name like that, and Vivian wasn't sure she liked it. She wasn't sure she didn't like it, either, but it was somewhat unsettling when he said it that way, looking at her that way. Simon called her Viv, and Flynn called her Miss V, when he didn't just call her girl. She picked up the piece of chicken and retreated a step. "And I shall call you a knave, just as I always have."

He grinned, leaning forward again. "I've been called worse. The way you say it is so charming, though. I think I like it." She stared at him in disbelief. The blighter was mad, that's what he was; he was flirting with her. With *her*! "In case you should ever grow tired of it, though," he went on casually, "my proper name is David. David Reece, at your service, madam."

She curled her lip at him in disdain. "You're a wretched host, Mr. Reece."

"How so?"

She dropped the chicken bone back on the plate. "You took the only chair, that's how. Not much of a gentleman, are you?" She smirked. "Not that I expect you're much worth the name, being a lying, cheating, guttersnipe of a kidnapper as you are."

He looked thunderstruck for a moment, then slapped his hand down on the table with a crack, making her jump. "By Jove, you're right!" He was on his feet and at her side before Vivian could move. "Allow me, madam." He caught her arms and steered her toward the chair, where he all but pushed her into it. His hands were big and strong, and Vivian was again aware how easily he could pick her up and do whatever he wished with her person. Although . . . His grip was firm but not rough. He had never really hurt her, and Vivian realized he wouldn't. She had no good reason for it, but somehow she was certain he wouldn't hurt her—unless perhaps she provoked him, and she had learned her lesson on that score. Still, she sat as far back as possible in the chair as he towered over her. Then she gave a squeak of alarm as he went down on his knee in front of her, folded his arms, and rested his elbows on the ends of the chair arms.

"Better?" he asked, his eyes alight with devilish amusement. "May I assist you in any other way? More chocolate, perhaps?"

"Aye," Vivian gasped, clutching at anything that would make him move away from her. Instead, he leaned closer, and Vivian retreated, digging her toes into the carpet in a vain effort to push herself even further backward.

"Tell me your name," he said softly. His face was on level with hers, and Vivian couldn't see anything else.

"Why do you want to know?"

He cocked his head, those piercing dark eyes fixed on hers. "Because I like you, Vivian," he said slowly. "Believe me or not, I do."

"I'm not a trinket you can keep just because you like me!"

The corner of his mouth went up, and his gaze turned lazy, speculative and seductive. "No, you're not," he said in a low voice. "By God, you are not."

She flushed. He sounded rather more appreciative of that fact than she'd intended. He sounded as though he would like to explore just what she was, with great thoroughness. She jerked her head away, fixing her gaze on the door. "Aye," she said flatly. "Then go away and leave me in peace, if you're wanting to be so gentlemanly all of a sudden."

"Ah, but you've not finished your chocolate." He

reached back to the table and picked up the little cup. Steam no longer rose from the surface, but it still smelled wonderful. He held the little cup up between them. "All I want is your name, Vivian," he coaxed.

Vivian drew a strangled breath; she felt closed in by his presence. Up close he even smelled rich, and overpoweringly male. She could see the pulse in his neck where his cravat had been pulled loose, a strong steady beat that made her own heart beat faster. The bloody knave had to be one of the handsomest rogues she'd ever laid eyes on, for all that he was a black-hearted devil, she thought in helpless fury.

"Beecham," she said at last, hating her voice for being so scratchy and quavering. He'd think she was swooning in a passion for him! "Vivian Beecham. Take your ruddy chocolate and leave me alone." She was determined not to look at him, but when he didn't move, she lost her patience and shot him a poisonous glare. "*Now* what?"

The heat had faded from his face. He searched her expression for a moment, then lifted one of her hands and placed the warm cup in it. "A very fine pleasure to meet you, Miss Beecham," was all he said. Without another word, he got to his feet and left, sketching a little bow at the door.

Vivian frowned in unease. What had she done? What had he done? Mr. Reece, she remembered he was named: David Reece. David. She lifted the cup and drained it. Her eyes fell on the chocolate pot still on the table, and when she lifted it, it was promisingly heavy. She poured some more, but it wasn't frothy, as it had been when he poured it, and it was getting cold. She put the cup aside and regarded the two trays, the half-empty dinner tray and the other one. The chocolate tray for a highway thief who wouldn't give him what he wanted.

For the first time since he'd locked her up, Vivian wasn't hungry anymore.

David rang for his own dinner, his mood at once euphoric and strangely thoughtful. He'd gotten Mrs. Gray to talk, and mostly she'd said just what he expected: a string of curses and slurs on his character, no more nor less than he deserved. He had a proper name for her now, though: Vivian Beecham. An oddly fanciful name for a common thief, he thought, but somehow it suited her. A face like hers was far from common.

It was that expressive face that was giving him pause. He'd seen the scorn in those fine blue eyes when he had asked about starving. He knew she must have been hungry just from looking at her, a little slip of a woman with none of the soft roundness a well-fed lady would have. But knowing it and hearing her admit it, almost defiantly, as if it were his fault in some way, were different things. Suppose she was starving when she got on the coach that day. Suppose she'd viewed his signet ring as nothing more than a month of good food. What else could a starving girl do to feed herself? She was too pretty, he supposed, to be hired in any decent household. She had the talent for Drury Lane, but perhaps not the temperament. What else was there? Seamstress work, perhaps, or selling things in the market. Selling herself in the market would bring her the most money, though, and David didn't like that image at all. His instinct said she didn't do that; she was uncomfortable when he moved close to her, and she never once tried to charm anything out of him.

He finished his dinner and sat with his feet stretched out to the fire while he drank his wine, the bottle nestled in the chair beside him. The nights were beginning to carry a chill of autumn, and he made a note to lay a fire in her room.

She was quite a puzzle to David. She was a thief, and by rights he ought to deliver her to the authorities. It was highly doubtful he would ever see that ring again—odds were it had already been sold and melted down—and there was almost surely nothing to gain by keeping her locked in his house. A wiser, more practical man would let her go.

But David had never been particularly wise or practical. It was true what he had told her: he did like her. The range of emotion that showed on her face made him want to laugh, from her fiery outrage at him to her sly satisfaction when she thought she'd bested him to her rapturous pleasure when he offered her a taste of the chocolate. David wanted to see that last expression again, and not over a cup of chocolate.

He poured the last of the wine into his glass. He would deal with the question of letting her go later. For now, he was too pleased at finally getting her to speak to him to contemplate her leaving. Tomorrow he'd get her to smile, and the day after, to laugh. He wanted to see her laugh, with her head thrown back and her eyes alight with it. Her skin flushed with it. Her chest heaving. Her hands pressed to her bosom, pulling at the fastenings of her dress. His mouth, pressed to the beating pulse at the base of her throat . . .

David slid a little lower in his chair and smiled in tipsy contemplation. No, he most certainly wasn't ready to let go of Vivian Beecham yet.

Chapter Ten

From that night on, he came to visit her more often. Every evening, in fact, and often he stayed and talked to her for hours. Some nights he seemed bent on teasing her until Vivian wanted to scream and throw things at him, which appeared to amuse him to no end. Some nights he asked her opinions of things she had never considered a man would think important, and listened to her with every appearance of attention. Some nights he told her stories about his youth and family in which his role was less than noble. She was hard put not to laugh when he told her about the time he cut all the roses in the garden and was chased into the lake by an irate gardener. She did laugh when he related how his younger sister, at the time a small child, smeared his face with her mother's rouge in retaliation for his eating the last of the currant buns. "I'd no idea they were promised to her," he protested with a wounded air as Vivian laughed. "And I was utterly famished."

"You wicked knave," she said, picturing him with streaks of red across his face, and finding it very entertaining and strangely endearing.

"My dear, if you think that's wicked, I shall have to spare you the rest of my life history."

"Aye, that's wicked, I say, eating the last of someone's currant buns. I expect the rest is a mere trifle next to it."

He chuckled. "If only the rest of my family were so understanding! Celia eventually forgave me for the currant buns, but not until I apologized on my knees and promised to let her have my custard at dinner."

Vivian laughed, too, finding with some surprise that she wasn't angry with him anymore, either. True, he had locked her up; but she had never been so pampered in her life. Not only fine food and a fine bed, but hot baths, chocolate, and amusing conversation, all things she could become accustomed to in no time. She didn't know if he was aware that his servant smuggled books out of his library for her, but Vivian somehow didn't think he would mind. He no longer tried to tease the whereabouts of his ring out of her, and at times Vivian even forgot why she was in his house in the first place. She didn't quite know what he was about, bringing her sweets and spending hours charming her, but she was not immune to it. She was beginning to like the bloody rogue, damn him.

She still thought about how she would escape, of course. There was still Simon to consider, as well as the fact that Vivian trusted no one, let alone the too-charming David Reece. But she thought about escape far less often, and about David far more often. It was perhaps weak and disloyal of her, but she couldn't help it. Her antipathy was waning, and she was no longer certain that was wrong. The truth of the matter was, David was *nice* to her—nicer than anyone had been in a long time. It was hard to hate him under those circumstances, no matter what his motive.

He was nice to her, *and* he made her laugh regularly. She knew he was striving to amuse her, and she initially tried not to let him, but he kept at it until she succumbed. She couldn't guess why he cared to make her laugh, but he did. She also found it was hard to hate someone who lifted her spirits so much. The harder she tried to resist his good humor, the more droll he grew, until she would collapse in helpless laughter. It simply wasn't fair, she thought in frustration. Her life before seemed completely dour and grim, and now she found herself anticipating his arrival every day with something very near pleasure. She never knew quite what to expect from him, but he managed not to disappoint her once.

"Congratulate me," he demanded one night upon bursting into her room, throwing his arms wide. "I've gone and done a brilliant thing today." Without waiting for her reply, he swept an elegant bow and caught her hand, bringing it to his lips for a courtly kiss. "Never let anyone say I haven't got any genius, because today, I proved I have." He strode back across the room and flung open the door, shouting for his servant to bring another chair. Then he swung around to face her again. "I hope you don't mind, I've decided to dine with you tonight."

Vivian clutched her kissed hand to her stomach and watched in confusion as the creaky old servant dragged in another chair and shoved it up to the table. Brilliant? Genius? What on earth was he talking of? The servant carried in a tray, staggering under the weight of it, and David took it from him. "Go on, then, Bannet," he declared. "Take yourself off for the evening, and have a glass of port as well."

"Yes, sir." The man bowed slightly, then left the room.

David turned to her again, grinning broadly, and produced a bottle of wine.

"A celebration of sorts," he said, uncorking it and filling two glasses. "It's a near miracle when I amaze myself, so the occasion must be observed in some fashion. A toast." He raised his glass.

Vivian took the glass he handed her. "What did you do?"

"Don't sound so suspicious." He shook his head in reproach.

"And why shouldn't I?" She sniffed the wine in the glass. "Have you got another woman locked up now?"

He lowered his glass, looking genuinely shocked. "No. Of course not. That was an exceptional circumstance . . ." He flipped one hand, and cleared his throat. "No, indeed, it is something much better than that. I have bought Dashing Dancer." He extended his arms again and bowed, as an actor might after giving a brilliant performance. Vivian waited, but he said nothing more, simply stood there expectantly.

"What dashing dancer?" she asked.

"What Dashing Dancer?" he repeated. "The *only* Dashing Dancer. The finest colt ever to run the Ascot. He lost out to an inferior horse because his rider was an absolute incompetent, but that horse has blood that will sire a legion of champions. My brother's been after him for a year, but old Camden wouldn't sell. And now, he has—to me."

"You bought a horse?" she said cautiously. "That's how you amaze yourself?"

He threw up his hand in exasperation. "It *is* amazing! I might have known a woman wouldn't grasp the significance."

Vivian cocked her head. "Did you get him on the cheap, then?"

He laughed. "Most certainly not."

"Then no, I don't grasp the significance."

David sighed loudly. "My brother has wanted that horse for his stables for a long time," he explained. "A very long time. He's made at least two offers for the horse, both of which were refused. Very few people refuse my brother anything, ever. And now I have succeeded where he failed. It is quite possible I have never in my life been able to say that before now."

"Oh," said Vivian. "All right. Congratulations to you."

He peered at her a moment longer in disbelief, then threw back his head and laughed. "I was well pleased by it at least, if you are not. Come, shall we dine?"

"I don't mean to make light of it," said Vivian as he pulled out a chair.

"No, no. I suppose in the sweep of life, it's nothing." He smiled wryly. "It was merely the achievement of finally, at long last, besting my brother. We're twins, you see. He is the good one, I am the wicked one."

A twin. Lord help the women of London, with two such men about. "He's all good, and you're all wicked?" She said it with a grin, intending to tease him. But he considered it, then nodded.

"Yes, I believe most people would say that's so."

Vivian frowned. "No one is all good."

"I notice you don't dispute one can be all wicked." He bowed slightly. "Won't you be seated?"

Oh Lord. He was holding out the chair for *her*. Vivian walked around the table and sat, reduced to shy silence by the gesture. He took the other chair and poured more wine, though she'd taken but a sip of hers. She stole a glance at him in the candlelight as he busied himself arranging the rest of the table, clearing away the trays and covers. For a fine gentleman, he seemed well able to take care of himself. She'd always supposed such folk were unable and unwilling to do aught for themselves, but had twenty servants lined up to do everything. So far, David had tended to her as devotedly as a man to his bride.

The unwitting thought made her eyes grow wide and her heart hammer at the very idiocy of the idea. Lord, what was she thinking now? The wine and the kiss on her hand must have made her lightheaded. Just because they were sitting here in some semblance of intimacy was no reason for her to get ideas. She knew very well what sort of relationship a man of his station would have with a girl of her station.

"I suppose one can be all wicked," she said, trying to regain her senses. "It's just harder to be all good."

"Do you think? I wouldn't know about it," he said. "Being all wicked is so much more fun."

"But you envy your brother," she pointed out. David paused, his wine glass in midair.

"Perhaps," he said thoughtfully. "At times. But usually, no."

"You must, if you're so pleased to have gotten something he could not."

"Most of what he has, I would happily do without. It is rare that our interests align, but in this one case, they did. I believe it is quite natural for one brother to revel in a triumph over the other."

"Aye," Vivian conceded that point. "So now you've got the horse, what do you propose to do with him?"

"I shall offer him for sale to my brother," he said promptly. "For an outrageous sum, of course."

"You've a rogue's soul," she said with a helpless smile. "If you hadn't been born so rich, you'd have been a pirate."

"Not at all," he said.

"Aye," she insisted. "I can see it clear, you with a cutlass in one hand and a pistol in the other, always on the run from the navy with a load of rum and stolen jewels."

David laughed, but deep inside himself thought, *Yes.* He could have been a pirate, if Reeces hadn't been born to such splendor. He liked the image more than he could possibly admit out loud. "The rum, for certain. Stolen jewels? Not likely."

"And how would you have come by the rum, then?" she shot back.

He winked at her. "A sympathetic tavern owner."

She scoffed. "And who are tavern keepers sympathetic to, but those with money?"

He chuckled, recalling how many taverns he and his friends had been thrown out of for raucous behavior. "Not always."

"Always," she said. "Those with money can drink until they're flat on their backs, snoring to wake the dead. Or start a brawl that disrupts everyone else's rest. Or distract the serving wenches and demand the best rooms, even if other folk must be turned out of them. And those with no money are fortunate to get a place at a table in the public room and a bowl of cold soup before they're shown the door."

He leaned back in his chair and studied her. "You've dealt with some miserly tavern keepers, I see."

"The worst." She said it with a peculiar grimace on her face, and David wondered again what her life had been like. He had never before known a woman who would call him a pirate and have unfortunate experiences with tavern keepers. It was odd just to discuss such things with a woman. But David was discovering he liked being able to talk so freely with Vivian. Not because of her hard history, but because of his own; to hold a decent conversation with a proper young lady, David would have to omit the vast majority of his life and doings. He didn't think he could manage more than a quarter hour of acceptable conversation with a sheltered lady of his own class, and at least half that time would no doubt be devoted to a discussion of the weather. Then he would have absolutely nothing left to say to her that wouldn't leave her swooning in shock or gasping in outrage. Disregarding for a moment whether or not it was proper to discuss such things at all, David found it easier to talk to Vivian Beecham simply because he didn't have to fear slipping up and saying something that would shock and repel her. In all truth, she was probably more likely to shock and horrify him, were she to share her life story. He wondered just how callous those tavern keepers had been to her.

The next day David was still feeling quite pleased with his coup. It had been a rare stroke of luck persuading Camden to sell Dashing Dancer. David still wasn't entirely certain how he had accomplished it, but over a bottle of port at White's, he had made the offer and to his immense surprise it had been accepted. Perhaps it was a sign that his luck had turned, or that his good intentions of reform were bearing fruit.

He didn't have a stable worthy of Dashing Dancer, unfortunately. The horse was too old to race, although David remained convinced he would be a champion sire. He knew Marcus believed it as well and, with Blessing Hill, Marcus could put Dashing Dancer to stud immediately. David had only been slightly exaggerating when he told Vivian he meant to sell the horse to Marcus. He did;

but the price he planned to ask was a number of Dashing Dancer's offspring, so that he could establish his own stable. The only mildly respectable pursuit David had any aptitude for was fine horses, breeding them and racing them. If he were to choose something to occupy himself with, a quality stable was the best choice.

When he arrived at Exeter House, he began hunting for the stud book from Blessing Hill, already considering breeding possibilities he could suggest to Marcus. The book, though, seemed to have disappeared from its usual place. David sighed in aggravation. There would be a copy at Blessing Hill, but he didn't want to wait while it was fetched. He sent Mr. Adams to look in his small office, and then turned to the cabinet behind the desk. Perhaps Marcus had put it away in there, with his personal papers. He opened a number of doors and drawers, until he found a slim leather-bound book that looked much like David remembered the stud book looking. "There you are," he muttered, pulling it out and flipping it open.

A sheaf of paper slid to the floor. David stooped to pick it up, and something caught his attention: the name of the man who had attempted to kill Marcus and cause David to be the suspected murderer. For a moment David just held it, taken completely off guard. He hadn't thought about that plot at all in several days. Perhaps it wasn't a good idea to read more . . . But then, with a mixture of dread and interest, he began to read, the stud book forgotten.

It was a report from Mr. John Stafford of Bow Street, addressed to Marcus and dated two months past. It began by thanking the duke for his invaluable assistance, then went on to relate the confession extorted from Mr. Bentley Reece after his arrest. Bentley admitted to printing counterfeit banknotes, but not to spending them; that,

Mr. Stafford wrote delicately, Bentley blamed on "other persons unknown to Bow Street." David felt a curious numbness steal over him. *He* was the "other person." Bentley most certainly would have named him, and the fact that Mr. Stafford didn't mention it meant that Marcus had persuaded him to overlook it.

David read on, his fury growing in tandem with his sense of humiliation and loathing. Bentley admitted to spying on the duke of Exeter by means of a maid in the duke's household. Stafford had discovered the maid passed information to a tailor's assistant named Slocum, who in turn worked for an Irishman named Fergal Rourke, a so-called "family man" who ran a ring of thieves and pickpockets. Rourke was dead—David knew that, having seen Marcus shoot the man himself—but several of his criminal cohorts had been arrested with Bentley. Their confessions implicated Bentley in everything from petty thievery to murder, concluding with the planned usurpation of Marcus's title.

The papers fell from David's hands unnoticed to the desk. So Bentley had schemed to see David arrested and transported for counterfeiting whilst plotting to murder Marcus. It was nothing David hadn't already assumed and suspected, but he and Marcus had never really talked about it. Marcus had simply seemed to let the matter go after they left the dilapidated harbor house where Bentley had tried to kill them both. David had nursed his multiple injuries and ailments, and Marcus had planned an elaborate wedding trip for his bride.

Had there ever been a bigger fool? David ran his hands over his head, digging his fingers into the tense muscles at the base of his skull. It wasn't bad enough to fall into a counterfeiter's scheme. Oh, no, he danced like a puppet on strings for his own cousin, who knew him well enough to use his every weakness and vice against him. Bentley was a villain, but David had made himself an easy tool in the hands of the villain. For all he knew, Bentley had been waiting and watching for years, planning exactly when to spring the trap that David would walk right into.

He shoved away from the desk and lurched to his feet. For a moment he stood there, breathing hard, bracing his hands on the desk while the damning words danced before his eyes on the papers scattered in front of him: counterfeiting—plot to murder—transported—spies—tailor's assistant—other persons unknown to Bow Street . . . With a curse he swept everything back into the black leather book and jammed it onto the shelf. He knew it was true—reading more wouldn't serve any purpose. David looked around, suddenly stifled by his brother's house, his brother's study, his brother's ability to walk away from that debacle and build a happy life with his new bride. Whatever Marcus had done, his conscience was clear. It was David's that was rotted and black.

He walked straight out of the house, barely pausing to take his hat and gloves. For some time David walked, with no destination in mind, but hoping the exercise would relieve the ache in his head. He didn't know how to escape his sins, nor why they had recently begun to weigh so heavily on his soul. It seemed that he hadn't felt them accumulating for years, and now they had settled on his shoulders in one crushing load overnight. It was almost more than he could bear.

After quite some time he found himself outside White's. Dusk had fallen while he walked. He looked at the brightly lit windows with bleak eyes. Perhaps oblivion was the answer, at least for tonight. He mounted the steps and went in, seeking nothing more than a quiet corner to drink himself into a blind, forgetful stupor.

He told a footman to bring him a bottle of wine, and he went in search of a secluded seat. The club was filled, though, and he was beginning to despair in his search when he saw one, just past the betting books.

Standing in his way was a cluster of men. As David approached, some of them noticed him. More than one face broke into a curious smile as he came nearer. "Good evening," said David, giving a brief nod. There were several acquaintances of his in the group.

The smiles grew larger. "Good evening," one man drawled, standing aside and sweeping an arm toward the books. "Come to see the latest wagers?" David hesitated, on the brink of saying no. He only wanted to drink, and drink and drink. He wasn't in a sporting state of mind at the moment. But there was something odd here. Everyone seemed to be watching him with a great deal of unwarranted interest. He summoned up an attitude of careless disinterest, and walked up to the podium where the betting books lay, spread open and ready for additional wagers to be entered.

But this page was full. The wagers dated from weeks previous. He started to turn the page, until his own initials caught his eye. Then again, and again. His name featured in many—nearly all—of the wagers written there.

Capt. Evans bets Mr. Melvill fifty pounds to twenty pounds that Lord D. R. will be in custody of Bow Street within the month. Sir H. T. bets Mr. R. T. one hundred pounds to fifty that D. R. will lose the Exeter fortune at the gaming tables. Mr. Grentham bets Mr. Thomson twenty pounds that Lord B. will call out D. R. . . . twenty pounds to ten pounds that Sir W. A. will call out D. R. . . . twenty pounds to fifteen pounds that Lord M will call out D. R. . . . five hundred pounds to two hundred pounds that the duke of E. returns from abroad to find himself destitute.

Slowly, deliberately, David turned the page. His ears buzzed, almost but not quite drowning out the malicious whispers behind him. He pretended to read the next page, and the one after, though his vision was blurred and his hand couldn't seem to unclench from a fist. He was a laughingstock, among men whose sins outnumbered even his own. He was an object of scorn to his own class, to those who had gone along on his debauched jaunt through life and been pleased to let him pay for it. David would rather have had the cut direct from every single one of them. He turned to go.

"Nothing to add, Reece?" asked one man, Henry Trevenham, making little attempt to hide his smirk. David could have put a sword through his heart; Trev had once been a friend of his, and they'd lost and won fortunes together at the hazard tables. Trev's hands were no whiter than his own.

David looked at him for a long moment, until Trev's mouth tightened and he stood a little straighter. "No," said David. "Should I?"

"Quite a number of wagers you might take a stake in," he prodded. "You always were one for the wagers." A muffled snicker went around the group.

Somehow, David brought a slight smile to his face. "Oh? I must have overlooked any of interest." He made a show of turning back to the book. "Ah. Here we are. The duke of E. . . . . Could that be old Elkington?"

Trev's smile was hard and cold now. "Why, no," he said, affecting surprise. "I do believe it's your own brother, Exeter. He's gone off and left the reins of the estate in your hands, hasn't he?" It was more accusation than question. David forced his hands to relax, and didn't let them curl into fists and pummel the blighter's face to a pulp. He rested one elbow on the edge of the podium and tried to keep his expression neutral.

"He has."

His lack of anger seemed to incite Trev, as well as the others. George Evans stepped forward. "I must have overlooked that one. Here, let me make my wager." David watched as Evans scribbled in the book, wagering that the duke of E. would indeed be left destitute. He didn't even bother filling in another name, leaving that blank. "Have you come to give us a report on your progress in emptying the coffers?"

David raised one eyebrow. "They're far from empty. If these wagers refer to my brother, I should warn you gentlemen you're heading for a loss."

"It would be a loss well worth it to ruin you," charged one man bitterly. "Because of you, Bow Street suspected us all of counterfeiting!" His voice dropped and he spat the last word out as if it fouled his mouth. "Not a man among us will ever receive you again. Not a man will ever sit at a table with you again, nor take your wagers. You are finished, I tell you, for ruining our good names and sullying our reputations!" A hiss of agreement rose from his companions.

David straightened to his full height, taking advantage of the few extra inches he had on the man to look down on his accuser. "And here I thought passing your bastard off on old Melchester was the ruination of your good name." The man's mouth dropped open in slack surprise, and David smiled thinly. "Lady Melchester is so indiscreet in her boudoir." He hadn't actually gone to bed with Lady Melchester, although she had tried to lure him there—sleeping with another man's wife who was pregnant by yet a different man was just too much for even David. He raised his voice a little, so each and every one of the hypocrites could hear him. "If any man here blames me for his troubles, let him consider this: not everyone of my acquaintance was suspected. Why were you singled out? Could it be that they made a list of the most depraved gamesters in London, and it had nothing to do with your acquaintance with me? I certainly never accused anyone of counterfeiting."

"Exeter was shadowing us," snarled Trev. "All of us! He gambled like—like—"

"Like you did?" David asked coolly. "A lapse on his part, for certain. But perhaps I mistook your meaning. Did you mean to suggest Marcus accused you?"

They muttered among each other, no one wanting to accuse Marcus of anything.

"Then I bid you all good evening." David began to walk away, then stopped and turned back. "Good Lord—don't let me forget to enter my wager." With a flourish he signed his name under the last wager, taking the bet Evans has just entered for one pound. "That looks like a rum bet to me," he said, replacing the pen and facing the men with a lazy grin. "Destitute? Come, now; really." Shaking his head, he strolled away, past the scowling faces of his one-time companions in mischief, away from their self-righteous outrage and lies and even worse, the truths they spoke. It felt as if his body were operating on a different level, unrelated to his mind and spirit. It took everything he had to walk leisurely away, when he really wanted to punch someone, upset the tables, and throw things.

Someone laid a hand on his arm as he walked back through the club; he brushed it away, his vision narrowed to the door. If he could only make it out of here without losing his grip on his composure, it seemed, he would be all right. He would survive this—somehow. He would redeem himself—somehow. But how on earth he would manage either, David couldn't guess.

At the door, a servant caught up to him. "Your wine, sir," said the man breathlessly, presenting his tray with the wine David had ordered earlier. David lifted the glass, drained it in one draught, and then lifted the bottle. "Er . . . Shall I pour for you, my lord?" asked the startled waiter, but David waved him off. He slapped his hat on his head and walked out of the club, the bottle of wine snug in his grip. Again he turned and walked blindly, and as he walked he drank.

Two hours later the bottle was empty. His steps were dragging. David knew he was limping, but he didn't have the strength of mind or body to hide it. The burgundy had dulled his mind but not the despair he felt. Instead of raging about being betrayed by his own blood cousin or cut by rogues who never cared what he did until it threatened their own facades of respectability, all he wanted to do was forget. Wine had been as good a method of forgetting his troubles as David had ever found. He turned homeward, the bottle hanging from his fingertips.

Bannet met him at the door. "Good evening, sir," he said, taking David's hat as if his master came home every night lame and drunk. Perhaps he did, David thought sluggishly, and was simply too foolish to realize it.

"Here go." David handed him the empty wine bottle and stripped off his gloves. One of them turned inside out, and he dropped it on the floor. "Bring another bottle, would you?"

Bannet took the bottle. "Yes, sir. Will you take madam her dinner now?"

Madam. David swayed on his feet, remembering. He should tell Bannet to take Vivian her dinner. Lord knew he wasn't fit company for anyone tonight. "All right," he grumbled, stumping up the stairs.

Vivian heard the scrape in the lock and shoved the little book of poetry under the mattress. At last, David was here. She was hungry, but she was also looking forward to his visit. Her spirits lifted in anticipation. She scrambled to her feet, but the door didn't swing open as usual. Instead there was a muffled curse, some more scraping, and then a hard rattle of the latch.

She drew back a step, instinctively wiping any expression from her face. She knew those sounds. He was drunk, he was, and while Vivian had no idea what to expect, her experiences with Flynn warned her it wouldn't be good.

The door swung open, so hard it banged against the wall. David stood in the doorway, the tray in his unsteady hands. His eyes wandered around the room until he found her. "Dinner, m'dear," he mumbled, then stepped into the room. He closed the door by kicking it with his boot heel, and Vivian flinched as it slammed shut. He winced, hobbling across the room to set down the tray with a loud clank. "Eat up," he told her, and collapsed into the chair with a grimace.

She stayed where she was. "You're cup-shot."

He produced another bottle from the pocket of his greatcoat, which he still wore. "Yes, I am." He twisted out the cork and tipped it over a glass. "And getting more so every moment, love."

He didn't look like a dangerous drunk, like Flynn. He looked rather like a sad drunk, his head hanging forward as he watched the wine pour into the glass. Cautiously she moved forward. "Why?"

"Because I am a pathetic louse of a man," he replied, and tossed back half his glass. He waved one hand. "Come, eat. I shan't add to my sins by starving you."

"Why are you getting drunk and drunker?" She ignored his invitation to eat.

"I prefer it to being sober."

Vivian threw him a suspicious look. Since she'd never yet seen him drunk, that didn't sound true. "Why's that?"

He swirled the wine around his glass. "It helps one to forget, my dear."

She raised her eyebrows. "And what do you have to forget? Did your last fancy meal turn your stomach?"

His shoulders lifted with a sigh. "It's nothing you would understand. Don't let it trouble you."

Vivian stared at him for a moment. She ought to let him stew in whatever misery he'd undoubtedly brought on himself. She had no reason to feel any pity for him, and she didn't. Really, she didn't. It was pure idle curiosity that made her want to know why he was sitting here, drinking himself senseless, staring at the fire with no trace of the daring energy and damnable charm she'd always seen before. He looked . . . empty. "I suppose that's because you're a fancy gentleman and have troubles no one like me could ever imagine. The cook burned your dinner, or the tailor sewed your drawers too small."

He twisted in his chair until he was peering up at her from beneath his tousled hair. "You wish me to bare my black soul, do you? I didn't want to offend your delicate sensibilities, but if you insist . . ." He braced one foot against the table leg and pushed himself upright in the chair. "This spring, I let myself become a tool in the hands of a murderous traitor. Shocking, isn't it? I know you will doubt I, a model of propriety and elegance, could have stumbled so badly, but it's true. And now I am an object of scorn to London society. Men I have known since I was a boy are wagering about what shame I shall bring on my family next." He slumped again, his voice weary. "I am a fool, and a laughingstock."

Vivian said nothing. She sensed there was more to it than folks making sport of him, but didn't know what. As far as she had seen, he was far from an object of mockery. She had never seen him anything less than completely assured and recklessly confident, and could hardly believe he was truly laid so low by others' opinions of him. Surely not; the man had laughed outright when she insulted him and called him the vilest names she knew, and now he was undone by gossips' talk of him? Vivian supposed no one would enjoy such a thing, but she knew it wasn't the end of the world. She also didn't think he had ever done anything truly evil, at least not by her accounting. She'd punched him on a broken rib, and he'd not so much as raised his hand to her. Flynn would have knocked her senseless for the same action.

David seemed determined to pity himself tonight, though, and Vivian couldn't abide that. Particularly not when he had so little grounds. Her eyes went to his leg, the one he favored, now stretched out in front of him. "What did you do to get a limp?" she asked on impulse.

For a moment his face stiffened, then he sighed, pressing his fist, knuckles first, into his thigh as if to rub away the ache. "I broke my leg in a carriage accident," he said. "Racing a mate of mine. I hit a hole in the road. Flew thirty feet through the air, to hear Percy tell it, then rolled down a hill and into a bush. If I hadn't been thoroughly pickled, there's no telling what else might have broken." Bitterness laced his tone. "That was months ago, and I still limp like an old woman."

That, Vivian could understand. Being lame could

indeed ruin a man's life and livelihood, although she rather doubted the slight limp impaired him too much. "I'm sorry," she said. He waved one hand, his eyes dark and melancholy.

"You had nothing to do with it."

"Nay, but I can still be sorry you have a limp, can't I?" she retorted. He lifted one hand in a motion of indifference, still staring into his glass. She crossed the room to stand in front of him. "And you'll feel sorry for yourself forever because of it, will you," she said. "A fine figure you are. It's not enough you have a warm house and a man to black your boots. You've food in your belly and a fire to warm your toes. You have clothes and clothes and clothes; you keep your own carriage, ye daft fool! There's folks who would fall on their knees in thanks to have any of those things, and all you can patter on about is people talking about you and a limp that cuts your fine stride. You can't even take a bit of sympathy, but keep to your gloom about it." She flipped one hand at him in disgust. "You're naught but a spoiled lad."

He didn't stir. "You're right. I am. Do you think I don't know it?" He took a big gulp of wine, and drops of red spattered his cravat. He either didn't notice or didn't care. "It's the sad story of my entire life," he muttered. "Poor David. Without his name and family, he'd be nothing. Offended by something David does? His mother will apologize. Fleeced at card by David? His brother will pay. Don't take anything about David seriously, he's just a spoiled lad." His voice had grown harsh and savage at the end.

"Aye, spoiled indeed," Vivian said sharply. "Ye have a family that looks after you, even when you're in trouble and up to no good? Rotten luck, that."

David let his head fall back against the hard wood of

the chair. He knew how fortunate he was. That wasn't what he was lamenting. It was his wasted life he mourned, a life he was only just beginning to realize he had lost. Yesterday he had felt on top of the world, ready and able to take on anything that presented itself. Now . . . he rather wished his brother would return from Italy early and spare him the further humiliation of running Exeter so badly that gentlemen were betting on how destitute Marcus would be when he returned. David indulged in a moment's fantasy of just leaving it all; he could pack a valise and be gone by morning, off to his hunting lodge or one of the more distant Exeter properties where no one would require anything of him. He was sick of being responsible and honest. He didn't want to give a damn anymore.

"Well, I expect the only choice you have is to give it up," Vivian said, startling him out of his thoughts. "Will you run off and hide from all the fools who have naught better to do with themselves than mock another person? Go on, they won't laugh at you for it. They won't turn their noses in the air and say they knew all along you would turn tail. No, not at all. You'll really be showing them what you're made of."

"Thank you for that wise and caring counsel. The remaining shreds of my pride are in cinders at your feet." He gave her a sour look.

She rolled her eyes and made an impatient noise. "What else did you expect? Pity for how terrible you've had it?" David filled his glass again and said nothing. "Well, if you think I'll feel sorry for you, you've had too much to drink."

"I never asked you to feel pity for me." David drank some more. He *had* had too much to drink, not that it was her concern. He was definitely drunk, so why didn't he feel happier? David was a jolly drunk; he knew it, and counted on it. Why was the wine failing him now when he needed it the most? "It's the last thing I would expect from you, of all people." He heaved himself to his feet, adjusting his balance with care born of long practice. He put the bottle to his lips and finished the wine, doing away with the trouble of pouring it into a glass. Everyone saw him as a drunk, he might as well be one. Tonight he'd willingly trade away all his good intentions for a respite from his humiliations.

She didn't say anything as he made his way to the door. The operation of the knob seemed to elude him; his fingers closed on it, but he couldn't seem to turn it right. He took a deep breath and let it out, concentrating on his grip, and finally the latch clicked.

"I don't pity you," said Vivian suddenly. David paused on the threshold. "Not because I think they're right to bam you so; 'tis cruel and mean-spirited, of course. And not because you've had some troubles of late. 'Tis no worse than other folk endure, though, and you know it. Don't pity yourself and it won't matter much what other people do."

"Did you ever think it's not pity, but guilt?" He gave a half-hearted shrug. "I know what I've done. Should I not feel the weight of remorse? Should I not suffer the consequences of my actions?"

"I expect none of us can hope to escape the consequences of our actions for long," she said. "But that doesn't mean all of them are warranted. The punishment don't always right the crime, aye?"

He looked at her, a hardened thief with the face of a angel. She knew what she spoke of. "I agree," he said quietly. "But in my case, my dear . . . I am very much afraid this punishment is exactly what I deserve." She made no answer, and he let himself out of the room in silence.

Chapter Eleven

By the next morning, the drink had worn off, along with most of David's melancholy.

Vivian's words of the night before had run round and round his brain during the night. No one *should* feel sorry for him. He didn't deserve pity, and that included from himself. After all, if he did give up and take himself off to some distant Exeter estate, he would be admitting defeat, admitting all the slurs about his character were absolutely true. Perhaps they had once been true, but no longer. He was determined to prove it. While David didn't care a farthing for the good opinion of the hypocritical rogues at White's last evening, he refused to let them think they had cowed him and chased him out of town. He would stay, just to prove them wrong and to make them lose every single wager on the books. He would turn a profit for Marcus; he'd already landed Dashing Dancer, which was triumph enough in its own right. He would show them how a Reece responded to a challenge. And to that end, he intended to go out tonight and have a grand time. He planned to take Vivian with him.

To hell with Trevenham and Grentham and all the rest.

Vivian had more compassion and kindness in her than any of them had. In the proper gown, with some jewels at her neck and in her hair, those alleged gentlemen would be eating out of her hand—the same gentlemen who wouldn't speak to her if they knew her background.

The sharp-tongued little harpy had somehow won his respect. He had become accustomed to coming home to her every night. He loved to provoke her to see how she would fairly ignite with indignation and fury, and he loved to tease her until it was all she could do to keep from laughing. If he had met her under different circumstances . . .

If only . . .

David had made a fool of himself many times over a woman. He had been stupid and he had been indiscreet, but never had he lost his head and gone silly over a woman. He never thought he would. And yet, he suspected he would have been in very great danger of losing his head over Vivian Beecham had she been a lady of his own class.

Of course, then she wouldn't have been herself. She would have been a proper lady, not someone David would have ever spoken to and not someone who would have been interested in speaking to him. She likely would have been married already to a better man than David. As it was, he was terribly torn between thinking he ought to let her go and wanting to keep her with him forever.

He just didn't know what to make of her. She was still every bit as intriguing to him as she always had been. Her background led him to entertain fantasies of seducing her with luxuries, like the chocolate. He closed his eyes and saw again her expression as she sipped. Yes, he definitely wanted to ply her with luxury. What would her face look like as he rolled silk stockings on her legs, he wondered?

It was out of character for him to think things like that. David was generally more interested in rolling the stockings *off* a woman's legs. Of course, it was entirely possible to make love to a woman while she was wearing stockings. And David would be more than willing to do it, if he thought Vivian wanted him to.

He was becoming consumed by that question: did she want him to seduce her? Or rather—since David was fairly certain he knew the answer to that question—would she allow him to seduce her? God knew he wanted to. If he hadn't taken her prisoner, he already would have done his best to do so. By locking her up, though, he had put himself in her debt. It didn't seem fair that he try to seduce her when she was under duress.

That thought brought a smile to his face. Vivian, under duress. He had never known a woman who bore up under duress as she did. She could be as frosty cold as any duchess David knew, and as hot with fury as any fishwife. But it was her demeanor last night that had impressed him most. He needed someone, he supposed, to be brutally honest with him. The only other women David knew with any degree of familiarity were his stepmother, his sister, and his sister-in-law. The first would have gone on crusade to expose the hypocrisy of Evans, Trevenham, and the like, in defense of the family's name; the second would have comforted him and declared she would never speak to any of those men or their families again; and the last would have reminded him that all gossip was wicked and he shouldn't listen. Only Vivian told him to keep on as he was, with the additional instruction to stop bemoaning his lot in life, because it could be far, far worse, and to prove his detractors all wrong, because they *were* wrong.

He rather liked that about her.

The door creaked open, interrupting his contemplation. "Sir, some callers are arrived," said Bannet.

"Eh? Who?" demanded David in surprise.

"Mr. Percy, sir, and some companions." Bannet held out the little tray, but David was already on his feet.

"Show them in, Bannet."

Bannet nodded and left the room, but he could hardly have gotten halfway down the hall before David's friends burst through the door.

"And what's more, I'll take that bet," Edward Percy was saying with a laugh. "I do like taking your money, Brixton."

"So often it used to be yours," retorted Hal Brixton irritably. "I shall never take a wager of yours again. Ah, Reece!"

"Good morning to you." David waved one hand in invitation to be seated. "What brings you here so early in the morning?"

"Loyalty," said the third man, Anthony Hamilton.

"Our friendship of twenty years," said Percy.

"That, and you owe me one hundred twenty pounds," said Brixton.

"I hope you don't want it now," said David.

"Of course he doesn't," said Hamilton. "We are here in a show of support, old man. Brixton can afford the loss."

"Mighty free of you to say so," grumbled Brixton, before Hamilton shot him a hard look. "But of course I can. Think nothing of it, Reece."

David glanced from one to the other. "Seen the books at White's, I suppose."

"Beastly buggers," said Percy.

"Small-minded hypocrites," said Hamilton.

"Er—well, we saw them weeks ago," said Brixton. "We heard *you* saw them last night."

David flipped his hand. "Pay it no mind. Let them wager themselves into penury. I hope you all took Evans up on his wager that I'll leave Marcus destitute. I've never seen easier money."

"You're not angry?" exclaimed Brixton. "Why, we only called this morning to prevent you meeting Trevenham."

"If I had called out Trev, or he had called me out, we would have concluded our business long before now," said David dryly. "If you mean to stop a duel, I do believe you'll have to rise before dawn."

Hamilton cleared his throat. "No one thought it would come to that. Brixton is running his mouth. We're simply here to make it clear we had no part in the gossip, or the wagers."

"What gossip?" asked David, leaning back in his chair. "I've not been out to hear much of late."

"Oh, nothing of import. The usual suggestion of scandal without any facts to support it," murmured Hamilton.

"They say you've sold Exeter House bare," said Percy, without the least trace of discretion or tact. "They say your family has left London to avoid the scandal. They say you're to be arrested at any moment by Bow Street and sent to Newgate for thieving, counterfeiting, and treason."

"Treason?" David laughed. "What was I accused of, selling the latest cravat styles to the Americans?"

"I don't know. Do you think the Americans would pay well for the latest cravat styles?"

"Besides, don't they hang traitors?" David continued. "How fortunate for me, only to be sent to prison."

"Damned calm about all this," said Brixton. "Hamilton roused us from our beds, all in a lather that you'd be distraught."

"A fine friend you are," Hamilton told him. "Preferring your bed to standing with an old friend."

"Yes, yes, but I'm not in need of a bodyguard," said David lightly. "Trev is out of sorts with me. Let him and all the rest wager their funds away over women's gossip."

This clearly took some wind from their sails. "Well, that robs a bit of nobility from our mission," said Percy. "If you're not off selling the contents of Exeter House to the pawnbrokers, what have you been doing, Reece? It's not like you to avoid all society."

David put out his hands, palms up. "As I told you, I've undertaken the management of Exeter, and it's rather consuming."

"Oh," said Percy, clearly disappointed. "Right." There was a moment of silence, as David's friends contemplated the prospect of working, and working so hard a man had no time for society. "I say," said Percy hesitantly. "You're not turning into him, are you? Your brother?"

"Lord, no!" David pulled a face. "As soon as he returns, I shall be as useless and indolent as ever." Although he suspected that was untrue.

"We are relieved to hear it," said Hamilton. "Being a wastrel isn't half so enjoyable without good company."

They all laughed, so heartily David barely heard the soft tap at the door.

"Yes, Bannet, what is it?" called David, still grinning. His servant shuffled around the door.

"Madam is asking for another book, sir. Might I fetch her one?"

Hamilton's ears visibly pricked up. Brixton let out a long, lewd whistle. "Madam?" exclaimed Percy in delight. "Have you got a woman stashed upstairs, Reece?"

David pressed his lips together in a grim smile. "No, no,

no one of interest." He bounded out of his chair and across the room, practically shoving Bannet back out the door.

"No one of interest?" Percy laughed. "I'm thoroughly interested! Tell all, Reece."

"Yes," said Brixton. "Who is she? No wonder you've not been out at nights."

Bannet stumbled over his own feet into the hallway. "And the book, sir?"

"Yes, yes," said David in a low tone, throwing a glance over his shoulder. "Anything she wants." He closed the door and turned back to his friends, who had an alarmingly energetic air about them now.

"Let's meet her," said Hamilton bluntly. "Invite the lady down, Reece."

"No."

"Come, man, what's the problem? We promise not to steal her away from you." Brixton chuckled

"No," David repeated.

His friends glanced at each other. "Reece, you dog," said Percy, "you can't expect us to let this pass. If you've got a woman hidden upstairs in your own house awaiting your every pleasure, without having got yourself legshackled or aflame with scandal, you are a genius among men. Display your spoils and revel in your triumph. We are apostles at your feet."

"You've no idea what you're raving about," David told him. "Nor have I."

"It can't be a matron," mused Hamilton. "Certainly not one of the girls baiting the parson's mousetrap. We've not heard a word connecting you to any actress, opera singer, nor any demimonde. Who on earth have you got?"

"A visiting relation," David said, improvising. "A very, very distant relation. No one you'll have heard of."

"Oh, a relation," said Percy, his interest fading.

"Elderly?" asked Hamilton, as probing as any lawyer. David made a face and held his hands up as if he couldn't decide. "Young?" David wagged his head from side to side in more indecision. "Attractive?" Hamilton asked, drawing the word out speculatively.

"Cut line," said Brixton. "Hamilton wants to know if she's rich." They all laughed, and David, grinning determinedly, went back to his seat. Good Lord, what was Bannet thinking to announce her presence to his friends? To anyone, in fact? David really must get some proper servants.

"She's so far from rich, Hamilton, I should warn you off. But if you want to meet her, by all means. I'll send for her. You should know, however, that she is my responsibility, and if you so much as look at her the wrong way, you'll find yourself facing either the vicar or my pistol barrel before the end of the day." He reached for the bell, hesitating with his hand over it. "Shall I?"

"Good God, no!" Percy looked horrified. "How utterly appalling. You, responsible for a woman's virtue?"

"What is the world coming to?" Brixton laughed again. "Soon they'll put highwaymen in charge of the Royal Mail."

David's smile froze to his lips at the mention of that word, "highwaymen." "Indeed," he said, trying to hide his reaction. "On a similar note, I must be off. Exeter business waits for no man, you know, not even me." He got to his feet again. "I bid you all good day."

"Yes, yes." Brixton and Percy led the way from the room, making more jokes about setting the wolves to guard the lambs, the cats the cream, and so on. Hamilton lingered just inside the door, waiting for David.

"Who is she really?" he asked in a low voice. David just looked at him, his face deliberately blank. "You wouldn't have a female relation here, not when Exeter House sits a mile away in grand propriety. So who is she?" he asked again, his eyes sharp.

"No one you would know," said David. "A woman of no consequence."

"Is she?" Hamilton murmured after a significant pause. "I wonder."

David watched him stroll after the other two. Should he worry about that? His friends were curious. But what would they do if they discovered who she was, and why she was in his house? Nothing much; David was certain his friends wouldn't call the Runners to his house, and even scoundrels had enough honor not to steal away another man's mistress. Vivian wasn't his mistress, of course, but David would let them think that. Only if necessary for her protection, of course.

Not because he wished it were true.

Bannet returned with three small volumes that made Vivian's eyes grow wide. "The master said you may have whatever you wish," said the servant through the door as he slid them under. Vivian snatched up each one eagerly, reading their titles with a little chirp of glee. "I tried to choose some appropriate for a lady."

"Oh, thank you, thank you, Bannet!" she said in delight. "I'll look at them all."

"Be sure to let me know if you need any assistance, madam," Bannet reminded her. She smiled.

"Sure, and I will. You're a dear, Bannet."

His voice softened noticeably. "Thank you, ma'am. It's kind of you to say."

Vivian laid her hand on the door, leaning closer to whisper, "It's no more than the kindness you've done me."

All was quiet from the other side, then she heard the muffled sound of his footsteps down the hall. Vivian smiled to herself, feeling very kindly toward the servant. If he hadn't taken to bringing her books and sitting outside the door and talking to her from time to time, Vivian was certain she'd have gone mad from sitting and waiting for David to arrive.

Cuddling the books to her chest, she skipped across the room to the window seat and settled herself. She'd never known she liked to read before, and it was still difficult for her at times. She found she didn't like poetry, liked some novels though not others, but loved, above all, plays. For some reason David Reece had a large collection of plays in his library, and Vivian was happily reading all of them. The plays opened a world of delight to Vivian, a world so different from the one she had grown up in.

She was lost in that different world hours later when the familiar scrape in the lock intruded. For a moment she scowled, not wanting to put the book aside. It was unlike him to come see her in the middle of the day, though. What was about?

He wore a smile when he came in, a package in his hand. He saw the book she clutched almost at once, but said nothing. Vivian wondered why. What had Bannet said? *The master says you may have whatever you like.* That didn't sound like he minded. That didn't sound like he cared. But she read the stifled inquiry in that lingering look, and put the book on the table, tucking her hands behind her, just in case. "I've come to apologize," he said, standing before her like a penitent before the priest. "I was, as you observed, drunk as a lord last night. I ought not to have subjected you to that."

Vivian lifted one shoulder. He hadn't hit her, nor

touched her at all. She'd endured a lot worse than a man feeling sorry for himself, and mostly from people who didn't apologize the next day.

"I should like to make it up to you," he went on. "Tonight."

Now Vivian recoiled, drawing her feet up under her skirts and curling her body into a ball. "You don't have to."

A mischievous light glowed in his eyes. "I want to," he said. "You may even enjoy it." He reached out and picked up one of the books Bannet had just brought. "How many of these have you read?"

"A few," she murmured. Oh dear; she'd read a dozen if she'd read one. Was she in trouble now?

"Ah." For a moment he stood still, head bent over the book. "More than I've read from the library. Glad to see someone's putting it to good use." He laid the book back where it had been, on top of the others. "This is for you." He handed her the package. Vivian took it with a wary glance. "It won't hurt you," he said. "Look inside."

She pulled off the string and a mass of fabric tumbled into her hands. It was as blue as a summer sky and as soft as baby's hair. She held it up and beheld a dress, a lovely fashionable dress with lace around the neckline and a silver ribbon around the bodice, with a little cluster of silk flowers right in the center. More silk bands circled the edge of the skirt, and silk of the same color was ruched about the sleeves. She turned to him, her mouth agape with astonishment. "What is it?" she asked stupidly.

"It's a dress," he said. "I thought you might appreciate something other than that dreary gray thing. We're going out tonight."

"What? Where?" she demanded.

He raised his eyebrows and closed his eyes. "It's a secret," he told her.

"No," she said nervously. "I want to know where first. If you won't tell me, then, no."

His gaze flicked to the books, then back to her face. "The theater. I thought you might like to see a play."

He could not have offered anything more likely to catch Vivian's fancy. Her eyes also strayed to the books. "Like those?"

"Good Lord, I hope it's more entertaining than those." He grinned engagingly, then sobered. "What are you frightened of?"

Being caught by the constables—an old fear from her days of picking pockets on London streets. But Vivian acknowledged it was a little far-fetched. She hadn't been to any decent part of London in years and years, and doubted anyone would recognize her or connect her to the bone-thin waif she'd been then. "Nothing," she replied to David's question, a little belligerently in spite of herself. "Why do you want me to go?"

He just looked at her for so long she felt her nerves bristle again. "Has no one ever done anything nice for you?"

She snorted. "Well, I expect you could have had me dangling from the nearest tree by now, so I suppose that I'm not counts as a nice thing."

He shook his head, those dark intense eyes searching her face. "That's not what I mean. Your mother? Your father? Anyone?"

She shrugged, her gaze falling to the dress in her hands. To be honest, just getting to hold such a dress was a pretty nice thing, to Vivian's mind. She longed to rub it against her cheek. Someone *had* done nice things for her: David. But she certainly couldn't tell him that.

"My mum," she said. "She used to braid my hair." She remembered her mother's hands moving quickly through her hair, knotting a strip of old cloth around the ends to hold it. Mum had never had enough time for things like that, but Vivian remembered. "That was a long time ago," she said, looking up at him again.

"Ah." His gentle sigh sounded almost sad, and Vivian fought not to flare up at him again. She didn't want pity. "Well, this is just a nice thing," he said, in his more usual tone of voice. "I've a fancy to see a play. I hoped you'd do me the honor of accompanying me."

How was she supposed to answer that? Vivian stroked the soft fabric in her hands and thought. She *would* like to see a play. The only plays she'd ever seen had been at traveling fairs, short little scenes that never lasted long enough. What would a real one be like, in a proper theater, in a dress that felt as soft and light as a cloud, with a handsome man beside her?

She cast a glance at that man sideways from under her eyelashes. He was still waiting for her answer, his head to one side, watching her. She lifted one shoulder, her fingers curling into the dress. "All right."

"Is that yes?" he prompted. "Are we agreed?" She pursed her lips and nodded. A nice thing, he said. He was just trying to treat her. She didn't know why, but again, she was unable to resist him.

"Excellent." He grinned. "Seven o'clock."

As if she had any choice in the matter. Still, Vivian couldn't keep a small smile from her lips as she replied, "Seven o'clock, then."

Chapter Twelve

Vivian had seen the Drury Lane theater before; she had picked many pockets in front of its grand façade. But she had never been inside, and couldn't help being excited as the fancy closed carriage they were riding in slowed to a stop.

"Nervous?" David asked.

She glanced at him, sitting back from the edge of the seat where she'd been perched with her face all but pressed to the window. "Well—no. I suppose I ought to be, for I've never been inside a real theater before!"

He just smiled, his gaze fixed on her. Vivian felt a flush of pleasure that had nothing to do with the theater. It had nothing to do with the lovely hot bath Bannet had prepared for her, nor the finery she wore. It might be related to the fact that Vivian knew she looked fine tonight, wearing a silk dress with a white flower pinned in her hair and beaded slippers on her feet, but that was only part of it. Mostly, she thought, it was because David was smiling at her as if there weren't another woman in the world.

And he looked quite fine himself tonight, in gentlemen's evening clothes. Vivian was certain she had never seen a handsomer man, in fact, than David Reece. Even though he looked a perfect gentleman, there was still something about him that hinted at dangerous unpredictability. She supposed that was what had made him think up this mad idea to take her to the theater, but she had to admit she liked it. It made him compelling in a way other men weren't, as if one ought not to look away because one never knew when he would do something utterly unexpected with no warning. Vivian had made her way in life by taking advantage of people who were predictable, and the fact that she couldn't predict David at all made him fascinating.

He had certainly shocked her tonight. Just as she had begun worrying about how she would look, a girl from the dressmaker had come to help her dress, making tiny adjustments to the gown and helping her pin some flowers in her hair. She had stared at her reflection in amazement, barely believing that lovely girl was she. After a hot bath, with her hair braided and pinned up, she probably wasn't the same. And it was all due to David.

The door opened, and a servant let down the steps. David alighted, then turned back and put out his hand. Feeling like a princess in a fairy tale, Vivian stepped down, her eyes filled with the sight of the Theatre Royal rising several stories above her. Gaslight shone off white stone and sparkling windows; laughter and voices rang out in the crowd of people, elegant people and middle class people and vagabonds and whores. Every stripe of person London held seemed to be attending the theater— even her. An involuntary smile lit Vivian's face.

"That's more like it," said David, bending his head to murmur in her ear. "I was beginning to think you'd changed your mind."

"Changed my mind? You're mad," she whispered back. "I've never seen anything like it!"

He merely laughed quietly, tucking her hand around his arm and drawing her close to his side as they joined the throng streaming through the wide double doors.

Inside it was even more crowded. Dashing young men in very fine dress strolled through, a class to themselves, often with scandalously dressed, brightly rouged women who could only be whores hanging on their arms. Instinctively Vivian began to follow them, only to have David turn toward the grand staircase. "Not the pit," he said. "We've got my brother's box."

Her wide eyes grew even wider. A box at the Theatre Royal! People in the boxes were people who were written about in the newspapers. Members of the royal family had boxes. Dukes and earls had boxes. She shot a look at David, but he seemed unmoved by the prospect. Of course, if the box was his brother's, David had been here before; this was nothing new to him. She likely looked like an idiot with her eyes popping from her head and her mouth open in amazement. She nodded and followed where he led.

Near the foot of the stairs, a pair of gentlemen stopped them. "Reece!" called one, a tall fellow with pale blond hair who looked decidedly drunk. "God save me, man, I thought we'd never see you again in society! Thank God you've given up whatever doings of Exeter's and come into the world again." He stumbled over a number of words, and had to steady himself with an arm around his companion's shoulders. That man, not quite as tall and with rich chestnut hair and brown eyes, turned and called out a casual greeting to David. Then his eyes landed on Vivian.

"Some friends," David said in her ear. "I hope you don't mind."

Vivian shook her head. Who was she to mind? He could talk to his friends while she gawked at everything around her.

"I say, who is your lovely companion?" asked the darker man as they drew near. His eyes hadn't strayed from her face.

"May I present Mrs. Vivian Beecham," said David. He said her last name differently, as if it were French: bow-sham. "Mrs. Beecham is not from London, so I've undertaken to show her the finer points of our city."

"Indeed." Both men bowed, but it was the man with dark hair who took her hand and brushed his lips just above her knuckles. Vivian had a sudden thought what his expression would look like if he knew he'd just kissed the hand of a half-Irish pickpocket, and she almost snickered aloud. She managed to stop herself in time, pressing her lips together in a polite smile.

David wondered if she had any idea how enchanting she looked that way. He noticed the glint in her eyes, and the way her lips curled as if hiding a smirk behind her demure smile; he had a good guess what she might be thinking, and it made him want to laugh, too. "Mrs. Beecham, may I present to you two notorious rogues, and sometime friends of mine: Mr. Edward Percy and Mr. Anthony Hamilton."

"Sometime? Nonsense," said the darker man, Mr. Hamilton, with a charming smile. "We are the closest of friends. Almost brothers."

"Not quite, if he can hide a woman from us," exclaimed Mr. Percy. "Reece, you dog, you—"

"But who can blame him, in this instance?" interrupted

Mr. Hamilton again. "Do you plan to stay in London long, Mrs. Beecham?"

"I have not yet decided," she replied, caught off guard. "It depends . . ."

"We must persuade you to make a long visit to our city. Have you seen the sights yet?"

"Er . . . no." She glanced at David, who seemed oddly quiet and watchful.

"I would be delighted to escort you," offered Mr. Hamilton at once. He also glanced at David. "Should business prevent Reece from it."

"When has business ever prevented Reece from showing a lady a fine time?" blared Mr. Percy. His eyes were bloodshot, and he tipped a flask to his lips as soon as the words were out of his mouth. Vivian gauged it wouldn't be long before he passed out and snored for a day and a half.

"Percy, you're drunk," said Mr. Hamilton without looking at his friend.

Mr. Percy hiccupped. "Most likely. So's you, Ham. Now Reece, is this the wom—?"

"We don't want to miss a moment of the play," said David, inclining his head. "Sleep it off, Percy. Hamilton."

"Good evening, Mrs. Beecham," said Mr. Hamilton, who did not look drunk. He glanced briefly at David before returning his attention to Vivian. "Reece."

"Am not drunk," said Mr. Percy with a bleary look. "Not that drunk. Just curious. Not every day Reece brings a wom—"

"This way, my dear," said David, guiding her past his two friends. Vivian wondered what, precisely, Mr. Percy had been saying that David didn't want her to hear. She supposed his friends thought she was his bit of skirt now; his mistress, they would say, no doubt. She doubted men of their class took whores to the theater and sat in the fancy boxes.

"Have you got a mistress already?" she asked as they slowly made their way up the stairs. David stopped dead, almost tripping an elderly man behind him.

"Have I *what*?"

"Got a mistress already," she repeated, but quietly. "Your friends seem surprised to see you here with a woman they don't recognize. Do you usually bring another woman?" He stared at her with an odd expression, and Vivian realized she was prying. "Well, none of my business, I suppose," she muttered.

"No," he said, resuming their pace. "I never bring any women to the theater. That is what shocked them. And now they are perishing of curiosity about you."

Vivian glanced back uneasily, hoping that was not true. It was. In just the second she was looking at him, Mr. Hamilton looked up, right at her. His eyes met hers, and she could see the speculation there. His mouth curled a little, and he nodded at her. Vivian faced front again, her heart beating hard. It had been amusing when he bowed to her and kissed her hand. Now she thought it might not be so amusing, if he started asking questions which had no answers. He might not share David's appreciation of the joke.

"You have nothing to fear from either of them," he went on. "Percy is likely so drunk he shan't recall ever meeting you."

"The other one will," she said.

A funny smile crossed his face. "Hamilton won't disturb you, either."

"Have—have you told them?" she asked warily. "The truth?"

He stopped again, this time shaking his head in exasperation. "You wound me."

She turned, stumbling as the crowd swirled around them, pushing her into him. He put his hand under her elbow, steadying her and pulling her closer at the same time. "You might be a Russian archduchess for all these people know. My friends will leave you in peace because you are my guest." He put his hand over hers on his arm. "Shall we enjoy the play?"

Reproved, Vivian nodded. Why was she questioning him about every little thing, when he had brought her to the theater? He said he wanted to do something nice for her. She ought to accept it in better grace, she decided, and stop looking for all the ways he might be making sport of her.

They continued on their way, more slowly now as the crowd around them grew sluggish and more fashionable. Up the stairs, away from the raucous throngs streaming toward the pit, the elegant theater patrons seemed determined to see and be seen, with much less interest in taking their seats. Although Vivian still felt finer than she had ever been in her life, she could see that she was nothing next to these ladies, with their sparkling jewels and glowing silk gowns.

People looked at them. Vivian could see their eyes skip over her as if she weren't there—not elegant enough to take note of, she thought—then land on David, grow wide, and leap back to her. At first it made her nervous, but David showed no such hesitation. In fact, she would swear he seemed to relish it as he walked right toward the interested onlookers. Summoning up a smile, she followed him.

If she had known what he would do, she might not have done so. From the left and from the right, people hailed him. Some were jovial, some were snide, and some seemed simply amazed. All of them looked to her with intense curiosity. And to Vivian's astonishment, David introduced her a bit differently every time. One time she would be Madam Beauchamp, a recent émigré to England. The next she would be Mrs. Beecham again, with a strong implication that she was a lady of some fortune recently returned from abroad, and after that Miss Beecham, a distant cousin of his come to see London. Once he even subtly suggested she was connected to the royal family of Denmark, a lie which left her speechless with shock.

"Denmark?" she managed to squeak as they moved on from the beaming couple who now thought she was almost a princess. "Are you completely mad?"

He grinned. "No. Lady Winters has never been to Denmark. You could be the queen and she would never know."

"I'm not Danish! I'm not even sure where Denmark is!"

"Well, you're Irish, which rhymes with Danish," he said. "And Denmark is somewhere . . . north. East, I'm certain of that. It's close enough, don't you think?"

"Not really," she said, although trying not to laugh at how outrageous he was, and how calm he was about the lies he was telling.

"I doubt Lady Winters knows where Denmark is, either," he told her. "There's no harm in it."

"You're a charlatan," she said, almost gasping in disbelief at the things he was telling people.

He simply smiled, but it was a wicked smile, full of satisfaction. He was having the time of his life, she realized, and suddenly it dawned on her what he was doing. To some people he had merely introduced her by name;

to others he had told ever more fanciful and outlandish stories, all seemingly guaranteed to make the listener fawn over her in awe. He was showing them up, these people who whispered behind their hands about him and took pleasure in his misfortunes. He was making them fall over themselves to win the favor of a no-account thief who would as like as not lift their purse while they were bowing over her hand. And yet, by telling everyone a different name and background for her, he had ensured that no one would be able to find her again. The joke was entirely on them, with no danger to her.

Strangely, it made Vivian want to laugh. How many times had she longed to take people who thought too highly of themselves down a peg, and here he had done it. Of course the fools would never know, but David would know, and that seemed to be enough for him.

He led her into a fancy box with an astonishingly good view of the stage. Peering over the edge, Vivian thought she would see the sweat on the actors' brows. It was wonderful, and she pulled her chair closer, not wanting to miss a moment.

"I'm not such a charlatan," he said, taking the seat beside her and resuming the conversation. "They would never have believed it if you hadn't had such lovely manners and a beautiful accent."

"Where did I learn to ape my betters, you mean to ask?" She grinned.

"No," he corrected her at once. "Not your betters. Not a person here is your better."

She turned to face him, her eyebrows raised as high as they would go. He wasn't perturbed. "What did you say?" she asked in surprise.

"Not a person here is your better," he repeated.

She looked closely at him for any indication he was

making sport of her. He had to be, even though she couldn't see any sign of it. She frowned suspiciously, and turned her back on him. "Bloody liar," she muttered.

"It's not a lie," he said. "Why would you think so?"

She spun around again. "Why, it's clear to see! All these folk are so finely dressed, so elegant . . ."

"That sort of elegance can be obtained from a milliner, a maid or valet, and a tailor. Anyone with money can achieve it. It's not your fault you aren't elegant in that way." He put his head to one side, studying her. "You have your own elegance."

Vivian just stared at him, speechless. He smiled slightly, his dark eyes lingering on her face. "You're mad," she finally said, but inwardly she felt a tingling rush of warmth. Elegance? It wasn't true, of course, but it was lovely of him to say so. "I've an ear for languages and an eye for things like manners," she said, leaving that topic and returning to an easier one. "It came in handy more than once, being able to ape a lady, or at least a lady's companion."

"No doubt," he said, then adopted a slightly wounded tone. "Still, knowing you can behave so beautifully, I wonder why I am treated to the sharp edge of your temper at all times."

"Because you're a scoundrel," she said calmly. "And you like it."

He laughed. "You have caught me out."

She laughed with him, just as the lights on the stage came up, and the musicians began to play. At once her attention fixed on the stage, and she did not notice how David's eyes lingered on her in an oddly thoughtful way.

David watched her instead of the stage. She didn't seem to realize it, enraptured by the play. Emotions dashed across her face, a flicker of a frown, a flash of dismay, then a brilliant smile and delighted laugh that made David smile, too, when she glanced at him, even though he hadn't the faintest idea what had been amusing.

For the first time, he thought he was seeing Vivian without a trace of artifice, the way she would be if her nature hadn't been hardened from years of cruel life. For days she had sat in stubborn silence, her back to him, a wooden figure almost. Now she was still again, but from rapt attention to the play.

David had never expected to spend this much time in her company. Locking her up had been pure impulse; keeping her there had been pure stubbornness. If she had been a simple petty thief, she would have told him what he wanted to know and he would have released her. He would never have noticed the way she nibbled the inside corner of her lip when she was worried. He never would have known that she loved the small luxuries in life—a hot bath, a cozy mattress, a bit of lemon tart—the way most women liked jewels. He would never have suspected that something as simple as a play would make her eyes light up and shine like stars, when all around her people were more interested in who was sitting in whose box than in anything the actors were saying or doing.

Now he didn't know what to do with her. Instead of losing interest in her, he only wanted to know more about her. He was attracted to her still, but it was not strictly about taking her to bed; he wanted to make her laugh almost as much as he wanted to make love to her. No other woman had ever managed to intrigue him so, particularly not whilst calling him the names Vivian hurled at him regularly. Instead of being put off by it, David found it exhilarating. He liked a woman with spirit and wit. He even liked that he must be himself with her, or be mocked as a liar. Vivian, he realized, forced him to be honest.

It wasn't an altogether comfortable feeling for David. All his life, people around him had made him aware of his many failings. It had been easier for him to laugh off every scolding, make a joke of every disaster, and generally carry on as if he hadn't a care in the world. He couldn't remember the last time he had been utterly unguarded, and not braced himself for a lecture or recriminations in return. But Vivian seemed to have little patience for his insouciance, and refused to let him sulk about his problems. Strange to say, but she might actually have been a good influence on him.

At the end of the farce, she applauded enthusiastically before turning to him, her eyes shining. "Wasn't it lovely?"

"Completely," he confirmed, smiling back at her.

"Have you ever seen anything so amusing?" She began to laugh as she spoke. "I never saw anyone so clever as Miss Hardcastle."

"Indeed," he said wryly, "for perceiving a fundamental truth about gentlemen: we are all fools when it comes to women."

"You needn't add the last," she said. "Just leave it at fools."

David smiled. "Perhaps so. Would you care for some wine?"

His genteel manner made Vivian want to laugh again. "Aye," she said, then corrected herself. "Yes, thank you. That would be lovely."

This time he laughed. "I shall fetch some. Bar the door behind me, wench, to keep your admirers at bay."

"Admirers, here," she said with a sniff. "What a laugh."

David shook his head and left, pulling the door

securely closed behind him. He briskly strode off down the corridor. It had been amusing earlier to introduce Vivian to people, but now he just wanted to get back to her. He hoped Hamilton would have the good sense not to stop by and visit her.

"Reece," whispered a silky voice behind him. David turned without thinking, only realizing too late that he would have done better to pretend not to have heard.

Jocelyn, Lady Barlow strolled around him, too closely, a secretive smile on her lips. She had been his last lover, months ago. He hadn't seen her since the night Marcus narrowly saved him from her husband's wrath. "I thought that was you, half asleep in Exeter's box. Where on earth have you been, darling?" She walked her fingers over his arm.

David shifted his weight, easing just away from her hand. There were few people in the corridor at the moment, and she was taking full advantage of it. "Out of town, Jocelyn. You might remember I had to leave rather suddenly."

She pouted. "What a tempest over nothing. Barlow forgot about it within a fortnight."

"Perhaps because I quit the scene so promptly," David murmured.

She smiled, a coy smile that had once brought him running to her side. "But now you've returned."

"So I have," he said, stepping sideways again when her hand would have slid along his waistcoat. "Are you enjoying the play?"

"Play?" She laughed. "Oh yes, we are at the theater. Darling, you know I don't care for the theater . . . unless one is contemplating diversions of a private nature, in one's box . . ."

"The farce was terribly amusing," he told her, ignoring her every attempt to flirt with him, and avoiding her attempts to touch him.

Jocelyn rolled her eyes. "If I cared to attend," she said, stepping closer until David had to stand a little straighter. She tilted her head and looked him in the eye. Jocelyn was tall for a woman, taller than Vivian. "Shall we find a quiet corner and create our own entertainment?"

He looked at her. Once he had been mad for her. He had carried on with her past the point of prudence and let her use him to punish her husband for his indifference, until even the negligent Lord Barlow couldn't let it pass. David knew Barlow had been on the verge of calling him out, before Marcus intervened and sent him away. David wasn't fool enough to tempt the same irate husband twice, had he even wished to. "No."

Jocelyn blinked. "No? Why not?"

He inhaled deeply, and let it out. "We are done, my dear. We have been for months."

"That needn't be so," she began, but David held up one hand.

"Yes, it really must."

She looked ready to protest, then stopped, acceptance settling over her features. "Yes," she said at last. "I suppose it must. The young woman, I trust."

"Not at all." His protest was quick and instinctive.

She smiled wryly. "I think so. A woman can tell."

David raised one eyebrow. "Then why did you approach me, if you believe that?"

She sighed. "One can hope. You really were the sweetest . . ." She patted him on the arm. "That's that, then. Go back to her."

"It's not what you think," he tried once more.

"Not yet, perhaps." She wagged a finger at him. "You want it to be, though."

He did. He couldn't admit it, but neither could he deny it. David smiled, and raised her hand to brush his lips across her knuckles. "Good evening to you, Jocelyn."

"And to you, David," she said. He bowed and walked away without looking back. Vivian would be wondering where he had gone, and he didn't like to keep her waiting.

The next play had begun by the time he slipped back into his seat beside Vivian, and she only cast him a fleeting smile. She made no move to touch him, or cling to him, or push herself at him. A woman can tell, Jocelyn had said. Jocelyn could see that he wanted Vivian. The question was, could Vivian? And if she did, what would her reaction be? He watched her from the corner of his eye. Instead of setting to pursuing her with his usual determination, David felt an almost hesitant reserve. He had been rejected before, his advances declined. He had survived, and often come to appreciate that he had been luckier to be refused. It was ludicrous for him to worry about offending an admitted thief, but he did. He didn't want to offend her any more than he wanted his advances to be refused this time.

But now that someone had spoken the words out loud, David knew he had no choice but to chance it because he did want Vivian Beecham, very much.

Chapter Thirteen

Vivian was still talking about the play when they reached home late that night. Displaying an amazing memory, she had quoted long stretches of dialogue in the carriage, with such verve David couldn't help but laugh with her. In imitation of Kate Hardcastle, she twitched her skirt at him as she danced up the stairs, and just like Marlow, he followed, unable not to follow. Giggling, she twirled around in her room, hands clasped at her bosom. "Lord, did you ever imagine such a sight! It was like a dream come to life!"

"Did you really like it, then?" He grinned as she nodded vigorously.

"Better than anything I've ever seen in my life. The farce, that is; the other was maudlin for my taste. But oh—when Marlow realized his mistake— when Tony sent the carriage round and round—" She broke off, laughing again at the memory.

David felt something deep in his chest shift. Had he ever been that happy in all his life? And over something as simple as going to see a play? It was both humbling and enthralling to see such joy on her face. And when she stopped her dizzy waltzing right in front of him, and looked up at him with that luminous smile, David kissed her without stopping to think what he was doing.

It was a soft kiss, mild really. His mouth brushed against hers before she realized what he was about, and then he lifted his head before she could recover from the surprise. But as David looked down at her with harsh longing in his eyes, Vivian did what she had wanted to do for some time. She threw her arms around his neck and kissed him back.

He caught her face in his hands and met her kiss with a hungry one of his own. With three steps he backed her against the wall, holding her in place. His big hand slid down her throat to cup her breast, a little roughly. Vivian moaned as his fingers pinched and teased her nipple into stinging awareness. The dress was like nothing beneath his touch, nothing; she could feel every stroke of his fingers through the light silk. She arched her back, liking it more than she had expected to.

Then his hands moved, shaping and molding her body hard against his. He dropped tiny little kisses on her forehead, and when she opened her mouth to exclaim in delight, his lips captured hers again, his tongue taking advantage of the opportunity to invade her mouth. She tasted burgundy and him just as his hands closed around her hips and pulled her body into direct contact with his.

Vivian gasped, her heart beginning to pound. Her hands started to shake. Lord, he was good with his hands. He held her firmly, then released her to run his fingertips lightly over the curves of her hips and bottom. Her knees trembled; as if he knew, he grasped her thigh and pulled it up, curling his arm around her leg and stroking his fingers along the underside of her knee. Even through the dress it felt better than anything Vivian had ever felt in her life.

She clung to him, kissing him back as fervently as she could while pulling at his clothing with blind hands. He cooperated a little. His coat hit the floor with a small thud, followed by his waistcoat. She managed to unknot the cravat, but couldn't get it unwound from his neck while his wicked mouth was moving over her face, nipping at her ear, sliding down her shoulder, and his hands were maddeningly, teasingly, moving over her until she was sure she would lose her balance. In frustration, she grabbed handfuls of his shirt and pulled, relieved and aroused by the way he hissed in a breath as she spread her hands against his stomach. Eagerly, she reached for the fastenings on his trousers.

That finally penetrated the fog of lust filling David's brain. Stop, he told himself; wait just a moment. Vivian had gotten a few of the buttons undone, and her fingers were moving lower—closer—David sucked in his breath. He caught her hands. "Vivian," he said. She squirmed against him, her breasts rising and falling with every rapid breath, her lips rosy and full, her eyes dilated with desire. She leaned into him, and David almost expired as she pressed against his erection. "Stop," he gasped, setting her away from him while he still could. "There's no rush."

She blinked at him, ravishingly mussed. "That's the way folk do it," she said, sounding puzzled.

Yes. That was often the way David did it, as a matter of fact, ripping away just enough clothing to get to the key parts of his lover's anatomy, and not bothering to discard more of his own clothing than was absolutely necessary. But those encounters had been arousing in part because of their rushed nature: slipping out of a ball, taking an illicit carriage ride, and once in the cloakroom at the opera. Knowing that they must be quick or be caught had driven him and his past lovers. It could be exciting, to be sure—but tonight he had no reason, and even less inclination, to hurry.

And strangely, Vivian's rushing made him want to go even more slowly. They had complete privacy. No one would burst in on them, and no one would miss them if they remained in this room until morning—or even longer. He rather liked the idea of spending an entire night making love to Vivian. He doubted anyone else had ever taken the time to please her properly, and David was suddenly determined to be the first to do so. "Not tonight," he said quietly. "I want to savor you."

What on earth . . . ? Vivian frowned a little, but he distracted her by stroking her shoulders and bare arms, a feathery touch that made her feel both shivery and warm. "Trust me," he added in the same velvet voice. He was looking at her as if he were about to devour her, one small bite at a time, and the thought—even though it was a bit mysterious—sent little pinpricks of delight through her. No one had ever savored her. The two boys she'd let under her skirts before had both been as young and inexperienced as she was. It hadn't been horrible, those two times, but neither had it inspired the breathless anticipation she felt now.

"I don't know what you mean," she said nervously. "I—I don't know what to do."

He smiled a wicked smile. "I do."

With sure, unhurried hands he unfastened the dress. Vivian leaned her head back against the wall, letting her eyes drift closed as his dark, low voice murmured in her ear, promising things she'd only heard about, and some things she hadn't, all in words that made her feel lightheaded and hot and restless all at once. He loosened her bodice, the tips of his fingers skimming the tender flesh of her bosom and shoulders. Vivian shivered as the fabric slid away, exposing her to cooler air and his scorching gaze. With a soft swish the dress fell to the floor, followed by the light petticoat. The corset loosened as he pulled the lace out, and eventually joined the dress. When she felt his fingers untying her chemise, Vivian thought her heart might stop in her chest. She took a great gulping breath; he was going to make love to her. She'd had a moment to cool her head and realize it, but she hadn't the slightest bit of strength or will to stop him.

"Open your eyes," he ordered in a mesmerizing whisper. "Look at me."

With effort, she pried her eyes open. He loomed over her, the planes of his face painted gold in the firelight, his white shirt seeming to glow. She looked at him mutely, feeling her face heat.

"Don't hide from me," he whispered, sending her chemise the way of the dress and corset. Now she stood there in only her stockings and beaded slippers. She made to kick them off, but he stopped her. "Not yet," he told her, and then swept her into his arms.

He laid her on the bed and leaned over her, looking very large and powerful as he eclipsed everything else in the room. Vivian's stomach dipped as much as the mattress did under his weight. What was he going to do to her? Her knowledge of sexual congress was rather limited and crude. The gleam in his eyes and the tone of his voice promised sinful pleasures she had never even heard of; he would make her scream with pleasure? Vivian only screamed from fright, or for effect. He would bring her to the point of delirium, again and again, until she couldn't even remember her own name? Vivian never lost control of herself that way. And he promised to do this all night long? She'd never heard the like.

"I'm not a virgin," she blurted out as David brushed his lips against her temple. "No one in St. Giles reaches four-and-twenty a maid."

He met her gaze. "I'm not, either."

Her face grew hot. "But no one expects you to be."

His dark eyes searched hers. "Was it . . ." He hesitated. "Were you willing?"

Vivian felt a rush of shame. If she'd been willing, she'd been a trollop. "Willing enough," she snapped.

He blinked, then gave his head a tiny shake. "No one forced you, did they?"

She opened her mouth, then closed it. He didn't sound judgmental, but concerned. He cared that no one had forced her. "No," she said.

Still he didn't move. "No one's forcing you now," he said softly.

Vivian felt herself blushing all over again. He was waiting for her response. She should probably say stop. He could leave her with a babe in her belly, and she'd end up like her poor mum. But . . . well, *savored* . . . and by *him* . . . "I know." She wet her lips. "No one's forcing you, either."

David stared at her, then dropped his head. His shoulders shook with silent laughter. "Vivian," he said, resting his forehead on hers. "Vivian." He sighed, still smiling. "Don't you know, love, a team of horses couldn't drag me away at this moment." He kissed her again. "Unless you bid them to."

"Well, I wouldn't," she said, blushing harder. She never knew people talked so much before swiving. In the crowded rookeries, people mated with some fumbling under clothing, a bit of grunting, and a great deal of speed. Vivian had never seen what all the fuss was about. It was all right, she supposed, nothing more. But that was before tonight, when she suddenly began to see more to the act than a quick coupling of bodies.

"Well." That lazy, satisfied smile crept over David's face again. "That's good to know." He stroked her cheek, down her throat, and all the way to her belly. He did it again, just one lone fingertip trailing over her skin, and her nipples hardened as if in longing for the touch of that finger. "Tell me what you like," he said.

"I don't know . . ." She gasped as his fingertip retraced its path, but this time taking a slow circle around the very edge of her breast.

"Say yes if you like it." David moved, sliding down her body. "No, if you don't."

"Yes," Vivian whispered as his finger continued to blaze a path of sensation across her skin. It dipped into the hollow of her navel, and then climbed her ribs to skate along her collarbone. "Yes."

He traced the line of her breastbone, then slowed as he crossed her belly. He drew lazy circles there that made her hips rise of their own volition. "Do you like this?" he whispered.

"Yes," she said. "Yes!" She wanted him to move lower, to the place between her legs that she knew was his ultimate destination. It seemed to tingle in anticipation. She gave in to impulse and tilted her hips.

"No," he said with a smile in his voice. He spread his palm on her lower belly, gently holding her in place until she settled back into the mattress. "We'll get there, darling. Don't rush me."

So somehow, Vivian said nothing but "yes" as his

finger made a leisurely, sensuous progress over every inch of her body. She jumped when the backs of his knuckles grazed the swell of her breast, but she managed to moan only "yes." Her voice rose into a squeak as his finger finally passed over her tight nipple, and she barely heard his low chuckle. He was a devil, she thought wildly, but he made her feel so good she didn't have the voice to curse him for it.

David had never in his whole, debauched, life seen anything more arousing than Vivian Beecham, rookery pickpocket and highway robber, spread almost naked on the bed before him, saying "yes" in a voice that ranged from breathless to moaning to downright begging. Her limbs stirred and twitched as if his finger caught invisible strings beneath her skin. Her still-stockinged legs were propped up on either side of his chest, and David bent his head to press a lingering kiss to the inside of her knee. Her skin was hot through the silk of the stocking. He flipped off her slippers, then slowly rolled each stocking down her legs, dropping them on the floor as he feasted his eyes on her.

He levered himself over her, bracing his weight on his left arm. Holy God, she was beautiful, he thought again as her sky-blue eyes flashed at him, glowing bright with desire. Her skin was flushed everywhere his hand had touched. His hand trailed lower, and he touched his tongue to her nipple at the same moment he finally slid his fingers between her legs.

Her startled gasp turned into a moan. Feather-lightly, David circled the little nub hidden in soft brown curls. He suckled a little harder at her breast, and her fingers threaded themselves into his hair.

"Oh, yes," she whimpered. "Yes . . . What are you doing to me?" Her legs were trembling, and she draped one over David's side, drawing him into the embrace of her legs.

"Pleasing you." He shifted, sliding away from her, sitting back on his heels. His heart was thumping madly in his chest, and his breath was ragged. She was flushed and pink everywhere. He stroked his fingertips down the backs of her thighs, and when she moaned, "yes," he felt his control begin to crack.

"Touch yourself," he said, taking her hand and dragging her fingertips down the center of her chest, between her breasts. "Do what I did."

Clumsily, she did. Her eyes were closed now, her head thrown back, and she was definitely using more force than he had. She palmed her breast, and the fullness compressed beneath her hand. The muscles in David's neck grew taut. He licked his thumb and rubbed it over her nub again, still teasing her but more insistently. She was slick and wet, and so, so hot. Holding his breath, he slid one finger inside her.

Vivian felt him part her flesh, something she had expected and yet feeling completely unlike what she had expected. He was still stroking her there, in that one spot that seemed connected to every nerve in her body, and the finger—now two—he pushed inside her only made the feeling more intense. She grabbed fistfuls of the blanket beneath her to anchor herself to the bed. It seemed as though her body would explode from the pleasure. "Oh," she gasped. "I can't bear it!"

"You can," he said, and then shoved off the bed, shedding the rest of his clothes almost before Vivian could surface from her disorientation enough to figure out what he was doing. He slid back over her, naked now, and the feel of his skin against hers made her shudder again. Blimey, he was beautiful, she thought dazedly, taking in the golden expanse of male skin, the dark hair scattered on his chest, the light sheen of sweat on his shoulders, and the way his muscular arm flexed as he raised himself above her. Instinctively, she tensed.

"Vivian." He kissed her mouth gently as his fingers opened her. "Let go. Let me please you."

His fingers withdrew. Something else returned; his cock, she realized. He pushed inside her just a little, then pulled back. Again inside, then back out. His fingers circled around his entry, then settled back on that spot. He pushed forward again, just as he stroked her there, and Vivian's eyes rolled back in her head.

With maddening slowness he worked his way deeper, all the while stroking her. Vivian was ready to weep at the intensity of the feeling; he had to finish quickly or she'd die, it seemed. She grabbed at his arms and thrashed about, wordlessly urging him to go faster.

"Don't fight me," he said, his voice low and rough. "God, Vivian, let me show you how."

"I can't," she cried. He pushed once more, and then stopped, all the way inside her. She felt full, filled with him, and coiled so tightly with desire she whimpered from the exquisite agony of it.

He smoothed her hair back from her face and kissed her nose. "You can," he said quietly, and then he began to move.

Oh . . . This, *this* was the part she recognized. But it wasn't at all the same as it had been the other times. David's thrusts were slow, hard, and matched perfectly to the rhythm of his fingers on that aching spot. He made her feel as if she would come apart in his arms, as if she would drown, as if she would faint—

And then the hot, hard wave of pleasure broke, so astonishingly she gasped, almost unable to breathe. Dimly she heard David suck in his breath, felt him fall on her neck with a kiss. She held on to him as her entire being seemed to convulse.

"Bloody hell," she said weakly, once she had got her breath back. A laugh rumbled through David's chest. Vivian stroked him tentatively on the back. "I liked that very much," she told him.

He pushed himself up again, his black eyes glittering. "Good," he said. "You're going to do it again."

Her eyes widened as he thrust into her again, harder than before. He touched her again, too, as his eyes trapped hers. Incredibly, Vivian felt the same feelings mount in her again. The first time he had teased her to it, lightly and slowly. Now he was driving her to it, forcefully and inexorably. His arm beside her began to tremble. She heard someone crying out, again and again, and realized it was coming from her.

Then David shouted, his head sinking. He drove all the way inside her and then jerked away, holding himself tightly against her as his hips bucked. His fingers circled, and pressed, then pinched just so, and Vivian succumbed again, shrieking with the contraction of her body.

"Bloody hell," David said, muffled against her shoulder, and she gave a shaky laugh. He sucked in a ragged breath as she moved beneath him, then he rolled to one side, taking her with him.

She threw one arm over his shoulder, snuggling into him. David felt as though his very bones had melted. Lovemaking hadn't been that good for him in . . . he couldn't even remember when. The look on her face had been like kindling on the fire inside him. She wriggled a little in his arms, settling more comfortably, and he obliged, shifting his weight while still keeping his arm around her. He reached down and pulled the coverlet over them. She turned her head, pressing her lips to his jaw and running her fingers through his hair, and David sighed, so bloody filled with contentment he could hardly move.

God, he didn't want to let her go. He didn't understand why, but David had never had this almost desperate desire to hold on to a woman. Normally he was just as happy as his lover to part ways; normally the sexual act was all they had in common and all they wanted to share. But Vivian . . .

He didn't want Vivian to be the same.

David was well aware that he had begun badly—very badly—with her. Taking a woman prisoner was hardly the way to win her over. Had he even won her over? She had laughed and smiled at the theater tonight, and the joy on her face when they arrived home had looked very real to him. She had kissed him. But he had also thought her a lonely, frightened widow on the stage, and look how wrong he had been.

All the warmth and satisfaction inside him faded to a cold lump of dread. Perhaps she had let him make love to her because she thought she had no choice. Perhaps it had been gratitude. Perhaps it had been curiosity; it was clear to him no one had ever made love to her properly before. Perhaps it had meant nothing to her but a physical release.

For the first time in several years, David wanted it to mean something to her. When he had first discovered lovemaking, and the fact that a handsome fellow with money could always find a willing woman, David had rather vainly wanted to be the finest lover his partners had ever had. He had devoted himself to learning a woman's body, how to please her until she screamed from it and let him take his pleasure as he wished. But it was an accomplishment, the bargain he made with a woman for the right to have her any way he imagined. And most of the women he dallied with seemed to feel the same. They walked away without a backward glance, just the same as David did.

Would Vivian walk away, too? How would he know if she wanted to, or if she wanted to stay, when he was keeping her locked up? How would he know she wasn't pretending to like his touch if he didn't give her a chance to reject it? But he didn't want her to go. If he threw wide the doors and invited her to leave, he was too afraid she would.

David had never particularly prided himself on any sort of moral courage or standards. But this was a dilemma he could not ignore. Offer her the chance to leave, and run the risk she would go; or keep her locked up, and always wonder. He wanted to know—needed to know—but feared the answer.

Vivian lay awake for some time, warm and relaxed and utterly sated. David's arm was flung across her stomach, his head tucked against her shoulder, and she watched the flickering shadows on the ceiling as she absently ran her fingers through his hair. It was so soft, his hair, clean and long. This was like a dream, lying in a fine featherbed with a handsome man in her arms, no wind whistling through the windows, no mice skittering in the corners, the room silent except for the crackle of the fire. Imagine that, a large fire in the midst of summer, just because it was rainy. And it was just for her. She couldn't remember the last time she'd had a fire just for herself.

She closed her eyes. No, this was better than a dream.

A dream was guaranteed to end when she woke. This might go on for days.

She pushed aside the thought of what this might make her. In her life, Vivian had done many things to survive, and she knew some of them weren't exactly legal. She had never been a whore, though, and had even explained her other actions as a way of avoiding that short and wretched life. Instead of raising her skirts for men with money, she'd reasoned, she'd simply taken the money they would have paid her. That way at least she was sure of getting the money, and without leaving herself at their mercy.

But what was this? David stirred in her arms, his arms tightening about her, and Vivian snuggled closer to him. He was sound asleep. On impulse she pressed her lips gently to his cheek. This wasn't acting the whore, she thought; there was no thought of money changing hands. She had let him make love to her because she wanted it, and for no other reason.

Still, he was a gentleman, and she was a thief. As glorious as tonight had been, Vivian knew that it was a temporary thing. She turned her head and her gaze fell on the door. The key was in the lock, unturned. If she wanted to escape, now was the night.

Her eyes felt fixed on that key. Her freedom. She could slip out of bed, pull on her clothes, and be out the door before anyone knew she was gone. David would never be able to find her if she went to ground, found Flynn and Simon and the rest and told them what had happened. They could be in any county of England, or on their way to Ireland or Scotland, in a day or two. David would never find her.

Her heartbeat seemed loud in the quiet room. The fire snapped, and the light flickered as the log broke in a

little burst of sparks. A fire just for her. A warm featherbed just for her. A silk dress just for her. A passion-
ate kiss just for her. And the key in the lock.

Experimentally, Vivian slid one leg to the edge of the
mattress. David didn't move. She eased onto her side,
turning away from him, and his arm moved lax and
easily away from her waist. A few more wiggles and she
was completely out of his embrace. Her maneuvers
hadn't woken him at all. He still slept, his dark hair
falling about his face, his eyelashes black against his
cheeks. All she had to do was slide out from under the
coverlet, and she would be free.

She told herself to get moving as she lay rigid. Simon
must be wild to know what had become of her. Flynn
was no doubt treating him like a lackey and blaming
him for her absence. He had no one but her to look out
for him, and if she had a duty to anyone in this world
other than herself, it was to Simon. He'd die for her,
wouldn't he, and now all she had to do was get up and
walk out the door to get back to him.

Her hands fisted in the sheets. She squeezed her eyes
closed and pressed her head into the soft feather pillow.
She was soft, considering her own wicked comfort
while Simon was probably resting in a cold damp barn
with no pillow at all and mice running about his feet.
She opened her eyes and stole another glance at David.
He slept on, oblivious to her struggle. She wished he
didn't. If he woke up and reached for her again, or even
just watched her, the decision would be made for her.
She could persuade herself she hadn't left because he
was still preventing her.

She poked one foot out from under the covers and
reached down toward the floor. Even with the fire, the
floor felt cold after the warmth of the bed. She shivered.

With a burst of determination, she pushed her other foot out, then slid silently from the bed to stand, naked and trembling, on the rug. The fancy dress was there on the floor where David had thrown it. She could slip that back on and sneak down the back stairs, out into the neglected little garden, and disappear into the alleys. The dress would fetch a pretty penny . . . except that it was by far the loveliest dress she'd ever had, and she didn't want to give it up. Well, she could keep it, she argued with herself; she could carry it and wear her old gray dress. She could keep the lovely blue dress as a re-minder of this glorious night, when she'd finally discov-ered what it meant to make love.

She wrapped her arms around herself to ward off the chill, and cursed herself for her indecision. What was the matter with her? How long had she been waiting for an opportunity to escape? Now it was here, and she was dithering like a fool, over a dress. She took another glance at David, then forced her eyes away. Why did he have to do this to her? Things had been so simple when she could just hate him and think him a cruel, arrogant popinjay. Why did he have to bring her a beautiful dress, take her out for an evening straight from a dream, and kiss her like he meant it? Why did he have to treat her not like a thief and a beggar, but like a lady? Why did he have to make love to her as if he actually, somehow, cared for her? And why did she have to want it to go on and on forever?

Vivian curled her toes into the thick rug beneath her feet. If she were going to run, now was the moment. To delay would mean not only an opportunity wasted, but, she suspected—feared—an irreversible step toward let-ting herself feel something dangerous for David. God knew, if he continued treating her this way—if he continued kissing her this way—continued making love to her this way—Vivian knew it would be more than her freedom lost.

And she knew it would never mean as much to him. It couldn't. For all his gallant words and behavior tonight, David wouldn't be holding her a year from now. There would be some other fortunate woman in his arms, and Vivian would be lucky not to have her neck stretched. It was too much fairy tale, and just as improbable.

Still . . . She shifted her weight. All this was getting her was gooseflesh. *Buck up, girl,* she told herself sternly; *are you going or aren't you?*

For what seemed an eternity she stood there, her hands rubbing her elbows. She cast another glance at the door, then back at the bed. The log in the fire snapped again, breaking in half with a shower of sparks, and she flinched. Finally, shaking with shivers, she inched back to the bedside and eased between the covers, slipping into bed again. After a moment of wriggling, she gave a small sigh and was still.

And behind her back, David's eyes opened a slit. He regarded her for a moment before his eyes fluttered shut again in relief, and he fell asleep in truth.

Chapter Fourteen

The servants Adams had hired reported to work early the next morning. David came downstairs to find his new butler awaiting him at the head of a small group of footmen, maids, and kitchen staff. Hobbs was a tall impressive figure, suitably aged, his back as straight as any poker. He looked every bit the perfect butler. Since there had been no one running the household for several months, David himself had to instruct the man in what needed doing—in short, almost everything. But after all this time, it was such a relief to have someone to instruct, and several other servants to carry out those instructions, that David barely cared.

The sounds of scrubbing and sweeping filled the house, along with the unfamiliar tread of extra pairs of feet and new voices. After the calm of an almost empty house, it made David itch to leave. There were disputes over the proper method of polishing the banisters. The cook stormed from the kitchen three times in an hour, ranting about Bannet's treatment of the kettles. The third time, David caught sight of Bannet himself, standing at the back of the hall with a polishing rag in one hand, taking a terrific scolding. His slightly stooped shoulders seemed more slumped than usual, and his placid round face more woebegone than ever. David ducked out of the way of the footmen carrying out a rug to be beaten, and crossed the hall. "Bannet, may I have a word?"

Bannet nodded, shuffling around the irate cook and after David. Inside the study, David turned to the man, the only servant who hadn't left him in his more desperate hours. "Quite a fuss, eh?"

"Quite, sir," agreed Bannet.

"It occurs to me that I have no valet," David continued. "Will you take the post?"

Some time flickered in Bannet's eyes. "I'm not a young man, sir," he said. "I know little of fashions."

David lifted one shoulder. "Is that a refusal?" Bannet said nothing. "I appreciate that you have been loyal and steadfast these several months, even when my circumstances were not . . . ideal. I wish to reward that loyalty. The maids will see to the cleaning, and you need no longer cook. You may let me know if you want the position this evening."

"I do," said Bannet softly. "Thank you, my lord."

"Thank you," returned David. "I am aware that you have been most kind to Mrs. Beecham."

Bannet studied his toes. "Yes, sir."

"Thank you for that as well." He turned to go. "You may go."

"Thank you, sir."

David nodded and went back to his study, feeling more pleased than he had expected to feel. His offer to Bannet had been made on the spur of the moment; he knew he would not be the most fashionable gentleman with Bannet tending him. But Bannet had been tending him for weeks now, and David was perfectly content with the state of his linen. Why should he hire another valet?

In his study he contemplated his desk. Normally the only thing that appeared on top of it was dust. He was too shocking to get invitations by the basketful, as Marcus did, and he had no political or financial concerns that required extensive correspondence. Mainly, David received bills. For a time, even those had gone straight to Exeter House but, since his return to London, David had directed Adams to send them here. As part of his new vow of responsibility, David had decided to get his own affairs in order. He just hadn't quite gotten around to it yet. Straightening his shoulders and stiffening his resolve, he marched to the desk and began sorting through the mess.

The butler tapped at the door not long after.

"Yes," said David absently, still reading.

Hobbs came to stand at attention in front of the desk. "You have a houseguest, sir."

"Yes," said David, barely listening as he paged through the pile of bills from the tailor. He didn't even recall spending most of that money. Had he really ordered so many waistcoats?

"My lord," said Hobbs in an aggrieved tone, "Bannet tells me your guest is a young woman. A young woman, sir, who has been locked inside your house for some time now."

David paused and looked up. "What's that, Hobbs?"

His butler swelled with offense. "Sir, I cannot continue in your service," he declared. "It is unconscionable. It is ungentlemanly."

David fixed a weary gaze on the man. "I was told you were a man of excellent understanding and discretion."

"I am, sir." Hobbs's eyes were directed somewhere

over David's head. David sighed, running one hand over his face in aggravation. He hadn't thought about how to explain Vivian's presence to the butler, for God's sake. But he couldn't afford to have the man quit after a mere six hours in his employ, not when there wasn't another butler in London who would take the position in Hobbs's place.

"Then surely you will understand the need for discretion in this matter," he said. "My guest is a young woman with a very sad history. She has been . . . Well, suffice to say she has not led the purest of lives. But I am trying to save her from it, Hobbs. Her door has remained locked to prevent her from returning to her former wicked ways. Do you take my meaning?"

After a long moment the butler dared a quick, uncertain glance at him. "Do you mean to say, sir . . . ?"

David nodded, more patiently than he felt. Why did he, of all people, have to hire a moral butler? Weren't butlers supposed to accept, and if necessary conceal, their employer's faults? "Yes, Hobbs, it is for her own good. What sort of man would I be if I were to allow her to rejoin her associates in crime?"

The butler began to look uneasy. "Er . . ."

"She would be hanged within a month," David went on, sensing a change in the man's attitude and pressing his advantage. "She was on the brink of it when I discovered her. It is my Christian duty to exert myself to save her, is it not?"

"Yes, of course, sir," said Hobbs, his face growing red.

"But of course it would not be a service to her if word were to get out that she has been living in my home. And there are some uncharitable souls who would doubt my motives and malign my efforts. So I must trust to your discretion in this, as in all else regarding my household,

Hobbs." David got to his feet. "You came very highly recommended, so I have great faith you shall succeed."

"Yes, sir," said the butler. He cleared his throat. "Then, the lady, sir . . . She has not been harmed?"

"How dare you," said David with real affront.

The butler shifted his weight. "No, no, sir! I did not mean—That is, she is well-cared for?"

"I have seen to it myself," David said. "Speak to Bannet if you wish."

"Well then." Hobbs cleared his throat again. "I see, sir. Very good, sir."

"Excellent. I am delighted you understand my position. I trust we shall not have any further disturbances?"

"No, sir," said the butler quickly. "None."

"Splendid. Send for my carriage at once, then."

Hobbs bowed and all but ran from the room. David looked at the bills again, then shook his head and left the room. There was still a great deal of activity in the hall, maids mopping and dusting and a footman polishing furniture. David nodded as the maids stopped work to curtsey, and then took the stairs two at a time. He wasn't used to so many people in his house, and couldn't fight the urge to get away from them any longer. He went to Vivian's door and tapped.

She looked up from a large box as he opened the door. Mindful of Hobbs's censure, David left the door open and propped his shoulder against the doorframe. "Does everything suit?"

She didn't say a word. In reply, she lifted a bonnet from a hatbox at her side, her wide eyes veering from it to him. "It's for me?" she asked in hushed tones.

He laughed. "Who else? Do you like it?"

Vivian looked at the bonnet again with something like awe. She had never had such a lovely bonnet. When the maid had brought the boxes into her room earlier, she could not have been more surprised—until she opened them, and found two day dresses of fine cotton, a shawl, a complete set of undergarments, and this bonnet, this lovely little straw bonnet covered with silk and ribbons. She didn't know what to say. "Yes," she whispered, remembering to answer his question.

He pushed away from the wall. "Put away that wretched gray dress—better yet, burn it. I've a mind to go driving. They're cleaning the entire house, and I cannot work with the smell of polish about me. Would you care to come with me?"

She nodded, suddenly feeling rather shy and uncertain. He had been gone from her room before she woke, and then Bannet had brought her breakfast. Bannet had informed her there were more servants about the house now, and she had heard their noise. The key was also gone from the lock. Just to see, Vivian had opened the door and stepped into the hall. She was free. She stood there for a moment, tingling with nerves, before retreating into the room. Now she could leave, but she didn't want to, not yet. It seemed impossible things would not change, after last night, but she didn't know exactly how.

By the time she changed and made her way downstairs, past a maid who bobbed a faint curtsey even as she eyed Vivian curiously, David was standing in the open front door. He was simply standing there, watching the servants bustling about the hall, but Vivian had the sudden feeling he couldn't bear to be in the house a moment longer. She hurried down the last of the stairs, somewhat relieved to see his eyes light up when he saw her.

"How lovely you look," he said. "Shall we?" She nodded and let him lead her out to the tall, shiny carriage waiting in the street behind a pair of perfectly matched chestnuts. He helped her into it, then jumped up beside her.

"I thought I would never be free," he muttered, flicking the whip and setting the horses in motion. Vivian had never ridden in such an elegant vehicle, nor one driven so quickly, and for a while she simply hung on and savored the sun on her back.

He drove with a controlled recklessness, sending the horses through impossibly small gaps in the traffic. The first time she gasped and closed her eyes, bracing for a collision, but by the third time she realized he was doing it deliberately, and just laughed. His only reply was a slight smile, but the sight of it was terribly reassuring to her.

David drove west, out of the confines of London. He had no particular destination in mind. The only thing on his mind was Vivian. In her new dress and bonnet, Vivian Beecham did not look like a thief; she looked like a heavenly sprite in blue muslin, a smile of sheer joy on her lips as she tilted her face to the sun. He was pleased, and enthralled, and terrified. Pleased because she was delighted by his gift. Enthralled because he had never seen anyone so lovely in all his life. And terrified because . . . because . . .

He was from one of the oldest and grandest families in England. His entire life had been one of privilege and indulgence. The only thing expected of him was that he make a respectable marriage to a girl of decent family. David had made a habit of not living up to his family's expectations of him, but this, he knew, was an absolute. He had even expected he would do it, eventually. He had never expected to love the girl; he was not required to. If David had not seen his stiff and exacting brother fall head over heels in love just this year, he would have sworn it was not possible to both love a woman and find happiness with her. But he was beginning to fear that he was falling in love with Vivian. And he was damned happy when he was with her.

"You must be relieved to be out of London at last," he said when he had turned off the main road and onto a smaller, less crowded one.

He felt her glance at him. "Aye," she murmured.

"We should not have waited so long to take a drive." David turned off the road altogether and pulled the horses to a stop beside a small pond. He hesitated, then just said what he had been trying to frame in politic words since they left London. "You do not have to return with me, if you don't wish to."

She shifted in her seat, away from him. "I could try to find your ring—"

David gave a short, rueful laugh. "No. It's gone. I've known that for some time now. Don't worry," he added as she flinched. "It doesn't matter."

"I'm sorry," she said in a rush. "Truly I am. It's just not so simple . . ."

"Vivian." He took her hand in his. He had forgotten gloves for her. On impulse he peeled off his driving gloves and reclaimed her hand, drawing his fingertips along her palm. He closed his eyes at the skin-to-skin contact. "I don't give a damn about the ring any more." Her fingers were tense and stiff in his. "I don't. I didn't think of it once last night, and I wasn't thinking of it today."

She said nothing.

"My butler believes I'm saving you from a life of crime," he said after a moment.

"Well, you're keeping me from it, sure you are," she replied, her voice unsteady.

One corner of his mouth crooked upward. "Are you sorry?"

Vivian knew he was asking more. Was she sorry for last night? He feared she was. He hadn't looked at her in several minutes. All his attention was focused on her hand, his head bent forward as he caressed it in a way that made her stomach flutter. "No."

"It's not done, in my society, to—to have a female guest in a bachelor household."

That was no surprise. Vivian's mother had taught her some things. But in St. Giles it was common for a man and woman to live together without marriage. Usually it was loose women and bad men, but not always.

"A few more miles along this road is a coaching inn," he said. "We could be there in an hour."

"An hour," she echoed.

He nodded. "You could take passage from there to . . . anywhere." She didn't say anything. He blew out his breath. "I am offering to take you there. With fifty pounds you could travel to Scotland or back to Ireland or any place in England."

"Fifty pounds?"

He jerked his head. "I have it in my pocket."

"You daft fool," she said. "Haven't you learned not to travel with such funds? There's highwaymen who'll take it from you." That got a small, reluctant smile. Vivian grinned, even though her heart was thumping. "Take it home and hide it under your floorboard. You'll need it to pay all those new servants."

David sighed and laughed, shaking his head. "Vivian, I am letting you go. If you wish to. I was . . . I was wrong to keep you."

"I know." She plucked at a fold of the lovely new gown she wore. "Was this all a fare-thee-well gift, or payment for last night?"

"No," he said before she had even finished speaking.

"It was not payment. I thought—last night—I should not have done, perhaps . . ."

"Well, good. I didn't want payment."

For a moment both were silent. "Where to, then, madam?" David asked softly.

Vivian reflected. She should go. He was offering to drive her to a coaching inn—with fifty pounds! But her old life seemed long ago and far away, and never once had it offered her the prospect of sitting in the sunshine with him, hand in hand. "London, I suppose," she said.

He turned to face her. Vivian gazed back at him. Lord help her, but she was a fool. He made her laugh and he treated her like a lady and he made love to her like it really was love. For an instant she felt again his body moving over hers, his hands on her skin, and she knew it made her blush.

Slowly he leaned forward, his dark eyes intent on hers. His kiss was gentle and sweet, lingering. "You're not my prisoner," he whispered, his lips brushing against hers. "But I want you."

"Here and now?" She could almost consider it, her blood warming as more memories of last night flooded back. There was no one about, here by this small pond away from the road.

He smiled, drawing back. "But I should hate to see grass stains on your lovely new frock."

Vivian blushed harder, smiling back at him as he flicked the whip and turned the carriage back toward London. She rather suspected she was still his prisoner, although not as he had meant a moment ago. This drive had not really changed things between them, just made some things more clear and some things less. The only thing Vivian knew for certain was that she wasn't ready to leave him yet.

Chapter Fifteen

David spent the next few days in the happiest humor of his life. He couldn't recall any other time when everything in his world seemed to be going exactly as it ought. He seemed to have finally gotten the hang of most of Marcus's business affairs, aided slightly by the nearing close of the Season and the end of Parliament. There was less work, it was true, but what there was, David understood and, miraculously, felt competent to handle. Confident competence was not something David was accustomed to, and he found it oddly exhilarating.

His household began to run rather well. Meals were served on time, everything looked clean, and, most importantly, the servants weren't quitting at every turn. After Hobbs's misgivings were addressed, no servants expressed outrage over Vivian's presence. His house was beginning to look quite nice, and David found he liked it more than he had expected. It was rather surprising to find his own home was a more comfortable place than he had ever thought it.

And there was Vivian. Just the thought of her could bring a foolish grin to his face. He was behaving like a lovesick boy over her, but he didn't care. For the first time in his life, David was in love, truly, madly, blissfully in love, and it was a wondrous thing to him. He worked all day at Exeter House, then returned home for dinner with her. She would often be waiting in the drawing room, a brilliant smile on her face, ready to fling herself into his arms once the door was shut and they were alone. They dined together, spent the evening together, and then David would carry her off to bed for a night of pure bliss together. Even having to sneak behind his butler's back to do it didn't bother him. Every day he concocted some new outlandish explanation why he and Miss Beecham must stay up until the servants went to bed. He rather thought Hobbs suspected something was going on, but thankfully seemed to prefer to believe they were reading Scriptures and practicing elocution.

He thought he would never tire of looking at Vivian. She could convey such a range of feeling with a single glance, a quirk of her brow, a slight twist of her lips. He delighted in exasperating her, just so he could cajole her back into a good mood. He loved to make her laugh, just to see her nose wrinkle. He loved to make her eyes flutter closed and her head fall back as she moaned in pleasure. He loved to watch her pore over some book from his library with that fine crease between her eyes and her lip caught between her teeth. He loved the way her face lit up when he gave her a gift, even something as inconsequential as a single flower plucked from the Exeter House gardens. In every way he could think of, David loved her.

He didn't know if she loved him. It didn't seem possible she was feigning her affection entirely. She could have walked out of his house and never come back at any time in the last fortnight, taking half his silver with her, but she hadn't. Once he arrived home early to find the drawing room empty. For a moment he had stood there, shocked that she had gone and desolate to his very soul, before Hobbs informed him she was sitting in the garden. The relief he felt was akin to euphoria.

She fascinated him. She marveled at things he took for granted, and then showed no surprise at things that shocked him. He wanted to understand her, but thought he never could. He had poured out his guilty secrets to her, discovered that she was not horrified—indeed, she was even amused by some of them—and now found he was insatiably curious about hers.

"Why did you become a thief?" he asked her one night.

"I got a handsome invitation." Vivian rolled her eyes. She was reclining on the sofa while David sat on the floor, his back against the sofa and his feet stretched out toward the fire. It was rainy and cool, and rather late. "I was hungry, and had no money for food. Why else would a body steal?"

David lifted one shoulder. "Some do it because they have no wish to work."

"Some," she agreed. "And some have no wish to work because the only work they can get will kill them, and still won't pay enough to feed their babes."

David peeled an orange, separating a slice and holding it out. She put it in her mouth, her eyes closing in ecstasy as she chewed. David had bought a basket full of oranges after discovering she had never tasted them. He was spoiling her, perhaps, but he was enjoying it too much to stop.

"How old were you?"

She licked drops of orange juice from her fingers. "When I started stealing?"

"Yes."

She thought for a moment. "About ten. When my mum died."

"And you lived in St. Giles then?"

"Aye. She was honest, my mum. Worked her hands to the bone as a washerwoman." A sad, distant look drifted over her face. "Her pa was a farmer. I don't remember where; Derbyshire, perhaps. She followed a man to London. An Army man, she said, an officer. He got sent off and never came back. I don't really remember him, although I must have known him, and—" She stopped suddenly and blinked. David wondered what she'd been about to say.

"Your father?"

She nodded once. "He married her, he did. He just didn't leave her much money. She had to find a place to live, but it was hard, what with a small child. And she was never strong again after—after he died. I remember thinking she just faded away.

"When she died, it was the workhouse or worse," she rushed on. "I was a small brat, with quick fingers, and could get through tight crowds. Mother Tate took me in. She was a fence, but ran a dress shop as well. She'd sell the ribbons and lace, then I'd steal them back so she could sell them again. She dressed me in pretty little dresses, so I wouldn't be suspected. I was to pretend to be a rich little girl lost from my nanny. More than one person felt sorry for me, and led me around by the hand looking for a nanny. When they did that it was easy for me to nick a handkerchief or even their purse. Mother Tate liked that." Again she stopped short, seemingly on the verge of saying something else.

"Then I got too big to be a child missing a nanny. Mother Tate handed me over to a gang, because she had no more use for me. A few years after that, it got too hard. Most thieves don't last long in London. I was caught once and sent to a reform house, where they beat us. I ran away and didn't stop until London was far behind."

"Ah." David felt a surge of pity and outrage, which he tried to hide. She spoke of being "handed over" with calm acceptance, as if she were an old pair of boots one could simply give another person. But she ran away when she was beaten. He felt a stab of pride in her for that. "And took to the highway."

She snorted with laughter. "Oh, aye; the highway took to me, more like. For a while I went along the roads, picking pockets here and there. Once along the Dover road there was a fair, and I picked a few pockets, hoping to get some food for me and—for my dinner." Vivian could have bitten off her tongue. Several times now she'd almost gone and mentioned Simon. It was hard not to think of him as she recounted her life's history: that she had worked for Mother Tate because Mother Tate took care of Simon when he was a baby, after their mother died; that she had gone to the gang because Mother Tate agreed to keep Simon in exchange for a share of Vivian's take; that she'd run from the reform school not because of the beatings, but because they wanted to send Simon, only ten, to a workhouse. "I took a purse off a man named Flynn, and he caught me. Snagged my hand, quick as a blink. He said he could hand me over to the local constable that day, or I could join his business."

"Flynn was a highwayman," David said. "I see."

"Flynn was a common thief," she corrected. "He had aspirations. But he's none too clever. He needed help

and he knew it." She shrugged. "We made an agreement. It was better than starving again."

"He needed a pickpocket's help?" David asked with
a frown.

Vivian smiled, remembering how Flynn had tried to
bully her into working for him, then threatened to make
her his doxy. Vivian had stuck a knife into his shoulder
for that, and Flynn had kept his distance. "He fancied
the highway as more elegant," she said simply. "He
needed help setting up jobs. It's not hard to find folk
who have the nerve, but it's a tricky prospect to find folk
who have the smarts not to get caught."

"You planned every robbery, didn't you?" David
looked half impressed, half annoyed.

She laughed at him. "Aye, and a perfect target you
were! Fine clothes, flashy horses, tossing coins this way
and that. How was I to know you'd only a pair of guineas
on you?" David's eyes narrowed. "It was simple calcula-
tion," she explained. "Find a passenger who had funds.
We only took small valuables and money, see, so it was
best to find someone with both."

"I regret not being more profitable," he said dryly.

"Well, I can forgive you now," she said graciously.
David stared at her a moment, then threw back his head
and laughed. Vivian grinned.

"Little vixen," he said, shaking his head. "*You* can
forgive *me*?"

"And if you want to beg my pardon for locking me
up, I can give it also."

"Beg your pardon?" He caught her ankle and pulled.
Vivian shrieked and tried to scramble back on the sofa.
"I'll beg your pardon, minx. Come here."

"Nay!" Laughing, she twisted in his grip, flailing
about. David ducked her elbow, then sat back on the

floor and let go of her. She was beautiful when she laughed. He liked the sound of it too much to be angry that she had deliberately set out to rob him.

"Were you good at picking pockets?" he asked as she brushed her skirts back into place.

"More than good," she said without a flicker of modesty or embarrassment.

"Show me." Vivian smiled and shook her head. David turned to see her better, walking his fingertips over her exposed ankle again. "Show me, Vivian, please," he coaxed.

"You're daft," she said with a laugh. "Why do you want to see?"

He lifted one shoulder. "Perhaps I just want you to touch me. Although, I suppose I could content myself with touching you . . ."

She rolled her eyes, but got to her feet, skipping out of his reach as he made to catch her. "You've a wish to have your pockets drawn, have you? Then on your feet, sir. I can't do it whilst you lie on the floor."

David got to his feet. "What sorts of things did you steal?"

Vivian inspected him. "All sorts. Anything a man had. There's a market and a fence for everything. No doubt I've lost my touch for it."

David patted his pockets, and then produced a fine cambric handkerchief. "This?"

"Aye, that would fetch a few pennies," she said. "Fine cloth, no marks."

"Only a few pennies?" he exclaimed, remembering the bill for a dozen such handkerchiefs. "It's worth a pound at least."

She lifted a shoulder. "Not in St. Giles. A few pennies buys a day's worth of bread, enough to make it worth a body's while to steal."

That silenced him. David tucked it back into his pocket. He'd known she had been hungry, and he'd known she was a thief. It was easy to forget that the latter occupation kept away the former affliction. She stole to survive. And in her place, David wasn't sure he wouldn't do the same.

"Walk across the room," she said then, breaking into his thoughts. "Stuff it down more inside the pocket."

"Are you sure you can get it?" he asked, pushing the handkerchief deeper into his pocket.

Her lips curled. "We'll see," she said with a small smile. "Now walk."

"Why must I walk?"

"I can't do it if you just stand there," she explained. "First, a body doesn't notice being jostled and bumped as much while walking. And, your clothes move when you do. It's easier to reach into a pocket that's open a bit."

"As you say." David strolled across the room. Vivian watched him for a second, then walked past him. Their shoulders brushed, nothing more. In a crowded street, he wouldn't have noticed it at all. She didn't look at him but kept her face forward, and she walked briskly, yet not too quickly. David reached the end of the room and stopped. He was certain there was no earthly way she could have taken the handkerchief; he'd not felt a thing. He reached for his pocket, and found it empty. "You've got it," he said incredulously.

She turned and lowered her gaze demurely. "Have I?"

He pushed his fingers all the way to the bottom of the pocket, to make certain. "It's gone."

"Didn't you feel it?" Now she smiled at him, her eyes dancing with glee. "I thought sure a great fellow like you would know all the tricks."

"You only brushed against me," he said slowly. "I never would have suspected. Where is it?" Her hands were empty, clasped in front of her.

She widened her eyes. "Where is what?"

David knew then how she'd gotten away with it for so long. Who could doubt her innocence, with that open, guileless look on her face? Who would want her to be guilty, when she looked young and almost angelically virtuous? "You little devil."

Now she laughed, and the innocent look was gone. Now she was a woman flush with excitement and triumph. David started across the room toward her. "I wouldn't have it anymore, in the real case," she said. "I would have passed it off to someone within a few steps, to avoid being caught with it."

"But I know you do have it." He let his eyes slide over every inch of her, until her cheeks were deep pink. "The only question is . . . where?"

"You said you wanted to see how it was done," she said as she dodged his hands. "Don't you care to know?"

"Now I just want it back." He caught her this time, wrapping his arm around her waist and pulling her close. "Let's see . . . I should check your pockets." He slipped one hand into the side slit of her dress, making a show of running his hand all around, stroking her hip. Vivian laughed, wriggling a bit. "Hmm. Not there." He checked the other pocket just as thoroughly. "Nor there." His gaze fell to her bosom.

"Don't you dare," Vivian said.

"Dare? I dare anything," he said softly, as his fingers trailed up her side to skim the swell of her breast. "I've been robbed, my dear."

"At your request," she said, her breath catching as his finger dipped between her breasts.

"Most certainly," he whispered, drawing lightly on her skin with his fingertip. Vivian shuddered, unconsciously arching her back and pressing closer to him.

"I can't think what you'll ask next," she said, even as he unfastened the front of her bodice to slide his hand inside. "You're a demanding one."

He laughed softly at that. "You have no idea." Her bodice fell open; he had undone the front and now spread the sides apart, exposing her shift. "Untie it," he said in a low, wicked voice. Her fingers trembling, Vivian untied the string holding her shift closed. It loosened above her corset, revealing the handkerchief she had tucked deep between her breasts.

"Tsk, tsk," he murmured. "I've caught you with stolen property, madam."

Vivian blushed. "I suppose you'll want it back."

His eyes darkened as he examined the handkerchief, and its surroundings, closely. "No, I think it's well situated for the moment." With leisurely movements, he unfastened the dress and peeled it from her shoulders to send it to the floor in a puddle around her feet. He untied her corset, loosening it enough to free her breasts. Finally he pulled his handkerchief out, and Vivian shuddered as his fine linen whisked across her skin.

"Thieves must make retribution," he said, winding the kerchief around her wrists, joining them together and knotting the ends just below her thumbs. "Let us see how you can repay me for my lost kerchief."

"It's not lost," she protested. "You had it in your hands."

His smile was slow and dangerous. "Let's see to that, then." He lifted her hands and ducked his head through them, so that her arms were caught around his neck, held in place by the kerchief tying her hands together.

He was so much taller than she, he had to stoop, and even then Vivian felt stretched, almost on her toes.

"Are you going to hang me, then?" she asked breathlessly, as his breath on her exposed bosom turned all her skin to gooseflesh.

He chuckled. "Why, yes; I'll hang you around my neck."

Vivian couldn't help laughing. Her heart skipped a beat. She tugged and pulled against the handkerchief, and only succeeded in losing her balance and stumbling against him.

"Mmm, yes, do that some more," he said, watching her breasts as she twisted.

"Untie me," she said.

Pure deviltry sparkled in his eyes. "Not yet. And don't think you'll get free on your own. I'm frightfully good at tying people up."

"Oh? You've done this often, then?"

"No," he said. "Not often enough."

"I see. Now what, since you've got me at your mercy?" Vivian could see why he was a rake. Surely that roguish, wicked smile would tempt any woman to throw scruples to the wind and take whatever pleasures he offered. Here she was, standing in her shift and corset with her hands tied together, and her heart was pounding in anticipation of what he would do next.

"First, you shall be flogged." He pulled up the back of her shift, exposing her bottom. Gently he slapped her with one hand, then the other. It didn't hurt, but made her skin sting and tingle. "Do you repent?"

"You asked me to do it—ow!" she cried as he slapped her lightly again. "Stop that!"

He laughed under his breath. "Repent, fair sinner. Else you'll be drawn and quartered." He drew one finger firmly up the line of her spine, from between the curves of her bottom to the base of her neck, and then across her back. Vivian quivered. That also didn't hurt, but it sent a shock through her whole body.

"I won't," she whispered. "I'm not sorry . . ."

"Are you not?" His hand was on her hip, now between her legs. She gave a soft sigh, her knees relaxing to allow him. "Are you sorry?" he asked, probing with his fingertips.

"Nay," she said. "Not a bit."

"Wicked wench," he breathed, his lips grazing hers before settling over them.

His kiss was like a drug. Vivian threw herself against him, shamelessly allowing him to pull up her shift and caress her bared bottom and stomach. He was her own Blue Ruin, she thought. When he held her like this and touched her like this, she wasn't herself. Under his spell, she was neither alert, nor wary, nor suspicious. Bad things happened to girls who didn't keep their wits about them at all times, in Vivian's experience, but when David kissed her, the world around her could come to a fiery end and she wouldn't notice. Nor even care.

Oh, but who could blame her? Surely there wasn't a woman in the country who wouldn't lose her head when his clever hands were there, just so, moving over her belly and her ribs, her hips and her bottom, between her legs. She was barely balancing on her tiptoes as he ran his fingertips down the back of her thigh and raised her knee to his hip, exposing her completely.

"Are you sorry yet?" he murmured, sliding one long finger inside her.

"Yes," she choked. "No! Not a bit . . . not yet . . ."

He laughed softly, pushing another finger into her, his thumb teasing that too-sensitive spot until she gasped.

"You will be. Put your legs around my waist," he commanded in that low growl, releasing her and unfastening his trousers. Vivian lifted her shaking legs one at a time, and he caught her under the knees, pulling her up until her legs were snug around his waist and she was looking down at him. David's expression turned almost fierce as he slowly lowered her, one arm under her bottom, the other beneath her, guiding his rigid sex into her.

"That's it, hold on to me," he told her as he slid inside her. Vivian moaned, clinging to his neck. "Ride me as you wish . . ."

"I don't know how," she managed to say. He chuckled again, his palms cupping the curves of her bottom, and lifted her. He took a few steps, and Vivian felt the wall at her back.

"You'll learn," he said. "Like . . . this." He slipped his forearms under her thighs, bracing his hands against the wall. Vivian clung to his neck and flexed her legs, trying not to fall, and succeeded in raising herself a few inches. "Now relax," he said into her ear, and Vivian understood what he meant.

She took up the movement, slowly at first and then with enthusiasm, up and down again and again as he whispered wicked things in her ear. He told she was beautiful. He told her she drove him mad. He told her to go faster, he told her to go slower, and he told her to talk back to him and tell him what she wanted. Vivian wasn't sure if she did what he asked or not. All she was aware of was him, large and strong and beautiful, and the way she felt in his arms.

Abruptly he squeezed her around the waist, lifting her away from him and putting her back on her own feet. "Turn around." His voice was rough and he sounded out of breath. He ducked out of the circle of her arms and ripped the kerchief from her wrists. "Turn around." Unsteady, Vivian let him turn her around and press her to the wall. David pushed his knee between hers, his hands at her waist holding her up against him. Within a second he thrust into her again, and Vivian's stomach contracted; it felt different this time, deep inside her. He nudged her feet wider apart, his hands gripping her hips to hold her in place, and then he began to move, long hard driving thrusts that rocked Vivian onto her toes and made her feel lightheaded. She spread her hands flat on the wall and pushed against him, driving her body down onto his.

"Touch," he rasped in her ear, touching her earlobe with the tip of his tongue. His fingers wrapped around one of her wrists, dragged her hand down her belly. "Yourself. Me. Touch me." He pressed her fingers to the place where his body joined hers. Vivian felt the thick hot slide of him inside her, and spread her fingers, so that he thrust between them. David groaned in her ear. Again and again he moved, harder and faster, deeper and deeper until Vivian felt tears running down her face and realized she was sobbing. Her bones seemed to be vibrating with the pleasure. She thought she might faint, at any second—he pushed her hand out of the way then and replaced it with his own, his fingers finding that perfect spot with unerring accuracy. In the space of a heartbeat, he sent her over the edge, moaning, bucking, and crying with release. He pushed deeper inside her than ever, pinning her to the wall with his weight, and went still with a harsh exhalation.

Vivian felt shattered. How could he do this to her, so easily? She had never been a trollop. She had fended off the boys and men for years. Now she was completely undone by a sly sideways glance from him, this fine gentleman who seemed to know the deepest secrets of how her body worked. What had come over her?

The one thing she knew was that she was happy. Blissfully, recklessly, happy, in a way she had never before known in her life.

"Good Lord," she said faintly. "Never thought that would happen over a picked pocket."

He laughed, a deep rumble in his chest that made Vivian feel warm with contentment. His arms were still around her, one around her hips, the other around her chest, his fingers curved around her breast. She rested her cheek against the wall and smiled dreamily as he nuzzled the back of her neck. Never in all her life had she felt so at ease. So safe. So . . . peaceful.

David breathed deeply, his face pressed against her hair. His mind felt scrubbed clean. His body felt blissfully exhausted. His soul felt at ease. And his heart . . .

His heart, he knew, was no longer his own. The sharp-witted little thief in his arms had plucked it right out of his chest. She understood him; they were alike, in more ways than David had ever thought possible. And he understood her. David couldn't say that his life would have turned out any differently than hers, if he had been in her place and she in his, although he was quite certain she would have made a more respectable lady than he made a gentleman. She recognized the wilder side of him, and wasn't repulsed by it. She had compassion for his failings, and a tolerance for his mad impulses. She drove him wild, and made him laugh, and excited protective instincts he never knew he had. David wasn't certain he would ever meet another woman with all those characteristics.

Gently he lowered her back to the floor, holding her as she swayed a bit on her feet. She gave him a look full of lazy amusement, without a trace of outrage or dismay that he had just made love to her up against the drawing room wall, and David knew he was lost. Unable to speak, he stepped away from her and put his clothes to rights as she did the same for hers. He scooped up her dress from the floor and helped her back into it. It was rather a plain dress; he much preferred her in the blue silk gown. She did the buttons on the front and brushed off the skirt, back to normal to all appearances, except for the color in her face and the brilliant sparkle in her eyes.

"Well." She flashed a saucy grin. "There'd be a lot more crime, if all thieves were punished so."

David made himself laugh. A thief. She was a thief, and he kept forgetting it in wild flights of fancy. As she crossed the room, a light bounce to her step, David felt unmanned. He had unwittingly taken her from that life, but he couldn't send her back to it. He couldn't bear to think of her starving . . . getting caught with her fingers slipping into someone's pocket . . . catching a pistol ball in a highway robbery gone awry. He couldn't do that to her.

He just didn't know what he *could* do.

Chapter Sixteen

The end of the idyll came suddenly and without warning.

"My lord, the duke of Ware to see you." David frowned, and Hobbs extended his silver tray with Ware's card on it. Ware? They had once been friends, years ago, but he hadn't spoken to the man in years. Perhaps he did business with Marcus. "There are some men with him," added the butler then, his voice ever-so-slightly distasteful, and David felt a premonition of dread. "Some men" probably did not refer to bankers and solicitors calling to negotiate profitable business. "Some men" generally referred to ruffians, moneylenders, and Runners.

"Show them in," he said warily. Hobbs bowed and left, and David got to his feet. Which sort of men would they turn out to be? He went to the cabinet and got out a bottle of the whiskey he'd taken from Exeter House, poured a generous finger, and tossed it back. He rolled his shoulders and stretched his neck, feeling the familiar defensiveness creeping over him. It was like being summoned to his father's study all over again, even though—for the first time in years—he honestly had no idea what he could have done wrong. He'd cheated no one, wasn't in anyone's debt, and hadn't so much as flirted with another man's wife. There was just something, something he couldn't put into words, that gave him a bad feeling about this visit.

"The duke of Ware, my lord," Hobbs announced. His voice dropped a level. "And some other . . . gentlemen." It was clear from his tone that they weren't any sort of gentlemen at all, something David could clearly see for himself. They weren't gentlemen; if David had to lay money on it, he'd wager they were from Bow Street.

"Ware." He bowed his head, and Ware nodded back. No trace of expression betrayed his thoughts, but it was always that way with Ware now.

"Reece. I trust all is well with your brother."

David gave a faint smile. "Yes. I've never seen him happier."

Ware nodded again. "No man in London deserves it more."

"No," David agreed. The two other men hovered just at the edge of his vision. So far, David had avoided them, but now he cast a brief glance their way. Yes, most certainly legal authorities, and grim ones, too. He steeled himself to a coming disaster, wishing he had an inkling what it would be. "Won't you be seated?"

Ware took the seat closest to the desk, and his two companions crowded onto the tiny sofa behind it. "Care for a drink?" asked David, keeping up the unconcerned air. One of the strangers opened his mouth as Ware flicked his fingers in dismissal.

"Thank you, no." The man behind him closed his mouth with a distinct huff. Ware paid him no mind. "I have come on a mission of some delicacy. Some questions have arisen . . ." He paused. "Some distasteful questions," he amended. A clear rebuke to the men behind him. "I have offered my assistance in answering them."

The man who had wanted a drink reached the end of his patience. He lurched to his feet. "My lord," he began respectfully but forcefully, "we're charged with investigating some serious crimes."

David arched a brow. "Indeed."

"Yes, sir," the man charged ahead. "It's come to our attention that certain thieves have been stopping coaches and committing outrages against the passengers."

"Thieves committing outrages. Indeed."

"My lord, this is serious business we're about," retorted the man. "One of these thieves, the leader of the gang, is quite a distinctive fellow. He wears a large plumed hat and a gold ring. He calls himself the Black Duke."

Even though David's heart had fallen at the mention of a ring, he kept his face impassive. He waited without moving as the men peered closely at him, knowing they were expecting a guilty start of sorts. "And?" he drawled in his best imitation of Marcus. "Do you require my assistance in catching the fellow?"

The man's mouth thinned. "No, your lordship," he replied. "We've come to let you know that Bow Street is aware of his doings. Highway robbery, my lord, is a hanging offense."

"I should hope so," said David.

"We're also aware that the ring he wears bears your own family crest. Three witnesses described it." The man's jaw lifted in challenge.

David waited. He knew, from long experience, that simply being stared at did terrible things to one's composure. Usually, though, he was the one being stared at in disapproval, and it seemed his stare didn't have the same effect that Marcus's did. The Bow Street men didn't flinch or squirm. "How fascinating. Do you mean to accuse me?"

"It's a topic of interest to Bow Street, my lord. We'd like to know what you have to say on the topic."

Ware tilted his head back, as if admiring the ceiling. "Of course, you've substantial proof. Bow Street wouldn't dare accuse the duke of Exeter's brother of something so serious otherwise."

The man hesitated. "We've a great deal of proof, Your Grace," he said with a bit more deference. "We have several witnesses, all of whom saw the highwayman and his ring. Their descriptions of the ring agree quite closely. We know you, my lord, were yourself on a coach robbed quite recently in a manner very like the one employed by this villain. We know your finances are somewhat unsteady. We know you've not been out and about in town of late, as has been your habit."

"In other words, you've nothing conclusive." David leaned back in his chair. "My ring, bearing my family's crest, was stolen in the robbery you mentioned earlier. Perhaps the methods are the same because the villains responsible are the same."

"What we've come to ask, sir," said the second man, breaking his silence at last, "is an accounting of your doings of late." David let his eyebrows rise. "It's our duty, sir," added the man, respectfully but firmly. "The evidence is convincing. There is a great outcry for us to arrest this man at once. We have been most circumspect, sir, in calling on you. This villain wears a signet ring with your family crest. Your absence from certain places has been noted. And it is a well-known fact, sir, that your finances have been precarious for years, but of late they are greatly improved. In light of all these facts, sir, as well as others I'm not at liberty to disclose, we've a duty to inquire."

"I have been here, at home, and at Exeter House," David said.

"Is there anyone who might testify to that?"

"The staff," replied David, his voice even colder than before. "What is your name?"

"Collins, sir," said the man, unfazed. "Deputy to Mr. John Stafford of Bow Street."

"Collins," said David, "I would be the greatest fool in England were I to rob coaches on a public highway wearing a ring easily traced to me. Either you take me for a fool, or you are so desperate for any person to clap in irons you have leaped to conclusions which any barrister worth his periwig would tear to shreds. Which is it?"

Collins's chest filled, then deflated. "Neither, my lord. We are merely making an inquiry."

"Then you have had the answer to your inquiry." David rang for Hobbs, getting to his feet in the same motion. "Good day."

Collins and his companion bowed and left, followed out by Hobbs. Slowly, like a puppet being lowered to the ground, David sank back into his seat. Good God. Accused by Bow Street of highway robbery. This was a new low, even for him. "I hope you'll take a drink now, Ware, for I need one quite badly."

"Thank you, I will."

David got up and poured two more glasses, his hands only slightly unsteady. He handed one to the duke and resumed his own seat. Bow Street, in his own house. David still couldn't quite believe it, and sipped his drink without noticing.

"Someone is pressuring them," Ware said in the ensuing silence. "The scandal rags are hardly full of the

Black Duke. I daresay not one person in ten in London would recognize the name."

"Trevenham," said David.

Ware put his head to one side. "That is unlikely, if only because a man like Trevenham doesn't invite scrutiny, public or private, from Bow Street. If I were to hazard a guess—based purely on conjecture, you understand—I would name old Percy."

For a moment David was shocked; his good friend's father? But of course it was a very good possibility. Sir James Percy detested David as a bad influence on his son, and always had. From the moment they had met and become friends at school, Sir James had advised Percy to avoid scoundrels and rogues like David. Percy had read the letters aloud to all his friends, and everyone had been highly amused that David was considered the worst of the lot. David had never been invited to the Percy estate on holiday from university, and Percy had never been allowed to accept an invitation to Ainsley Park. Even now, Sir James regularly scolded Percy for his association with David.

"He's quite outspoken on the issue of prison reform," Ware went on. "He takes a keen interest in the workings of Bow Street, and constantly proposes improvements and funding for them. A highwayman posing as nobility would be sure to excite Percy's interest."

David nodded, fairly certain Ware knew why else old Percy might have pressed Bow Street to inquire into David's actions, but thankful the duke didn't say it. No doubt the latest gossip spread by Trevenham and others about David would enrage Sir James, particularly when his son continued to stand loyally at David's side. "I should hope Bow Street would operate on more solid grounds than the urgings of one man."

"No doubt they do. It was a rather polite invitation to confess. Had they any real proof, it would not have been so," said Ware idly, examining his empty glass.

"They have the wrong man," said David with an edge. Would no one believe him innocent? Of highway robbery, for God's sake?

"Of course," Ware agreed at once. "Still, men like Collins can be terribly . . . inconvenient. They are rather difficult to shake. I expect you're being watched."

That was probably true, he realized, and wondered what they'd seen. For the first time it occurred to him that he was not the only one who could be in danger. If they discovered Vivian, and linked her to the robberies— she, who was actually guilty of thieving—she would hang. There wouldn't be much he could do to help her, especially not if he himself were under suspicion as well. A familiar surge of resentment rose inside him, that a man like Marcus or Ware could step in and control events with just a glance or a word while he . . .

David let out his breath slowly. While he was suspected of being up to his old habits. Perhaps he might have some of that power if he hadn't wasted his life to date on drinking, gambling, womanizing, and other activities that were in fact illegal. He had no one to blame but himself for his situation, and no one to turn to for help but himself. Even if he wished to, Marcus was in Italy, more than a month's travel away. David would have to see to it himself.

"Ware," he said. "I am not the Black Duke."

"I never thought you were," said Ware. His voice was the same as before, but his gaze sharpened.

David leaned forward. "I want you to know. I am not the Black Duke. That ring was stolen from me weeks ago. I visited pawnbrokers all over London looking for it, but it never turned up. I had given it up for lost."

"I see," murmured Ware.

"I've not left London in weeks," David went on. "I have been occupied with Marcus's business as well as affairs of my own. Not only my servants but all Marcus's staff can vouch for my presence at Exeter House nearly every day, from morning until evening. I want you to know this, in case events conspire to prevent me from sharing it. On my word of honor, I would never debase my family name in such a manner."

"Of course not." With a graceful nod, Ware got to his feet. "I shall see what I can do."

David rose also. "My thanks."

The duke bowed slightly, and left. David stared at the door. Right. Ware would do what he could to shake up and slow down Bow Street. Ware had influence, and could do that much. But David would have to do the rest.

His feet heavy, David went up the stairs in search of Vivian. He found her in her room, sitting in the window seat with her knees pulled up in front of her, holding a book to the light. At his entrance, a glorious smile bloomed on her face.

"Have you read this?" she demanded. "Oh, it's marvelous—I never knew a man could write such lovely stuff, and about a woman, too! Listen:

> *That for they Insolence—And that for thy Jealously—And that for thy Infidelity!*
> *Oh happy Figaro— Take thy Revenge, my dear, kind, good Angel; Never did Man or Martyr suffer with such Extacy!*

Can you imagine a man saying such?" She laughed.

For a moment he couldn't speak. The excitement on her face as she read aloud, slowly and carefully, had tightened his throat until he could hardly breathe, let alone speak. She was like a landscape grown hard and coarse from lack of care; a little tending, a little encouragement, and her mind and spirit blossomed and flourished. To see her smile, with her hair unbound and her bare toes peeping from beneath her skirts, he would count the damned signet ring a good loss.

If only that were all there was to it.

Vivian's smile faded as the silence dragged on, and David simply stared at her, his eyes dark and bleak. "What is it?" she asked, pressing the little book closer to her chest as if to cling to its lovely words and funny characters and outrageous antics. "What's wrong?"

Without answering he pulled a chair over and sat on the edge, bracing his hands on his knees. "Vivian," he said in that low voice that made her skin tingle. "I'm in a spot of . . . trouble."

"Trouble?" She didn't like that word, not a bit.

He nodded once. "Someone, it seems . . . Someone has been robbing stages on Bromley Heath." He gave her a level look. "He calls himself the Black Duke and wears a signet ring remarkably like the one I lost."

Vivian felt her mouth fall open in dismay. "Flynn," she managed to say. David nodded, looking more and more grim. "That black bastard!"

"No doubt. Did he ever sell stolen goods himself?"

She shook her head. "I did. All of it."

He closed his eyes for a second. "Then he probably didn't sell the ring. He must still have it."

"Yes," she said, growing angry. How dare that fool do something so flashy, so bold, so stupid? And Simon— her heart contracted with fear. Simon would have to go along with it, for she wasn't there to shield him any longer. She put down the book and swung her feet to the floor. "That no-good rat-catcher's been flirting with the rope for years," she said. "Of all the—"

"Vivian." He gave the tiniest shake of his head. "That's not the problem."

She paused, wary. "No?"

"No." He pushed his hand through his hair in that gesture she secretly loved, the one that made him look a bit tousled and wild. "They think I'm doing it."

It was so shocking, she couldn't even frown in response. "That's the bloody stupidest thing I've ever heard," she blurted out.

"Isn't it?" he said wryly. "Unfortunately, it's true."

"No, it's not, it's a mark of lazy Runners," she snapped. "Why, you haven't left London in over a month!"

"I told them that. I have no proof, though."

"I can prove it," she declared. "Haven't I seen you here every day?"

"Yes, but." He sighed. "You can hardly march down to Bow Street and tell them. At best they'd think you were my mistress and not trustworthy, at worst they'd begin to wonder who you really are."

That shut Vivian's mouth. Oh, dear. That was a problem. It would hardly help David if people learned he was harboring a thief in his house. And it wouldn't do her any good, either.

"I can't let you risk that," he added. "And they're no doubt watching the house even now, to track me if I should leave."

"That's no problem," she said automatically. "If you want to leave, there are ways to get around the charleys."

He looked at her sideways. "Where were you when I was young," he muttered, then shook his head. "Just leaving the house isn't the question. They'll want to collect as much evidence as they can before arresting me—

I do have friends, and Marcus would likely take down the government if he were here. They won't do anything until they are absolutely certain."

"But they won't hang you," Vivian said. "You've got funds. It's true enough that a man with five hundred pounds is a man who won't hang."

He shook his head. "They might as well hang me if I have to live the rest of my life as a suspected highwayman. Society is not very gracious to those who take from them. I want to prove that this time, this *one* time, I am completely innocent. I intend to find the real Black Duke."

Vivian pursed her lips and said nothing.

"Will you help me?" he pressed, taking her hand and cradling it between his.

She tugged free. "Are you certain you want to? Flynn will hardly stroll into the magistrate's office with you and confess."

David laughed. "No? I was counting on that." She rolled her eyes, and he stopped laughing. "Of course he won't. But if I catch him wearing the ring, in the act . . ." He paused significantly as Vivian's mouth fell open in shock.

"Have you lost your bloody mind?" she gasped. "He's like to shoot you if he sees you again, just so you can't finger him to the constables."

"I wouldn't go out looking like this," he said. "I'll be a country farmer. You say he's not a bright fellow; he'll never guess it's I."

"Being a bloody idiot doesn't mean he's not observant," she argued. "He'd have been left to rot in chains and irons long ago if he hadn't kept his eyes and ears open, at least while doing a job."

"How else can I prove I'm innocent?"

Vivian paused. "Well, they must be out to catch

him—the Black Duke, that is. Just wait. Sooner or later the constables will get him. Then all will know it wasn't you."

David rocked back in his chair, beginning to look impatient. "Wait! Wait, while Bow Street becomes certain I'm the culprit. Wait, and hope the constables around London suddenly grow determined and vigilant. Oh, yes, and pray Flynn's fool enough to keep robbing coaches in the same area under the same guise. If he decides to decamp to York or Wales or Ireland tomorrow, they'll never catch him and I'll be suspect forever, if not arrested and convicted."

"If Flynn goes away, there'll be no more robberies," Vivian pointed out. "How could they arrest you then?"

"It will be better if I point them in Flynn's direction, or better yet, bring him to them. They may take me off to Newgate at any time. It's much harder to persuade people of one's innocence from inside the prison walls."

"You're daft," she insisted. "'Tis a daft idea."

"You've no love for Flynn," he said, puzzled. "Wouldn't you like to see him in prison?"

Vivian ran her finger up and down the spine of the book, avoiding David's eyes. "It's complicated."

"How?" He reached out and tipped up her chin, so she had to look at him.

She didn't want to tell him. Secrecy was so ingrained in Vivian, it felt physically difficult for her to open her mouth and explain that her brother was with Flynn, and that she'd die before she did anything to put her brother in prison. Flynn could rot there for a hundred years for all she cared, but not Simon. "There's others besides Flynn," she muttered. "I don't hate them all."

"Ah." He sat back. "The big man, and the boy."

She flinched at the last word, but merely nodded.

"All the more reason to go out looking for them myself, then," David said. "I only want the ring back, to put an end to the Black Duke. I wouldn't mind seeing Flynn sent to Botany Bay, for what he's done to you if nothing else, but if he just leaves off calling himself a duke and gives back the ring, I'll be satisfied."

Vivian closed her eyes and frowned. *For what he's done to you.* Simon was the only man she could ever recall being protective of her, and he was too young to be much protection. It made her heart ache all over again. "Flynn . . . He'll be angry to lose that ring. He's bull-headed, see, and has a temper, and he'll . . ." Her frown deepened into a scowl. "He'll take it out on the boy."

After a moment, the puzzlement faded from David's face, to be replaced by something more compassionate. He leaned forward. "Who is the boy, Vivian?"

She looked up fearfully. "He's my brother," she whispered. "My younger brother, Simon."

David's eyes closed. He nodded once, slowly. "I see now. You've been protecting him all this time."

"And I won't help the charleys to him now, no matter what!" she declared. "You can hand me over to them if you want, but leave Simon al—"

"All the more reason to go ourselves," he said as if she had not spoken. "We'll retrieve both my ring and your brother."

Vivian paused, her mouth still open in mid-sentence. She could only stare at David, dumbstruck, as he went on with growing enthusiasm.

"If Flynn's as you say, the boy—Simon, you called him?—Simon should be all too happy to come away with us. I've no ill will toward him."

"You might remember Simon's the one who gave you a great clout on the head," she said.

David waved it away. "And why shouldn't he? He likely thought I was about to maul your unconscious person." Vivian was so startled at the thought that she laughed. She choked it down at once, then sat quietly thinking. Perhaps this mad plan would work. What he proposed *was* definitely mad, but it was also quite tempting. Waiting until the constables caught Flynn with that blasted ring would have the unfortunate effect of leaving Simon to the constables as well. And Flynn certainly was fool enough to keep robbing coaches in the same area; how else was he to enjoy his new fame? Vivian would have wagered every farthing she had that Flynn went around to all the local pubs to drink and enjoy the recounting of his latest adventures, possibly even adding to them himself. It was doubtless only a matter of time until Flynn got caught.

"Will you help me find them?" he pressed her again.

"Do you give your promise not to turn Simon over to the constables?" she asked. "I can't help send my brother to prison."

"I wouldn't ask it of you," he said quietly. "I swear to do everything in my power to keep Simon from the constables."

Vivian stared at him, heart thumping. She felt completely at sea. It had always been her duty to look after Simon and keep him safe, or as safe as possible. Now she'd gone and put his fate in the hands of this man who   who . . . She managed a wobbly smile. It was done; she was committed now. "Then I'll help you find them."

Chapter Seventeen

David spent the next two days plotting. He stuck to his normal routine, going to Exeter House every morning, watching from the corners of his eyes to see if anyone followed him. Once he thought he spied the fellow, a man in a brown coat who looked a bit too aimless even for London. David took great delight in stopping in a dozen exclusive shops, where he knew the man couldn't possibly follow without being obvious. Of course, he had to justify his presence in so many shops, so he found himself buying gifts for Vivian. He bought hair ribbons and lace, a fine paisley shawl, two silk fans, and books. It made him ridiculously happy just to picture her expression when she opened the packages.

At Exeter House he rushed through any necessary work and sent Adams off to complete it. As usual with something new and urgent—and best of all, clandestine—David threw himself wholeheartedly into planning how he would find this Black Duke. Vivian was certain it was Flynn, and David saw no reason to doubt it, either. She knew Flynn, and declared he had taken a fancy to that ring and wouldn't sell it to another thief who could then be posing as the Black Duke. Flynn was a miserly man, she said, who was also extremely cocky and brash. Calling himself a duke of any color or sort would please him immensely.

David didn't want Bow Street to follow him, nor know of his intentions. He didn't like being accused—of something he hadn't actually done, that is—and didn't want any overzealous Runners wreaking havoc on his plans. David simply didn't trust them not to grow suspicious and blunder in to ruin things.

It didn't take long to decide that the best place to find the Black Duke was where he was last seen: on the roads to London, near a stagecoach. Vivian would be able to guess with some accuracy which coaches Flynn might select. They would simply purchase seats on those coaches and eventually, their path was certain to cross Flynn's. Then it would be a simple matter to follow Flynn and the others, and present a business proposition. David would ransom back his ring, buy Simon's freedom if necessary, and that would be the end of the Black Duke.

His planning became a bit more urgent when the duke of Ware called on him again. Ware's suggestion that Sir James Percy was behind Bow Street's visit had likely been correct. Through discreet inquiries, Ware had learned that Percy had been heard to rail against the recent rash of highway robberies, singling out the Black Duke as one particularly worthy of loathing. Not only was thieving illegal and wrong, Percy had declared, but to appropriate the title of a noble duke was nigh sacrilege. Percy was agitating for an immediate arrest.

"I hardly think I've done anything worth this," David muttered.

Ware smiled, a flicker of the roguish grin David suddenly remembered from years ago, when he and Ware had run in the same wild crowd. "His son, I hear, has gambled away a small fortune this year."

"He didn't lose it to me."

"Percy believes he lost most of it in your company."

That might be true. David sat back in his chair and frowned. "So I should expect Bow Street to call on me again soon."

"That would not be a surprise," Ware agreed. "I wasn't able to learn of any additional evidence they may have, but if they were to arrest you, even house arrest, it would cause a stir in the papers. People would begin to speak of it with more interest. Once a bit of mud accrues to a man's name, it's inevitable that more will follow."

David swore under his breath. He would be savaged if word spread that Bow Street was about to arrest him for highway robbery, and even worse, it would drag his family's name through the dirt in the process. It was bad enough the men at White's were wagering on how extravagant his ultimate disgrace would be, and calling him a counterfeiter among themselves. Trevenham and the others would descend on him with malicious glee if Bow Street took action, and that would be the end of whatever scraps of respectability David still possessed.

"Of course, Percy cannot press for your arrest too obviously, and he has no information that names you as the culprit," Ware added.

"Since when has that mattered to the gossips?"

"True." Ware nodded. "Have you made any plans yet?"

David glanced at him warily. "Plans?"

"Come now." That old smile crossed Ware's face again. "I cannot believe you intend to sit and wait for Bow Street to sort matters out."

"Er . . . Perhaps." David left it vague on purpose. Ware seemed to understand. His grin widened.

"I knew you would not disappoint." He got to his feet. "Someday, I do hope you write your memoirs. No doubt it would make very enlightening reading."

"Alarming reading, you mean." David ran his hands over his hair ruefully. "I should be declared a terrible example to all young bucks. It would kill my stepmother."

Ware grinned. "No doubt. But I should enjoy reading it all the same." He took his leave, and David went back to his plans.

They left London during a pounding rain, with Anthony Hamilton's help. Of all his friends, David judged Hamilton to be the one who could keep their departure secret. He had never been entirely certain Bow Street was following him, but it seemed wise not to take the chance. So David arranged for Hamilton to drive them to a posting inn on the outskirts of London where he had hired a carriage. From there they would set off on their search.

David realized Hamilton was studying Vivian with interest, though conversation was limited due to the rain and she said almost nothing. At the inn he jumped down into the rain and handed her down from Hamilton's carriage, directly into the one waiting for them. Hamilton stepped down beside him as his driver retrieved the luggage.

His friend's eyes followed her. "You once told me it would end with me facing a vicar or a pistol."

"The vicar is no longer a possibility," David told him. "Not with her."

Something that could only be a smirk spread across his friend's face. "Ah."

David nodded. "My thanks for your help."

"My pleasure," said Hamilton, sounding amused.

David just shook his head as he handed up the traveling valises packed with his and Vivian's things. Thoroughly drenched, he paused only to clasp Hamilton's hand for a moment. "Best of luck," his friend said.

David grinned. "Thank you."

"No one ever needed it more," Hamilton added as David stepped into the hired carriage.

David shook his head and closed the door, falling into the seat as the carriage lurched forward. Vivian gave him a questioning look, and he flashed a confident smile. He hoped they were lucky, but either way, they were off.

Vivian had marked four roads as the most likely places to find Flynn. The countryside was unfamiliar to David; usually he drove straight through on his way to or from London, or was driven through while he slept off some revelry. Vivian had a better sense of the land, but even she admitted her knowledge was thin, for a reason.

"We always move around, see," she explained to him over dinner the first night at a busy inn. "It wouldn't do to be recognized. Public houses won't allow known thieves and vagabonds to congregate, or they lose their license to operate. The tavern owners would call the constables on us as quick as anyone."

"But you did more than one robbery on Bromley," he said.

"Aye, and it was a damn foolish thing to do." Her

brows drew together in an annoyed frown. "Flynn refused to move on, just because I suggested it. Folk begin to talk when there's more than one job. And now, no doubt every night watchman and lamplighter will be looking for the Black Duke. Flynn might as well have posted notice he wants to be hanged."

David shrugged. "That wouldn't bother me a bit, as long as we discover him before they do."

Vivian nodded, thinking again of Simon. It wouldn't bother her to see Flynn hang, either, but he'd probably take Simon to the gallows with him. Any pretense of gallantry or nobility would come to an end the instant Flynn realized he was doomed. They simply *had* to find the gang first.

"Tell me about Simon," said David as if he could read her thoughts. "What sort of lad is he?"

"He's sixteen," she said, picking up her spoon and going back to her dinner. Her stew was getting cold while she sat here and moped. "A good boy. He always has been. You mustn't think too ill of him; I'm the one who took to thieving, not Simon. He's dreadful at it."

"Indeed. What is his role in this scheme?"

"Well, he's mostly Flynn's dog," she said apologetically. "He's got charge of the horses. I suppose he might have stolen one or two. He goes with me to set up the jobs, and then takes word back to Flynn and Crum. Crum's the big man. But he's a good heart, Simon has. It's my fault he's in this mess." She sighed.

"Why is that?" David leaned one elbow on the table, watching her with dark attentive eyes.

Vivian flushed. "He was only a child when our mum died. I wanted to keep him with me, and the only way I could do that was to steal. Mother Tate agreed to take

Simon in, too, so long as I stole for her. What chance had Simon then, raised by a fence and a pickpocket?"

"Are you sorry you kept him with you?" David asked. "Do you ever wish you'd handed him over to an orphanage?"

"No," she said before he even finished speaking. "Never."

He lifted one shoulder. "Then you can't blame yourself. You did the only thing you could."

She ducked her head and nodded. Yes, she'd known it was the right thing to do, just because she couldn't have done it any other way. "Luckily I was good at it—picking pockets, I mean. I'm certain Mother Tate wouldn't have kept him for so long if I hadn't been quick-fingered. It was clear from the start that Simon wasn't so good. She sent him out, too, but he couldn't do it. More than once I had to toss his stealings into the river or into an alley and help him get away. He was so bad I almost had to go with him and do it for him." Realizing just how much she was confessing to, for both herself and her brother, Vivian glanced up. "You gave your word not to give him over to the charleys," she said.

A trace of smile bent David's mouth, a smile that didn't reach his eyes. "I did," he agreed. "Did you think I had forgotten?"

"No." Not really. She was just reassuring herself that it had truly happened.

"It will be a pleasure to meet your brother," he said, as if they were going to take tea with Simon tomorrow. "I've never met an incompetent thief."

"You met me," she pointed out.

He laughed. "You, my love, are the most competent of the lot."

"Let's hope I can manage to find them, then."

"Of course we shall," he said. "I have great confidence in you."

It flustered her, this confidence of his. It ought to please her, but somehow it seemed wrong. He was wrong for this, a fine gentleman out looking for thieves. He ought to be back in London, attending the theater instead of helping a pickpocket track her horse thief of a brother. "We must work on your accent," she said to change the subject. "You sound too proper."

David leaned back in his chair, propping one booted foot on the opposite knee. "Nonsense. I shall just grunt and mumble."

"What if you're required to speak? One sensible word from you, and all in hearing will know you're a gentleman."

"Oh, come now," he said, still obviously not concerned. "How difficult can it be? I've been told for years I don't speak like a gentleman."

"You don't sound like a country farmer, either." Vivian scooted to the edge of her chair and swirled the crust of her bread around the inside of the wooden bowl to get the last bit of stew. "This is just another lark to you, isn't it?"

David laughed. "Worried about me? How kind you are." Vivian wiggled her shoulders noncommittally. "Then come here, my vagabond," he said, hooking his boot around one leg of her chair. With a sharp jerk of his foot, he turned her chair to face his, then took hold of the chair arms and dragged it closer. "Teach me."

"Aye, I'll teach you," she muttered with a sharp look. "What do you wish to sound like?"

"Any sort of country bumpkin will do."

"It's an important question," she said tartly. "Do you wish to be Irish?" She let her vowels swell into an Irish lilt. "A Welshman? Cornish farmer? Kentish drover?"

With each query she mimicked the accent she spoke of. "Your accent will determine how people treat you, so mind your choice."

"I say," he said admiringly. "That's quite a useful trick."

Vivian grinned. "Isn't it? The only useful thing to come out of living in St. Giles." Thieves came from everywhere. It wasn't hard for Vivian to hear any number of accents in the rookeries and pick them up for use when she needed them. An Irish maid might steal the apples, but when the outraged merchant caught up to her, he'd only find a Derbyshire farm girl come to sell her own apples in the market.

"I see I'm in the presence of a master." He leaned forward, clasping his hands and resting his elbows on his knees. His face was only inches from her own. "Teach me, then."

Flustered, Vivian shifted in her chair. It was hard to think with his dark eyes fixed on her so intently, and so near. "Say 'ta.'"

"Tuh."

She shook her head. "No, shorter. Ta, not tah."

"Tah."

Vivian took a deep breath and let it out. "Don't you hear the difference? Thou want a shorter sound." To emphasize, she said it in strong Yorkshire dialect.

"You sound like a completely different person," David murmured, his eyes on her lips.

"Aye, that's the point, love." *Ey, tha's th' pooint, luv.*

For a moment he was silent. "I haven't got a chance at this, have I?"

"Yes, you have," she said. "Just listen and say it. 'One ticket to London, please.'"

"Woon ticket tuh Lundon, plase."

She sighed. "Folk will think thou a pillock."

"Hm." His eyes never left her mouth.

Vivian tried to ignore that look and keep her mind on the matter at hand—namely, trying to disguise him even the tiniest bit. Perhaps if she could just get him to clip his words . . . People wouldn't be able to identify his dialect, but they wouldn't think him a London dandy, either. "Try this. When you speak, stop the words short in the back of your throat," she said, laying her finger on his neck to illustrate. "Try to close your throat here—"

"Kiss me," he murmured, leaning forward even more.

"—if you can." She stopped and then laughed helplessly. "This is no time for a kiss!"

"Yes, it is," he whispered, his lips now brushing hers. "It's always time to kiss you." And he did, cutting off her next protest before it could even begin.

Vivian gave in, letting him kiss away her doubts. Who knew how much longer he would kiss her? She had determinedly ignored that question for days now, but could do so no longer. Tomorrow, or the next day, or the day after they would catch up with Flynn. David would have his ring back and put an end to this Black Duke nonsense, but where would that leave *her*?

Even if David were willing to take her back to London with him, there was no future for her there. And chances were, to get the ring back she'd have to bargain with Flynn. Vivian knew Flynn didn't retreat lightly or easily; he would demand a heavy price, especially after she'd been gone for so many weeks from his gang. It hadn't been her fault, at least at first, but Flynn wouldn't care. Vivian doubted he would just hand over the ring, even for a nice fat purse. He'd take her back as well, back to a life of thieving and hiding and lying. Now that she had been away from it for a few weeks, it seemed the cruelest fate imaginable to go back to it.

But what else could she do? Her life wouldn't be worth living if David ended up on the gallows for Flynn's crimes and Simon's crimes and, worst of all, her crimes. Vivian knew she would rather feel the rope about her own neck than know she had let an innocent man—the man she loved—suffer in her place. Thieving had been her lot in life. She would use it this one last time, to get that bloody ring back and save David from being suspected, and then she would suffer the consequences she had only brought upon herself.

So she let David kiss her, and when he pulled her into his lap and cradled her head to hold her there, she only pressed closer. She pushed her hands under his coarse woolen jacket, running her hands over the worn linen shirt, memorizing the feel of his warm, strong body. *I love you*, she told him silently. He smoothed a hand down her cheek, over her shoulder and around to her back, turning her to face him. His hands spanned her waist and he lifted her, settling her again astride his lap, her skirt bunching around her knees. It took him only a few moments to unfasten her sturdy work dress and take it off. Vivian sighed and let her head fall back as he kissed a path down one side of her neck, across the bare skin exposed above her shift, and into the valley between her breasts. It was quite magical, what he could do with a kiss.

"What about your lessons?" she sighed.

"I'm learning a great deal," he murmured against her collarbone. "This is the best lesson I've ever had."

She laughed, draping her arms around his neck. "This is not what I meant to teach you."

His fingers undid the string at her shift neckline. It slipped down her shoulder, and his mouth was there, feather-light. Vivian shivered. "I've accepted the fact that I'm a difficult pupil," he said matter-of-factly. "My tutors used to thrash me weekly."

"They must not have been good teachers."

"Not nearly as good as you are," he said with feeling. Vivian's laugh caught in her throat as he pushed the shift further down. His fingers pulled at the strings of her short corset, and then he pulled the undergarment off, tossing it aside. The untied shift pooled in her lap as she pulled her arms free and wound them around his neck again.

"You're a hopeless case," she said, wiggling closer. His hands cupped her hips and pulled her belly against his. She could feel him growing harder beneath her, and she wiggled a little more, just to see his eyes darken.

"I'm hopeless?" he repeated in that velvet voice that sent shivers down her spine. "I'm not sitting naked in a man's lap, tormenting him past all endurance." His hands were sliding up her thighs, draped over his, and gathering the edge of the shift as he spoke. Vivian smiled, her heart skipping a beat. He made her stomach clench with anticipation when he used that voice.

"I'm not naked."

"Let's remedy that." He slipped the shift over her head, leaving her in only her stockings. "Say, 'kiss me, David,' in that strange accent," he murmured.

"Which one?"

"Welsh," he said. "Cornish. It doesn't matter."

"Kiss me, David," she whispered, and he did. "Kiss me again. And again."

"Demanding wench," he said with a low laugh. "What shall I do next?"

"Make love to me." She cupped his face in her hands. "Please."

The merriment in his face faded, and he took her

hands in his, kissing her knuckles. "You shall never have to beg for that." He carried her to the bed, and did everything she asked him to do, as well as some things she would have never thought to ask for. And as he made her body fairly sing with pleasure, Vivian could only think one thing:

Kiss me again and again, David, for I do love you.

David waited until they were lying in drowsy lassitude, tangled in the bed linens. His conscience, heretofore mute and meek, had asserted itself with sudden vigor, so strongly he couldn't ignore it until the feeling passed. Vivian lay curled in his arm, and he stroked her back. "I want you to stay here tomorrow," he whispered.

She stirred. "Don't be daft," came her sleepy voice.

"It's not safe for you to go along." His hold tightened on her unconsciously. "Don't think I haven't realized how dangerous it is for you to do this."

Her hand slipped free of the sheets, groping for his until she found it and laced her fingers between his. David closed his eyes against the wave of feeling that action caused within him. He couldn't bear to lose her. "You'll need help," she said in the same relaxed tone. "D'you think Flynn will just hand over the ring with a tip of his hat?"

David was silent. He was afraid Flynn would try to take her along with him. He was afraid Flynn would be angry at her prolonged absence and shoot her. He was afraid something, some vague thing he couldn't put his finger on but feared immensely, would happen to endanger Vivian in some way. He knew what Flynn looked like, and was confident he would be able to track the man down once they located him. David wasn't afraid of anything for himself.

But for Vivian . . . he was terrified.

"I would feel better if you stayed here," he tried again.

"David." With a sigh she twisted in his arms to face him. "You don't know what you're doing. Don't rush off on your own like a fool. Flynn would be too happy to put a pistol to your head for ransom, or just to scare you to death." She cupped his cheek in one hand and gave him a sleepy smile. "We've got our plan, aye? Stick to it."

He didn't smile back. "I'm frightened for you."

Something flickered for a moment in her eyes, then she gave a brief laugh. "Me? You're frightened for me? Where was that thought when you were locking me in your house?"

He closed his eyes and rested his forehead against hers. "Swear to me you'll be cautious. I just want to find them, not confront them there on the road with my hands in the air."

"Oh, David." She sighed and touched his mouth with her fingertip. "I know all that. I've done this before, you remember?"

He noticed the Irish brogue slipping back into her speech, bit by bit. He noticed she seemed to grow calmer and more serene even as he began to regret ever suggesting such a plan. What had seemed perfectly justified and thrillingly daring back in his London home suddenly, in a small country inn, began to appear foolhardy and dangerous. What on earth was he thinking, asking a wanted woman to put herself in the middle of danger, over a blasted ring?

He had always been a reckless sort; no danger was too daunting, no adventure too risky. David had risked his neck many times, his fortune many more, and his reputation . . . his reputation had been risked so many times, there wasn't much left to lose at this point. Often it was just the thrill of doing something wicked, something forbidden, that drove him onward. Knowing that he had gotten away with something, even something as small as filching the last tart from the tray when he'd been told he mustn't, had brought an unparalleled rush of energy and excitement.

But now David realized perhaps that thrill had been bolstered by the knowledge, never fully acknowledged but there all the same, that he *would* get away with it. He was a Reece. His father, and then his brother, was the duke of Exeter. His very name was a shield from the consequences of his actions. No matter what he had done, he had never been in any real danger. He could have killed himself in one of his escapades, no doubt, but even then he wouldn't have had to suffer through any consequences of his own death. His fortune would return, thanks to a generous income from his brother, and just in the last few weeks, he had seen how easily he could reclaim his reputation, if he so desired. With a modest effort, David knew he could regain his standing in society, obliterating a lifetime of debauchery and hell-raising.

Vivian didn't have anything like that. If she were arrested and charged with highway robbery, no powerful family would step forward to protect her. David could try, but the rage against thieves was so potent, and justice so swift and severe, that it would be a lost cause. The only way to keep her truly safe was to keep her from being arrested at all, and the best way to do that was for him to take the stagecoach alone.

"Please, Vivian," he whispered.

"Go to sleep," she replied, and wouldn't say another word.

Chapter Eighteen

For five days they rumbled about the English countryside on public stagecoaches. David, much to Vivian's relief, had managed to absorb some of what she said and coarsened his voice and manner. He still wasn't quite rustic; she supposed people might take him for a gentry farmer, or perhaps a prosperous merchant with airs. Either way, no one seemed unduly suspicious of them, and best of all, neither David nor Vivian saw any sign of constables watching the coaches.

They maintained the same pose throughout, David a man of some modest means and Vivian a poor gentlewoman, traveling to and from London. Upon reaching the end of a stage, David would hire a cart and horse, gallantly offering a ride to Vivian. They would circle around, keeping a respectable distance from London's outskirts, until they got to the next coaching inn on Vivian's list. He would let her down well outside of town, so they would arrive independently, and then late at night he would sneak into her room and make love to her, slipping out again before the morning to preserve their attitude of strangers.

It had almost become a version of normalcy for Vivian. Every day she woke alone, met David as though for the first time, allowed him to be increasingly polite and solicitous to her, until finally he slipped into her bed that night. This left her tired during the days, of course. It was hard not to fall asleep on the coach, even rocked and jolted about as she was. Even harder was keeping her composure when David, often seated across from her, gave her sly little looks, as though he were remembering what he had done to her the night before.

The sixth day began no differently. She was stifling a yawn behind one hand when a shot rang out and the coach lurched sideways as the driver reacted. Although she had been waiting for it, hoping for it, Vivian's heart leaped into her throat. This had always been her cue, the moment when her role began in earnest. Today, though, there was more meaning and importance in it.

Under the folds of her skirt, David, seated beside her today, pressed her hand. She longed to squeeze it back, but his hand slid away before she could move. She wet her dry lips, scrupulously keeping her eyes away from him. They didn't know each other—she must remember that—and she needed to keep her mind clear.

"What's that?" asked someone indignantly.

"Highwaymen!"

"Highwaymen?" echoed David. "Surely not."

"As sure as I can see," answered the first man, leaning out the window. "Riding hard after us."

The coach swayed and rocked some more, picking up speed. The man opposite Vivian hung on the straps as he was nearly catapulted off his seat. The interior of the coach was a cacophony of cursing, shouts, and cries for help. David threw out his arm in front of her as they were tossed forward and back by the coach's motion, to keep her from being thrown to the floor.

"What's going on?" roared one passenger.

"The bloody driver's tryin' to outrun them," shouted

another, risking life and limb by leaning out the window again to see. Vivian clutched at David's restraining arm gratefully, instinctively slipping back into her frightened widow pose. After so many weeks away from it, the terror of the robbery was fresh and new to her. Even though she knew who pursued them, it had been a long time since Vivian had truly appreciated how frightening it felt to be robbed.

David was handling it beautifully. Of course he, too, was prepared this time, but Vivian honestly couldn't see a difference between his reaction this time and that other time. His mouth was set in a firm line, his eyes narrowed and watchful. He looked braced for anything and slightly put out at the inconvenience of it all. Unwittingly Vivian saw again his body lying sprawled in the dirt, blood trickling down his face from where Simon had struck him. She swallowed and let go of his arm.

Another shot rang out, directly above the coach from the sound of it. The man who had been leaning out the window jerked his head back in with a startled oath, and the coach began to slow.

"Why are we stopping?" demanded one man.

"Because they've caught us," said the man who'd been watching out the window. "Not much sense in racing to our deaths, now that they're near enough to hit the driver."

"I say we fight them," warbled a young man in the corner, who'd been a sickly shade of pale green just a few minutes ago. "I don't fancy being robbed by highwaymen, I don't . . ."

"All right, then," said David. "Draw your pistols, lad, and aim well, for there's more than one of them." He spoke in the coarser tone she had coached him in, and Vivian felt a thrill of pride, along with a little flutter in her stomach at the memory of how he had distracted her from the lesson. His retort silenced the young man, and all the passengers fell silent as the vehicle shuddered to a stop.

Vivian clasped her hands together, her palms perspiring inside her gloves. The door swung open. Crum, as usual, pointed his pistol at them. "Out," he muttered. Purposely, Vivian kept her head down. Her mind had blanked. She had brought it off this far, but everything depended on the next few minutes.

As usual, Crum stepped into the doorway of the coach and began throwing down the luggage. As usual, Simon stepped forward with his sack. Behind him, Vivian caught sight of Flynn. Also as usual, he still sat on his horse, but now he was wearing a large plumed hat, the white feather bright in the darkness. The bloody fool, she thought in contempt, making a spectacle of himself. As the other passengers began grudgingly dropping their valuables into Simon's bag, Flynn spurred his horse and trotted over to them.

"Good evening, gents," he said in his rusty voice, sweeping off the ridiculous hat. The signet ring on his finger flashed ostentatiously. "And my lady," he added. Vivian kept her face averted. She wanted to speak to Simon first, before Flynn or Crum had a chance to recognize her. "My thanks for contributin' to the coffers o' the Black Duke."

"Scoundrel," muttered the young man beside her. Flynn heard, for he chuckled.

"Aye, that and more!" With another grand gesture, he wheeled his horse around and circled to the front of the coach, no doubt to subject the driver and his men to the same show.

Simon turned from taking the thin man's watch and purse. "Any jewels, mum?" he asked.

Vivian finally lifted her face and stared grimly at him as she opened her reticule and added a few coins to the bag. Simon glanced at her, then glanced back again. His eyes widened. She compressed her lips; don't say anything, she willed. He blinked, and for half a second a smile crossed his face, his teeth white in his blackened visage. She glared intensely at him. He coughed, shuffled backward, and thrust the sack at David. "Valuables, guv," he barked, barely looking at David.

Vivian breathed a little easier. There. She'd let him know. He would tell Flynn, and then she could meet them later. With luck, she could persuade Flynn to give back the blasted ring, and have it back to David tonight. And then he could prove his innocence, and she could persuade Simon to leave Flynn. One way or another they had to get away from this life. And then . . .

"Hold!" A new voice rang across the clearing. Simon spun around, his mouth falling open. Flynn jerked his head up. Crum looked up from kicking open trunks and running his dirty hands through them. Vivian's heart fell into her shoes. A number of well-armed mounted men were circling them, pistols out. The Bow Street horse patrol, it seemed, had finally caught the Black Duke.

For a few minutes confusion reigned. Flynn shot off both his pistols, shouting at the top of his lungs, but one of the mounted men put an end to that by shooting Flynn's horse. The animal went down with a scream. Flynn jumped free and tried to run, but was quickly caught.

More men moved toward Crum and Simon. At the first report of Flynn's pistol, Crum took to his heels and ran with a speed Vivian had never guessed he could achieve, vanishing into the shadows. Half a dozen horsemen thundered after him. Simon made no effort to flee. He whirled to face Vivian again, his eyes incredulous, but her expression must have indicated her alarm and dismay. Simon's face relaxed in defeat, and he bowed his head as the men approached, his pistol hanging limply from his fingers. He surrendered without resistance, and was led away, across the road to where Flynn was scuffling with the constables. He didn't look back.

Once rescued from the highwaymen, the passengers broke into an excited babble. David took advantage of the uproar to turn to her. "Are you hurt?" he said in a whisper. Vivian gave a barely perceptible shake of her head. He looked relieved. "Not quite what we planned," he said under his breath. "What now?"

Vivian didn't say anything; she didn't know what they should do next. One man detached himself from the crowd of constables and horsemen, and came over to them, hands up, gesturing for quiet. Everyone quieted quickly, waiting with palpable eagerness for the word. "Gentlemen, madam," announced the man pretentiously, "we have caught the Black Duke."

A murmur went through the passengers. Standing on tiptoe, Vivian glanced toward the prisoners. She saw Flynn and Simon, arms tied behind their backs. Someone shoved Simon, knocking him to his knees in the mud. Her brother slumped over, hiding his face, and she swallowed a moan of anguish for him. She'd put a bullet in Flynn's black heart for dragging a boy along on this dangerous a job. Her eyes caught on the constables then, standing to the side. They were talking to a tall, thin man who'd been on the coach. That man was gesturing wildly with both hands at the other passengers, and Vivian knew, with a blinding flash of realization, what he was telling them.

She caught David's coat sleeve. This might be her last chance to speak to him. Crowded together, he too had been looking around, but bent at her second tug on his arm. "Thank you," she said softly.

A slight frown creased his face. "Don't worry," he said distractedly. "I mean to have a word with the constable, about your brother."

Vivian gave a tiny shake of her head even as her heart twisted. He thought she was worried about her brother, and was already trying to help. Darling David didn't realize what she was saying. "I didn't mean that," she said. From the corner of her eye she saw the constables turning to look their way, scanning the passengers as their planted man continued to speak and point right at her. "I meant . . . for everything else. For the happiest weeks of my life."

That caught his attention. "It was my pleasure," he said, surprised, "but can't we discuss it later?"

Her laugh caught in her throat. "Perhaps," she said wistfully. "I hope." But the constables were now striding in her direction. She pulled at David's arm again, drawing him nearer still. "But if not . . . it meant more to me than you could ever know. Remember that, please?"

"I'll never forget it," he said, sounding thoroughly bewildered. "But let me—"

"Good-bye," she whispered.

"I say, miss." The biggest constable shouldered his way through the knot of passengers and took her arm roughly. "Mr. Spikes is wantin' a word."

"Here, now," David protested as the burly man hauled Vivian after him. "What the devil do you think you're doing?"

The man didn't stop. "Mr. Spikes wants a word," he repeated. The other passengers scurried out of his way, and for some reason Vivian allowed herself to be pulled along without protest. David took a step after them, only to find that another of the constable's men was blocking his way.

"Let me by," he said.

"Can't," said the man, who looked stupid but strong. "Mr. Spikes'll have his word."

David pressed his lips together and watched, determined not to leave her. To his astonishment, Mr.

Spikes's word consisted of irons locked around her wrists. "Stand aside," he said to the man in a stern voice.

The man laid a pistol along his forearm. All the constables were thrumming with excitement, and belatedly David realized the thrill of catching the Black Duke was blinding them to all else. "Stay where ye are, guv," he replied. "Mr. Spikes's orders."

David fumed. Mr. Spikes would suffer for this. Dragging a woman off in irons! A flicker of alarm crossed his mind. Vivian had been among the passengers; they couldn't possibly think she was one of the thieves. Could they? It had been as clear as day to David that her brother had recognized Vivian, but could anyone else in the coach have observed it? At all costs, David mustn't give her away now. He tried again with the man.

"Who is this Spikes, who's taking a woman away in irons?" he asked, trying to sound merely outraged at the principle. "Some sort of constable you have. Look, they've shackled her legs, too. No man could stand by and see a woman treated so badly."

The man didn't even look. "Mr. Spikes tells us he'll handle it his way, and so he shall. If he's abusin' a woman, no doubt but that he's got cause. Just bide your time, sir, and all will be well."

David continued to frown, watching as Vivian was handed up to the seat of a wagon. The male prisoners were already in the bed of the wagon, trussed and on their bellies. Vivian turned, and David almost shoved past the idiot in front of him to go to her, appearances be damned. She looked frightened. For the first time he saw fear in her face. Did she know, he wondered. But of course she did. That's why she had said good-bye.

"Well, I intend to have a word with the local magistrate about it," he said loudly. "It's not proper and not right, shackling a woman."

"That woman's one of them," said the man who had announced the capture of the Black Duke. He was fairly preening with pride, and puffed out his chest as the passengers all turned to him again. "We got them, we did, the Black Duke and two of his accomplices."

"The lady was a passenger on the coach," David protested. "Just as we were." The other passengers murmured behind him, but David ignored them.

"She was an accomplice, and we've got her," retorted the constable. "One of our men was on the coach, and he saw the signal she gave to the outlaws." He tapped the side of his nose smugly. "We're not fooled by a pretty face, no, sir."

Dismay kept David silent as the rest of the passengers all began to chatter at once, and the constable went on congratulating himself. Holy Christ. What was he to do now? Say too much, and he might make things worse for her. Say nothing, and watch her be driven to her hanging anyway. What was he to do to help her, he wondered in anguish. What could he do? If Marcus were here . . . Perhaps Ware could intercede, although these were not his lands. Perhaps David could borrow some money from Marcus's funds and bribe the man to let her go . . . But if he failed, her situation would be worse, and he would have lost his chance to save her.

For what seemed an eternity, the constables kept them there, standing in the deepening dusk, writing down names and statements by torchlight. David was frantic with fury by the time they got to him. "I think it's dreadful what you did to that poor woman," he said right off.

The constable grunted. "No doubt." He looked up, his sallow face gleaming with sweat. "Fancied her, eh? Two others told me you had your eyes on her."

"How dare you," said David. "Such a quiet lady. I'm sure I never did anything improper—"

"Right. Name, sir?"

David swallowed a furious retort. "John Palmer," he said, giving the false name he'd been using.

"Direction?"

"Kent," he said. "Near Maidstone."

The man's head bobbed slightly as he made a note. "Business?"

"I say, what's the reason for these questions? Am I a suspect?"

"No." The constable looked up. "Ought you be, sir?"

David's indignation was real. "Of course not! I was robbed! Of fifteen shillings, by a man who seems to have run wild about these parts for some time."

"Not anymore," said the man with malicious satisfaction. "He'll not run anywhere no more. What was your business, sir?"

Unsettled, David said the first thing that came into his head. "I am on business for my employer, the duke of Exeter."

The constable's pencil paused. "The duke of Exeter?" he repeated.

"Yes, and I shall be sure to tell him of this."

The man put away his pencil. "Yes, sir. You're free to go."

"I should hope so." David glared at him. "What will happen to her now?"

Impatience sparked in his eyes, but the constable replied civilly enough. "She'll go with the others, to Newgate. Bow Street will sort them out quick enough. You're free to go, sir."

That was it. There was nothing he could say now. David jerked his head in a nod and made himself walk away, without the slightest idea what he would do next.

Chapter Nineteen

David rode back to London, proceeding directly to Exeter House when he reached town. All through the journey he had tried desperately to think of a way to rescue Vivian, and had come up with absolutely nothing within reason. He had a feeling he would need to drink a lot of wine to dull the pain in his chest and quiet the relentless pounding of his thoughts, and Marcus had by far the better cellar. He tossed the reins of his horse to a stable boy and went inside the house, his steps dragging. Somehow this was all his fault. Somehow, he had mucked things up yet again, only this time he hadn't put himself in the muddle, he'd put Vivian there. He of all people had known how precarious her position was, and yet he'd pushed her right back into the path of trouble and suspicion. David had never felt lower in his life. If he could have exchanged places with her and put his own neck in the noose, he would have. Didn't he deserve it?

He paused at the bottom of the stairs. There was a lot more activity in the household than there should have been for this time of night, he finally noticed. He turned to the butler, who hovered a step behind him. "What's about, Harper?"

Harper bowed. "Her Grace the dowager duchess has returned to town, my lord."

David almost groaned out loud. Just bloody wonderful, his stepmother was here. What on earth had brought her to town now? She was supposed to be at Ainsley Park with Celia, spoiling Molly. Rosalind was the last person David wanted to see at the moment, Rosalind who had always stood up for him and believed in him and trusted him, even when he didn't deserve it. Like now. If she tried to console and comfort him that it wasn't his fault, that there was nothing he could do now, David thought he might have to exile himself from England.

He slunk into Marcus's study, hoping she wouldn't find him there. Perhaps he ought to have told Harper not to reveal his presence. He carried the decanter of whiskey and a glass to the desk, hoping the drink would spur his brain into some useful course of action, or if not, into a stupor so he wouldn't remember. His chances of the latter were much better, he thought grimly, pouring a full glass.

He winced at the knock on the door, and then his stepmother swept in before he could say anything. "David, there you are," she cried, bearing down on him. He tried to muster a smile, getting to his feet. "I would have written that I was coming to town, but I simply couldn't wait," Rosalind went on after kissing his cheek. "Lady Winters wrote and told me the happy news, and I could not contain myself."

David had no idea what she was talking about, and wished she would go. He really wasn't fit company at the moment. "Oh?" he said vaguely.

She beamed at him. "And you shan't tell me it's another of your larks, for Lady Winters was quite specific. I thought you and your brother would leave me waiting forever, and here both of you, gone in the same year! Oh, David, I am so very happy for you."

David clutched the glass of whiskey and stared at her, completely befuddled.

"So." She seated herself on the sofa across from the desk. "Shall you tell me about her over tea?"

"Her?" he repeated.

"The woman you were with at the theater a fortnight ago," Rosalind said with a laugh. "The theater! If I'd known, I would have persuaded Marcus to give you his box years ago! Oh, David, I do believe marriage will be the saving of you. I must confess, since your father died, there have been moments when I worried about you. Of course young men must sow their wild oats, but at times, particularly earlier this year, I did worry that you would never settle down." A servant tapped on the door, and Rosalind stopped long enough for the maid to bring in tea. David felt as though he'd already consumed the bottle of whiskey, and gave his head a small shake to clear it. The servant left, and Rosalind beckoned him to her side with a bright smile. "Come, tell me all."

He went, warily, still holding his glass and the decanter. "I confess, I know not what to tell."

"What is her name?" Rosalind prompted, pouring a cup of tea. "Lady Winters didn't know her."

Because she was a thief from the rookeries, no doubt. David gave a bitter laugh. "No, she didn't." He took a large swallow of his drink.

"Well, what is her name?" Rosalind asked again.

David stared into his glass. "Her name is Vivian."

"A lovely name. And her family?"

A band of outlaws. "She has a brother," he mumbled.

"I see. And I don't suppose I've ever chanced to meet either of them?" She gave a tinkling laugh.

Were you ever robbed on the Bromley stage? "I doubt it," David said.

Rosalind huffed. "David, you're being infuriating. Tell me about her! I want to know everything."

"There's not much to tell," he said, trying to avoid the question. "I'm rather surprised you came to London just because I was at the theater with a woman. Gossip must be dear these days, if Lady Winters found it so exciting."

"It is true Lucretia Winters loves a bit of gossip, but she doesn't make things up out of whole cloth." She shook her finger teasingly at him. "Don't try to fool me that you weren't there, young man."

David drank some more. "You're right. I was in fact at the theater with a woman." A woman who promptly unearthed a copy of the play from his unused library and read it again, word by word, because she thought it was funny.

"I am sure there is more than you are telling me," Rosalind said. "Come, David. I would not have come all the way to London if I'd merely heard you were escorting a woman to the theater. That, in itself, would not be terribly interesting. But Lady Winters said it appeared to be more than your usual . . ." She stopped short, delicately avoiding saying that David usually escorted courtesans or married women, when he escorted anyone at all. "What I truly came to London to discover is why you were looking at her as though you couldn't take your eyes off her."

Because I couldn't, thought David hopelessly. *And now I may never see her again.*

He drained his glass. "You've never met her, Rosalind," he confessed. "You wouldn't have. She's not a lady."

"That is not a problem," said his stepmother without missing a beat. "Hannah was born a commoner and is a wonderful duchess."

David sighed. "No, Rosalind. Not a lady in any sense of the word. Her mother was a farm girl, and her father was most likely an Army captain who never returned from Spain. Her brother is her only family, and he's currently in jail for robbing stagecoaches. Which, by the by, is where Vivian herself is, thanks to my bungling. And if I can't scrape up some wits soon, she'll hang with him, because I met her when she helped him rob the coach I took to London."

Rosalind regarded him in silence for a moment, her mouth agape. Then she set down her teacup, picked up the decanter, and poured a generous amount of the liquor into her tea. "I see," she said in an unnaturally bright voice, lifting the cup with trembling fingers. "How . . . unusual."

David's lips twisted. "Isn't it?"

For a moment there was silence as Rosalind gulped her very potent tea and David drank the last of the whiskey in his glass.

"Good heavens." Rosalind set the cup down at last. "Indeed. I never expected . . . That is to say . . ." Her voice cracked, and failed. "David," she said a moment later, very carefully, "what have you been up to?"

"I didn't do it deliberately," he said instinctively.

She waved one hand. "I didn't ask why. I asked *what*."

He sighed. "One of my chestnuts went lame on my journey from Ainsley Park to London. I took a place on the stagecoach in order to reach town in time."

"In time for what?"

"Marcus had arranged for his banker and solicitors to meet me and go over his concerns," David said. "Did he not tell you?"

"Oh, yes, yes," said his stepmother, looking a little surprised. "You took the public stage. My word. And then?"

"It was robbed." David stopped; that wasn't quite "what then." "She was, I thought, merely another passenger. She was so lovely, and when the highwaymen were collecting our purses, she had only one shilling to give them. One of them knocked her down, and I . . ." He lifted one hand and then let it fall. "They took the signet ring Marcus gave me, and I was determined to get it back. I called on every pawnbroker I knew—"

"How many?"

"At least two dozen," he said, somewhat ashamed.

She gasped. "So many! But why?"

"I had need of funds, from time to time."

"Marcus—" she began, but David shook his head.

"I would have gone to the Fleet before asking Marcus for money. And it was a near thing, at times." She looked as though he'd struck her. Perhaps he had. David knew his stepmother had a special affection for him; he knew she had stood up for him when no one else had, had believed in him when no one else did. He knew she was misguided and wrong many of those times. "I've been every bit as wicked as people say, Rosalind. Why do you think Bentley chose me for his plot?"

"Do not speak that name to me, ever again," she ordered. "He is no longer family."

"He's not an idiot, though," said David, slumping lower on the sofa. "He chose well. I gambled a lot, and lost often. I was bull-headed and arrogant about it, and I deserved what he did to me."

His stepmother's lips parted in silent surprise, and she looked at him in wonder.

"But I was determined to get that ring back. It seemed shameful to repay Marcus by losing the thing and not even tending to business on a timely schedule. One pawnbroker sent word that he'd seen the ring, and would not only help me get it back, but help catch the thief who tried to sell it. So I went, thinking I would solve my own problem and remedy some social ills at the same time.

"But it was she, Vivian, who tried to sell the ring. I dragged her back to my home and locked her up—"

"David!" gasped Rosalind. He nodded.

"I thought it would frighten her to death and she'd simply give me the ring." A smile lit his face as he recalled how wrong that had been. "But she didn't have it and refused to get it, and I refused to let her go until she did, so there we were."

Rosalind pressed her fingertips to her forehead. "I fail to see . . ."

"She's lovely," he said softly. "Beautiful. And clever. With a sharp wit, and spirit, and charm."

"Oh, dear." She poured herself more tea, without whiskey this time. "A common . . . thief."

"There's nothing common about her," he said, and meant it.

She sighed, shaking her head, and sipped her tea for several moments. "Then, why, pray, is she back in prison?"

"Bow Street came to call on me," he said, continuing the story. "Someone was robbing stagecoaches wearing a gold signet ring and calling himself the Black Duke. They made it clear they were considering arresting me for it."

Her eyes narrowed. "That is inconceivable."

He grimaced. "No, not really. I doubt they'd have hanged me—yet—but I didn't fancy going to prison at all. Bow Street had clearly decided I was the villain, and they weren't looking very hard for another. So I decided to go catch the fellow myself, at least long enough to retrieve my ring, and that would be the end of it. There would be no more Black Duke robberies, and thus no reason for anyone to arrest me. It seemed a good plan."

"Oh, David," she said on a sigh.

"I convinced Vivian to help me find them," he plowed onward, heaping the guilt on his own head. "I suspected the man calling himself the Black Duke was one of the highwaymen who had stolen my ring with her. I dragged her off an a foolhardy mission to find a notorious criminal."

"But—the pawnbrokers," said Rosalind distastefully.

"Never recovered the ring. I gave it up for lost, and rather forgot about it." He paused, wishing now that he had just let it go. If he hadn't gone looking for the bloody ring, none of this would have happened. "But we went after it, and not only did we find the Black Duke, Bow Street found him, too. And in the uproar, they took Vivian away with the rest of the highwaymen, one of whom is her brother. They are headed for Newgate, and will probably be hanged in short order. And that is the sum of my latest, pudding-headed, scrape."

"Oh, David," she said after a moment, her voice full of dismay. He threw up one hand to stop her.

"It is my fault. All mine. I have led a woman to her death. I ought to have let Bow Street arrest me. It would have been better that way." He closed his eyes. "I took her to the theater because she'd never been. She was enchanting that night, delighted by everything."

He let his head fall back, staring bleakly at the ceiling.

Rosalind murmured a few words, and then mercifully left him. Even she didn't feel sorry for him anymore. David was glad.

For a while he just sat, staring blindly upward. His head hurt. It felt as though a drum had begun beating inside his skull, urging him on toward something. He must do something. He just didn't know what.

With a lurch he flung himself off the sofa. He strode through the hall and out of the house, through the streets until he reached his own house. He climbed the steps, feeling a twinge in his bad leg again, only to almost run into Anthony Hamilton, just departing.

"Reece." Hamilton bowed his head, his sharp eyes taking in David's rough clothing. "I called to see how the excursion ended."

"It's not ended." David led the way inside, Hamilton following. Hobbs took his guest's hat and gloves again, as well as David's own cap, without a word. Limping slightly, David made his way to his drawing room, taking a seat in front of the fire with a small grimace of relief.

"What remains?" Hamilton took the opposite seat, helping himself to a glass of brandy from the tray still sitting on a nearby table. "You said the excursion is not yet ended."

"We found the Black Duke."

Hamilton's eyebrow arched. "Excellent work. I rated that possibility at only one chance in three."

"The Bow Street horse patrol also found him, at the same moment."

"Ah." Hamilton sat back. "Who would have thought it."

"Beastly timing," David agreed. "It could hardly have been worse. And in the excitement, they took Vivian away with the rest of the highwaymen."

"The rest of the highwaymen," repeated Hamilton, laying a slight stress on the second word. "Yes, I see now."

"Yes, yes, she's a thief," David said impatiently. "Or she was. How else was she to survive? If you say prostitution, I shall cut your throat." Hamilton merely smiled and shook his head. "Now they've gone and taken her off to Newgate, or will in the morning, and I've got to think of a way to get her free."

"Pose as your brother again," suggested Hamilton. "Exeter could get a murderer out of Newgate."

David grunted. "No."

"Why not?" asked his friend in mild surprise. "Ought to be easy enough to do."

"Enough people know he's on the Continent." David continued to scowl at the fire. Vivian certainly wouldn't have a fire tonight, nor the soft feather mattress he knew she adored. "And I don't like it."

"What has that got to do with anything?" There was a clink of crystal as Hamilton poured himself more brandy. "Do you want the girl or not?"

David did. He wanted the girl more than anything he had ever wanted before, and he was mortally afraid he would fail her, when he was her only chance. But he didn't want to pose as his brother again. He'd only done that once when it mattered, and it had almost gotten him killed. He couldn't afford that this time, for Vivian's sake; he was her only hope. The burden of that phrase sat on David's head, and heart, like a giant boulder. He couldn't recall any other moment in his life when he had felt such a responsibility, and such a helplessness regarding it. "I'll have to think of another way," he muttered.

Anthony Hamilton leaned back, stretching his legs out toward the hearth. "Bribery? Trickery? A prison break? What other choices do you have?"

David frowned at the implication. "It has to be legal," he said. "I can't get her out, only to have the Runners swarm London looking for her. We'd both end up in Newgate, and as you have already pointed out with exceedingly helpful clarity, Marcus is hundreds of miles away and unable to save my neck yet again."

"Indeed," said Hamilton in tones of wounded surprise. "It seems to me then you might as well just walk into the place and ask for her back."

David's scowl slowly eased. The instinctive rude retort faded from his lips. Like an oracle from on high, a plan sprang to life in his mind. He'd been thinking too hard, he realized; the best plan was not complicated, but very, very simple. He thought quickly, trying to catch any fatal flaws before he committed himself to a course of action, but didn't see one. There were flaws, to be sure, but none fatal—he thought. He hoped. He didn't really have much time to think of something better, but he must use his head this time. "Yes," he said slowly. "I think I might just do that."

Chapter Twenty

Vivian sat on the floor, curled into the corner of the holding cell. She, Simon, and Flynn were locked in a small, filthy country jail, apparently for the night. The constables and the horsemen, who were, she believed, from Bow Street, had departed in a roaring chorus of self-congratulation, no doubt for the local pub. Vivian had feared they would be taken straight to Newgate and hanged at the dawn, but this was only slightly better. The floor was wet, and she could hear the wretched scratching of mice nearby. She thought they were at the other end of the narrow room, in the pile of straw covered with a thin blanket that passed for a bed. She refused to go near it. After so many nights in a warm soft bed and no mice to be seen or heard, she preferred the hard cold floor to that vermin-infested straw.

She wondered where David was, and what he was doing. When they locked the irons on her wrists and ankles, then tossed her onto the wagon like a hog for market, she hadn't been able to look back, not wanting to feel the shame of being seen like that. Now she wished she had. It might be the last she ever saw of

David, and she oughtn't to have let pride steal those last few glimpses from her. She closed her eyes against the squalor of her current situation and tried to summon up the memory of last night instead. Last night, when she had been warm and secure and loved.

"Viv?" She opened her eyes at the soft query. Simon sounded tired and worried. She scrambled across the floor to the wall that divided the holding cells, and ran her fingers over it, looking for a hole. "Are you there?" His voice cracked. "Are you awake?"

"I'm here," she whispered back, locating a seam where mortar had crumbled away between the bricks. "Are you hurt?"

His sigh was faint through the wall. "Not compared to what comes next." Vivian shuddered. There was a scuffling on the other side. "Viv?" he asked, slightly louder. "What are they going to do with us?"

She ground her teeth together, thinking about what to say. Her heart ached for him; he sounded scared, but he was trying to be brave. She had failed them both, but especially him. Simon never would have joined Flynn's band if she hadn't brought him into it when he was a boy. And if she had managed to escape David's house earlier, she might have found her brother and warned him of the danger and gotten him away. "I don't know, Si," she said at last, hating that she had nothing else to say. If only David . . . But no. What could he possibly have done?

He was quiet for a long moment. "Where've you been, Viv?" he finally asked. She closed her eyes and rested her forehead against the wall. The stone was rough and cold. "That bloke, he was on the other job, wasn't he," Simon went on when she said nothing. "The one I hit. The time I knocked you down." His voice cracked again, in anguish. "He caught you, didn't he?"

Vivian sighed. "In a way," she said softly. Caught her, and caught her heart. "He's a good sort," she added, not wanting Simon to worry. "He didn't hurt me."

"I'm sorry, Viv," her brother whispered back. "If I hadn't been such a sapskull, I wouldn't have taken his ring. You were right, I shouldn't have done it. Aw, Viv, I've gone and got us all killed!"

"Simon, it was a small mistake, and you haven't gotten us killed," she said firmly. "We're still talking, aren't we? Dead people don't talk, so we can't be dead." Whether that would still be true tomorrow, she wasn't sure, and didn't mention. "It doesn't matter now that you took his ring." She paused. "Flynn's got it, I expect? What happened after I . . . left?"

"Aye, Flynn kept the ring," said Simon. "He fancied it, you see? So he took to wearing it, and admiring it . . . Well, you always knew he weren't too clever, but he started telling people he was a duke's bastard, a proper gentleman, just on the wrong side of the blanket. Crum, he didn't care, because Flynn took to paying for ale and such when he was wearing that ring."

"What did he do to you?" she wanted to know.

"Nothing he hadn't done before," said Simon, avoiding the question. "It didn't matter. I was sore sick about you, though. I feared the bawds had got you, or you'd been murdered by some ruffian. And Flynn wouldn't let me go to look for you, nor would he send Crum. He said you'd run off and taken the profit for yourself and we were well rid of you." In spite of herself Vivian scowled. She and Simon might end on the gallows, but at least Flynn would, too.

It was cold comfort, but solace nonetheless to her vengeful heart. Simon's voice dropped. "I missed you, Viv."

Guilt speared her. "I missed you, too," she replied, trying not to think about the theater, the long days exploring David's library, the long nights spent in David's bed.

"So that cull," he said, homing in on the topic she didn't know how to discuss. "He didn't hurt you, you say; what did he do?"

Thinking hard, and trying not to grow maudlin at the same time, Vivian shifted. Tiny feet skittered nearby, and she sprang back to her feet, shaking out her skirts before kneeling down by the crack in the wall again. "He caught me trying to sell the goods, and said he wouldn't let me go until I returned his ring." But then he had let her go. At any time in the last fortnight, Vivian knew she could have walked out of the house, and he wouldn't have stopped her . . . or at least not on account of his ring.

"So why'd you turn up on the stage with him?" Simon asked.

Vivian sighed. "It's complicated, Simon."

"You let him hump you, didn't you." It wasn't a question.

Vivian bristled. "Don't you speak to me like that! Mind your tongue, Simon!"

"It's true, isn't it," he shot back. "When they put the irons on you, he argued with the charleys. A man don't argue over a filching mort for no reason."

"Well, he's gone now, and it's not your concern," she said, brutally putting down the small thrill of happiness that David had made some effort to help her. But of course there had been nothing he could do.

"It would've been bloody useful to have his help," Simon mumbled. "A flash cove like that ought to have the ready to spring us."

"Aye, and why should he? So you can hit him again?"

"I wouldn't knock him around if he got us out of here," Simon retorted. Then he heaved a sigh. "I'm just . . . Well, I'm not scared, you ken; just a bit nervous, is all."

Vivian gave a dry laugh. "I'm scared."

There was a pause. "You are?"

"Bloody scared enough to cry," she admitted. "It's my fault you're here, Si. Mum told me to look out for you, and look where I brought you. Into a gang of no-account ruffians without enough wits to rob a coach properly. And now . . . Well, I haven't got a plan just yet, but I don't know what to do. Flynn went and made certain they'd be quick to tie the hangman's rope, and I don't know how to stall them until I can think of a way out." She sighed. "So, aye, I'm scared."

A long silence was her only answer. Vivian leaned against the wall, exhausted. What was the point in consoling Simon when she really didn't see any hope for them? In all the tight spots she'd ever been in, Vivian had always refused to give in to the despair and panic. That only ensured a bad ending. So long as she kept her calm and her wits, she always thought she had a chance—until now. She was tired. Her brain felt sluggish and fogged. She'd gotten soft, sleeping in a warm, cozy bed, because now she felt stiff and cold and so miserable she wanted to cry. Something ran across the toe of her shoe, and she kicked it in frustration. Let the ruddy mice wait until she was actually dead before they nibbled at her.

"Where's Flynn?" she whispered, when she couldn't bear the silence any longer. "Si?" Nothing. "Simon?"

"He's in another cell," mumbled her brother. She heard a faint snuffle. "He's likely proud, being treated like a real duke, and all . . ." Vivian wanted to laugh, incredibly. "He was talking at me through the wall for a bit, but he's sound asleep now," Simon went on. "I can hear him snoring."

Just like always. She shook her head. "What about Crum?"

"Don't know. He took off like a rabbit, didn't he?" Simon gave a shaky, choking laugh. "Back to Alice, probably."

That was fine with Vivian. If the constables never caught Crum, she wouldn't care. Alice needed him. At least they all wouldn't suffer for Flynn's idiocy. "Get some sleep, Simon," she said gently.

"What for?" He snuffled again, and her heart clenched. He was crying. "I expect we'll get enough sleep tomorrow, and the day after, and every day after that."

Another truth she couldn't counter. She hunched her shoulders and propped herself against the wall more securely. When the mice ran past again, she didn't move.

It looked bleak indeed. She at least had had a taste of heaven before the end; her poor brother had not.

"I'm sorry, Simon," she whispered again. "So sorry."

More sniffles, and a scraping noise. "Me, too, Viv," came her brother's voice, a little louder than before. "Me, too."

Chapter Twenty-one

David found the Moresham jail without much difficulty. He pulled up his horse, and Harris, the Exeter coachman, brought the Exeter town coach in all its lumbering glory to a halt behind him. David had judged it a necessary part of the show he intended to put on, but couldn't bear to be trapped inside it. He studied the building that held Vivian. It was an old dingy building with stone walls and small windows. It was certain to be damp and cold inside. David dismounted, handing the reins to one of the footmen who sprang off the back of the coach. He glanced at the man climbing down from the coach.

"Do you remember what we discussed?"

Mr. Adams shook his head eagerly. "Yes, sir. Every word."

"Good." David took a deep breath. "Let's to it, then."

He paused in front of the coach, tugging at his gloves. Adams handed him a walking stick. Then David walked up to the door of the jail and began rapping as loudly as he could.

After several minutes it opened, revealing a pudgy,

yawning constable scratching his belly. "What the bloody hell do you want?" he complained. His barely-open eyes were bloodshot and his breath reeked of ale. David judged it had been a night of celebration.

"You are the constable, I presume." David leaned elegantly on his walking stick.

The man blinked at him a few more times. "Aye, sir, that I am, sir. Constable Chawley."

"Excellent." David made no attempt to hurry things along, letting his appearance and manner work on the fellow. The man's eyes flitted around, taking in the heavy town coach, the liveried footmen, and Adams standing a respectful step behind David. He noticed the man's eyes lingering on one point for a moment; the crest on the coach door, no doubt. The constable's throat worked, and he gave a little bow.

"How can I serve you, sir?"

David arched one brow. "Must I discuss it on the front step?"

Chawley jumped. "Aye! I mean, nay. Right this way, sir." He held the door open and David strolled inside, Adams at his heels. Chawley trotted around in front of them, hitching up his trousers as he went, and showed them into a small office.

David took a seat without waiting to be invited. Chawley, now flushed, repeated his earlier question. "How can I serve you, sir?"

"You have something of mine, I believe."

The constable's mouth opened, flapping once, twice, like a fish's. "I'm sure not, sir," he said in a tone that was not certain at all.

"A ring," said David. "Made of gold, bearing my family crest. It was stolen from me in a robbery on the Bromley stage some weeks ago and has not been seen since. Or rather, *I* have not seen it since. Bow Street informed me a villain . . ." He paused, head cocked.

"The Black Duke, my lord," supplied Adams.

David raised his eyes to the ceiling for a moment before focusing on the constable again. "Yes. Just so. This . . . person has been wearing my ring, calling himself this preposterous name, and then robbing stagecoaches." He pulled a slight grimace of distaste. "I should like to have it back now."

The constable's ruddy color had faded from his pockmarked cheeks. "Ah . . . well. Erm, right, sir. Could—could you describe the crest?"

David inclined his head again. On cue, Adams stepped forward and drew out a sheet of paper from his folio. "The arms of His Grace the duke of Exeter," murmured the secretary.

Constable Chawley's eyes rounded with alarm. He glanced sideways at David. "Are you—that is, begging pardon, sir—"

"No, I am not Exeter," said David with an amused look. "I am his brother." The constable's eyes swung to Adams, who bowed his head in discreet confirmation.

"I see." Chawley's fingers left little damp marks on the paper as he turned it around again. His mouth was screwed up in concentration. David waited. Somewhere a door opened, and a tuneless humming drifted in through the door.

"Lord bless me, that'll be Mr. Spikes," said the constable, relief flooding his face. "He'll know what's what, sir." And he hurried from the room.

David sat back in his chair and listened. The humming abruptly stopped, followed by a rush of whispered conversation. Footsteps clattered in the outer office, followed by another bout of loud whispers. Then footsteps came toward the office where he waited until the door was thrown open again.

"Sir, good morning," said an oily new voice. David turned his head to see the new arrival, the bowlegged man who had strutted before him last evening in the torchlight and crowed about catching the Black Duke. This would be Mr. Spikes, the man who had put Vivian in irons. "Allow me to bid you welcome to our town—"

David looked him up and down. "Yes."

The man paused, nonplussed, then hurried on. "I am Mr. Samuel Spikes, good sir, sheriff of this county."

"Indeed," David said. "Then you have my signet ring."

"I do have that ring, sir, but you understand, I can't simply hand it over to the first gentleman who walks in and asks . . ." His voice died as David got to his feet and faced him. "For it," he finished weakly.

"Of course," said David. "What proof do you require?"

"Er . . ." Spikes seemed unprepared for this. "Proof."

David cast his eyes upward and sighed, and Adams rushed forward to present the documents again.

"Who are *you*?" hissed Spikes at him.

"Private secretary to His Grace the duke of Exeter," said Adams. "Assisting his lordship in His Grace's absence."

"Absence?" Spikes frowned at David.

"Lord David Reece," murmured Adams. "His Grace's brother has the management of the estate at present."

Spikes continued frowning. "Does he."

"Ainsley Park," piped up the constable, who had been watching with bleary eyes. "My cousin's an undergardener there."

"Ainsley Park in Kent, as well as several other properties and estates in England and Scotland," said Adams. "You are quite fortunate his lordship came in person this morning. He is a very busy man."

David simply stood there and watched them, the paunchy, sour-faced sheriff and the plump, half-drunk constable. This should be an easy game for him, persuading these two bumpkins to give him what he wanted. Still, he couldn't afford to lose, which always made things more difficult.

Mr. Spikes exchanged an uneasy look with the constable, then hunched his shoulders over the papers Adams had brought. After examining them for several moments, even turning them sideways, the sheriff thrust them back into Adams's hands. "Hmmph. Well, right then. I'll just go fetch it for you." He jerked his head at Chawley, who twitched in surprise, then followed the sheriff from the room.

"Thank you." David waited until they closed the door behind them. Then he turned to Adams. "Well done."

The secretary's eyes shone. "Thank you, sir!"

"They'll be talking it over," said David, almost to himself. "Trying to decide between handing things over to Bow Street or currying favor for themselves. Stroke of luck, really, that the constable's cousin is an undergardener."

"Even more importantly, sir, they have no wish to bring disfavor on themselves."

David smiled faintly. "Well, I shall give them every opportunity to avoid that."

Spikes and the constable returned again in a few minutes. His manner considerably more restrained now, Mr. Spikes held out a small grimy pouch. "I believe this is what you're seeking, m'lord." He gave an awkward little bow.

David took the pouch and opened it. Out rolled the heavy gold signet ring Marcus had given him so many weeks ago. He tossed the pouch aside and put the ring on his hand.

The cool weight of it slipped easily onto his finger, at once reassuring and foreign. He breathed a mental sigh of relief; the first part of his plan had been accomplished. David favored Mr. Spikes with a smile. "Yes, indeed. Mr. Adams, see to it the reward for its return is sent at once."

"Yes, my lord." Adams flipped open his folio and made a note. Mr. Spikes couldn't conceal his delight and relief.

"Thank you, sir, though it's not necessary, of course. It's our duty to protect the good folks of—"

"Yes." David cut him off. "There is something else."

The sheriff closed his mouth, glancing uncertainly at Adams. His skinny throat worked twice as he faced David again. "How else can I serve you, sir?"

"I am looking for someone," said David. "A woman."

Something surprised and uneasy flashed across Spikes's features. He didn't move.

"Brown hair, blue eyes," David went on. "So high." He held up his hand to indicate. "Have you seen her?"

Spikes looked unwilling to open his mouth. "Who is she?" he muttered at last. David raised one eyebrow in reproach. The sheriff flushed. "Begging your pardon, m'lord, but I can't just hand over my prisoners to anyone who asks."

David's face cleared. "You have seen her, then. Excellent." Then he frowned again. "Prisoner?"

Spikes was the color of turnips. "Who else would I have, here in the jail?"

"I see." David let his impatience show. "Bring her out at once, if you please."

"I have to ask who you're looking for," said Spikes stubbornly. "I got only prisoners here, and I ain't giving over any of them without good cause. Caught robbing a public stage, they were—"

"A female, engaged in highway robbery?"

Spikes flushed even deeper. "She was with 'em! Part of the gang, most like."

"The woman I am seeking would be a passenger, not a thief," said David. "Perhaps this is not the same woman."

"Who is she?" Spikes growled, although he looked more and more wretched about protesting.

David leaned on his walking stick and fixed an intent stare on the man. "I hardly think that is your concern," he said softly.

For a long moment they stared at each other, as if in silent combat. David didn't move; neither did Mr. Spikes, aside from the clenching of his fist.

"Let me be very clear," said David at last, speaking very slowly. "If you have arrested the lady in question, I shall be most displeased. Perhaps the only way to mitigate my displeasure would be to produce her, posthaste, and pray she is unharmed. Do you understand?"

Spikes wet his lips. "Her name?" he asked through his teeth.

David bent his head very slightly toward Mr. Adams, without taking his eyes off the sheriff. "Gray," said Adams at once. "Mrs. Mary Gray."

"Posthaste," David repeated.

"What makes you think this particular female is here, sir?" argued the sheriff.

"A man"—David glanced to Adams again.

"Mr. John Palmer," supplied Adams.

"Yes. Mr. Palmer is employed by my brother. Mr. Palmer informed me that a woman of her description was on a stagecoach with him yesterday."

Spikes looked as though he'd eaten something very

bitter. "Very well, sir," he muttered. "I'll go have a look." He ducked back out of the room.

Samuel Spikes was not having a good day. It had begun well enough. He woke to remember, quite proudly, that he had personally apprehended the most notorious villain in all the shire, the Black Duke, not to mention the highwayman's gang. The Bow Street horse patrol had commended him for his assistance. He was certain to receive a citation from the Home Secretary. Mr. Spikes had himself bought a round for all the constables and officers at The Bear and Bull in celebration last night.

Today was to have been one of the finest in Samuel Spikes's life, and now this lordship fellow was spoiling it. It was bad enough he had come to claim the Black Duke's ring. Spikes had suspected that was a real ring, stolen of course, and would be returned. He had expected to present it to the men from Bow Street, though, when they returned today to remove his prisoners to Newgate. Now he had been forced to give it to the gentleman waiting in his private office, and there would be no triumphant presentation to the magistrate.

That was bad enough. This lord wanted one of his prisoners now. Grinding his teeth, Spikes stomped down the hall to where Chawley waited, scratching his belly and looking stupid. "What's her name?" he snapped. "The girl."

Chawley gaped at him. "Eh . . ."

"Go check." Spikes stood fuming while Chawley retrieved his records.

"Gray, sir. Mary Gray."

Mr. Spikes ground his teeth. "Here, Chawley. Gutterson was dead certain about her, wasn't he? He wasn't drunk yesterday, was he?" Amos Gutterson, the man who had told them one of the thieves had recognized the female passenger, was well-known in Moresham for his fondness for ale. At the time, Mr. Spikes had been so pleased to capture the Black Duke and his mates, he'd ordered the woman taken away, too, as a person of interest if nothing else. Now, however, that didn't seem so farsighted.

Chawley hesitated, confirming his suspicions. "I don't think much," he mumbled.

"Damn it!" Mr. Spikes glanced around and lowered his voice. "That gentleman in there says he wants her. Won't say why, or what gives him the right to demand a prisoner's release, but he's a duke's brother and I don't know how to refuse him, not based only on Amos's word." He slashed one hand through the air. "Go fetch her, then. But not a word to her about why she's coming out. I'll not lose a prisoner if I can help it. This bunch is clever, and she might see an opportunity to give the hangman the slip." Chawley nodded and hurried off.

Mr. Spikes took a moment to compose himself. What on earth could a nobleman want with a young woman who knew thieves? Spikes wished he had time to send to London and ask Bow Street what to do. The notices sent around to all the local sheriffs had described the Black Duke in detail, and made only passing reference to his gang. A woman had not been mentioned. If this gent insisted, Spikes supposed he'd have to choose between defying the man, with who knew what consequences—the fellow likely had friends in the Home Office and Parliament who could remove Spikes from his post—or giving up a prisoner of uncertain value.

Facing a choice between awful and worse, Spikes stomped back to his unexpected and unwanted visitor.

* * *

The clang of the lock woke Vivian. Blinking, she sat up from where she had fallen asleep leaning against the wall, and saw the stocky constable who had shoved her into the cell last night opening the door. "Come," he said. "You're wanted."

By whom? Slowly she got to her feet, thinking frantically. It was early, she guessed from the light. Was the magistrate already here to pass judgment and sentence her? She stepped into the corridor, her muscles stiff and sore from a night spent huddled in the cold, and the constable banged the door closed behind her. With a wave of his hand, he motioned her down the hallway—treating her rather kindly this time, she thought. Last night he'd dragged her by the arm, pushing her from side to side with great enthusiasm.

Simon's face appeared in the tiny barred window in his cell door. "Where are you taking her?" he demanded. The constable rapped on his door and grunted in reply. "Don't hurt her!" Simon said shrilly.

Her throat felt stuffed with wool. Silently, she gave him a quavering smile before the constable nudged her forward. Vivian looked back at her brother as long as she could, until they rounded the corner. It could conceivably be the last time she ever saw Simon. She clenched her jaw and blinked, trying not to humiliate herself by crying.

The constable opened another locked door, then led her down a short corridor into a small plain room. He opened the door for her, then stood aside and motioned for her to walk in. He'd been strangely quiet on this walk, and Vivian had to force herself to step into the room, fully expecting to see the hangman waiting for her, noose in hand.

Instead she saw David, as she had seen him the night

he escorted her to the theater. His clothing elegant, his demeanor composed, the sight was too much for her. She stopped short, blinking hard. It was one last cruel joke of fate, to see him here now.

"Ah," he said calmly. "That's the one."

The prune-faced sheriff gave her an angry glare. "Certain of that, sir?"

David looked at him. "Are you questioning my eyesight, or my judgment?"

"No," muttered the sheriff. "But see here—I can't just release her on your word."

"Why not?" asked David, soundly mildly surprised.

"She's—she's a highway thief!"

"Don't be ridiculous. She was a passenger on the coach, was she not?"

"Yes," the sheriff admitted.

"Did she take anything from any other passenger?"

"No," the sheriff admitted.

"What evidence of guilt do you have, then?"

"One of the thieves recognized her," said the sheriff defiantly. "Our man saw it quite clearly."

"So you are taking the word of a third party, who believes a thief made some sign he recognized this woman, over my word that she is innocent."

The sheriff opened his mouth, and then he closed it. He glared at Vivian again.

"Are you injured, my dear?" asked David in the same calm, unhurried tone. Vivian knew he was up to something, but she had no idea what, and so merely shook her head. It wasn't clear her voice would function at the moment anyway.

"Very good. Let's be on our way, then." He said it looking right at her, but he didn't move.

Neither did Vivian. "No," she heard herself blurt out. "I can't."

David rocked back on his heels and looked at her. "Whyever not? I should think you eager to be quit of the place."

"There's a boy," she said, her voice trembling a little. "Just a boy. In the jail."

David turned that inquiring look on the sheriff, who flushed.

"He was very kind to me last night," Vivian went on, her eyes filling with tears quite involuntarily. "I can't bear to think what will happen to him." She had unconsciously slipped into one of her familiar poses, making her voice young and her manner tragic.

"The sheriff says he is a thief, my dear," remarked David, as if he did not care. But he was playing along, and Vivian clutched at it.

A tear slipped from her eye. "He did not want to be a thief! His parents died and he was sold to thieves, and beaten if he did not do as they told him!"

"Your heart is too soft, madam."

"And you have none, if you can abandon a boy barely out of shortcoats to a terrible fate. I believe he is a good lad. He stood up for me when the constable's men pushed me. I cannot simply leave him here to hang."

"They pushed you?" David turned to glare coldly at the Mr. Spikes

"Madam, he's a thief," said Mr. Spikes impatiently. "Thieves hang. I beg your pardon for any roughness of my men, but we are upholding the law, pursuing violent criminals—"

"I'm certain he is not!" Tears began to roll down her cheeks again. She turned a solemn face to David. "If he must hang, I must stay here until the end, to comfort him and try to save his soul."

David pressed his lips together and looked wildly annoyed. "Of course you shan't. We are returning to London this instant."

"No! How can you be so heartless?" Vivian covered her face with her hands and began to weep in earnest, heart-wrenching sobs that shook her shoulders.

His expression grim, David turned to Spikes. "Ten guineas to release the boy."

"I should say not," said Spikes indignantly. "He's a highwayman, and he'll hang for it."

"Fifteen guineas."

"No, sir, I cannot." Spikes lifted his chin and folded his arms.

David dug in his coat pocket and opened his purse. One by one, he began stacking bright golden guineas on the desk. "I am quite certain the hangman will not miss one lad." David made a stack of five and set it aside, beginning a new one. "I shall know no peace if she does not have her way in this." Vivian wept more loudly than ever. Now ten guineas sat on the desk. Spikes's eyes strayed to them and lingered. David placed five more guineas beside the ten. "I should hate to trouble my solicitors to come all this way to set him free." With five soft clinks, five more golden guineas dropped onto the desk.

Mr. Spikes looked at the coins again and sighed. "How can I release him?" he asked plaintively. "Bow Street wants them all fetched to London this day."

David took out one of his cards and placed it on the desk. "You may send them to me."

The sheriff looked almost pitiable in his helpless fury. "That's most irregular, sir."

"Is it?" David smiled thinly.

For a moment it was quiet in the small room, as Spikes looked from the money to Vivian to David and back to the money, seeming to shrink with every passing second. "Chawley, bring the lad," he said at last.

With a surprised grunt, the constable waddled from the room again. "You'll not be wanting anything else, will you, m'lord?" asked Spikes in despair.

David smiled faintly. "I don't believe so."

Spikes let out a breath of relief. Vivian wiped her eyes with her fingers, barely breathing at all. She strained her ears for footsteps, and soon enough heard them, two sets, coming toward them.

And then Simon walked into the room, his thin shoulders hunched and chains rattling from his wrists. White showed around the blue of his eyes as he looked all around the room, finally fixing his gaze on her.

"Do you wish to give up a life of crime and become an honest lad?" she asked him in her sweetest, clearest voice.

Simon eyed her as if she'd gone mad. "Aye," he said in a hoarse croak. She clapped her hands together and turned to beam at David. David sighed and waved one hand toward the door. Another man, standing just behind David, stepped forward then, making Vivian start; she hadn't even noticed him. He murmured something to the defeated Mr. Spikes, who just nodded once, his expression more sour than ever. The golden guineas had disappeared from the desk.

"Shall we?" David drawled, and Vivian nodded. The constable opened the door for them, and they filed out. In the outer room Vivian could hear someone shouting; Flynn, she realized. He must have seen them bring out her and Simon, and put together what was happening.

"How dare you keep me and let them go," bellowed Flynn from the recesses of the jail. "I deserve to go, not those brats! You're being played for a fool, you fat noddy! They planned the whole thing! A fraud, I tell you, fraud! It's a job they're pulling on you, right this minute!"

David stopped and listened for a moment, turning to Mr. Spikes. "What on earth is that?"

Mr. Spikes puffed up his chest in spite of himself. "The Black Duke. Or rather," he amended hastily, "him what calls himself the Black Duke."

"Are you certain?" David asked.

"Quite, sir," said Spikes with pride. "I took that ring from his finger myself."

David flexed his hand that wore the signet. "Excellent. My commendation, Mr. Spikes. Hang him high, would you?"

Evidently deciding it was best to rescue what he could of a nobleman's good opinion, or relieved that David wasn't asking for any other prisoners to be released, Mr. Spikes bowed. "That we shall, m'lord."

The constable rushed to open the door for them, and David led the way into the glorious sunshine of morning. Vivian took a deep breath, trying not to shake. It seemed unreal, that she was walking out of the jail, free, when she had expected to be climbing the steps of the gallows when next she saw the sky above her. And Simon was right behind her, still cowed into silence by uncertainty but with her all the same. Somehow, David had come for her and gotten them both out of jail.

An enormous coach, gleaming lacquered black with four equally glossy black horses in front, stood waiting. A servant in gray and blue velvet jumped to open the door, and David paused, putting out his hand to her.

Vivian put her grimy hand in his spotless gloved hand, and let him help her up the step into the carriage. Simon followed, and then the other man who had been with David. Vivian waited, but the door swung shut. She tugged aside the velvet curtain at the window and peeked out to see David mounting a splendid gray horse. Without a glance her way, he nodded, and the coach started forward. Mr. Spikes remained where he was, and the last Vivian saw of him was his sour expression easing as he plunged one hand into his bulging pocket.

Chapter Twenty-two

For a moment there was silence in the coach. Then the man across from them let out a whoop.

"What an adventure! Why, I'm certain my uncle never saw the like!"

Simon's hand took hold of hers, and squeezed. Vivian squeezed back, cautioning him to stay quiet. "What do you mean?"

The man leaned forward, his face alight. "Getting you out of jail! I vow, when his lordship told me his plan it seemed incredible. But it worked. It worked!" He beamed at them for a moment as Vivian and Simon exchanged fleeting, alarmed, glances. "But I beg your pardon, madam," said the man suddenly, his demeanor growing anxious. "You must not have known what was planned."

"No," said Vivian. "And I'm not at all certain I understand what happened."

"Allow me to introduce myself," he said quickly. "I am Roger Adams, private secretary to His Grace the duke of Exeter."

Vivian stared at him without blinking. The duke of Exeter? Who the ruddy hell was he? "Are you, now?"

The young man nodded. "Yes, indeed. I have been assisting Lord David these past weeks during His Grace's absence. I must say, nothing prepared me for the plan he proposed when he woke me last night!"

"Which was?" Vivian prompted, still digesting the fact that David's brother was, apparently, a duke. A bloody duke!

"He declared we were going to rescue a lady from imprisonment," exclaimed Mr. Adams. "And I was to play a vital role, although it didn't proceed quite as his lordship said. Quite a challenge, to keep up with the workings of his mind. I daresay even His Grace could not have been more poised and patient, to say nothing of clever."

Vivian's eyes widened, and she tucked her chin down to hide her amazement. "That he was," she mumbled in agreement, as Mr. Adams seemed to be waiting for her to acknowledge David's cleverness. Clever! It was David's sheer nerve Vivian had to admire most. Simon squeezed her hand again, demandingly, and she shook her head a little, telling him to wait. She didn't know how to answer his questions in any event. "What's he planned next?"

The delight faded from Mr. Adams's face. "Well . . . well, madam, I don't precisely know."

She exhaled softly without realizing she had been holding her breath. "What next" was the main question that mattered to her now. She supposed she should be grateful if he just let them go and called the accounts even. There was no way she could ever repay him for her life and Simon's. That pile of bright gold coins lingered in her memory. "Where are we going?"

"Back to London, I presume." He sat back and beamed at them some more, as if now everything were right with the world. Vivian rolled her lower lip between her teeth and continued to ignore her brother's repeated attempts to get her attention without Mr. Adams knowing about it. After a night in jail, she was filthy and tired, and no doubt stank of mildew and rotting straw. Simon could only be called a great deal more unkempt. What a sight they'd make, parading down David's elegant, well-swept street: two thieves snatched from the hangman's rope.

She pulled her hand free of Simon's grip and clasped her fingers together in her lap, her eyes fixed on them. She was a fool. She hadn't regretted anything she'd done up to this moment, when she realized that her hopes and fantasies had somehow built up a fairy tale kind of future for her and a duke's brother. Just a "lordship" was bad enough, but a duke? When she'd seen David leaning elegantly against the constable's desk, her heart had taken a leap like never before in her life: he'd come for her. Surely that meant . . . surely it *must* mean . . .

But it didn't. It couldn't. She was ten times a fool for having ever allowed the idea to enter her head, even unwittingly.

It was a long ride into London, but Vivian was still surprised when they arrived. She glanced at Simon nervously as the carriage stopped in front of the familiar town house, and she caught the indistinct sound of David's voice outside. "Where are we?" asked Simon in a barely audible whisper.

"London, sir," said Mr. Adams before Vivian could. "His lordship's home, I believe."

"Oh, aye," said Simon wryly. "O' course."

The door swung open then, and his lordship himself stood in the opening. "Has everyone made it safely?" he asked, his gaze jumping around before landing on Vivian. "No one ill or unwell?"

"No, sir," said Mr. Adams, who seemed eager to talk after the long, quiet journey. "Everything went off splendidly, just as you planned."

"Close enough, at any rate." David finally glanced away from Vivian. "Mr. Adams, I am hiring you away from my brother. Whatever he is paying you . . ." He paused, thinking. "I will pay you the same. Will you take the position?"

The secretary's eyes went round. "Y-y-yes, sir," he stammered. David nodded once.

"Very good. Give your notice the day he returns."

"Yes, sir," repeated Adams, beginning to smile again. "I will, sir!"

"Excellent. Take the coach back to Exeter House, would you?"

"Yes, sir. I will, sir." Adams was now beaming idiotically. "Good day, madam," he said to Vivian as David waited in the doorway, his hand outstretched to help her down.

She looked from that hand to the secretary, still almost too stunned to move. "Where are we?" muttered Simon insistently in her ear. Vivian shook herself.

"London." She took David's hand and let him help her down. She still didn't quite understand what was happening, but there was nothing to be gained by sitting in the carriage pondering it. Simon jumped down behind her as David, still holding tight to her hand, turned and started up the steps. The carriage started off again, with Mr. Adams giving one last wave out the window. He, if no one else, seemed quite satisfied and pleased by the day's events.

"Here, where are we going?" said Simon suspiciously. "Where are we?"

David paused, turning to face him as the door opened behind him. "My home," he said. "Won't you come in, Mr. Beecham?"

Simon's eyes nearly started from his head, and he looked at his sister in amazement. She bit her lip and made a quick motion with her hand, for him to follow, and let David lead her inside.

Simon only followed as far as the hall, though, and there he planted his feet and assumed a stubborn expression that was startlingly familiar. "What's happening, Viv?" he asked her. "How'd he get us out o' jail, and why'd he bring us here? How d'you know this cove?"

David took his time replying. He hadn't thought very far ahead of getting them out of jail, and was still somewhat shocked he had succeeded in that. No doubt Bow Street would call on him again, once Mr. Spikes informed them what he had done, but that was later. In London, David was in his element, with the prestige of his family name to see him through, not to mention the Exeter solicitors at his command. But in many ways, the next minutes would be the most delicate part of the business. "Welcome to London," he said at last. "I trust it will be more agreeable than your last abode."

Simon's eyes narrowed warily. "Who the bloody hell are you?" he asked.

David opened his mouth, but Vivian cut in. "He saved your ungrateful neck," she said swiftly. "Do you need to know more?"

Simon cast another glance at David, then looked closer at his sister. "Yeah," he growled. "I think I do. What's he to you, Viv?"

David was quietly satisfied to see her blush bright pink. "He's—he's—you hush!" she stammered.

"There will be a meal in the kitchen for you," David said then to Simon. "And a hot bath drawn upstairs in a guest room. Hobbs will direct you and see to your needs while I discuss something with your sister." The butler, waiting discreetly nearby, stepped forward at his name.

"Discuss what?" Simon's hands were in fists at his sides, and his blue eyes burned suspiciously in his pale, thin face. David was six inches taller, several stone heavier, and had no doubt the boy was ready to attack him to defend his sister's honor.

"The solution to all our problems," he answered honestly. The more he thought about it, the more David believed that. If Vivian agreed to his proposal, he could save both her and Simon from the hangman.

"You go on, Simon," Vivian said at the same time. The boy glanced uncertainly between the two of them. "It's all right," she added. "Go on."

"Well . . ." He hunched his shoulders and suddenly looked very young. "You call if you need me," he told her almost plaintively.

She nodded, her expression as serious as his. David glanced at his new butler, and the man bowed his head.

"This way, sir," said Hobbs, indicating the way to the kitchen. Simon hesitated another moment, then turned and went. David stepped away from Vivian for a moment, lowering his voice. "Hobbs," he said, "the young man is another soul just saved from the wickedness of crime. I depend on you to look after him, making certain he is comfortable and well-settled. He shall be my guest for a time, until I can find him an honest place."

The butler's eyes shone. "Yes, my lord," he whispered in reply. "I shall see to him myself." David nodded and turned to go, but the butler spoke again. "Sir—if I may be so bold—I heard things, after I entered your employ, that suggested you consorted with immoral people. I never guessed that your motive—"

"Yes, yes," said David with uneasy heartiness.

"Was so steeped in Christian charity and purity." Hobbs gazed at him with something like reverence. "I am honored to serve you, sir."

"Splendid," said David. "I shan't make a habit of this,

you know. It has mostly proceeded from the impulse of the moment—and, of course, Christian charity. But see to the lad, would you?" The butler bowed very smartly, and hurried off with Simon. David let out his breath in relief, vowing to himself not to carouse at home anymore.

He turned to Vivian and held out his hand. "Come."

Vivian gave him a somber nod, and together they went into the drawing room. David closed the doors behind him, and turned to see her standing stiff and anxious. He knew her well enough to see the tension in her now.

"It was a wonderful thing you did for us," she said. "For me. I can never thank you enough for myself, let alone for Simon—"

"I did nothing for Simon," he said. "I kept my promise to you."

Her face grew pinker. "A promise you didn't have to make, let alone keep."

He put his head to one side. "Did you think I wouldn't?"

Vivian's lower lip trembled. "No," she said. "That is, I knew you would *want* to keep it, but I never dreamed—I never imagined the lengths you'd go to."

It brought a faint smile to his lips. "Odd, how many people have said that to me of late."

"And I'll repay you," she went on as if he hadn't spoken. "I will, somehow."

"Ah," he said. "Excellent. I was counting on that."

She opened her mouth, then closed it without a word. He put out his hand. "Shall we sit down?"

Vivian had never felt so unsteady in her life. She crossed the room and took the seat he indicated. David sat opposite her, on the edge of the small sofa. Their knees were almost touching. She tucked her hands into the folds of her skirt and waited.

"Vivian," he began, then stopped. David sighed, running his hands through his hair and letting his head hang forward. "I'm a thorough scoundrel," he confessed. "The sad truth is that I've spent my life no better than you've spent yours—perhaps worse, in many ways. I had the advantages of wealth and family who looked out for me and saved me from my worse mistakes, advantages I gained through nothing more than the good fortune of being born to them. If my brother hadn't risked his own life to help me, I would have been transported or killed this very year. I've been a thief, a liar, a man so consumed with his own pleasure that I've had affairs with other men's wives and laughed about it. I even proposed to a woman once and then tricked her into thinking I was marrying her when I had changed my mind." Vivian felt her eyes growing wide. This was not what she had expected him to tell her.

"I'm not an eligible match," he went on. "Or if I am, it's due only to my name and my brother's fortune, and I don't particularly fancy being wanted for either of those reasons. I'm . . . I'm a fairly disreputable person." He cast a wary glance her way, but Vivian couldn't make any reply. "And I'm not rich. I would be, if I hadn't spent every last farthing my brother gave me and then some. I have this house" —Vivian couldn't help sneaking a quick glance around in disbelief—"which means I'm not poor," he allowed, seeing that glance. "I shall always have a place to live and enough to eat. And my brother, for whatever reason, still trusts me and seems ready to give me yet another chance, so I have hopes of rebuilding a fortune to support myself." He paused for a moment. "It will take me a while to be comfortable," he said. "And I may never be received in society again."

He was watching her as if he wanted her thoughts on this. Vivian swallowed. "Oh."

"But I love you," he said, his voice yearning. "I love

your spirit and courage and the way you aren't afraid to risk everything for someone you love."

Her breath came out in a sob. "Oh, but how could I not? They might have hanged you in my place, *my* place, David, and I couldn't live with it . . ."

He blinked. "I meant for Simon."

She slipped to her knees, taking his hand between hers. "But didn't you know?" she asked shyly. "Didn't you know that I loved you?"

Never in her life had a man looked at her the way he was looking at her. "I love you," he repeated, bringing her hands to his lips and pressing a gentle kiss on her knuckles. "Then you'll marry me?"

Vivian gasped, so startled she almost toppled backwards. "Marry you? But—no, but—I never thought you meant that!"

He pulled her back, leaning forward at the same time until their faces were bare inches apart. "What did you think I meant?"

"Well—well," she floundered; what *had* she expected him to say? "I don't know! But I'm not the sort of girl a man like you marries."

"And I'm not the sort of man a woman like you marries," he replied. "You'd be taking an awful risk."

She stared at him, her lips pressed together. "What sort of woman am I?"

"A clever one," he said at once. "A bright, courageous, loyal woman who could surely do better than an irresponsible jackanapes like me."

Her eyes narrowed. "An irresponsible jackanapes who had the nerve to go tell a sheriff to let me out of jail or you'd be displeased. And then act as if he ought to cower in fear at the thought!"

"He should have," said David. "My next plan involved detonating a powder keg outside the building and snatching you from the rubble."

Vivian choked on laughter at the ridiculousness of the idea. "You're daft," she said.

"Don't laugh," he replied. "I've done some very daft things."

Proposing to marry her had to be the daftest of them all. That's what this was, then, another lark. She sighed, bittersweetly. Her first—and perhaps only—marriage proposal, and it was a joke. For a moment, just a moment there . . . "No," she said, glad to hear her voice sounded normal. "Of course I won't marry you."

He looked severely disconcerted. "You won't? Why not?"

"Better to ask why you thought I would," she retorted. "What a ridiculous notion, me marrying you. Why, you already know I'll let you under my skirt. What more do you want?"

Instead of a smart answer, David cocked his head to one side and just looked at her, a slight frown on his face. After a moment Vivian drew back, unsettled by his silence. "I like that part, you know," she rattled on. "It's quite . . ." *Heavenly,* she thought longingly. "Nice."

David got to his feet. "Nice?" he echoed.

Her face burned, and she scrambled to her feet and out of his reach. "Lovely," she said. "Pleasurable! You know what I mean."

He took a step toward her. "No," he said. "I don't believe I do." She made to retreat, to put some distance between them, but he caught her hand and wouldn't let go, even when she tugged. "I have never declared my love to a woman, asked her most sincerely to marry me, and been refused. Not just refused, but mocked even for asking."

"Mocked?" She twisted, trying to get away from him

as he slowly pulled her closer. "It's just your vanity hurt from being refused."

"My vanity," he said. Vivian lost the tug-of-war between them then, and stumbled into him. His arm went around her waist before she could recover her balance. She put her hands against his chest and pushed, uselessly. "Assuming I had any vanity left after baring my soul to you just now, it would have been well nigh crushed when you said it was merely 'nice' and 'lovely' to make love to me. It's not nice for me. It's not lovely. It's as close to paradise as I've ever been." He caught her chin with his fingertips, snaring her gaze, even though Vivian couldn't have looked away if she had wanted to. "I've been under enough skirts to know the difference," he said softly. "I never cared for any other woman the way I care for you." He paused, searching her face. Vivian felt all a-jumble, wanting to laugh it off and push him away before he made her cry, and at the same time wanting so much to believe him and fling her arms around him and accept what he was offering her. "You don't have to be afraid," he whispered.

She blinked. "I'm not afraid!" she almost shouted. "Not of you, not of . . ." Her voice trailed off as he put his finger on her lips.

"Aren't you?"

She was. Deathly afraid. Afraid this was too good to be true, that he would change his mind, that he would realize how terribly unsuited she was to his life and society and family. Afraid of losing him, after she'd gone and lost her heart and soul to him. "Not much," she whispered.

"Well," he said. "I took you prisoner once before. Perhaps I shall do it again, until you say yes."

Her face grew hot. "Simon—"

"Oh, Simon may come and go as he pleases," David

said easily. "He's my guest and, I hope, future brother-in-law. You, however, are not going anywhere."

"Your family won't approve," she said.

"It won't be the first time. They'll come around."

"But your brother is a duke!"

"You mustn't hold it against him, love. He truly had no say in the matter."

Vivian gave a gulp of hysterical laughter, that he could say such a thing at a moment like this. "I'm just a novelty to you! You'll grow tired of me."

"Perhaps, in a few decades," he conceded. "Although I should like to tire you every night in the meantime."

"People will be scandalized," she said. "They'll laugh at you."

He laughed. "Why, that I married the Danish princess?"

Vivian scowled. "Don't laugh at me! I'm trying to make you see reason."

David stopped laughing. "Vivian," he said. "If you don't want me, say it. I won't tease you if you truly don't wish to marry me."

"That's better," she said, only to be cut off as his hands began wandering over her back, holding her against him. "Stop it," she protested, weakening as always.

"I shan't tease you but I shall try to persuade you." He cupped her cheek, his eyes moving intently over her face.

"I'll sleep on it," she said, in one last effort to resist. If he truly wanted her . . . why shouldn't she say yes? Perhaps they would never be a fashionable couple, but Vivian didn't care for that. It was too tempting. Who could fault her for accepting him, especially when he asked so nicely?

His smile grew faintly wicked. "But you'll never sleep apart from me again, darling Vivian. Say yes."

She blushed. "When have I ever said no to you?"

"Hmm. First you said I should go to the devil. For

days you said nothing at all. Then you said I was a wretched, lying guttersnipe—"

"But you hadn't kissed me then," she cried, putting her hand over his mouth to stop the recital.

He smiled under her hand. "Oh, is that all I had to do?" With a thump he sat back on the sofa, pulling her down into his lap and holding her tightly. "Marry me and make an honest man of me in my butler's eyes." He kissed her. "Marry me and save me from having to chase loose women for the rest of my life." He kissed her again. "Marry me, darling," he said once more against her lips. "Because I adore you."

She pulled back to look at him. "Do you really?"

He stopped, tracing the curve of her lower lip with the tip of his finger. "I do. Really, truly, I do." Her chin began to tremble. A trace of that cocky smile crossed his face again. "Just as much as you adore me."

She rolled her eyes upward, swiping at her eyes. "Don't be daft."

"Now, that's why you've got to marry me. You keep saying things you know will only provoke me to do worse." He flipped up a handful of skirts. "For instance, shall I prove just how much you adore me?"

She gasped, then laughed, then simply sighed as his hand slid up her leg, over her knee. "Worse? This is your meaning of worse?"

He laughed. "No, but it can get even better."

Vivian knew that. She let her head fall back against his arm and stared up into the face of the man she did adore. "All right, then," she said on a sigh. "I'll marry you. Just kiss me again."

Please turn the page for an exciting peek of
Caroline Linden's next historical romance,
coming soon from Zebra Books!

Anthony Hamilton had been born scandalous, and his reputation did not improve as he grew.

He was the only son of the earl of Lynley, but it was almost a proven fact that he was not Lynley's own child. Lady Lynley, a much younger woman than her husband, had not born a child in the first ten years of her marriage, and then, out of the blue, gave birth to a strapping, handsome lad who didn't look a thing like Lord Lynley, nor any of the Hamiltons for that matter. Lynley had not repudiated his wife or the child, but the fact that Lady Lynley and her son spent most of their time away from Lynley Manor seemed proof of . . . something.

Mr. Hamilton had been a thoroughly wild boy as well. He was asked to leave no fewer than three schools—mostly for fighting, but once for cheating a professor at cards. He had finished his education at Oxford in record time, then set himself up in London to begin a life that could only be called, in hushed tones, depraved and immoral. That was when he had stopped using his courtesy title as well; he no longer allowed people to call him Viscount Langford, as befitted the

Lynley heir, but insisted on being plain Mr. Hamilton. That, combined with his regular appearances at high stakes gaming tables and the steady stream of wealthy widows and matrons he kept company with, painted him blacker than black, utterly irredeemable, and absolutely, deliciously, fascinating to the *ton*.

There was the time he wagered everything he owned, including the clothing he was wearing at the time, at the hazard table, and somehow walked away with a small fortune. There was his infamous, but vague, wager with Lady Nicols—no one quite seemed to know the precise details—which ended with Lady Nicols handing him her priceless rubies in the midst of a ball at Carleton House. There was the time Sir Henry Milton accused him of siring the child Lady Milton carried at the time; Mr. Hamilton simply smiled, murmured a few words in Sir Henry's ear, and within an hour the two men were sharing a bottle of wine, for all the world as if they were bosom friends. He was reputed to be on the verge of being taken to the Fleet one night, and as rich as Croesus the next. He was a complete contradiction, and he only inflamed the gossips' interest by being utterly discreet. For such a wicked man, he was remarkably guarded.

Celia Reece heard all the stories about him. Despite her mother's admonitions, Celia had developed a fondness for gossip in her first Season in London, and all the best bits seemed to involve him in one way or another. While Anthony Hamilton might not be—quite—the most scandalous person in London, he was the most scandalous person she knew, and as such she found his exploits hugely entertaining.

He had been friends with her brother David for as long as Celia could remember, and had often come to

Ainsley Park, the Reece family estate, for school holidays. As he had grown more and more disreputable, he had stopped visiting—Celia suspected her mother banned him from coming—but she still remembered him fondly, almost as an extra brother. He had tied her fishing lines and helped launch her kites, and it gave her no end of amusement that he was now so wicked, young ladies were afraid to walk past him alone.

Naturally, his reputation meant that she was never to speak to him again. Celia's mother, Rosalind, had drummed it into her daughter's head that proper young ladies did not associate with wicked gentlemen. Celia had restrained herself from pointing out that her own brother was every bit as wild as Mr. Hamilton, but she had obeyed her mother for the most part. She was having a grand time in her first Season, and didn't want to do anything to spoil it, particularly not anything that would get her sent back to Ainsley Park in disgrace for associating with wicked gentlemen.

Fortunately, there were so many other gentlemen to choose from. As the daughter and now sister of the duke of Exeter, Celia was a very eligible young lady. The Earl of Cumberland sent her lilies every week. Sir Henry Avenall sent her roses. The duke of Ware had asked her to dance more than once, Viscount Graves had taken her driving in the Park, and Lord Andrew Bertram wrote sonnets to her. It was nothing less than exhilarating, being courted by so many gentlemen.

Tonight, for instance, Lord Euston was being very attentive. The handsome young earl was a prime catch, with an estate in Derbyshire and a respectable fortune. He was also a wonderful dancer, and Celia loved to dance. When he approached her for the third time, she smiled at him.

"Lady Celia, I should like to have this dance." He bowed very smartly. He had handsome manners, too.

Celia blushed. He must know she couldn't possibly dance with him again. "Indeed, sir, I think I must refuse."

He didn't look surprised or disappointed. "Would you consent to take a turn on the terrace with me instead?"

A turn on the terrace—alone with a gentleman! She darted a glance at her mother, several feet away. Rosalind was watching, and gave a tiny nod of permission, with an approving look at Lord Euston. Her stomach jumped. She had never taken a private stroll with a gentleman. She excused herself from her friends, all of whom watched enviously, and put her hand on Lord Euston's arm.

"I am honored you would walk with me," he said as they skirted the edge of the ballroom.

"It is my pleasure, sir." She smiled at him, but he merely nodded and didn't speak again. They stepped through the open doors, into the wonderfully fresh and cool night air. Instead of remaining near the doors, though, Lord Euston kept walking, leading her toward the far end of the terrace, where it was darker and less crowded. Far less crowded; almost deserted, really. Celia's heart skipped a beat. What did he intend? None of her other admirers had kissed her. Lord Euston wasn't quite her favorite among them, but it would be immensely flattering if he tried to kiss her. And shouldn't she have some practice at kissing? Celia's curiosity flared to life, and she stole a glance at her companion. He was a little handsomer in the moonlight, she thought, trying to imagine what his lips would feel like. Would it be pleasant or awkward? Should she be modest and retiring, or more forward? Should she even allow him the liberty at all? Should—?

"There is something I must say to you." Celia wet her

lips, preparing herself, still trying to decide if she would allow it. But he made no move toward her. "Lady Celia," he began, "I must tell you how passionately I adore you."

She hadn't quite expected that. "Oh. Er . . . Oh, indeed?"

"Since the moment I first saw you, I have thought of nothing but you," he went on with growing fervor. "My will is overruled by fate. To deliberate would demean my love, which blossomed at first sight." He took her hand, looking at her expectantly.

"I—I am flattered, sir," she said after a pregnant pause.

"And do you adore me?" he prompted. Celia's eyes widened in confusion.

"I—Well, that is . . . I . . ." She cleared her throat. "What?"

"Do you adore me?" he repeated with unnerving intensity.

No. Of course she didn't. He was handsome and a wonderful dancer, and she probably would have let him steal a chaste kiss on the cheek, but adore him? No. She wished she hadn't let him lead her all the way out here. "Lord Euston, I don't think this is a proper thing to discuss."

He resisted her gentle attempts to pull free of his grasp. "If it is maidenly reserve that prevents you saying it, I understand. If it is fear of your family's disapproval, I understand. You have but to say one word, and I will wait a thousand years for you."

"Oh, please don't." She pulled a little harder, and he squeezed her hand a little tighter.

"Or you might say another word, and we could go to His Grace tonight. We could be married before the end of the Season, my dearest Lady Celia."

"Ah, but—but my brother's away from town," she

said, edging backward. Euston followed, pulling her toward him, now gripping her one hand in his two.

"I shall call on him the moment he returns."

"I wish you wouldn't."

"Your modesty enthralls me." He crowded nearer, his eyes feverish.

"Oh dear . . ."

"Sweet Celia, make me immortal with a kiss!" Celia grimaced, and turned her face aside from his. She was never going to dance with Lord Euston again. What a wretched first kiss this would be.

"Good evening," said an affable new voice just then.

Lord Euston released her at once, recoiling a step as he spun around toward the intruder. Celia put her freed hands behind her, suddenly horrified at what she had done. Goodness—she was alone, in the dark, with an unmarried gentleman—if they were discovered here, she could be ruined.

"Lovely evening, isn't it?" said Anthony Hamilton as he strolled over, a glass of champagne in each hand.

"Yes," said Euston stiffly. Celia closed her eyes, relief flooding her as she recognized her savior. Surely he, of all people, would understand and not cause trouble for her.

"Lady Celia. A pleasure to see you again." He gave her a secretive smile, as if he knew very well what he had interrupted and found it highly amusing.

"Mr. Hamilton," she murmured, bobbing a curtsey. For a moment everyone stood in awkward silence.

"We should return to the ball." Lord Euston extended his hand to her, pointedly not looking at the other man.

"No!" Celia exclaimed without thinking. Euston froze, startled. She flushed. "I shall return in a moment, sir," she said more politely, grasping for any excuse not to go with him. "The air is so fresh and cool."

"Yes," said Euston grimly. He didn't look nearly so handsome anymore. "Yes. I see. Good evening, Lady Celia."

Celia murmured a reply, willing him to leave. "Good evening, Euston," added Mr. Hamilton.

Lord Euston jerked, darting a suspicious glance at Mr. Hamilton. "Good evening, sir." He hesitated, gave Celia a deeply disappointed look, then walked away.

Celia swung around, bracing her hands on the balustrade that encircled the terrace. Good heavens. That had not turned out at all the way she had expected. Why had her mother approved of him?

"That," said Mr. Hamilton, leaning against the balustrade beside her, "may be the worst marriage proposal I have ever heard."

She closed her eyes, and took a deep breath. It didn't work. The giggle bubbled up inside her, and finally burst free. She pressed one hand to her mouth. "I suppose you heard everything he said?"

"I suppose," he agreed. "Including the part he stole from Marlowe."

"No! Really?" Celia gasped. He just smiled, and she groaned. "You mustn't repeat it to anyone."

"Of course not," he said in mild affront. "I should be ashamed to say such things aloud. It would quite ruin my reputation." Celia laughed again, and he smiled. "Would you care for some champagne?"

"Thank you." She took the glass he offered, and sipped gratefully.

He set the other glass on the balustrade and leaned on his elbows, surveying the dark gardens in front of them. "So you weren't trying to bring Euston up to scratch?"

"Don't be ridiculous." She snorted, then remembered

she wasn't supposed to do that. "I would never have walked out with him if I'd thought he meant to propose."

"Why did you then?" He glanced at her, his expression open and relaxed, inviting confidence. Celia sighed, sipping more champagne.

"He's a wonderful dancer," she said.

"And a dreadful bore," he said in the same regretful tone. Celia looked at him in shock, then burst out laughing.

"That's dreadful of you to say, but—but—well, perhaps he is."

"Perhaps," he murmured.

"And now he is probably telling my mother." She sighed. Walking out with Lord Euston, with her mother's permission, was one thing; lingering in the darkness with a man—let alone a notorious rake her mother strenuously disapproved of—was another. "I really should return."

"Did you want him to kiss you, then?"

She stopped in the act of turning to go. He was still facing the gardens, away from her, but after a moment passed and she said nothing, he glanced at her. "Did you?" he asked again, his voice a shade deeper.

Celia drew closer. He turned, now leaning on one elbow, his full attention fixed on her. She didn't know another gentleman who could appear so approachable. She had forgotten how easy he was to talk to. "You mustn't laugh at me, Anthony," she warned, unconsciously using his Christian name as she had done for years. "I—I've never been kissed before, and it seemed like the perfect night for it, and . . . well, until he started demanding to know if I adored him, it was quite romantic. It *was*," she protested as his mouth curved. "We can't all be disreputable, with all sorts of scandalous adventures."

His smile stiffened. "Nor should you be."

"But you should?" She grinned, glad to be teasing him instead of the other way around. "Every gossip in London adores you, you know."

He sighed, shaking his head. "I'm neither so daring nor so foolish as they like to think. Perhaps you, as a pillar of propriety, can tell me how to escape their pernicious notice."

"Why, that is easy," she said with a wave of one hand. "Find a girl, fall desperately in love with her, and settle down to have six children and raise dogs. No one will say a word about you then."

Anthony chuckled. "Ah, there's the rub. What you suggest is more easily said than done, miss."

"Have you ever tried?"

He shrugged. "No."

"Then how can you say it's so difficult?" she exclaimed. "There are dozens of young ladies looking for a husband, you must simply ask one—"

He gave a soft *tsk*. "I couldn't possibly."

"You could."

"I couldn't."

Celia's eyes lit. "That sounds almost like a challenge."

He glanced at her from the corner of his eye, then grinned. "It's not. Don't try your matchmaking on me. I'm a hopeless case."

"Of course you're not," she said stoutly. "Why, any lady in London—"

"Would not suit me, nor I her."

"Miss Weatherby," said Celia.

"Too thin."

"Lady Jane Cranston."

"Too tall."

"Miss Alcomb."

"Too . . ." He paused, his gaze sharpening on her as he thought, and Celia opened her mouth, ready to exclaim in delight that he could find no fault with Lucinda Alcomb, who was a very nice girl. "Too merry," he said at last.

"Who would please you, then?" she burst out laughing at his pleasant obstinacy.

He shifted, his eyes skipping across the garden again. "No one, perhaps."

"You aren't even trying to be fair. I know so many nice young ladies—" Anthony gave a sharp huff.

"This is quite a boring topic of conversation. We've had very fine weather this spring, don't you think?"

"Anyone who took the trouble to know you would accept you," Celia insisted, ignoring his efforts to turn the subject.

"You've gone and ruled out every woman in England." He leaned over the railing, squinting into the darkness.

"Except myself," Celia declared, and then she stopped. Good heavens, what had she just said?

Anthony seemed shocked as well. His head whipped around, and he stared at her with raised eyebrows. "I beg your pardon?"

Heat rushed to her face. "I—I meant that I know you, and know you're not half so bad as you pretend to be."

His gaze was riveted on her, so dark and intense Celia scarcely recognized him for a moment. Goodness, it was just Anthony, but for a moment, he was looking at her almost like . . .

"Not half so bad," he murmured speculatively. "A rare compliment, if I do say so myself."

She burst out laughing again, relieved that he was merely teasing her. That expression on his face—rather like a wolf's before he sprang—unsettled her; it had made her think, for one mad moment, that he might, in fact, spring on her. And even worse, Celia realized that a small, naughty part of her was somewhat curious. No, rampantly curious. She might have let Lord Euston kiss her, but only for the satisfaction of being able to say she had been kissed. She had never expected to be swept away with passion by Lord Euston, who was, as Anthony had said, a dreadful bore. But a kiss from one of the most talked-about rakes in London . . . now, *that* would be something else altogether.

"You know what I meant," she said. "I know you've quite a soft heart, although you hide it very well. As proof, I must point out that you've stood out here with me for some time now, trying to make me feel better after receiving the most appalling marriage proposal of all time. David would have laughed until he couldn't stand upright, and then retold the tale to everyone he met."

"Ah, but I am not your brother," he replied, smiling easily although his gaze lingered on her face.

"No, indeed! But because you are not"—she took the last sip of champagne from her glass before setting it on the balustrade—"I must return to the ballroom. I suppose you'll continue to skulk in the shadows out here, and be appropriately wicked?"

"You know me too well."

Celia laughed once more. "Good night, Anthony. And thank you." She flashed him a parting smile, and hurried away. Perhaps if she could make her mother see the humor, and idiocy, in Lord Euston's proposal, Mama wouldn't ask too many questions about where she'd been ever since.

* * *

Anthony listened to her rapid footsteps die away, counting every one. Seventeen steps, and then she was gone. He folded his arms on the balustrade once again, taking a deep breath. The faint scent of lemons lingered in the air. He wondered why she smelled of lemons and not rosewater or something other ladies wore.

"You gave away my champagne, I see," said a voice behind him.

Anthony smiled and held out the untouched glass sitting next to his elbow. "No. I gave away mine."

Fanny, Lady Drummond, took it with a coy look. "Indeed." She turned, looking back at the house. "A bit young for your taste."

"An old friend," he said evenly. "The younger sister of a friend. Euston was giving her a spot of trouble."

"Better and better," exclaimed Fanny. "You are a knight in shining armor."

Anthony shrugged. "Hardly."

"Now, darling, I wouldn't blame you." She ran her fingers down his arm. "She's the catch of the Season. Rumor holds her marriage portion is two hundred thousand pounds."

"How *do* the gossips ferret out such information?"

"Persistent spying, I believe. Fouché's agents would have been put to shame by the matrons of London." Fanny rested the tip of her fan next to her mouth, studying him. "For a moment, I thought you had spotted your chance."

Anthony tightened his lips and said nothing. The less said on this topic, the better. The scent of lemons was gone, banished by Fanny's heavier perfume. "Have you?" pressed Fanny as the silence lengthened. She moved closer, her face lighting up with interest. "Good Lord. The greatest lover in London, pining for a girl?"

He turned to her. "She's just a girl," he said. "I've

known her since she was practically a babe; and yes, I am fond of her. Fanny, you would understand if you'd heard what Euston was saying to her. I spoke as much to close his mouth as anything else."

"And yet, there *was* something else," she replied archly. He sighed in exasperation. She laughed, laying her hand on his. "Admit it, you've thought of it. She would solve all your problems, wouldn't she? Money, connection, respectability . . ."

He pulled his hand free. "Yes, all I would have to do is persuade the duke of Exeter to give his consent, overcome the dowager duchess's extreme dislike of me, and then ask the lady herself to choose me above all her respectable, eligible suitors. I don't take odds that long, Fanny."

She smirked. "She was a girl a moment ago. Now she's a lady." Anthony looked at her in undisguised irritation. Fanny moved closer, so close her breath warmed his ear. "I wouldn't fault you for trying, darling," she murmured. "It needn't alter our relationship in any way . . ."

"You'll want to hear the news from Cornwall, I expect."

Fanny pouted at his deliberate change of subject, but she let it go. "I don't believe I would have let you seduce me if I'd known you simply wanted me to invest in some mining venture." He cocked a brow at her. "All right," she gave in with a knowing smile. "I would have still let you seduce me, but I would have asked for better terms."

"I like to think we shall always be on the best of terms with each other." He brought her hand to his mouth and pressed his lips to the inside of her wrist. Fanny's expression softened even more.

"I suppose we shall. Interest terms . . . and other terms."

Anthony smiled, ruthlessly forcing his moment of gallantry from his mind, along with everything else related to Celia Reece. Fanny might make light of it, but he needed every farthing she would invest, and Anthony knew how to work to protect that.

He related the report from the mine manager, knowing Fanny, unlike many women, truly wanted to know how her money was faring. She had a sharp mind for business, and they shared a profitable relationship. Their other relationship was almost as valuable to him—Fanny lived in the present, and didn't dwell on the past, especially not *his* past. That mattered a great deal to Anthony.

But when Fanny had gone back to the ball, Anthony found his mind wandering. Although Fanny was nearly fifteen years older than he, she was still a very handsome woman, with a tart wit and a marvelous sense of humor. She had a sophistication no young lady just making her debut could claim, and Anthony genuinely liked her. He liked the way her money made his financial schemes successful. He liked her acceptance of their intermittent affair with no recriminations or demands. But she didn't smell of lemons.

He pushed away from the balustrade, restless and tired at the same time. His plans for the evening had included some time in the card room, where he hoped to win a few months' rent, but he suspected he couldn't concentrate on his cards now. Damn lemons.

With a deep sigh, Anthony turned back toward the house. He repeated in his mind what he had told Fanny: Celia was just a girl; he spoke to her out of mere kindness. He tried not to hear the echo of Celia's words, that she was the only woman in England who thought him . . . how had she put it . . . *not half so bad as he pretended.*

He slipped into the overheated ballroom, lingering near the door. Without meaning to, he saw her. She was dancing with another young buck like Euston. Her pink gown swirled around her as her partner turned her, her golden curls gleaming in the candlelight. Anthony's gaze lingered on her back, where her partner's hand was spread in a wide, proprietary grip. The young man was delighted to be dancing with her—and why shouldn't he be? She beamed up at him, smiling at whatever he'd said to her, and Anthony realized, with a small shock of alarm, that she was breathtaking. No longer a child or a young girl, but a beautiful young woman who would walk out with a gentleman in hopes of a kiss and end up fending off a marriage proposal.

About the Author

Caroline Linden earned a math degree from Harvard College and worked as a programmer at a financial services firm before realizing that writing romance novels is much more interesting and exciting than writing code. She threw away her actuarial textbooks, unchained her Inner Vixen, and never looked back. She lives in New England with her family. Please visit her online at www.carolinelinden.com.